Taken

A Bicultural Series

Book One

Kera C. Munnings

2026

Disclaimer

This book is a work of fiction. Unless otherwise indicated, all the names, characters, places, events, and incidents in this book are the product of the author's imagination and used in a fictitious manner. Any resemblance to actual people, living or dead, or actual events is purely coincidental.

Author: Shakera Munnings

www.sommersetwaynovels.com

TAKEN – A Bicultural Series Book One

RAVAGED – A Bicultural Series Book Two

FATE – A Bicultural Series Book Three

Content Advisory

This novel contains depictions of violence, emotional and psychological trauma, abuse of authority, and mature romantic themes that may be unsettling for some readers. These elements reflect the historical realities portrayed in the story. Reader discretion is advised.

Dedication

Gia, when I first began drafting this book, your words were the ones that carried me forward. You told me, "Don't give up. See it through till the end." I held onto those words, and I did see it through. I finished this book, even though you are no longer here to read it.

I dedicate this story to you so the world may know how much you meant to me. As your younger sister, your encouragement gave me strength when I doubted myself. You reminded me to reach further, to believe more deeply, and to become more than I thought I could be.

This book stands in honor of you and the legacy you left behind.

Rest well.

Nadera Yiesha Munnings

'Gia'

1980-2022

Prologue

Mbemba Kingdom, 1620

*N*zingha ran with the certainty of someone who understood pursuit.

She did not look back. Sound told her everything she needed to know as the weight of boots struck the earth too heavily, breath drawn too loud by men unused to hunting on this land. Fifteen of them, by her count. Foreign men, already angry that the ground did not yield to them.

She cleared the six-foot wall in one clean motion, hands finding stone by memory rather than sight. The landing jarred her ankle sharply, pain flashing hot and immediate, but she did not slow. Pain could be carried. Hesitation could not.

Two men broke from the garrison behind her. They were faster. She accepted that without panic, adjusted her stride, her breathing, the angle of her escape.

Ahead, the torches of the castle burned, close enough to tempt, too far to promise safety.

Her foot caught on a fallen palm. The cry tore from her before discipline could still it, and heat ripped through her leg with the sickening certainty of injury. For a dangerous moment, the world pitched beneath her.

She stood anyway.

She always did.

Laughter followed her, sharp, careless, confident. That sound decided the matter.

Nzingha slowed and turned.

The bow slid from her back into her hands as though it had always belonged there. She planted her feet, letting the night fall quiet around her, breath settling, pulse steadying. Training rose where fear did not.

"Simameni," she called, her voice carrying calm authority through the dark. *Stand.*

They answered in a foreign tongue, laughter thick with disbelief, and came on anyway.

She drew the bowstring back until it brushed her cheek.

"Nkenda ve," she warned softly. *Do not come.*

The first arrow struck before the laughter had finished echoing. Precision marked the second one's follow-up. The third fell as understanding finally reached them, too late to matter.

They rushed her then.

The bow became a staff in her hands, wood cracking against bone as she moved with ruthless economy, striking, turning, never wasting motion. One man dropped without a sound. Another collapsed in confusion before his body caught up with the blow.

A blade came down hard enough to shatter the bow.

She swore once and turned the loss into a weapon, the broken shaft slashing across a face, the other hurled blind into the night. A scream split the air as it found its mark.

Arms locked around her throat from behind. She reached without looking, fingers closing around the knife strapped to her thigh, and drove it back into flesh. The grip loosened. She climbed his back and ended him without ceremony.

She ran again.

The torches burned brighter now, oil and smoke thick in the air.

"Nisaidie," she cried *in Swahili*, her voice breaking free at last. *Help me.*
"Nisaidie tafadhali."

Not a plea.

A call torn raw from blood and breath.

The blow came from the side, heavy and exact. Sound rang through her skull like struck iron, and the world tipped, folded, and fell away.

As darkness claimed her, Nzingha did not scream.

She held one thought steady, like a hand pressed flat against her spine.

I will survive this. Then, the night closed over her

Chapter 1

The Princess and the Guard

*N*zingha vanished from the castle after the evening meal, not in haste, and not unseen.

She waited until the drums softened and the wine loosened tongues, until laughter spilled too freely and hands wandered where they ought not. The court was loud tonight, perfumed with oil and arrogance. Nobles drifted through the inner gardens, trailing silk and entitlement, convinced the world ended where torchlight did.

Nzingha knew better.

She moved when no one thought to look for her, slipping behind carved pillars, pausing beneath hanging vines, counting her breaths the way warriors did before battle. Reaching the outer gardens, she gathered her skirts high enough to move; her pulse was steady, and she already measured shadow and distance.

The warriors' quarters sat low against the far wall, firelight flickering lazily from the tents. Two guards lounged near one of them, seated far too comfortably for men entrusted with vigilance. A jug of rum rested between them, its contents sloshing with each careless laugh.

Nzingha crouched, listening.

"I swear, the Princess is full of herself. Such a shrew, with that bitter tongue," one guard said.

The other snorted. "May the gods help the man foolish enough to make her his wife."

Nzingha stepped out of the darkness.

Not abruptly.
Not loudly.

She let them notice her.

Both men jumped so hard one nearly spilled his drink.

"Ahh, Princess!" one laughed far too quickly, already reaching for humor as armor. "By the Gods, you'll be the death of us. If the King knew you were out here…"

"He'd cut out your tongues," Nzingha finished pleasantly, as though completing a shared thought rather than issuing a threat.

The guards froze.

She tilted her head, studying their faces as if weighing something delicate. The pause stretched just long enough to make them uneasy. Then she reached into the fold of her sash and placed a gold coin into the first man's palm. Another into the second.

"And if a word of this reaches his ears," she continued lightly, her tone almost conversational, "I will cut out your tongues myself and feed them to Asha for supper."

Neither man laughed.

Asha.

The name settled between them like a weight.

The lioness was not a story told to frighten children. She was not a rumor. She was very real, very large, and bound to Nzingha by something no one dared question.

Both guards clutched themselves at once instinctively.

"No need, Princess," one said quickly, voice pitching higher than he meant it to. "Only jesting."

"Good," Nzingha replied. "I dislike repeating myself."

She passed them smiling, as if she'd said nothing more threatening than good evening.

At Mikel's tent, she paused.

The night breathed around her, distant waves, low voices, the crackle of a dying fire. She listened to the movements. For armor. For footsteps that did not belong.

Satisfied, she slipped inside.

Mikel lay sprawled across his pallet, bare-chested, leopard skin tangled low around his waist, one arm flung above his head. He was fast asleep.

Nzingha shook her head, amused despite herself.

"Sleep when you're dead," she said, tossing his shirt onto his chest.

He jerked awake with a curse, hand flying toward a blade that wasn't there. "By the ancestors, Nzingha! Do you always arrive like an omen?"

"A warrior should not sleep so deeply," she replied, already leaning down, already close.

He caught her wrist, thumb brushing the pulse at her throat. His grip lingered longer than necessary, as if reassuring himself she was real.

"One day," he murmured, still half-dreaming, "you will be the end of me."

"And yet," she said, meeting his eyes, "you slept. Knowing I was coming."

A low warning growl cut through the tent.

Asha's massive head pushed through the flap, golden eyes bright, unimpressed.

Mikel groaned and dropped back against the pallet. "Even the lion has come to judge me."

Asha licked his face, slowly and deliberately.

"Traitor," he muttered, rubbing behind her ears despite himself.

Nzingha folded her arms, watching the exchange with open fondness. "So I torment you?"

"Never," he breathed, the humor fading from his voice. "Not once."

They emerged moments later, laughter still clinging to them like heat.

Mikel brushed past her and smacked her hip in passing, a familiar, reckless affection.

Nzingha shot him a look that promised violence.

He only smiled wider, entirely unrepentant.

One guard snickered. "Careful," he warned. "The lion may disapprove of such liberties."

Asha appeared instantly.

Nzingha smiled sweetly. "She may also be hungry."

The guards yelped as Asha bounded past them, utterly uninterested.

"Insolent fools." She walked ahead not looking back.

Run Away with Me

Under the moon and stars, Mikel and Nzingha walked the shoreline of Mbemba. The tide rolled in slow, patient breaths, moonlight breaking across the water like scattered silver. They stopped without planning to, standing side by side, the sea stretching before them.

Mikel turned to her and studied her face as she watched the waves, the quiet strength in her posture. The distance in her gaze no crown could erase.

"How does a man like me become so fortunate to walk beside a woman like you?" he asked. "You know I love you."

She smiled, small and knowing. "And cheetahs have spots," she said, "This I know. I love you too."

Relief loosened something in him. He kissed her, first quick, then lingering, and she rose into it, her hands resting against his chest, familiar as breath. His hair brushed her fingers, scented with coconut oil and salt, and for a moment she allowed herself the dangerous comfort of imagining a life without consequence.

It frightened her.

At last, he said, "I want you for my wife. I cannot bear it. The thought of you being promised to another..." His voice dropped. "We could run."

She lifted her hand gently, stopping him. "Mikel... we have spoken of this." Her voice turned careful. "My father is King of these lands. He will not allow..." She faltered, then steadied herself. "Before we reached the border, his soldiers would find us. And he would have you killed."

Mikel turned away, anger and hurt warring in his silence. He bent, picked up a stone, and hurled it into the sea. It skipped twice, then vanished.

Regret tightened her chest. She crossed the sand and wrapped her arms around him from behind, resting her cheek between his shoulders.

"But you are my warrior," she whispered. "You fight for me every day. You remind me that love is not weakness."

She kissed him, once, then deeper.

"Earn my father's favor," she said at last. "Fight well. This war has lasted two years. Too many of our people vanish into chains." She drew a breath. "Before he gives my hand to Oyomo, I will speak. And if he refuses..." Her voice hardened with resolve. "Then I will run with you."

A tear slipped free.

Mikel caught it gently, kissing her with hunger edged by fear.

A growl broke the moment.

Asha emerged from the trees, muscles tense, and then the guards appeared. Nzingha stepped back at once, command already settling into her spine.

"Asha," she whispered. "Stand down."

The lioness obeyed.

"Nzingha," one guard said respectfully, "The King questions your absence."

She turned back to Mikel. "Give me a single night," she whispered. "I will speak to my father."

He nodded, watching until she disappeared between the guards.

When Mikel finally turned toward the quarters, six soldiers stepped into his path.

The night ended in fists and boots.

And then, in darkness.

Silent Death

Mikel's captors presented him to the King before sunrise, during which the palace held shadows and stone, and the world retained its silence.

A warrior forced him to his knees at the center of the chamber. The chains at his wrists were ceremonial, unnecessary. He did not look up. He did not need to.

The King did not sit.

He stood, hands clasped behind his back, and when he finally spoke, his voice filled the chamber without effort.

"You were not dragged here because you were careless," the King said. "Nor because you were ignorant of the consequences. You stand before me because you believed that proximity to power granted you permission to feel. Because you mistook access for intimacy, duty for invitation, and silence for consent.

I raised you from obscurity and gave you function. I placed you where knowledge moves quietly, where discretion is not virtue, but law. Men of higher caliber would have guarded such favor with their lives. You devalued it by expecting the world to cater to your desires.

Sentiment does not govern Mbemba Kingdom. Containment governs it. Men who understand power know this: love, left untethered, is not poetry but ruin. Kingdoms do not fall to armies first. They fall to unchecked desire.

And you would have made my household vulnerable to that weakness. You would have turned a daughter of my blood into a symbol of your private awakening. You would have reduced her existence to a lesson meant for you.

Do not mistake my restraint for mercy. I have listened to every whisper, every silence you believed unseen. I have measured not only your actions, but the intent behind them. You did not test the waters. You circled them like a beast of the sea. Again and again, you chose her, even when obedience stood waiting.

You believed sincerity might absolve you. That the truth of your feeling could sanctify your disobedience.

It cannot.

Sincerity does not cleanse treason. It only makes it more dangerous."

The King drew a slow breath, then continued, his voice lower now, heavier.

"And yet, before judgment is sealed, you will speak. Not to defend yourself. Not to romanticize your ruin. You will speak once, and what you say will stand as the sum of you."

The chamber held its breath.
Mikel lifted his head.

"My love for Nzingha is my confession," he said, his voice steady. "There is nothing that could have made my choice wiser. She gave me the true meaning of love, not possession, not reward, no expectation. Only recognition. If I were to live another life, I would still wish to meet her again. Even knowing this end."

Silence followed, dense and final.

The King's fury broke like a blade drawn too fast.

"You do not get to immortalize your disobedience by calling it love."

Steel flashed. Mikel's head rolled. King Afonso flicked gore from metal, ignoring it.

The chamber did not react. No gasp followed. No cry rose.

When he returned the blade to its sheath, the space reclaimed its stillness, as though the man who had knelt there had already vanished.

"Remove him," the King said coldly. There is no record. No name. No echo."

Mikel vanished before the palace woke.

No one spoke of his death.

No one admitted his absence.

And so, a silent death sealed his end.

The King's Judgment

Two weeks later, Nzingha stormed into the training yard.

Her uncle was already at work, bare arms slick with sweat, staff moving in sharp, efficient arcs as his men circled him. Femi, brother to King Afonso, Prince of the western and eastern lands, and general of the Mbemba and Tafarian armies, did not slow when she approached, his focus locked on the discipline of the drill as if her presence were merely another distraction to be endured.

"Uncle," Nzingha demanded, her voice slicing through the clash of wood and grunts of exertion. "I have searched the quarters, the training fields, and the outer villages. Mikel is gone. His post is empty, his weapons untouched, and no one will give me a straight answer. I am asking you now, not as a child, but as the Princess of Mbemba. Where has he gone?"

She kicked a stone across the packed earth and planted her hands on her hips, waiting for him to acknowledge her.

Femi disarmed his opponent with a final, efficient twist before stepping back. Only then did he turn to her, his expression carved from patience long exhausted.

"Nzingha," he said, drawing her name out slowly, "you arrive in the middle of a drill as though the world bends to your urgency. You demand answers without first considering what you have set in motion. I do not know where Mikel has gone. But I know this much. Your father summoned him. And when the King of Mbemba summons a man in silence, it is never for conversation."

The ground seemed to tilt beneath her feet.

"Perhaps," she said quickly, grasping for reason, "perhaps they sent him to another village. Or dispatched to Tafaria for reinforcement. You know how my father moves his men without notice. It does not mean harm. It does not mean punishment."

Femi studied her then, and the pity in his eyes cut deeper than anger ever could.

"There is talk," he whispered. "Whispers carried too freely by men who forget their place. Someone saw you and Mikel on the beach. Not training. Not speaking. Seen." His jaw tightened. "If those whispers reached your father, then you already know the truth of it. A king who fears weakness does not forgive disobedience. He eradicates it. Go, speak to my brother. I wish you strength."

She turned away without answering, her stomach twisting violently as dread settled into certainty.

My Daughter the Princess

The throne room swallowed her whole.
Her father sat upon the carved seat of Mbemba, two servants fanning him with broad ostrich feathers as he read a missive. King Afonso the First did not look up when she entered. He did not need to.

"I need a moment with my father," Nzingha said, her voice sharp with urgency and restrained fury.

The King lifted one hand.
The servants bowed and withdrew.

Only then did he raise his eyes, and the weight of his attention pressed down on her like a physical force.

"You stand before me agitated and reckless," Afonso said coolly. "You interrupt counsel and demand privacy as if you can summon kings whenever you want." Speak quickly, daughter. My patience is not endless."

Nzingha curtsied, though her heart hammered against her ribs. "Father, Mikel is gone. He has not returned to his post, and no one will tell me where he is. You summoned him, I know. I know you have the power to end this uncertainty. I am asking you now, tell me what you have done with him."

Afonso rose slowly, descending the steps that led to his throne with deliberate calm.

"You ask as though love excuses negligence," he said, "As though indulgence entitles you to answers reserved for rulers. You humiliate yourself further by pretending ignorance. I allowed that man to train you because I believed discipline would temper your impulses.

Instead, you turned instruction into spectacle. Touching. Kissing. Parading yourself before guards who know better than to keep your secrets."

Nzingha's voice trembled despite her effort to steady it. "We love each other. That is not a crime. He has served this kingdom faithfully. If you have punished him for affection, then you have punished loyalty."

Afonso's expression hardened.

"You confuse loyalty with possession," he said, "You confuse affection with consequence. That man forgot his place. You encouraged him to forget it. And now you stand here offended that a king acted as a king must."

He stepped closer.

"You will never see him again. You will not speak his name. And you will learn, at last, that your mother's restraint did not survive in you."

Something broke.

"I will never marry that bastard from Oyomo," Nzingha said, her voice shaking with grief and fury. "You speak of duty while selling me like…"

His hand came down.

The sound of the slap echoed through the throne room.

Once.

Then again.

Nzingha stepped back, white light briefly sparking across her vision.
She steadied herself, jaw set, breath measured.

Her strength did not falter.
Her bravery did not yield.

"Guards," Afonso said calmly. "Escort my daughter to her quarters.
Guard her door. Before she mistakes leniency for freedom."

Nzingha turned and left the hall without another word, blood sharp
on her tongue, fury contained only by silence.

At the threshold, she caught sight of Iney, her best friend, and the
one who had guarded her longest, standing watch at the entrance to
the throne room.
Their eyes met.

Nzingha did not slow. She did not speak. She passed her with a look
so cold and deliberate it struck deeper than any command.

Something in Iney's chest tightened as she watched her go.

Vengeance moved beneath Nzingha's skin, hot and pulsing, a living thing she did not yet give voice to.

That night, alone in her quarters, she refused dinner and imagined the whispers already taking shape.

"Damn him," she whispered.
"He made me a fool."

Defiance

Nzingha moved as if her body had already decided; her heart was still resisting.
Her hands did not shake as she reached for her longbow, but something inside her did; a quiet tearing, the kind that comes when grief has not yet found its name. She slung the bow over her shoulder and gathered her arrows, counting them not for readiness, but to anchor herself to something that still made sense.
Her sword followed. The familiar weight settled against her hip, steady and known, and she breathed a little easier for it. She lifted her skirts and tied the fabric into a braid, baring her legs for movement, then secured her knives where they always belonged. The motions were rituals. Protective. Necessary.
Prepared because not being prepared had already cost her too much.

She bound her hair tightly back, fingers lingering for a moment longer than needed, as though she were saying farewell to the softness of a princess.

She climbed onto the canopy of her bed and eased the hidden panel aside. The opening waited for her, faithful as ever. For a heartbeat, memory rose unbidden, quiet laughter, shared breath, a presence that had once made the dark feel less heavy.

Mikel.

She closed the panel behind that thought and pulled herself upward. On the rooftop, she paused and looked down at the guards posted outside her quarters. They stood exactly where they were meant to stand.

Watching the door.

Never the absence.

Nzingha slid down the far side of the wall and landed lightly, breath leaving her in a controlled exhale. When she straightened, she did not look back at the castle. If she did, she would not leave.

She walked at first, then faster, the sand cool beneath her feet as the world widened and the sea breathed ahead of her.

"I love my kingdom," she whispered, the words trembling despite her effort to steady them. "But I will not let it take everything. Mikel, I will find you; I swear it."

Her steps lengthened. The walk became a run.

She heard it then, the soft, familiar rhythm of padded feet behind her.

Nzingha stopped so abruptly that her breath caught in her chest. Asha emerged from the darkness, eyes bright, body loose and trusting, moving as if following her was the most natural thing in the world.

"No," Nzingha breathed.

She dropped to her knees, the anger that had carried her this far dissolving into something far more fragile. She gathered the lioness's face between her hands, pressing her forehead to warm fur, breathing her in as if she could memorize the weight of her.

"You cannot come," she whispered, voice breaking despite herself. "This is not for you."

Asha huffed softly, nudging her chin, unbothered by reason.

Nzingha smiled despite the ache rising sharply in her throat. "You are too brave," she murmured. "You always were."

She kissed the lioness's brow, lingering there longer than she should have, as though some part of her already knew.

"I will come back," she promised. "I swear it."

Asha broke from her the moment she was told no.

The lioness sprang away into the dark, her powerful stride carrying her fast and silent, vanishing between palm and shadow. Nzingha watched her go, something sharp pulling tight in her chest.

Asha, her child.

She forced herself to move, steps measured, breath controlled, the ache pressed down and buried where it would not slow her. She had gone only a short distance when the night shifted.

Movement.

She dropped low at once, instincts flaring, eyes narrowing as the shoreline resolved into shapes that did not belong. Too late. A shout cut the air, sharp and foreign, and she knew she had been seen.

The first rush came hard and fast.

Steel flashed. Bodies closed in. Nzingha loosed an arrow and then another, already moving, already cutting her way through the press as sand churned beneath her feet. A blow struck her shoulder. Two hands dragged her down. She fought on, breath burning, the world narrowing to motion and survival.

She faltered.

A heavy roar tore through the night.

Asha came out of nowhere.

The lioness slammed into a man with crushing force, jaws closing as another fell beneath the weight of her paw. Chaos rippled outward as the beast tore through them, feral and furious, placing herself between Nzingha and the blades without hesitation.

"Asha!" Nzingha cried, scrambling to her feet. "Go! Get away from here!"

The lioness did not listen.

She never had.

Nzingha cut down the man nearest her and turned...

Just for a breath.

Just long enough.

The crack of a musket split the air.

Asha went down.

The lioness hit the sand hard, breath tearing from her in ragged pants, blood dark against her fur. She tried to rise. Failed. Tried again.

"No... no..." Nzingha screamed, fighting like something unbound, driving forward through the bodies between her and the one thing that mattered. She struck and shoved and tore her way ahead, vision blurring, heart hammering in her ears.

Beyond the chaos, she glimpsed movement, a figure cutting through men with terrifying efficiency, blades flashing, bodies dropping without sound. The sight barely registered before the world surged back around her.

More men poured in.

Asha roared again, the sound broken now, desperate and raw.

"My child!" Nzingha screamed, voice ripping free of her. "My baby!"

She ran.
A blow struck the side of her head.
The sky tilted. The sand rose. The sound of the world fell away.

Darkness took her mid-stride; and that was the end of before.

Chapter 2

The Second Son - Tantallon Castle, Scotland, 1620

*A*ndrew Barton had never been meant to lead.

That truth followed him like a shadow, present in every room, every decision, every quiet moment where weight settled on his shoulders and refused to lift. He was the second son of Barton's Keep, born to support, not command. To stand beside, not before.

And yet command had found him all the same.

On land, he bore the title of Second Laird, charged with the care of the estate and its people when his elder brother proved unable. The work was unglamorous and unending. Crofters needed coin. Walls needed mending. Names needed answering. Andrew carried it without complaint because someone had to.

At sea, he answered another name.

Drake.

A name earned not through inheritance, but through action. Through salt, blood, and decisions made far from the safety of shore. Captain Drake was known across open waters for hunting Portuguese slavers and pirate vessels alike; his sails recognized before his colors, his reputation arriving long before his ship.

Men whispered the name with care.

His crew, the Sea Dogs, followed him not because of blood, but because he never asked of them what he would not do himself. Among them sailed his brother, Alex Barton, and his closest guard, Haemish McTavish, men bound to him by loyalty forged in weather and steel.

Though Andrew was younger by two summers, authority had settled on him as if it had always known where it belonged.

That knowledge did not make the burden lighter.
It only made it permanent.

God's Work

This time, duty led him not to the docks, but to the kirk. Father McPherson stood at the altar, lighting candles when Andrew entered, the quiet broken only by the soft scrape of flame and wick.

"Good morrow, Father McPherson."

The priest turned with a smile that had weathered many confessions. "Laird Andrew. A fine morrow indeed."

"Have ye the items drawn up for the voyage?" Andrew asked, slowing his stride as they crossed the nave. "We cast off in a sen night."

"Aye," Father McPherson replied. "I retrieved the list whilst dining with His Grace."

Andrew took the parchment and scanned it as he walked. His brows climbed steadily with each line.

"Sixty-five barrels of wine from Venice," he read slowly. "Five hundred yards of printed cloth. Thirty stones of ivory." He lowered the page and looked at the priest. "Father, there are only fifteen men aboard this vessel."

He paced once, the list fluttering in his hand. "By the time we return, it'll be past six moons, if the seas favor us. Half of this will take a fortnight just to stow. Christ,"

He stopped mid-step, crossed himself, and murmured a Hail Mary before glancing toward the altar. "Forgive me."

Father McPherson clasped his hands, unbothered. "Ye are doing God's work, Laird Barton. The Crown is grateful. In fact, your wages have been increased."

Andrew paused. "Pray tell... and that comes to?"

"Five hundred crowns for the journey. Another twelve hundred for labor."

"And provisions?"

"Fifteen barrels of food. Fifty of water and ale."

Andrew exhaled slowly, the tension easing just enough to matter. "Now ye speak sense," he said, "My thanks."

Mid-September weighed heavy on his mind. October seas showed little mercy, and the debts from a lost shipment still lingered like a bruise that refused to fade.

"We sail in a week," he said, folding the parchment. "I'll have the men begin loading at once."

"God keep ye, Andrew."

He nodded once and turned toward the door.

God had never kept anyone at sea.
But he accepted the blessing all the same.

Barton Brothers

Andrew had only just stepped from the kirk when something small and fast collided with his side.

"Laird Andrew! Laird Andrew!"

He caught the boy by the shoulder before he could bowl straight into the road. "Young Amos?" Andrew sighed under his breath. "Darnation. What now?"

Amos bent double, hands braced on his knees, gulping air like he had run from the devil himself. "It's yer brother, my Laird. Chieftain Alex. He's at my Da's alehouse, deep in his cups. Got into a row over a card wager, accused a man of cheatin', called him a cheatin' bastard…"

Andrew fixed him with a look.

"Mind yer tongue."

Amos winced. "Aye. Sorry, my Laird. I meant a cheatin' dog."

He hesitated. "Which is still bad, I ken."

Andrew pinched the bridge of his nose.

Amos rushed on, "Next thing I knew, yer brother threw a punch and all hell…"

Andrew's eyes lifted.

"…all went daft," Amos finished quickly. "Very daft. Da sent me to fetch ye before someone lost an eye."

"And where is my brother now?" Andrew asked, already turning toward the village.

Amos grimaced. "Passed out on the tavern porch. Folks steppin' over him to get inside. One lady tucked a coin in his boot, thinkin' he was beggin'."

Andrew stopped and closed his eyes. "Christ."

Then he turned toward the road. "Damn it all, Alex."

Since their parents' deaths, grief had hollowed Alex rather than sharpened him. Responsibility had not waited for him to recover, and he had not risen to meet it. Andrew had carried what Alex could not.

Grief twisted inward. When it could no longer be borne, Alex drowned it in whisky and laughter and women who asked no questions. Andrew knew this was not the man his brother had been.

The fracture had begun long before the drink took hold. Before the castle fell quiet.

There had been Sophie.

Alex's first love, or what passed for it in a young man who wanted something in the world to be his. She had clever eyes. A practiced smile. She laughed at his devotion even as she took from it. By morning she was gone, along with his horse, his boots, his sword, and his dagger.

Alex went looking for her, only to find her lifeless body, or what was left of it after the wolves were done.

Andrew brought him home that night. His brother was broken. Quieter than Andrew had ever known him to be. A man who once filled every awkward silence now said nothing at all. He only stared at the blood on his knuckles, blood that had nothing to do with a fight.

Alex never spoke of her again.

Something essential had gone missing with her.

After that, drinking came easier.

Trust did not.

Whiskey and Grief

At the alehouse, Andrew found his brother exactly where he expected him to be.
Alex lay sprawled across the threshold, one boot missing, the other hanging on by stubborn habit, hair fallen loose across his face, like a man who had fought the ground and lost. Patrons stepped over him on their way inside, careful not to trip, less careful not to stare.

Andrew sighed through his nose and nudged him with his boot. "Darnation."

Alex groaned. "If that's the devil, tell him I'm busy. I'm out tonight."

Andrew bent, hauled his brother upright by the collar, and propped him against the wall before turning at once to young Amos. "Run to the stables. Fetch Haemish. Bring the buggy."

"Aye, Laird Andrew." The boy bolted, relieved to be anywhere else.

Andrew tapped Alex's cheek. Not gently. "Alex. Open yer eyes."

"Ouch! Leave me be," Alex swatted weakly. He squinted, struggling for focus. "Why d'ye look so disappointed? Did I forget a birthday? A funeral? Or did I promise somethin' important again?"

"It's me, yer brother, Drake," he said flatly.

Recognition flickered. Alex scoffed. "Andrew! Why're ye usin' yer sea name in public?" A hiccup escaped him. "Go away, Drake. Ye smell like rules and responsibility."

Andrew pinched the bridge of his nose. "Bloody hell. We sail in a week. A week. And here ye are, drinkin' yerself into the stones like a dockhand with no name to lose."

"To hell with yer cockhand," Alex slurred, waving a hand. "Can ye not see I'm occupied? I'm in deep negotiations with the floor."

Andrew answered by flinging cold water into his face.

"JESUS, MARY, AND ALL THE SAINTS!" Alex roared. "What in God's frozen arse was that for?" He wiped his eyes, sputtered once, then laughed. "Oh. That woke me."

"You're drunk," Andrew snapped. "And makin' a spectacle of yerself."

"I am inspired," Alex corrected, drawing himself upright with far more confidence than balance. "I am a man. Not a wee bairn." He jabbed a finger at his chest. "And if Da wanted the business run proper, he'd've stayed longer."

He laughed once, too loudly.
The sound died.

Andrew didn't answer. His jaw tightened as he stepped aside.

Though Alex was the elder, the weight of the Barton name had settled squarely on Andrew's shoulders these past two years. Estates, accounts, alliances, the obligations of the family had passed to him without ceremony.

The fracture had begun long before the drink took hold. Before the house fell quiet.

There had been a girl once.

Not a lady of court, not someone his father would ever have approved of, but someone Alex had loved with the earnest, foolish intensity of youth. He had promised her things he had not yet learned how to keep. When he returned for her, years later, she was already gone from the life he had imagined.

Alex never spoke her name aloud. Some losses did not need words to rot a man from the inside.

Grief twisted inward, quiet and corrosive, and when it could no longer be borne, he drowned it in whisky and laughter and women who asked no questions. Andrew knew this was not the man his brother had been.

Alex blinked, as if only then realizing he'd gone too far. He opened his mouth, thought better of it, and took one proud step forward, only to pitch flat onto his face.

"Ouch," he muttered into the stones. "The ground jumped me."

Andrew looked down at him. "Ye are a drunken fool."

"Aye," Alex said, lifting one hand and pointing without looking up. "But I'm yer drunken fool."

Andrew exhaled and bent to lift him anyway.

Haemish arrived just then. "Drunk again?"

"Aye," Andrew muttered. "But this time the arse has a black eye."

"At least he's nae covered in piss," Haemish said, laughing as he hoisted Alex over his shoulder like a sack of wool.

"Ouch," Alex groaned. "Easy, ye big oaf."

The Weight of Blood

Andrew stepped onto the dais and took his seat. Food appeared at once, bread still warm, eggs, sausages, porridge, and a jug of apple cider set down with quiet efficiency.

"Good morrow, my Laird," the girls said together.

"Good morrow," Andrew replied, already reaching for the bread. "Where is Laird Alex?"

One of them hesitated. "Still abed, I believe."

Andrew paused, butter knife hovering. His jaw tightened, only a little, then he finished the motion as though nothing had been said. He glanced toward Haemish. "Any word from Edinburgh?"

"Nae," Haemish replied. "Not a whisper."

Andrew exhaled through his nose. "Christ. King James kens we sail within the week. Without the King's seal, we're pirates the moment we clear open water."

"Aye," Haemish said mildly. "And pirates tend to die young."

"The English or the Spanish'll string us up by our cocks," Andrew muttered.

Haemish snorted. "Aye. So what's the plan, then?"

"We sail at first light. Slip the firth quietly. You and I ride to Edinburgh while the men hold fast."

Haemish nodded once. "I'll have the supplies finished by eve. We'll be ready."

Andrew raked a hand through his hair. "Alex will nae like this."

"Alex will nae like what?"

Alex appeared at the top of the stairs, hair wild, shirt unlaced, descending with the reckless confidence of a man who had never been properly punished by consequence. He plucked an apple from a passing tray and dropped into the chair beside Andrew.

"What will I nae like?" he asked, already chewing.

Andrew closed his eyes for a brief, prayerless moment. "We sail on the morrow."

Apple and spittle flew.

"On the morrow?" Alex wiped his mouth. "Are ye daft? We've just returned. 'Tis nae even a new moon. The crofters are waitin' on coin, the keep needs repairs." He jabbed a thumb at his chest. "They think we've forgotten them."

"I'm glad to see ye sober and suddenly civic-minded," Andrew said. "But we've debts to settle. Two new galleys to purchase. Business does nae pause because ye've discovered responsibility overnight." He leaned back. "And before we sail, we must ride to Edinburgh for the King's seal. Without it, we're dead men the moment we clear open water."

Alex's grin softened. "This time, I wish to remain behind."

Andrew didn't look at him.

"I ken I've disappointed ye. And Da. And Ma." Alex swallowed. "I've been grieving."

Silence settled. Andrew kept eating.

"I ken," he said at last.

Alex set the apple down. "I'll mind the keep. From this day, nae more spirits will touch my lips."

Andrew raised one brow. "That's a bold oath before breakfast."

Alex grinned. "Have faith, Drake. I'm the heir Da trained since I could stand and piss straight."

Andrew huffed despite himself and stood, pulling Alex into a brief, fierce embrace.

"I'm givin' ye one last chance, brother. Do right."

They pressed foreheads together, a gesture older than pride.

"I ken Ma and Da would be proud," Andrew murmured. He stepped back. "Lay off the whisky and the wenches. Let yer cock rest and yer mind do the thinking."

Alex laughed. "Speak for yerself and take that big oaf Haemish with ye. And dinnae bring back some exotic lass claimin' she's yer wife."

Andrew waved him off. "Oh, to be different, brother. Oh, to be different."

Chapter 3

Captured - Atlantic Ocean, 1620

*P*ain dragged Nzingha back into the world.

It pulsed outward from the base of her skull, slow and relentless, each throb pulling her farther from the mercy of darkness. The ground beneath her swayed. No. The world. She groaned, nausea rising as though her body had forgotten which way was down.
She opened her eyes.

Light cut through her vision in dull, unfocused flashes, sharp enough to make her squeeze them shut again. The air was thick with salt and rot, old water and something fouler beneath it. Wood creaked. Water rushed.

Her stomach dropped.
She was at sea.

Nzingha raised a hand to her head. Her fingers brushed a swollen knot near the back of her skull, and she hissed softly. When she lowered her hand, the sound that followed stopped her breath altogether.

Metal.

She looked down.
Iron shackles bound her wrists. Chains wrapped her ankles, heavy and unforgiving, their weight pressing into bone and tendon alike.

"No," she whispered. "No... this cannot be."

Panic surged, sharp and sudden, threatening to drown her where she sat. She drew her knees close as the chains allowed and forced herself to breathe. Slowly, her eyes adjusted to the dim.

She was inside a cage.

Rough wooden bars enclosed her on all sides, splintered and thick, hay scattered across the floor like bedding meant for animals. The smell told her the rest; livestock had been kept here before her.

She was not a prisoner.
She was cargo.

A shadow moved beyond the bars.

"Cala a boca!"

A man struck the cage with a stick. The sound cracked through her skull, and something hot and violent flared in her chest. Nzingha lifted her chin and met his gaze through the bars, her voice low and measured.

"When my arms are free," she said, enunciating each word, "I am going to kill you."

The man laughed and moved on.

Nzingha retreated to the corner of the cage, pressing her back to the wood, wrapping her arms around herself. Her body shook, not with fear, but fury.

The Truth Beneath the Deck

From the darkness beyond the reach of the lantern light came a whisper.

"Princess Nzingha."

Her head snapped up.

"Yes," she breathed. "Who speaks?"

"'Tis me," the voice answered softly. "Iney."

"Oh, Iney..." Nzingha whispered, crawling toward the bars as far as her chains allowed.

A hand slipped through the narrow space between the slats and gripped her fingers tightly.

"My Princess," Iney murmured. "I feared you were dead. You slept for three days."

Nzingha swallowed. Her mouth was dry, her throat burning. "Water."

"I saved this," Iney said quickly. "Each time the men came below, they passed you by. I hoped..."

She pressed a small ration to Nzingha's lips. The water was stale, but it eased the ache enough to let her speak.

"I wish I had died instead of waking here."

Iney's grip tightened. "Why did you flee your quarters? I saw you leave and followed from a distance. There were intruders on the shore. When they chased you, I was forced into a skirmish. By the time I reached you, they had already struck you down."

Nzingha's gaze dropped to Iney's arm. "You're wounded."

"I pulled the arrow free. I had herbs hidden on my person. They took my weapons, but not my knowledge. I have no fever."

Nzingha scanned the shadows. "Are there others?"

"No. Only us."

The weight of that settled heavily between them.

"We must escape," Nzingha said.

Iney shook her head. "We have sailed for days. These chains weigh nearly five stone."

Nzingha's voice wavered despite herself. "I fled to find Mikel. I believe my father sold him."

Iney hesitated. Her grip tightened, then loosened, as if she could not decide whether to hold on or let go.

"My Princess..." Her voice broke. She tried again. "Princess... A fortnight ago, King Afonso ordered Mikel's execution."

The words did not fall so much as strike.

"Mikel?" Nzingha breathed. The name barely made it past her lips. "A fortnight... and no one told me?"

"I could not," Iney whispered. "Your father would have killed anyone who spoke it."

Something inside Nzingha gave way. She sobbed openly now, grief tearing through her without restraint.

"I hate him," she cried. "He may be my father by blood, but I hate him."

Iney leaned close. "You must be silent."

Keys rattled in the darkness.

Blood in the Hold

A man stormed into the hold, shouting, the jangle of keys growing closer. Nzingha bowed her head, tears still slipping free as the cage door creaked open.
The man raised his hand.

Instinct answered first.

She thrust her shackled feet forward, catching his legs and sending him crashing to the deck. Before he could recover, Iney looped her chains through the bars and pulled them tight around his neck, bracing herself as he gasped and clawed uselessly at the iron.

Nzingha surged forward.

She seized the dagger from his belt and drove it home, once, clean and final. His body went still.

Silence rushed in.

She stripped him of the keys and freed herself, then Iney. Her breath caught when she found her belongings among the corpses; Mikel's sapphire necklace, her mother's ruby ring, the gold bands of her people, the twin daggers her uncle had forged for her.

She kicked the body once.

"Rot in this cage, like the beast you are."

Iney's voice was tight. "There are near twenty men above."

Nzingha listened to the ship breathe, the groan of wood, the snap of sail.

"Then we do not fight them all, we move like shadows."

They crept toward the stairs, bodies low, bare feet silent against the planks as the ship rolled beneath them. Lantern light swayed overhead, casting long, unsteady shadows. Two men slept near the rail, mouths slack with drink. Above them, silhouettes laughed in the crow's nest, unaware, unwatchful.

Iney lifted three fingers.

They moved.

The first man never woke. The kill was swift and soundless, steel finding flesh before breath could turn into a warning. His body sagged, taken by the dark.

The rowboat lay ahead.

They cut the ropes together, quick and precise, but the sea betrayed them. The boat struck the water with a hard, echoing splash.

For a heartbeat, the world held its breath.

Then shouts erupted.

CRACK. CRACK.

Musket fire lit the dark, sudden and wild, shots tearing across the deck as men surged toward the rail.

"Jump!" Nzingha screamed.

They leaped without hesitation, plunging into the black ocean below, no plan left now but survival, or die trying.

Between Sea and Dark Sky

The water swallowed them whole.

Cold slammed into Nzingha's lungs as she sank, the weight of her weapons dragging her down. She kicked hard, fighting upward until she burst back into the air, gasping.

"Iney!"

Panic sliced through her voice. "Can you see the boat?"

The night pressed in from all sides, sky and sea indistinguishable, gunfire flashing briefly behind them.

"I see it!" Iney shouted. "To the left, swim!"

Musket fire cracked across the water. Balls struck the surrounding surface, sending violent sprays into the air as arrows hissed past, slicing the dark. They swam hard, arms burning, the current tugging at them while the ship loomed behind like a shadowed beast.

Nzingha reached the boat first and turned back just in time to see Iney falter. Her injured arm dragged uselessly at her side, her head dipping beneath the surface.

"Iney!"

She lunged, seized her warrior's shoulder, and hauled her close. "Hold on to me." Using her body as leverage, Nzingha climbed into the boat and braced herself, then reached down again, fingers straining until she caught Iney's wrist. With a guttural cry, she heaved herself up and over the side.

Iney collapsed at the bottom of the boat, coughing violently, clutching her wounded arm. Nzingha seized the oars and rowed.

She did not look back.

Arrows splashed behind them. Shouts faded. The ship shrank, swallowed by distance and darkness, until it vanished entirely. Only the sea remained.

Iney lay trembling at her feet, breath ragged but alive. After a long moment, she let out a weak laugh. "We did it."

Nzingha kept rowing.

Tears slipped down her face, unnoticed, as the sky stretched endlessly above them. Somewhere between the oar strokes, Mikel's voice rose from memory, soft, teasing, and now cruel in its absence.

You will be the death of me.

"Yet... I was," she whispered.

The sea carried them forward. She would never return to Mbemba, not for alliance, not for war, not for her father's throne.

Only forward remained.

Four Moons at Sea - Atlantic Ocean-

1620

Andrew Barton had deemed it wise to bring Haemish along once Alex chose to remain behind. If his elder brother would not steady the keep, then Andrew would steady the seas. Quartermaster Denton McKoy joined them in the captain's quarters as the ship pressed onward through unsettled waters, their course plotted along the Atlantic route skirting the Canary Islands.

Crates of silk and printed cloth were secured below deck, alongside pink sea salt and sea sponges packed tight against moisture. Fragrant oils, hibiscus, coconut, jasmine, rested sealed in clay jars. Tropical fruits followed, strange oranges and pineapples prized by nobles who had never tasted the sun. Wine and spirits filled the remaining space, gathered from ports that understood trade and indulgence in equal measures.

Barton & Sons had been built on such ventures. Scotland's markets thrived on it. The King's table was stocked by it. Andrew took pride in knowing that through him, the world reached beyond stone walls and cold shores.

At sea, he let his beard grow and his name fade. Andrew remained on land. Here he was Captain. Drake.

Denton traced the map with a careful finger, eyes narrowed in thought. "Captain," he said at last, "I advise we turn for home. The rain's held a sen night now, and the sea's turning sour. We've enough cargo for the kirk and the castle, and more than enough to trade without tempting God's patience."

Haemish leaned back in his chair, tipping it onto two legs, boots planted square on the desk as though it belonged to him. "Aye?" he said, glancing sideways at Andrew. "That sounds like a man with a lass waitin' ashore, or a creditor breathin' down his neck."

Andrew shoved Haemish's boots aside without looking at him. "We've one sen night left," he said evenly. "And Father McPherson's list is still short. I didnae promise half-measures, and I willnae return with excuses."

Denton studied Andrew's face a moment longer, then nodded once. He'd sailed long enough to know when a decision had already been made.

A sudden swell slammed into the hull, throwing the ship hard to port.

Glasses skidded. Plates leaped from the table and shattered at their feet. All three men caught their whiskey just in time.

Haemish laughed under his breath. "That's the sea tellin' ye she's heard you."

Andrew drank deep, the burn steadying him as thunder rolled beyond the hull. "We ride the storm tonight," he said calmly. "Home on the morrow."

Thunder answered him.

Later, cards slapped against the table as rain hammered the deck above. The lantern swayed, casting wild shadows as the ship groaned like a living thing straining against its own bones.

Haemish grinned, dealing with easy confidence. "Rummy in three, ye bastards."

Andrew said nothing, hiding his final card behind his knuckles while Denton watched him with suspicion earned over many voyages.

Haemish drained his glass and slammed it down. "Just play the damn card. Yer not negotiatin' with the King. Yer playin' cards."

Andrew laid the card on the table. "Rummy."

Haemish swore, then barked a laugh as he shoved back his chair. "That's twice this week. I'm sleepin' before I lose my boots too."

He turned to leave.

The crash came before his foot hit the floor.

The ship screamed as timber split somewhere above, the deck pitching hard beneath them.

"St. Christopher's cross," Haemish breathed.

The Storm

The first jolt came without warning.

The ship lurched hard to port, timbers groaning as though the hull itself had drawn breath and decided to scream. Plates skidded across the table inside the quarters, shattering against the bulkhead. Somewhere above, a shout rang out, sharp and startling. Another rang clearly.

Andrew was on his feet before the second cry finished. So were Haemish and Denton. For one brief instant they looked at one another, three men who had weathered too much sea together to mistake the sound. No orders were given. Chairs scraped back.

Hands reached for belts and blades as they moved as one, already running for the ladder.

Andrew reached the door first.

Before his hand touched the latch, the wind struck, ripping the door inward and nearly tearing it from its hinges.

Wind exploded into the passage, ripping breath from his lungs as rain lashed sideways, stinging his face. Loose charts and parchment tore free, whipping past him in a frenzy of paper and spray.

"What the devil...."

Andrew staggered back half a step, bracing himself against the frame. "None of ye arselings thought to alert us?!"

Thunder cracked so close it rattled bone.

He shoved forward anyway and forced his way onto the deck.

Chaos reigned.

A mast cracked with a thunderous report, not the clean break of battle, but the brutal snap of wood pushed past its limits. It tore free and slammed into the bow, exploding into splinters. Men scattered, boots slipping on the flooded planks as ropes snapped loose and whipped through the air like striking serpents.

"Hold fast!" Andrew roared, already moving. "Close the sails! Tie those bloody knots before they tear us apart!"

The deck pitched beneath him, water surging in sheets. He severed a tangled line in one clean strike; the rope recoiled as it fell away. Above, sails thundered and flapped, threatening to rip free entirely as the rigging screamed in protest.

"Aye, Captain!" voices shouted back, thin, edged with panic, but obeying.

Lightning split the sky.

For a heartbeat, the sea stood revealed, towering black walls of water rolling toward them, relentless, merciless. Thunder followed, close enough to shake bone. The rain came down harder, blinding, soaking wool and leather until everything weighed twice as much.

Andrew wiped water from his eyes and scanned the deck.

"HEAVE!" Haemish roared.

He was near the rail, shoulder to shoulder with half a dozen men, shoving broken timber toward the edge to keep it from battering the hull. He shouted orders of his own, voice carrying even over the storm.

Andrew took a step and froze. No rope. No line at Haemish's waist. His stomach dropped.

"Haemish!" Andrew bellowed, fighting the wind as he looped a rope around himself with swift, practiced movements.

"Are ye daft?! Tie in!" Andrew shouted, hurling the free end toward him.

A dark, towering wall rose from the sea itself, as if torn upward from the ocean floor, higher than the deck, higher than the mast that still clung to the ship, its vast shadow swallowing sky and sail alike as it reared over them.

For one suspended moment, everything went silent.

Then it crashed.

The deck vanished beneath a roaring flood. Andrew felt the rope wrench violently, his feet lifting as the force dragged him forward. His shoulder smashed into the rail. His head struck iron-hard wood.

Stars burst behind his eyes as cold swallowed him whole, water crushing in from all sides, spinning him end over end while he kicked blindly, lungs burning, fighting for an up that no longer existed.

He broke the surface with a gasp.

The ship was gone, nothing left but shattered timber to prove it had ever existed at all.

Rain hammered his face as the sea tossed him like flotsam. He heard shouting once, faint and distant, Haemish's voice, carried and stolen by the wind.

"Captain!"

"HAEMISH!" Andrew roared, forcing the name from his lungs. "HAEMISH, HOLD FAST!"

The rope wrenched hard, then fell slack in his hands.

Fear locked tight around his chest as he fumbled along the line, fingers numb, searching for resistance, for weight, for life.

Nothing.

Blood ran warm down his brow, mixing with rain and salt as he clung to a floating length of timber, every muscle trembling with exhaustion. The storm drifted off as suddenly as it had come, leaving rolling water and a vast, roaring silence in its wake.

The sea rocked him, almost gently.

Against his will, his eyes slid shut.

And the darkness took him.

Castaway

Andrew woke choking, air tearing into his lungs in a harsh, burning rush that left him gagging and clawing at the ground. His fingers sank into grit so hot it stung, and he coughed hard, rolling onto his side as saltwater spilled from his mouth and nose. His throat felt scraped raw, hollowed out, as though he had swallowed the sea itself, and when he dragged in another breath, it burned just as badly. He lay there, chest heaving, heart hammering too fast for a body that had not yet caught up with the fact that it still lived.

Above him, the sky stretched wide and mercilessly, an endless blue broken by slow-moving clouds drifting past as if nothing violent had occurred beneath them. The sun bore down on his face and chest without pity, heating his wet clothes until they clung and burned, while beneath him the tide crept close, cool water lapping at his boots before retreating again, only to return a moment later, steady as a pulse. Hot and cold chased one another across his skin, leaving him shivering despite the heat.

His head throbbed with a deep, punishing ache. When Andrew lifted a hand to his brow, he hissed as his fingers came away slick with blood. The world swam, and memory returned in fragments, the rail beneath his hands, the scream of the wind, the sickening crack of his skull against iron.

"Christ," he muttered, though the word sounded thin and useless in his own ears.

Getting upright took longer than it should have. Every inch was won through pain. His vision tilted, steadied, then tilted again. He spat sand from his mouth and wiped his lips, already split and dry, thirst clawing hard at the back of his throat. It felt as though whatever the sea had not taken, it had wrung dry and left behind.

He stopped and listened.

There was no creaking of timber. No canvas snapping. No shouted orders carried on the wind. Only the steady hush of surf rolling in and pulling back, again and again, patient and indifferent, and the faint creak of palms somewhere inland. No answering call came when he strained for it. No Haemish.

Andrew turned his head slowly, scanning the beach. There was no wreckage strewn along the shore, no shattered hull half-buried in sand, no bodies dragged up by the tide. No ship. No men.

"No," he breathed, the word barely leaving him.

The shoreline stretched pale and empty in both directions, endless sand meeting endless water, and beyond it the jungle pressed thick and green, alive in a way that set his nerves on edge. The air felt heavy and wet, closing around his lungs. He tried to swallow and found his mouth dry as wool.

"Where the bloody hell am I?" he rasped.

The words vanished into the open heat.

His sword came free next, dropped to the sand with a dull, final sound. Then the dirks. The scabbard. Each piece felt heavier than the last, his arms trembling as though they belonged to someone else. He stripped off his doublet, then his blouse, until his skin could breathe beneath the sun's assault.

Andrew staggered toward the water, boots sinking as the tide washed over his feet. With clumsy fingers, he untied his cravat and soaked it in the sea, pressing the cool cloth to his neck and brow. The relief was brief, almost insulting in how little it offered.

His head still pounded. His stomach churned. His limbs felt wrong, heavy and slow, as though the ocean had not quite released its claim on him.

This was not Scotland. He knew it without thinking, in the heat, the sand, the way the air pressed thick against his chest with every breath. Wherever the storm had thrown him, it had carried him far from home.

Andrew Barton.
Drake of the open seas.

He had survived the storm.

He stood alone at the edge of the world, blood drying on his skin, salt crusting his lashes, staring into a land that did not know his name and would not care to learn it.

Now he would discover whether survival had ended with the sea or merely changed its shape.

The Tropical Paradise

Nzingha ducked into the hut she had built from palm limbs and thick branches, the kind of shelter a princess should never have had to learn to make.
Six months had passed since the sea had thrown them onto this island, reducing the world to sand, jungle, and a horizon that never offered a ship. The land had no one, absolutely no one, and still, it had taken nearly everything.

When they first arrived, Iney fell ill. Fever took her hard and fast, and the wound in her arm, earned protection from her princess, began to turn foul. Weeks passed. Then more weeks. Some days she rallied. Other days she lay still, staring as though her spirit had already begun to loosen its grip.

Iney coughed, a wet sound that shook her ribs.

Nzingha was at her side at once, pressing a cloth to Iney's brow as she began unwrapping the bandages torn from her own clothing. The moment the fabric pulled free, the smell rose. Rot, heat, a sickness thick enough to claw at the throat. Pus seeped from the wound, pale and heavy, and Nzingha swallowed hard, twice, before steadying herself.

"You have the face of a child smelling her first spoiled fish," Iney rasped.

Nzingha blinked, then breathed out through her nose. "You are lucky I love you."

"You love me because I am too ill to run away."

The sound Nzingha made fell somewhere between a laugh and a sob. She reached for the clay pot she had fashioned from mud and dried straw, the water inside boiling over the small fire. She had washed the rags in the sea earlier, scrubbing until her fingers burned, doing everything she could to keep the wound from claiming Iney outright.

Using two sticks, she lifted a steaming rag and pressed it to the infected flesh.

Iney screamed into her own palm, eyes squeezed shut, the sound muffled but raw.

"I know," Nzingha said quickly, already working. "I know. You are brave. The bravest woman I have ever known. But the infection must come out, or it will eat you from the inside."

"You say that as though it is an inconvenience," Iney muttered, her voice thin with pain.

Nzingha's mouth tightened as she wiped the wound clean. "I found aloe bushes five miles from camp."

Iney's eyes fluttered open. "Five miles."

"Yes."

"That is too far."

"Did I not come back?"

A cough cracked through Iney's chest. "Those men could be anywhere."

Nzingha softened then, brushing her knuckles along Iney's cheek. "We are safe. I set traps around the camp. Beast or man, we will know."

Iney tried to push herself upright, stubborn even now, but her strength failed her halfway and she sank back with a curse.

Nzingha spoke too brightly, as though cheer might plug the holes grief kept tearing open.
"Found plantain trees today, oh… and I caught four fish this morning. We will have soup for supper."

Iney stared at her.

Nzingha leaned closer, conspiratorially. "And guess what."

"What."

She held up a small cloth sack, shaking it like treasure. "Salt. Dried from the ocean rocks. We have salt."

Her smile was wide, the kind that once lit a throne room.
It did not reach her eyes.

Iney watched her for a long moment before speaking. "For someone who lost her love, was chained like an animal, and sleeps in palm branches, you are far too pleased with yourself."

The smile faltered.

"You have not spoken of returning," Iney continued, quieter now. "Not once. You speak of soup and salt as if that is a life."

Nzingha's fingers tightened around the sack. "Because it is."

"It is hiding."

"No. It is peace."

Iney shook her head, irritation flickering through her fatigue. "It is running."

The wind moved through the palm trees. The sea whispered like a secret.

"Do you think I do not know what I have lost?" Nzingha asked, her voice low and sharp.

Iney's gaze softened, fever loosening her restraint. "Then stop pretending you do not care."

Nzingha rose so fast that the woven mat shifted. "I care so much it tears me open."

Silence pressed on.

"Mikel's necklace should still be on my skin," Nzingha said, her voice breaking open now. "His hands on my face. His voice in my ears. Instead, I have this island and a sky that does not answer."

"Princess…"

"Do not call me that," she snapped. "Not when I am living like a ghost."

Iney stepped closer despite the pain. "Your father acted to protect your bloodline."

"Protection?" Nzingha laughed, sharp and bitter. "He executed my love."

Iney flinched.

"He stole my future and named it duty," Nzingha said. "Ripped away my happiness as if it were nothing."

"He feared you would be ruined," Iney said gently.

"Ruined." Nzingha repeated the word as though tasting poison. She stepped back. "Is that what you think?"

She dusted her hands in the sharp, insulting gesture of her people.

"Silence your mouth," she said, fury breaking through grief. "I am not ruined. Even if I had given myself freely, it was no one's business."

Her chest heaved. "He is no better than the men who captured us. No better than slavers."

Iney faltered then, dizziness finally winning. "Nzingha," she whispered. "I cannot lose you too."

The words struck harder than any blow.

Nzingha turned away quickly, ashamed of her tears. "I am never going back."

She pointed towards the trees. "The boat is hidden east, five miles inland. If you wish to return, you may."

Her voice shook, but she did not turn.

"I am not going anywhere."

And she stormed off.

Unexpected Guest

Nzingha, heated by the argument, stormed away.

She hiked toward the lake, needing distance, needing air, needing a world that did not contain Iney's fevered eyes or Mikel's absence.

Two miles from camp, the ground softened beneath her feet, the mud catching where it should not have.

She slowed without thinking, eyes lowering, breath tightening as the shape resolved itself. Before she had words for it.

A boot print. Too large. Too fresh.

Her stomach turned hard enough to make her swallow. "No," she whispered. "It cannot be."

She knew this island. Every ridge, every break in the brush, every place a man might hide. Until now, it had been empty.

She moved as Asha once had, silent and deliberate, each step chosen with care. No leaves stirred. No branches betrayed her. Reaching the brush, she sank low and watched from the shadows.

A white man knelt on one knee, one hand braced against the earth, the other clamped tight to his side. His breathing came in broken pulls, chest heaving so hard it looked painful.

Sunburn blistered his shoulders and back, the skin angry and raw, sweat running freely down the hard line of his spine as he knelt there, braced against the earth like a man held upright by stubbornness alone. He looked as though he had crawled out of the sea and regretted surviving it.

Something stirred in the trees.

His head lifted slowly, eyes tracking the undergrowth, the shadows between leaves, the places a man learned to watch when life had already taught him what waited there. He searched the jungle as though expecting it to answer him.

Then he saw her.

She knelt among the branches, still as stone, peering through the leaves like a lioness at rest before the strike. One knee pressed into the earth, staff balanced easily in her palm, her body quiet in a way that spoke of patience and calculation rather than fear.

Their eyes met.

For a breath, the world held.

Nzingha shifted, already rising, already dismissing him as no threat worth her time.

That was when he dragged his sword free.

The blade scraped softly as it left its sheath, trembling in his grip as he forced himself upright, pride doing what strength could not.

"Halt," he croaked, the word shaped more by habit than authority.

Blood seeped through the cloth bound around his head, trailing down his temple. His gaze wavered, faltered, then fixed on her again, stubborn as the man himself.

Only then did the truth break through him.

"Water," he rasped, the word tearing free before he could stop it. His jaw tightened as if angered by the weakness of it.

"Where… where am I?"

The question fractured, breath breaking between syllables.

She did not answer.

"I am Captain Drake of Scotland."

He took a single step toward her.

That was a huge mistake.

Nzingha lunged.

The staff struck fast and clean, wood cracking against steel as he barely wrenched his sword up in time. The impact shuddered through his arm, rattling bone. She came again without pause, driving him backward with relentless precision.

"Christ," he muttered as his boots slipped in the loose dirt.

She pressed harder.

He parried left, then right, each movement slower than the last, his shoulders already sagging beneath exhaustion. Sweat stung his eyes. His mouth tasted of ash. He circled, trying to read her, trying to catch the rhythm of her strikes, angling his blade to hook her weapon and wrench it free.

She saw the attempt before it finished forming.

Nzingha dropped low and spun.

Her leg swept clean beneath him. The ground vanished. The world tilted, and he hit hard, landing squarely on his backside with a grunt that drove the breath from his lungs.

Before he could rise, the staff was there.

Its tip hovered a breath from his right eye.

He froze.

Slowly, carefully, he lifted his hands. "Fine… fine," he said, breathless. "I can see I'm nae welcome."

She did not answer.

He drew out a breath. "I'm lost, Hungry. Thirsty. And in no fit state tae fight a woman who could put me in the dirt twice over."

Still, she said nothing.

"If ye'd just point me toward water," he added more quietly, "I'll take it and be on my way."

The pause stretched.

Then Nzingha lowered the staff.

That was her mistake.

He moved with sudden speed, hooking her ankle and yanking hard. She hit the ground with a sharp breath as he surged up, teeth clenched, sword snapping back into his grip.

He stood over her, blade angled toward her chest, then extended his free hand.

"Easy," he said, "I'm no here tae harm ye."

She slapped it aside and rose in one smooth motion, eyes blazing.

He exhaled slowly now, the effort visible, shoulders sagging again as the borrowed strength bled out of him. He hesitated, then lifted his hand and tipped it toward his mouth, the gesture clumsy, nearly desperate.

"Water," he rasped. "Please."

Nzingha lifted one brow.

He looked like a beggar who had forgotten the language of men.

She held his gaze a moment longer than necessary, measuring him, then turned away without a word. One brief motion of her hand.

Follow.

They walked in silence until the jungle opened onto a waterfall spilling into a clear pool, lush and green and impossibly alive.

He stopped short. "I'd drink the devil himself for that," he breathed.

He dropped to his knees and plunged his head beneath the water, drinking like a man pulled back from the grave. A quiet laugh escaped him before he submerged fully beneath the falls, washing salt, blood, and sand from his skin.

When he surfaced, he pressed his palms together briefly, eyes closed. "God bless ye," he murmured.

He noticed her watching and offered a faint, grateful smile. "Aye," he said softly. "That'll do."

Nzingha stood in the shade, chewing sea grapes, watching him with calculating eyes, the question forming unbidden beneath the quiet of her face.

She thought to herself, *just who the hell are you?*

His complexion was not pale but bronze, burned dark by the sun. His back was lean, muscular. He looked better than any pirate she had seen, and that made her more suspicious, not less.

When he emerged from the water and approached her, hunger returned with urgency. He rubbed his stomach. "Food."

Nzingha pointed toward the sea grape trees.

He plucked a green one, bit into it, and immediately spat it out. "Bloody hell."

She held up a purple one without expression.

He took it, chewed, then smiled slowly. "That is far better. What do you call this?"

He kept eating, slower now, savoring, his face settling into a peace that unsettled her.

Then Mikel's face flashed through her mind so suddenly she stepped back, breath catching hard in her chest.

When she blinked, the stranger stood watching her with quiet concern, the smile gone.

Something shifted inside her. She ignored it.

Sending him away would be wiser. A stranger had no place in their survival, in Iney's sickness, or within her grief.

But he was starving.

And he had not harmed her when he could have.

Nzingha drew a steady breath and motioned for Captain Drake of Scotland to follow.

Chapter 4

The First Appraisal

*T*he almond-skinned woman took the lead, and Drake had the sudden, inconvenient thought that God was testing him.

She moved as though the jungle belonged to her. Not cautiously, not timidly, but with the steady assurance of someone who had walked through worse than thorn and vine and survived it. He followed where she led, branches brushing his shoulders, the heat pressing close, the air thick with birdsong and damp earth.

Christ, he thought.

If she ever wore such attire in Christendom, the kirk would call her a harlot before she reached the first pew.

He grabbed his beard and pressed his lips together as she guided him onward, her back exposed beneath a white wrap that dipped low and tied at her neck, the fabric thin enough to catch the sun, modest enough to pretend.

He had sailed to ports thick with perfume and trouble, to islands where men paid in gold and lied in three tongues, but he had never seen a Black beauty move with such cold certainty, leading the way as though the world itself made room for her.

She was striking, and not only because of her skin, though the bronze glow of it made her look carved from something precious. It was the way she carried herself. The slim waist. The curving hips. The posture that said she did not ask permission to exist. Her bosom sat full and high beneath the cloth, and he forced his gaze back to the trail because a man had to have some decency, even if his pride was bruised and his throat still felt packed with sand.

He noticed the small scar on her shoulder, faint but real, the sort that came from consequence, not accident. That pleased him in a way he could not explain. Softness was easy to desire. A mark like that hinted at survival.

He gave thought, "How could such a tiny lass fight like a she-wolf?"

Her eyes were honey-brown and catlike, shaped in a way that made every glance feel like judgment. Long lashes framed a steady, unsmiling stare that warned men to keep their distance.

At her wrists gleamed gold bracelets, and a heavy necklace rested at her throat, set with a sapphire the size of a musket ball. The daggers at her waist bore jeweled handles that marked her as neither peasant nor island wildling.

It dawned on him slowly, like a ship emerging from fog.

This woman was no common wanderer.

She was royalty or rich blood, and either way, she was dangerous.

He cleared his throat, trying for lightness, as though curiosity were the only thing stirring him.

"Are ye from here?"

Nzingha did not answer. She stepped around roots and fallen vines with the ease of someone who had memorized the land.

He waited a moment, then added, ""I've walked a fair stretch of this island and seen no one yet, only you, moving as though you own the ground beneath you."

Still nothing.

He huffed a breath through his nose. "Right then," he muttered. Louder, he tried again. "Do ye speak the king's English, or am I talking to the trees now?"

She flicked a glance at him from the corner of her eye, quick as a blade, then returned her gaze to the path.

Drake smiled faintly. She heard him. That was something.

He ducked beneath a branch and cursed when a vine snapped back and slapped his face. There was no village here. No path cut by men. Only dense jungle and birds that never seemed to shut their mouths. He was growing tired of ducking and dodging branches thick as arms.

"Beggin' your pardon, miss," he tried again, keeping his voice polite though his patience thinned. "Where d'ye hail from?"

Silence.

He pressed on, because she clearly had no intention of saving him from himself. "I can tell ye're nobility."

She stopped so abruptly he nearly collided with her.

When she turned, her expression was calm, but it was the calm of someone deciding whether a blade was necessary.

"You do not need to know anything about me," she said evenly. "So stop asking."

Then she turned and continued walking.

Drake blinked once, then smiled as though she had handed him a gift.
"Oh, so ye do speak English."

She kept walking, mute as stone.

"Miss," he called again, intentionally. He was a bastard and he knew it, and her silence was beginning to feel like a challenge. "I am the last person tae be a thorn in one's side, but I cannae help noticing ye're skilled with a weapon. That staff's no ornament."
His voice dropped just enough to carry. "But the stick up yer ass is."

She scowled at his rude banter, though it did not bother her. She heard warriors bad-mouth her behavior all the time. Nzingha took it as a compliment. She slowed just enough for it to be noticed, then decided to play nice.

"Thank you for the compliment," she said, still not looking at him.

He exhaled softly. "Saints preserve. She speaks. Are ye some sort of warrior?"

She stopped again. Not with irritation this time, but with consideration.

"I was part of our defense," she said at last, her voice measured, careful, as though speaking of home required a steady hand.
"In my lands, many women fight. We do not wait to be protected."

"Defense," Drake repeated. "Of a kingdom, I take it."

"Yes. Mbemba Kingdom. Africa."

He let out a low breath. "Africa," he murmured. "And here I thought I'd sailed past the edge of the world."

The humor faded as the truth settled. A woman from Africa alone on an island, armed like a commander, wearing jewels like a queen. He had seen ships full of stolen bodies. He had cut down men who laughed while they chained women. He had escorted vessels back toward African shores before, but always with blood in the water.

His voice softened without his permission.

"Lass… were ye taken?"

She slowed, drew a breath, and nodded once.

"Yes."

The word sounded bitter.

"About six moons ago," she said, "I was on my land, searching for someone after nightfall when I heard men moving through the trees, more than I could fight alone. I fought anyway, killed some of them, and ran until my lungs burned and my legs failed me, but still it was not enough, and I was captured. They put me on a ship, iron everywhere, darkness below deck, men who laughed as though suffering were sport. We escaped in the dead of night, stole a rowboat, and rowed until our hands bled, drifting so long we no longer knew whether land or death would find us first. Then… land came."

He caught on the word immediately.

"We?" he said,

"One other," she replied without hesitation. "A comrade. She aided me the night I was taken. She was wounded and captured as well."

"I'm sorry," Drake said quietly, and meant it.

She glanced at him then, assessing, her expression unreadable.

"What are you sorry for? You did not bring me here." Her gaze sharpened as the question turned. "So how did you come to be here, bloodied, lying in the mud, with no food to eat and no water to drink?"

He let out a small huff of breath and lifted a hand toward the cloth at his head. "Och, ye mean this wee scratch? 'Tis nothing. I'm Highland strong."

She looked him over once, unimpressed. "You did not look strong. You looked as though you were birthing a child."

The laugh burst out of him before he could stop it. "Christ," he said, shaking his head. "Ye've a wicked tongue."

"And you speak nonsense," she replied evenly. "What is 'Highland strong'?"

"It means hard land," he said, "Cold rain. Mountains that don't forgive. Folk who learn young that pain doesnae stop the work."

As they walked, he spoke more freely, of narrow valleys and stone paths, of hunting through weather that cut to the bone, of bruises treated as inconveniences and blood wiped away so the work could continue. He told her of sailing as well, of carrying the world home so his people might know more than the edges of their own shores.

"What is it like in Scotland?" she asked at last, curiosity easing into her voice.

He told her the summers were kind and the winters brutal.

"Winter," she repeated, then laughed softly. "Mbemba has none. We pray for rain."

"In Scotland," he said with a faint grin, "ye never know what ye'll get."

"I have never seen snow," she said, "What does it feel like?"

"Cold enough to bite," he answered. "And so white it blinds ye."

Her gaze drifted to his plaid, fingers pinching the cloth as though testing its truth.

"Do you not wear garments called trousers?" she asked. "That is what foreign men wore when they came to our lands. Where are yours? Were they lost at sea?"

He stared at her, then laughed outright, the sound loud enough to startle a bird from the canopy. "Nae," he managed. "'Tis called a kilt."

"A kilt," she repeated, tasting the word.

"Aye. Clan colors."

She walked on in silence for a time, thoughtful, before asking quietly, "Have you ever taken people and put them aboard a ship?"

Drake stopped.

"On my honor," he said, his voice low and steady, "and on the souls of my parents, I never have. Nor would I." He swallowed. "What's done to your people is an abomination."

She kept her gaze forward, anger softening into something wetter, more dangerous. "Then why is it done?"

"Greed," he said, "Men stealing lives and calling it trade." He pressed his hand to his chest. "My God teaches that all souls are equal."

She drew a steady breath and smiled, small but true. "Then your God and ours may yet speak the same tongue," she said, "Oshun. Goddess of love."

And when she smiled fully, her lashes lowering as her eyes closed, the hardness in her face easing just long enough to reveal what lived beneath it, Drake felt something shift within him that had nothing to do with thirst or injury.

He should have left it untouched.

Misjudgments

They were nearing her shelter when Nzingha slowed and turned to face him, her face settling into seriousness.

"We are close," she said, lifting a hand to stop him. "From here on, you step where I step and nowhere else. Do as I do. If you do not, you will regret it. Have a care."

Drake followed her gaze to the ground, scanning the roots and leaf litter with exaggerated seriousness. "Why?" he asked.

"There are snares and traps all around us."

He looked again, unconvinced, and took two careless steps. "What animal snar..."

The vine snapped tight.

"BLOODY HELL FIRE," Drake roared as his feet left the ground. "DAMNATION. AM I THE BLOODY MEAL? WHY DID YE NO WARN ME?"

Nzingha froze.
Then she broke.

She bent double, clutching her stomach, laughter tearing out of her in helpless bursts, so violent she nearly lost her footing. She tried to straighten, failed, and laughed harder, the sound bright and unrestrained in a way he had not yet heard from her.

"You think this is funny," Drake barked, swinging slightly. "Help me down before the blood drains from my cock and makes a desperate escape through my nose."

That only made it worse.

She wheezed, one hand braced against a tree, the other pressed to her mouth as though she might actually choke. Tears gathered at the corners of her eyes.

"Oh…" she managed, then turned too fast.

Drake's plaid had flipped clean up to his chest.
The jungle received a full, uninvited education.

"Ah, hell," he snapped, swinging once. "That's unfortunate."

He tried to tug the cloth down one-handed, failed, and cursed with feeling. "Any chance ye could stop laughin' long enough tae help me," he demanded. "This is not funny."

"Then stop swingin'," she gasped.

"I'm tied tae a bloody tree," he roared. "What choice do I have?"

"Please," she said, breathless, swiping at her eyes. "Cover yourself, and I shall climb up to assist you."

He gathered his plaid with one hand, muttering dark curses while watching her from upside down, baffled by the height of the knot.

"How did ye even tie this vine so high?" he demanded. "There's nae footing for six feet."

Nzingha stepped back several paces, removed her sandals, and took a measured breath.
Then she ran.

Drake's eyes widened as she sprinted and leapt, striking the tree nearly six feet up, feet planting against the bark like a beast. She pushed off, caught a thick branch, and swung up with a grace that did not look human.

"What the hell," Drake breathed.

Within moments she was above him, cutting vines with calm precision.

"I will cut the vine," she called down. "Throw me the extra length hanging beside you."

He tossed it up. She secured it around a log, tested the knot, then signaled him.

When she cut the final vine, Drake caught himself and hauled up onto the branch, breathing hard.

"If I had fallen," he muttered, "I could've snapped me neck."

They sat for a moment, the jungle settling around them, Drake trying to regain both breath and dignity. Nzingha leaned closer, studying his face.

"Your wound," she said, "It is bleeding heavily. Allow me to look."

She examined the slice at his hairline and frowned. "It is not deep. From the way it bleeds, I thought it worse."

As she wrapped the cloth around his head, Drake's gaze betrayed him, drawn to the curve of her breast as she leaned close, the drape of her clothing offering a view he did not deserve.

The smirk slipped out before he could stop it.

Nzingha caught it instantly.

She rolled her eyes, tugged her wrap into place with sharp efficiency, and frowned. "I will see to it properly once we reach the hut."

He lifted a hand in surrender. "I am fine. 'Tis a scratch."

"I have herbs," she said flatly. "I will make certain it does not go putrid."

"My thanks," Drake said, sincere. "How many traps do ye have about here?"

She considered. "About twenty."

"Twenty," he repeated, impressed despite himself. "I have never met a lass like you. A fierce fighter, an excellent climber. What else can ye do?"

She smiled, brief and proud. "As a child, all the women of my tribe were taught to defend themselves. My father would not allow me such freedoms, so I watched and learned. When I begged to fight, he introduced me to a warrior who trained me at fifteen."

"Your father must be wealthy," Drake said. "Most wealthy men prefer servants do the work."

"Mm-hmm," she said, "He is."

He studied her. "How many summers are ye?"

"One and twenty."

He blinked. "Younger than ye look."

She turned the question on him. "And you?"

"Five and twenty."

"Are you married?"

"Nae."

The word came too quickly. He frowned at it himself.

"Not for lack of interest," he added. "I'm nae home long enough to stand still. The sea makes a poor wife, but she's greedy for time."

He glanced at her. "And you?"

She paused.

A tear slipped free, sudden and unwelcome. She wiped it away so quickly it nearly did not exist.

"No," she said, sharp, and seized the vine to climb down.

Drake's worry flickered. "Are ye hale?"

She ignored him. "Come. Iney will be worried."

Chapter 5

The Reveal

After a long walk, they reached a clearing.

A small hut stood there, built of bamboo poles and coconut branches woven tight, banana leaves laid at the entrance to keep animals out. It was simple, sturdy, and clearly lived in.

Nzingha entered first.

Inside, Iney lay coughing. At the sound of footsteps, she propped herself onto one elbow, her face lighting with fragile relief when she saw who it was.

"My Princess," Iney said.

Drake stopped cold.

"Princess?"

In an instant, everything aligned. The gold at her throat. The jeweled daggers. The way she carried herself, the sharpness of her tongue when he'd called it wicked. None of it had been ornament or accident. And the truth that burned hottest of all was this...

She had seen him hanging upside down fully exposed.

"Christ."

His mouth opened, then closed again as he pressed a fist to his lips, as though shame were something he might still contain.

Nzingha closed her eyes for a brief moment, irritation flickering and gone just as quickly, then she moved with the ease of a woman long practiced at recovering from unwanted truth.

"Yes," she said calmly as she knelt beside Iney, pressing a hand to her forehead. "I am hale."

Then, without looking at him, she extended a hand toward Drake, presenting him as one might an object of passing relevance.

"This is Captain Drake Barton of Scotland," she said, "He was capsized from his ship and washed ashore."

Drake bowed stiffly. "Good day to you."

Iney's eyes widened, surprise hardening into a small, tight scowl, the sort that said she already disliked him on principle.

"My Princess," she said again, her voice trembling. "I grew worried. I cannot protect you."

A coughing fit seized her, wracking her whole body. Nzingha pressed a finger gently to her lips.

"Save your strength," she said,

She moved to the fire and began working with quiet purpose, gathering bitter vine and green leaves, crushing them between her palms before steeping them into a clay pot of water. The liquid darkened as it heated.

"This will break the fever," she said,

Drake watched the water change. "And what manner o' vine is that, Your Grace?"

She did not look up. "One that works."

"Aye," he muttered. "It smells like it intends to punish whoever drinks it."

She ignored him and crossed back to Iney, examining her arm. Her expression tightened at once.

"Oh, Iney," she said softly, and the gentleness in her voice was the most troubling thing Drake had heard from her all day. "This does not look good."

He stepped closer and immediately regretted it. The hut was not built for a man his size. He crouched awkwardly, trying to be useful without being in the way.

"Is there anything I can do?"

"Yes," she said, "Hold her steady while I squeeze the wound and clean it. I must relieve the fluid that has built up."

Drake nodded once. "Aye, Your Grace."

Nzingha's lips pressed together.

Drake smiled. He knew exactly what he was doing, and she knew it too.

"I will need salt water from the shore," she said, ignoring him. "It will help with the infection. When I return I will lance it, wash it, and set a healing leaf to it."

Drake reached for his sword out of habit. "Let me accompany you, Princess."

"No need," she snapped.

She turned and stormed out through the hut's opening.

Drake watched her go, then looked to Iney.

Iney looked back at him with the expression of a woman who would gladly watch him die if it meant her princess remained safe.

He swallowed.

It occurred to him that he might have survived the sea only to be killed by two women and a clay pot.

And somehow, that felt fair.

Strangers in a Borrowed Home

Drake crossed toward the fire pit at the center of the hut, drawn by the clay pot Nzingha had suspended above the flames. The herbs inside boiled heavily now, the mixture thick and dark as though it had reached its final stage, steam curling upward in slow, deliberate breaths. Curiosity tugged him closer despite the heat.
He leaned in, careful this time, breathing deep.

The scent was unmistakable, sharp and alive with promise, the sort of medicine men guarded with prayer and secrecy. It smelled powerful enough to heal what ought not be healed.

His attention drifted.

Nearby lay a small pile of unfamiliar fruit, long and thick, yellow-skinned and mottled with black. He picked one up and turned it in his hands, peeling back the skin and sniffing cautiously. It reminded him of a yellow fruit he had once seen traded in warmer ports, though this one felt heavier, more substantial.

He took a bite.

Drake closed his eyes.

"Mmm," he murmured, voice reverent. "Oh, Mother of God. That's a fine taste."

He finished it in two generous bites, savoring the sweetness before reaching for another.

"You do know that is our dinner."

He turned smoothly, already smiling.

"Oh, my apologies," he said easily. "I'm starvin', and I've never tasted a fruit like this. Truly, it's a mercy."

"'Tis plantain," Iney said.

"Excuse me," he replied mildly. "A what?"

"Banana's cousin."

Drake frowned, considering. "Whose cousin?"

She paused, then shook her head, a faint smile slipping through despite herself. "Never mind."

He set the peel aside, suddenly aware of himself. "Very well," he said lightly. "I shall behave."

The pot bubbled softly over the fire. Drake lifted it just long enough to pour the dark liquid into a broad shell set nearby, the steam curling as it settled. He set it aside to cool, watching until the surface stilled.

Iney shifted, trying to push herself upright, but the effort stole her strength, her breath hitching as she spoke. "Why are you here? I thought we outran your kind."

In two quick strides Drake was at her side. He slid an arm behind her shoulders and helped her sit upright, careful of the wound, then lifted the shell and held it steady before her.

"Easy now," he said quietly. "I heard of yer escape from the Portuguese, and besides, I am nae one of those bastards."

She took the shell with trembling hands and drank, wincing at the bitterness. When she finished, Drake took it back and eased her down again, settling her as gently as the narrow space allowed.

Her breathing slowed.

Only then did he step back.

"Glad to hear it," Iney said flatly. "But you still havenae told me why you are here."

He chuckled softly. "Straight to the point, are ye?" He settled onto one knee beside her. "I'm a sailor and a merchant. We were bound for another stop in the eastern world, harvestin' tobacco and salt along the channel. On the return, we sailed straight into a storm."

His gaze drifted, the memory tightening his voice. "I went overboard tryin' to haul one of my men back aboard. Drifted longer than I care to guess. Woke half-dead atop a log, sunburned, throat dry as sand, with nae notion where I'd landed."

Iney listened without interrupting.

"The thirst near finished me," he went on. "I went in search of a loch."

"A what?" she asked faintly.

"Water," he said quickly. "River. Lake."

"Oh," she said, "I see."

"Nzingha found me near passed out," he continued. "Her first instinct was to run me through. Cannae say I blame her. But once she saw I was no threat, she showed mercy."

Iney smiled, despite herself. "That is Nzingha. A warrior princess with a trusting heart."

Drake nodded. "Do ye ken if there's a village nearby? A dock? Somewhere I might find passage?"

She coughed softly, the sound thin. "I have not seen beyond this hut. Besides, the princess wishes to remain unseen. If I were you, I would stay near the shore. Your men will find you. I am certain they are searching."

Drake considered that. He could not have been adrift so long.

He opened his mouth to ask about a skiff, but her breathing had already evened.

She was asleep.

Saltwater and Sense

Nzingha followed the narrow path toward the beach in the late afternoon, a woven basket resting against her hip as she went to gather saltwater for Iney's wound. The sun had begun its slow descent, casting warm light through the palms, and she moved quietly, as though the island itself listened, the air heavy with heat and the promise of night.

Her feet splashed softly as she reached the shallow creek that fed into the sea. She bent between the rocks and lifted the first fish trap, peering inside. The bait still hung where she had tied it.

She frowned. "Oh gods," she murmured, "could you favor me with at least one."

She set the basket aside and stepped carefully between two larger stones where the second trap lay hidden.

Something moved.

A large fish thrashed inside, its yellow tail flashing in the light.

Nzingha smiled despite herself. "A quickly answered prayer," she said softly. "My, what a big one." She lowered her voice. "Forgive me, my friend, but I must eat you."

She secured the traps beneath one arm and lifted the clay pot toward her head. The weight shifted awkwardly as she tried to balance it, her grip slipping just enough for the pot to tumble from her hands and shatter against the sand, water spilling uselessly at her feet.

Before she could curse herself, a pale hand reached down and lifted the pot.

Nzingha gasped and jumped back, heart racing.

"'Tis only me," Drake said, already smiling.

She looked up just as the sun broke through the clouds, striking his face. The light caught in his dark hair and made his skin glisten, and though he carried himself like a common sailor, she could not deny the fact of him. His eyes were a vivid blue, bright as open sea, and they held her a breath longer than she expected.

She steadied herself and pressed a hand to her chest. "My thanks. You startled me."

He chuckled. "No need to be afraid. I'm certain ye can defend yerself better than most men I ken."

They shared a brief laugh, the tension easing.

"I was foolish to think I could carry it all alone," she said, reaching for the traps.

"Well then," Drake replied easily, "'tis fortunate I decided to see whether ye needed help."

She turned away, avoiding his eyes. "How is Iney?"

"She's restin'," he said, "Though she made a point before driftin' off."

"Oh?" Nzingha asked, tossing another trap into the sea. "And what point might that be?"

"She said I should stay near the shore, in case my men are searchin' for me."

She looked at him once.

"That is a stupid idea. Do not suggest it again."

His brows lifted, and then he laughed under his breath. "Ye've a sharp mouth, I'll give ye that."

She resumed tying the traps without looking at him. "Anyone can see fires from the sea. You could be attacked, outnumbered, captured, or worse. And by drawing attention to yourself, you would place Iney and me in grave danger." She paused only long enough to add, "So yes. Stupid."

Drake tugged thoughtfully at his beard. "A fair argument," he conceded. "But I could leave a sign at the beach. A crest or broach. If my men come ashore, they will follow it, or think it washed up by chance. Either way, it gives them direction."

He gestured toward a hill overlooking the ocean. "I could keep watch from there."

Nzingha smiled then, slow and approving. "Now that," she said, "is a clever idea."

She bent to gather the remaining fish, lifting the largest with effort. Drake's eyes widened.

"Christ," he said, "That's a massive fish."

"One of the largest I've seen since arriving," she replied.

"What did ye use for bait?"

"Fish guts and sea snail meat."

He set his hands at his waist, impressed. "Ye're royalty, yet ye build shelters, shape clay pots, hunt, fish, and heal. Most noble women in Scotland complain their stays are tied too tight."

Nzingha continued working. "Iney and I must survive. Without shelter, we would be eaten alive by insects or soaked through by rain. Without food, we starve. There are no servants here, Captain. Only work."

"I'm certain yer father would be proud."

She scowled faintly. "My father believed my status should shield me from labor. I never agreed. If I had not learned these skills, Iney and I would have perished within the first week."

Drake drew his dagger and stepped closer. "Then let me help."

They moved to a rock jutting from the shallows, where he laid the fish and began to scale and gut it with practiced ease.

Nzingha waded waist-deep into the water to fill the clay pots.

Drake's gaze followed her despite himself.

The wet fabric clung to her as though it had been poured onto her skin, pale and nearly translucent now, tracing the lines of her body with an intimacy he had no right to witness. The curve of her hips. The long strength of her legs. The subtle swell where her waist gave way. He forgot, for a breath too long, that he was meant to look elsewhere.

He whispered, "Christ above, she's shapely."

He forced air into his lungs, dragged his attention back to his hands, to the fish, to anything that was not her, but it was already too late.

When she emerged from the water, she balanced one pot atop her head and tucked the other beneath her arm, the movement drawing her body into a slow, unconscious sway. Each step set her hips in motion, measured and unhurried, as though she were wholly unaware of the effect she carried with her.

Drake snapped his eyes away, jaw tightening.

This was dangerous ground.

Catching his stare, she said evenly as she passed him, "I am returning to the shelter."

He nodded, forcing his eyes elsewhere. Only when she had disappeared into the greenery did he allow himself a final glance.

Drake steadied himself. She was a noblewoman cast into hardship, burdened by grief and responsibility. Whatever stirred in him had no place here.

Still, he could not help wondering what pain she carried beneath that warrior's skin.

And if the men who had taken her had laid hands where they should not have, he knew, quietly, with certainty, that he would hunt them to the ends of the world.

Firelight Confessions

Nzingha returned to the shelter as dusk settled over the island. The light faded slowly, the sky turning burnished gold before surrendering to violet shadow. Smoke rose in a thin, steady line from the fire pit, carrying the scent of herbs and simmering soup into the cooling air.

She set the clay pots down and did not hesitate. Plantains were peeled and broken apart with quick, unforgiving motions, thrown into the pot hard enough to make it hiss and splash. The work came fast, almost rough, her hands moving as if anger had found a place to settle when her chest would not hold it.

Her thoughts strayed anyway.

She could still feel Drake's eyes on her from the shore.

"Foolish," she muttered under her breath. "I am foolish. And selfish."

It had not yet been six full moons since Mikel's death, and already her thoughts strayed where they should not. She saw his eyes as clearly as if he stood before her, dark and steady, and guilt followed close behind.

She stirred the pot harder.

Mikel was gone. Gone beyond reach, beyond argument. She would never hear his laughter again, never feel his presence beside her in the quiet hours. The island made sense in a way the world beyond it no longer did. If she returned to Mbemba, every stone and corridor would echo with his absence. Here, grief had room to breathe.

She had never given him her maidenhead, believing restraint might somehow keep him alive. He had taught her pleasure without possession, affection without claim. Their moments together had been secret and precious, held carefully in stolen hours.

Her throat tightened.

"How can I let you go," she whispered.

The tears came before she could stop them. She folded forward, rocking as one hand clamped over her mouth in a futile attempt at silence. Soft cries escaped anyway, breaking through her fingers, pressing hard against her chest until it hurt. Her shoulders shook, and no matter how tightly she tried to hold it in, grief refused to be quiet.

She wiped her face with the back of her hand and drew in a steady breath, pressing her lips together until control returned. When she turned, a smile was already in place. It held... barely.

Drake came through the brush carrying the cleaned fish wrapped in palm leaves, pride plain on his face. He lifted the bundle slightly.

Her voice wavered when she spoke. "You finished already. That was quick."

"Ye brought in a beast of a catch," he said, pleased. "That fish near fought me even after it was dead. We'll have ourselves a proper feast tonight." He chuckled. "I cut it into pieces already. Thought it might suit a stew. Soup seems wise, especially for In..."

He stopped.

His gaze lifted fully to her face.

Her eyes were red. Her lashes still wet.

Drake said nothing.

He stood there, words abandoned, understanding enough to know better than to speak.

She reached for a pot and added water and herbs, her movements slower now, more careful. When she finally looked at him, her voice had softened.

"May I have the fish, please. I shall cook it with the rest."

"Aye," he said gently, handing it over.

She added the fish, sea salt, and chunks of plantain. The broth thickened, rich and fragrant as it simmered.

Drake watched her for a moment before speaking. "Lass... all well? How is Iney?"

"I am fine," she replied evenly. "Iney is fine. I was thinking of home."

He knew she was not telling him everything, but he did not press.

"Aye," he said quietly. "I ken that feelin' well enough."

He knelt beside her as she stirred. "I miss my home too. My brother most of all. Our parents passed two years gone. He took it hard. Took to drinkin'. Grief makes fools of good men."

He rested a hand briefly on her shoulder. "It does ease, with time. Or at least, it learns where to sit."

She smiled faintly.

After a moment, he spoke more carefully. "Ye ken ye can speak to me. I mean no harm. Did those men hurt ye?"

She looked at him sharply. "No."

She tasted the broth and added a pinch of salt. "I told you. I am fine."

She moved to a nearby log, gathering green herbs and crushing them in her palm before packing them into a carved wooden pipe.

Drake frowned. "What is that ye have there?"

"Cannabis," she said, a small smile touching her mouth. "The island offers much, if you know where to look." She held it out. "Care to join me?"

He had heard sailors speak of it in low voices, of its use for pain and breath. He sat beside her.

She lit the herbs, inhaled deeply, and passed the pipe to him.

The world softened.

The sea whispered against the shore. Insects hummed. The fire crackled low as the last light disappeared.

"I was fifteen when I met Mikel," she said at last. "My trainer. I begged my father to let me learn to fight after my brother died. I wished to protect myself. To protect my people." Her gaze fixed on the flames. "Mikel taught me discipline. Strength. And how to love myself."

Drake swallowed and passed the pipe back.

"My father learned of us through gossip," she continued. "Soon after, Mikel vanished."

"I am sorry," Drake said quietly. "What did your father do to him?"

She did not answer. She stared past him, letting the silence carry what she would not. After a moment, she spoke instead.

"What is a lass?"

Drake blinked, then laughed softly. "A woman. A girl. Sometimes a bonnie one, if she's earned it."

She nudged his arm. "I thought it an insult at first."

He smiled. "Nae. Never that."

Her gaze returned to the fire. "You asked what my father did to him."

Drake nodded once.

"He was taken."

She rose and fetched a clay pot filled with liquid, pouring it into coconut shells before handing one to Drake.

"I once had a lion cub," she said suddenly. "Her name was Asha."

Drake stared. "A lion?"

"Yes," she said, pride lighting her face. "She was fierce. Loyal. She followed me everywhere. The night I escaped, she fought for me. Bought me time."

Her voice broke. "They killed her."

Drake's jaw clenched.

She continued. "That night, I fought harder than I ever have. Fifteen men, perhaps more. I killed six before they overwhelmed me. When I woke, I was chained aboard a ship. Iney was there too."

"How did ye escape?" he asked.

"One of them tried to ravish me," she said calmly. "He failed."

Drake exhaled slowly.

"He carried the keys to our shackles. I took them. We freed ourselves, lowered a skiff, and pushed off under fire." She lifted her shell. "To loss. And to freedom."

Drake took a deep swallow and immediately choked, coughing hard.

"Christ Almighty," he rasped. "That's good, but it's got the bite of the devil himself. What in God's name is it?"

"Sugared rum," she said evenly. "Fermented from what the island gives. It has been fermenting for months."

He wiped his mouth, eyes watering. "Months. That explains why it near sent me to my Maker."

She shook her head. "Eat first. Your stomach is empty."

"Aye," he said, smiling. "I see now that would have been wise."

She handed him a bowl of soup. Drake took a careful bite, then another. His shoulders eased, and his eyes closed without thought.

"Lass," he said quietly, "if I were in the Highlands, I would take you as both warrior and cook."

She laughed, and this time it came easily.

The sound lingered between them, easing what had been tight and heavy moments before. For all the uncertainty that lay ahead, Drake could not deny the simple truth of it.

"I am done in," he said, "That soup and that drink have near finished me."

"You may share the hut. I will burn herbs to keep the insects away."

"Aye," he replied, already heavy with sleep. "That sounds like mercy."

They stepped into the shelter together as night settled fully over the island.

Chapter 6

Fast Friends

Drake woke with a dull ache pounding behind his eyes, the

lingering consequence of sugar rum and cannabis. For a moment he lay still, letting the throb settle, then turned his head and saw Iney asleep on her pallet. Sweat beaded her brow, her face drawn tight with pain even in rest.

He rose slowly, stiff and dusty from the leaves and coconut palms beneath him, brushed the debris from his hair, and stepped outside. The clearing was quiet. Too quiet.

Nzingha was nowhere in sight.

"She must be at the beach," he muttered, adjusting his clothing as unease crept in. He cut through the dense woods toward the shoreline, only to find the sand empty. The knot in his chest tightened.

"Zingha," he called. "Zingha."

No answer.

He turned back inland, following the sound of rushing water until the roar grew louder and he realized he had come out near the falls. Then he heard it. Her voice, carrying through the mist and thunder of water, steady and unbroken.

His eyes searched below and caught a flash of white.

Her dress lay spread across a sun-warmed rock, clean now, free of dirt and travel stains.

Drake swallowed.

He picked his way down toward the water, shedding his clothes as he went. He wanted the bath. He smelled of smoke, fish, salt, and yesterday's indulgence, every inch the castaway.

Slipping into the river, he submerged fully, letting the cool wash over his skin until the ache eased and his breath steadied.

When he surfaced, he dragged a hand through his hair and shook the water free. Even now, her singing carried through the air.

He swam toward a broad boulder rising from the current and surfaced again near the falls, eyes closed, letting sunlight strike his face. When he opened them, he froze and ducked instinctively.

"Holy shite."

He had not expected this.

Nzingha stood naked beneath the waterfall, the water pounding her back as she tipped her head from side to side, eyes closed, surrendering to the force of it.
He drifted toward another boulder, keeping distance though his gaze betrayed him.

She bent and lifted a coconut shell filled with a pale, grainy mixture and scooped it over her skin, scrubbing her inner thighs in slow, deliberate strokes.

His breath caught.

Her body was lush and powerful, curves softened by strength. Her hips flared generously, her breasts full and firm, dark nipples cresting as they moved with her rhythm. A neat, straight line of hair marked her sex.

"Christ Almighty," he breathed under his breath. "Did she shave?"

He hardened instantly.

As she lifted her arms, he saw there was no hair beneath them either.
Drake stared, stunned.

"Saint Christopher's Cross, I've fallen off my ship and washed up in Heaven."

Her skin glowed beneath the water, smooth and almond-dark, sculpted as though by deliberate hands. A scar marked her back.

"I wonder, is that from war?" he whispered, "Or the bastards who captured her?"

He stayed hidden near the rock, heart thudding.

Her hair, freed from its braids, spilled thick and curling down her back. Strength lived beneath the softness of her stomach, the quiet proof of training.
Nzingha was no ordinary woman. She was a trained killer, and his smooth words would do him no good. She would gut him with a dagger long before he ever thought to steal a kiss.

Only then did another, less sensible thought intrude.

He had known women across the seas, Oriental, Indigenous, Roman, more than he cared to count. A rogue by reputation, aye, but still a Scotsman through and through, possessed of curiosity and an unfortunate habit of tempting fate.

The question, he supposed, was whether his death would be a fair price for unwelcome curiosity.

She stilled suddenly, sensing movement. Covering her breasts, she turned her head just enough to see him.

"Do you always spy on naked women?"

She lowered herself until the water reached her waist. Drake stepped forward, hands lifting slightly.

"Can I help you, Captain?" Her gaze sharpened. "Is Iney well?"

"Aye, she's taken a fever." He swallowed. "I'm sorry. I didnae see ye there. I was caught off guard."

She rose fully, granting him an unobstructed view before turning her back and continuing her wash.

"Oh, you knew," she said, cool and unimpressed.

Had this been Mbemba, he would already be dead, by guards or by her late lion, Asha.

Bathing held no shame for her. Royal attendants had seen to her until her eighteenth summer, and even then only ceased when Mikel objected. She washed her arms, her stomach, then lifted one leg onto a rock to scrub her thigh and calf.

Drake cleared his throat. "What is it ye're doing?"

"Bathing," she replied easily. "It is not a difficult thing."

She turned into the waterfall, letting it rinse her clean.

Drake looked away, though the image burned behind his eyes.

Is this what they do in Africa?

No Scottish noblewoman would dare such boldness. Only tavern wenches or whores behaved so freely.

"I beg your pardon," she said coolly, "but you are interrupting my bath."

She fixed him with a sharp look. "Do not insult me by pretending modesty. You were caught staring. Where I come from, men who spy are either laughed at... or corrected."

Her head tilted slightly. "Tell me, Captain. Do you suffer more from wandering eyes, or from waiting for permission you lack the courage to ask for."

She lifted the coconut shell.

"Crushed coconut and sea salt," she said, "For your sunburn. Not for your lack of discipline."

His face burned. "Aye. My back's red enough."

He stepped beneath the falls.

She scooped a handful and rubbed it across his blistered skin, slow and firm.

He hissed. "It stings... but it smells incredible."

"It is the best I can do in the wild."

"I dinnae frighten ye? Ye're no exactly covered."

"No. I've seen how you fight."

His brows lifted. "Ye're a brave lass."

"Bravery has nothing to do with it." She tapped the dagger resting nearby. "I can defend myself."

"In Scotland," he said carefully, "it's ungodly for a woman tae bathe with a man who isnae her husband."

She laughed, low and untroubled, hands never leaving his shoulders. "Oh, stop it. In Mbemba Kingdom, warriors bathe together. It is a matter of respect. Man or woman, we are treated as equals."

She glanced at him then, a faint curve at her mouth. "Perhaps that is the trouble in the ways of foreign men of the west. Do they not respect women as such?"

He huffed. "Aye, some men are weak in the head, but others mind themselves. So, pray tell, ye've no perverted bastards wanderin' about?"

"In my lands, if a man desires a woman, he may take her as his wife. A man may have many wives if he wishes. There is no need to harm a woman when marriage is an option. And the punishment for perversion is severe."

Her smile thinned, sharpened, eyes never leaving him.

"A man who rapes a woman loses his manhood while watching it fed to a crocodile. Then he joins it."

Drake blinked once. "Well... I'm all for feedin' rapists tae crocodiles. But that many women?" He shook his head. "I can barely manage the thought of one."

She flicked water at his face. "Where I come from, men are free to choose."

He splashed her in answer.

She gasped, then laughed, already slipping beneath the surface as the water closed over her head. Drake followed at once, less graceful but no less eager, and learned too late that she was faster than she looked. He caught her foot; she kicked by instinct, heel glancing hard against his jaw.

He broke the surface with a curse, palm pressed to his face. "That's no fair."

She rose a few paces away, water streaming down her hair and shoulders, a grin already waiting for him. "You sound wounded, Captain."

He dove again, determination overtaking caution, and this time caught her properly, hauling her up as she laughed and protested, breathless and unguarded.

"Enough, enough," she said between breaths. "I yield."

He released her, and she dropped back into the river with a splash, resurfacing still laughing as she slicked her hair from her face. "I thought you a gentleman."

"Only when it suits me," he said, smiling. "Race ye tae the shore."

They broke for the bank together, water churning behind them, Drake reaching it first with Nzingha close on his heels. She dropped beside him, breathless and smiling as she tugged her dress over damp skin.

"I have not laughed like that in a very long time," she said quietly. "My thanks."

"Och," he replied, still catching his breath. "I'm only a playful son of Scotland."

She wrung out her hair and began to braid it, wet and gleaming in the light, while Drake turned his gaze back toward the river, letting the moment settle.

"This place is bonnie."

She glanced at him. "Bon-nie?" She rolled the sound slowly, as if learning it.

"Beautiful," he said softly. "Like ye."

She looked away, smiling despite herself.

After a moment, his voice shifted, the play giving way to purpose. "Ye mentioned a skiff. A rowboat. Is it still here? I'd like tae scout the island for my men."

Her smile faded, then steadied. "Yes. Let us dress. I'll show you where it's hidden."

She took a step, then stopped.

"Drake."

"Aye?"

"If you do find your men... and leave, I shall miss you terribly."

He did not answer at once. Then he nodded.

They dressed in silence and set off toward the hidden skiff, the river murmuring behind them as though it, too, had noticed the change.

Cliff Grief Release

Nzingha led him along a narrow rise until the trees thickened and the land fell away to a cliff overlooking the water. There, hidden deep beneath overhanging branches, lay the skiff.

Drake slowed, taking it in. "Why hide it here?"

"If it were left tied to a rock, a passing ship might find it," she said calmly. "I have no intention of being captured... nor of returning home."

He turned toward her then. "Ye dinnae wish tae go back tae yer kingdom?"

She lowered her head, shook it once. "No. My father betrayed me. There can be no forgiveness."

"Because he disagreed with ye and Mikel?"

She looked away, as though she was steadying herself against the thought. The memory of Mikel's laugh came to her then, bright, careless, alive. Her chest tightened, as though the sound still lingered in the air between them. For a breath, she said nothing. Then she turned back to him.

Whatever strength she carried fell from her face.

"No," she said quietly.

She held his gaze now, unflinching. "He was beheaded."

She paused.

"For loving me."

Drake drew in a slow breath, the weight of it tightening his brow. "Oh, lass... I'm so, so sorry."
He stepped forward, meaning only to comfort her, but the moment they touched, her restraint gave way. The strength she carried so carefully collapsed, and the sobs came hard and uncontrolled. She had borne her grief in silence and pride for too long. No one had understood her love for Mikel, nor the cost of it. The sound tore from her chest, raw and unguarded.
At last she pulled back, fighting for composure, wiping her face as she struggled for breath.

"Forgive me. There was no one to console me. Iney believes I was foolish for loving a commoner. If I return home, my father will torture me... then wed me to one of the western king's sons to secure his alliances. My people will see only scandals and ruin. Yet Mikel and I were never intimate. I cannot go back."

The words emptied her. What strength she had left wavered, then steadied.
The truth of it settled between them, heavy and inescapable.

Drake drew her close, his hand steady at her back, holding her as though she might break apart if he did not. Beneath the bearing of royalty and the discipline of a warrior, she was grieving, still sharp, even as she came undone.

"There, there now, bonnie princess. This pain ye carry willnae always feel so sharp. One day it'll be a memory, not a wound. Until then, ye've a shoulder here."

"My thanks," she whispered.

He pulled off his shirt and pressed it gently to her face. She sniffed, then laughed weakly despite herself. "I am sorry."
"Och," he said softly. "It'll wash in the sea."

The sound that left her then was small, broken, but lighter than before.

Drake stepped back, circling the skiff, one hand resting at his hip. "I ken I cannae row this wee thing back tae Scotland. But I can be a friend while I find my way." His mouth curved faintly. "Truth be told, this isle's growin' on me. So is yer cookin'."

She let out a slow breath. "Truly?"
"Aye."

Her gaze drifted toward the water. "Thank you. I've always been strong. I forgot how it feels to mourn."
"What are friends for?" he said lightly.

She smiled then. "I should return to the shelter. Iney will need me."
"Very well," he nodded. "I'll be back near dusk. Shouldnae take long tae circle the isle."

She stepped forward and embraced him. "Have a care."

The hug lasted only a moment, yet she pressed her face against his chest, and he rested his chin atop her head. For that brief span, she felt safe, also something she could not yet name.

She pulled away with a small smile. "I shall see you anon."

As she disappeared into the trees, Drake lifted the skiff and began the slow task of carrying it back toward the sea.

Silent Promises to a Friend

Back at the shelter, Nzingha prepared a bowl of leftover soup and knelt beside Iney. Her breathing was shallow and uneven.

"Iney?" she whispered. "Are you awake?"

She tipped water onto a broad leaf and touched it gently to Iney's lips.

Iney stirred, her fingers lifting weakly to brush Nzingha's cheek. When she spoke, her voice was soft but certain.

"My princess... do not grieve before the time comes. I have walked beside you since you were small. I guarded you when you slept, stood between you and danger, and loved you as my own. Whatever awaits me now is only the closing of a long and faithful road. But you must live. You must return home. Mbemba Kingdom needs you. Make peace with your father, even if he does not deserve it. Carry the kingdom forward, as you were born to do."

Nzingha shook her head, tears already burning. "Do not speak of leaving me. You will be set to rights. I will not lose you too."

She drew back the cloth.

The darkened flesh along Iney's arm crept upward toward her chest, cruel and unmistakable. Hope faltered, but still she knelt there, unwilling to surrender it.

Iney's gaze never wavered. "Promise me this, child of my heart. Do not let grief or anger turn you from who you are. Do not let love become shame. What you gave was pure. What you lost was real. Return home one day, when you are able, and stand tall."

Nzingha collapsed against her then, the words tearing free at last.

"I am so sorry. If I had not fled, you would not be wounded. Asha would still live. All of this is my doing. Forgive me. Forgive me."

Iney's hand moved slowly through her hair, steady and familiar, offering comfort even now.

Sometime later, Nzingha's sobs softened, grief ebbing into exhaustion. She slept there beside her, curled close, holding on as though love itself might yet keep death at bay.

Silent Promises to a Friend

Back at the shelter, Nzingha prepared a bowl of leftover soup and knelt beside Iney. Her breathing was shallow and uneven.

"Iney?" she whispered. "Are you awake?"

She tipped water onto a broad leaf and touched it gently to Iney's lips.

Iney stirred, her fingers lifting weakly to brush Nzingha's cheek. When she spoke, her voice was soft but certain.

"My princess... do not grieve before the time comes. I have walked beside you since you were small. I guarded you when you slept, stood between you and danger, and loved you as my own. Whatever awaits me now is only the closing of a long and faithful road. But you must live. You must return home. Mbemba Kingdom needs you. Make peace with your father, even if he does not deserve it. Carry the kingdom forward, as you were born to do."

Nzingha shook her head, tears already burning. "Do not speak of leaving me. You will be set to rights. I will not lose you too."

She drew back the cloth.

The darkened flesh along Iney's arm crept upward toward her chest, cruel and unmistakable. Hope faltered, but still she knelt there, unwilling to surrender it.

Iney's gaze never wavered. "Promise me this, child of my heart. Do not let grief or anger turn you from who you are. Do not let love become shame. What you gave was pure. What you lost was real. Return home one day, when you are able, and stand tall."

Nzingha collapsed against her then, the words tearing free at last.

"I am so sorry. If I had not fled, you would not be wounded. Asha would still live. All of this is my doing. Forgive me. Forgive me."

Iney's hand moved slowly through her hair, steady and familiar, offering comfort even now.

Sometime later, Nzingha's sobs softened, grief ebbing into exhaustion. She slept there beside her, curled close, holding on as though love itself might yet keep death at bay.

Discovery

Drake let the skiff drift along the curve of the island, the oars resting loose in his hands. Dusk had begun its slow claim on the sky, the sun sinking low enough that its warmth no longer comforted, only lingered. The light thinned to amber and shadow, stretching the jungle into long, watchful shapes.

His stomach churned sourly. Salt still burned his throat. His head ached with a dull, distant pressure, as though his thoughts were wrapped in wool and slow to answer him. Each breath carried the faint taste of rot and brine, the air heavier now, closer.

No village revealed itself. No smoke lifted into the evening air. No voices carried on the wind. Nothing but the press of green closing in and the steady hush of the surf behind him, growing more distant by the moment.

Just as hope began to thin, something ahead caught what little light remained.

Drake squinted, blinking hard. A pale flash surfaced again between the darkening leaves, brief and uncertain, as though the island itself had shifted and shown its hand for a heartbeat before closing it once more.

"What in the devil is that?" he muttered, more to steady himself than to ask.

He guided the skiff toward shore and beached it gently, boots sinking into damp sand. A narrow path wound inland, half-swallowed by brush. He followed it, swaying slightly as he went, his balance not yet his own. The earth felt too soft beneath his feet, as though it might give way.

A rough fence emerged from the growth, sharpened stakes driven into the ground with purpose rather than haste.

"Please God," he murmured, voice rough, "let this be a village."

Beyond the fence lay an animal pen, empty now, its gate hanging loose. No tracks marred the dirt. No sound stirred the air. The quiet pressed in on him, heavy and expectant.

Farther on stood a small, hand-built home, made of driftwood and packed clay. Its roof was woven thick with grass, carefully layered against rain. The windows were latticed with sticks and coconut palm, and a fine net stretched across the doorway to keep the insects at bay. Even the door itself had been shaped with care, wood fitted to clay, smoothed by patient hands.

Drake knocked once. "Hello the home."

The sound echoed strangely, then died.

He stepped inside.

The air was stale, thick with dust and age, yet the place had not been stripped bare. A driftwood table stood near the wall. Two barrels stuffed with cushions served as seats, their fabric faded but mended. A pair of rocking chairs faced a small hearth, ash long cold. In the corner rested a box bed.

Drake pressed his hand to the mattress. Dust rose, catching the light, but beneath it the stuffing was soft.

Feathers.

Nearby lay folded cloth. He sifted through it slowly. Two dresses, neatly kept. A blouse. A pair of men's trousers, patched at the knee. Not abandoned in haste. Not looted.

He straightened, hand resting at his hip, brow tightening.

"Where in God's name are ye?"

Outside, behind the dwelling, stood an almond tree so large it seemed ancient, its branches spreading wide in quiet dominion. Beneath it sat rain barrels and a wooden bathing tub, the rim smoothed by repeated use.

For the first time since waking on the island, Drake smiled faintly.

The place felt lived in. Considered. Ordered.

Someone had known peace here.

He walked farther, noting fruit trees planted with care, their spacing deliberate, and a simple outdoor kitchen long unused. Stone blackened by old fires. Clay pots stacked neatly, waiting.

Still, no sign of life.

Then he saw the hill.

Crude wooden crosses marked the rise, their edges weathered, their lines uneven but earnest.

He crossed himself and moved closer.

The smell struck him all at once.

Sweet and rotten, thick enough to taste, it rose from the earth and wrapped itself around his throat. Drake retched hard, the sound tearing from him before he could stop it. He turned away, bracing his hands on his knees as his stomach heaved again, empty and burning, his vision swimming until he forced himself to breathe through it.

"Christ..." he rasped.

With shaking hands, he tore the cravat from his neck and bound it across his mouth and nose, drawing the cloth tight until the worst of it dulled. Even then, the air pressed heavy and foul against his chest.

Beneath a coconut tree sat a body.

Not laid out. Not buried.

Simply left where strength had failed.

Time and heat had taken what they would. Flesh had surrendered to bone, the remains drawn in upon themselves as though the man had folded inward at the end. Flies swarmed thickly, their low hum constant and unrelenting, rising and falling with the breeze.

Drake crossed himself, the gesture slow, reverent. "I'm sorry, sir," he said quietly. "Ye deserved better than this."

His gaze shifted then, taking in the ground around him, the crude crosses on the rise beyond, the careful spacing, the effort it must have taken.

Understanding settled, heavy and unmistakable.

This man had buried the others.

All of them.

There had been no one left to bury him.

He swallowed hard, the truth of it tightening something deep in his chest as dusk pressed closer, the island holding its silence.

He fetched a length of driftwood and began to dig beside one of the marked graves. The soil was stubborn, tangled with roots. Each thrust of the wood released more of the stench, turning his stomach until sweat beaded at his brow.

"How long have ye lain here, and why alone?"

By the time the grave was finished, his hands trembled. He washed them at the rain barrel, then his face, leaning heavily on the rim until the world steadied. Returning with a clean bed cloth, he covered the remains as best he could and eased them into the earth.

"Forgive me," he said quietly.

Dusk settled in while he worked, the light thinning to gold and then to gray, shadows stretching long across the ground as the island drew itself inward. When he turned back toward the skiff, the world felt quieter somehow, as though it were holding its breath.

Then the sound reached him.

Soft at first, little more than a pulse beneath the wind.

Bum. Bum. Bum.

His foot halted mid-step, muscles locking before thought could catch up. The rhythm rolled again, low and deliberate, rising from the island's darkening spine, not hurried, not wild, measured, it was lively.

Drake did not move.

"Is that... drums." He froze. "Please God," he whispered, "let it be a village."

The sound rose and fell from the mountains north of the home, and Drake followed it, letting the rhythm guide his steps as he climbed the rising ground. He kept to the shadow of the brush until the slope steepened beneath his hands, then pulled himself higher. At the crest, he dropped low, flattening himself against the earth.

When he reached the ridge, he slowed.

The ground fell away on the other side.

Firelight flickered below.

A village.

Men patrolled the perimeter with bows and spears, their movements practiced and deliberate, as though the paths beneath their feet had been walked this way for generations. Their bodies bore markings in ink and scar, not chaotic but patterned, laid with care and meaning earned over time. Women moved among the fires, cloth wrapped low about their hips, breasts bare as they carried their bairns or tended the flames, their faces calm, alert, accustomed to watching the edges of their world.

Drake watched from the ridge, unsettled by the order of it, by how easily life and vigilance coexisted here.

They were people who knew their land and guarded it.

Then he noticed the trees.

From their branches hung skulls, bleached and bound, set high enough to be seen from a distance. Nearby, the remains of a body had been tied upright against the trunk of another, bone drawn tight with cord, left not in chaos but in warning.

The message was unmistakable.

This ground was claimed.

And trespass was remembered.

His stomach turned.

"This isnae right," he murmured. "And they're nae the friendly kind."

Slowly, he withdrew, retracing his steps down the mountain. By the time he reached the skiff, night had fallen.

He pushed off into the dark, rowing by moonlight alone, the steady pull of the oars grounding him as the certainty settled deep in his chest.

The island held more than refuge.

It held memory, grief, and men who had learned to live inside terror.

And he was not the first stranger to wash ashore.

Chapter 7

The Quiet That Breaks

*N*zingha rose from the floor where she had been lying beside Iney,

her limbs stiff, her throat raw with grief and salt air. The hut was

black as pitch. When she peered through the opening, she saw that

night had fallen fully, the jungle pressing close, and Drake had not

returned. The quiet unsettled her more than the darkness.

She turned back toward the pallet and spoke her name once, softly.

"Iney?"

No answer came.

She knelt and fed the fire a few dry fronds until it caught, the flame

lifting just enough to cast a thin, wavering light across the hut. Iney

lay as she had been left, her face turned slightly to the side, her hair

damp against her temples.

"Iney, are you awake?"

Still nothing.

Nzingha crossed the hut and crouched beside her, touching her cheek. The skin beneath her fingers was cold. Not the ebbing warmth of fever, not the clammy chill of sickness. Cold in a way that did not belong to sleep.

Her breath caught. She tapped Iney's face once, then again, gentler than fear, as if tenderness alone might summon breath.

"Iney... wake up."

She pressed her fingers to Iney's throat. Then lowered her head to her chest, ear against ribs that had once held stubborn breath and sharper words. She went very still, listening with all of herself, as though her own heartbeat might drown the truth if she did not.

There was nothing.

For a moment her mind refused it, sliding away from the truth like a blade from oil. Then the sound tore out of her, broken and animal.

"No."

She folded over Iney, cheek pressed to her breastbone, arms wrapping around a body that would not return the hold. Her shoulders shook. She breathed in hard, as if air itself might bring Iney back with it. It did not. Tears came hot, then violent, and she sobbed into her friend's chest until her throat burned, rocking there in half-prayer, half-denial, fingers clutching cloth as though she could hold the world in place.

Something shifted behind her.

A touch.

Not Iney's.

Instinct moved faster than grief. Nzingha surged up in one swift motion, steel flashing from the knife strapped high to her thigh. She was on her feet before thought caught up, blade at a throat, eyes wild, breath cutting.

Drake froze where he stood, hands lifting slowly, palms open. The firelight caught his face, worry etched deep in the lines of it.

"Easy, lass," he said quietly. "Easy. 'Tis only me."

Recognition struck like a blow. Her arm went slack. The dagger fell to the floor as if it had turned to ash in her grip. She stared at him once, blinking hard, and then the last of her control broke clean through. A wail tore out of her, raw and unguarded, and she stumbled forward.

Drake caught her without hesitation, arms closing around her, bracing himself as she shook and clung and broke against his chest.

"Shhhh," he murmured. "'Tis only me. I'm here. I'm here."

Her words came in jagged pieces between sobs.

"Iney's dead. She's cold. I could not save her."

His hold tightened, one hand moving slowly over her back, a steady rhythm meant to anchor her to something solid.

"Oh, lass, I'm so sorry."

He did not offer small comforts. He did not soften her pain. He stayed, solid and unmoving, until grief turned savage and had nowhere left to go.

She shoved at his chest, tears streaking her face.

"I can take care of myself. You are leaving. You said so. You will leave."

Drake did not flinch.

"Aye, and that is what terrifies me."

She turned away before her face could betray how much she needed him to stay. Kneeling once more beside Iney, her hands trembling, she found the oath wrap she wore as a Mbemba guard, woven in green, gold, and black. With careful reverence she drew it up and laid it across Iney's face, granting her privacy even in death.

"She made me promise to go back. To my kingdom. To him."

Drake lowered himself beside her, cautious, as if one wrong movement might shatter what little composure remained.

"Is that what ye wish?"

"No. I do not wish to see my father again. I want to stay here. I wish for peace. But Iney made me promise."

She folded her arms around herself, rocking once. "I am losing everyone I care about. The only choice left to me is to remain... and take care of myself."

Drake's gaze went to Iney's covered face, then back to Nzingha. He brushed a loose lock of hair from her cheek, tucking it back with care.

"Come back with me," he said, "To Scotland. I ken it's a world that isnae yours, but I can keep ye safe there. Ye would have peace at my home. Stay at my keep as long as ye need. My people will learn tae respect ye."

Nzingha rose so fast the fire snapped in protest.

"No. I do not know how your people would look upon someone like me. And I do not share your faith. Your God."

Drake drew a breath.

"Christ, ye're stubborn. No one is trying tae command ye. Iney and I wanted one thing only, yer safety. And if my men find me and I must leave, I would be leaving ye here. Alone." He held her gaze. "Lass, we are not alone on this island."

She went very still.

"What do you mean?"

"I took the skiff north. There's a village there. From what I saw, they wouldnae welcome ye. Human skulls hanging from trees." The fire cracked softly between them. "Think on that before ye decide solitude is safer than company."

Her voice dropped.

"I do not know what to do. I cannot speak of this now."

Drake nodded once.

"Very well. We'll finish it another time." He rose, his gaze resting on Iney. "I'll prepare what needs preparing. For Iney."

He turned to go, and she caught his arm.

"Give me time."

"Aye. Of course."

"Also... we burn the deceased. As an offering."

Drake inclined his head.

"Very well."

He stepped out into the night, leaving the firelight to hold her, and leaving Nzingha beside the covered face of the woman who had guarded her until her last breath.

The Fire Offering

Within the hour, Iney's body was laid upon the pyre. The night had grown heavy and unmoving, the air already thick with smoke, as though the earth itself had stilled to witness what must be done.

Drake stood beside Nzingha as she accepted the torch. Her spine was straight, her posture ceremonial, grief held behind the discipline of duty. When she spoke, it was in her native tongue, her voice steady even as tears gathered and clung to her lashes.

"Mother Earth, I present Iney Abebe.

Warrior of Mbemba Kingdom.

Loyal daughter of the eastern lands of Tafaria.

Born to breathe.

Born to serve her people.

Born to die without fear."

The words settled into the night like vows offered to something ancient and listening.

Tears slipped free at last, tracing silent paths down Nzingha's cheeks, yet she did not falter. She lowered the torch and lit the pyre, watching as flame caught and climbed, the fire crackling softly as it claimed Iney's body. Drake felt her fingers curl into his arm. She leaned into him without a word, seeking strength without asking for it, and he remained still, letting himself become an anchor while she wept.

When the fire burned down and only embers remained, Nzingha knelt. With careful hands, she gathered Iney's ashes, scooping them into a small clay pot with reverence born of love and loss.

Drake watched, confused.

"Lass," he said gently, "what are ye doin'?"

She did not look up. "I will take her to Yemaya, she belongs to Mother Earth and to the sea. Yemaya guards the souls of those who drowned seeking freedom." Her voice trembled. "For decades she has protected our fallen brothers and sisters. Iney will be safe with her. She will be..."

Her words broke. Fresh tears fell as she sealed the pot. She lit two torches and turned toward the beach without another word.

Drake followed.

She stopped abruptly and lifted her hand. "No. I wish to be alone."

"Nzingha, 'tis dangerous out there."

She spun on him, grief flaring into anger. "I can take care of my bloody self."

"Ye've not seen what I've seen. We dinnae ken who, or what, walks this land. Stop actin' daft and listen for once. Ye cannae go alone."

The command in his voice struck her hard. Only two men had ever spoken to her that way. Her father, and Mikel.

She met his gaze, her voice suddenly quiet. "Please, Drake. Leave me be."

Then she turned and walked away.

He stood there, counting the slow pull of seconds, cursing under his breath. "Bloody stubborn woman. Like a young tree that refuses tae bend."

When he followed at last, the moon had climbed higher, spilling silver across the sea. The water glowed with ghostly color, the sand beneath visible as though the ocean itself were lit from within. Nzingha stood at the shoreline, the clay pot cradled in her hands.

He stopped several paces behind her, leaning against a tree, arms crossed, eyes scanning the darkness as instinct demanded.

She set the pot upon the sand and began to undress.

Naked and unashamed, she lifted the vessel and walked into the ocean. The water closed over her as she submerged.

"Ye daft princess," Drake muttered, already pulling off his shirt.

Before he could take another step, she surfaced and swam back toward shore, emerging from the sea like something reborn. Water streamed down her skin as she reached the sand. She gathered her dress and passed him without slowing.

He caught her arm just long enough to press his kilt into her hands. "Here, for warmth."

Then he snapped. "What in God's name were ye thinkin'? 'Tis nae safe tae swim at night."

"Stop being so bloody overbearing," she said over her shoulder as she wrapped the cloth around herself. "I asked you to leave me be."

She disappeared toward the hut, his kilt clenched in her fist.

Inside, Nzingha curled into herself, the last of her restraint finally breaking. Drake entered quietly, dressed only in the long shirt that brushed his knees, and sat beside her.

"I am sorry I shouted," he said, "But I promised Iney..."

She turned away, pretending not to hear.

He noticed but continued. "I promised her I would protect ye. When my men find me, I'll take ye back tae yer kin. Ye dinnae wish tae go tae Scotland, and I willnae leave ye here. I'll take ye home. Or as near tae it as I can."

She remained silent.

Respecting her space, he rose and stepped away.

Immediately, she sat up and caught his shirt. "Please. Do not leave."

He sank back down, and they curled together.

She whispered. "Hold me. Please?" Her tears returned, heavier now.

"Shh, I'll hold ye as long as ye need."

He rocked her gently, rubbing slow circles into her back as she spoke again, her voice quiet but resolute.

"I laid Iney to rest with the others taken from our lands."

"'Tis a cruel thing man has made," Drake said softly.

"Slavery?" she asked.

"Aye," he replied. "One man claimin' ownership of another. I hate it. Some of my own people were taken as well. Sold. Never returned home."

He drew a breath. "English, Scottish, Irish, many sold their own. Sent them away as punishment. Then carried the same cruelty forward." His voice lowered. "I've done business with folk from the east. Traded goods. Broken bread. They are intelligent, capable people. None deserve such treatment."

"Really?" she asked softly. "You have met those from my world?"

"Aye," he said quietly. "What does it profit a man tae gain the world if he loses his soul?"

She tilted her head. "Did you make that up?"

"Nae. Scripture."

"The Bible?" she asked.

"You ken of it?"

"No," she said, "But an English priest once came to our shores. He spoke of a man named Jesus Christ."

A faint smile touched her mouth. "I thought it merely a figure of speech. You say his name so often when vexed."

Drake let out a low breath, almost a laugh. "Sometimes it is."

Sleep softened her voice, though her mind remained bright and wandering.

"We do not believe in just one man," she murmured. "We believe in Mother Earth, and in the deities who guard her. They watch over the air, the sea, the trees, the whole of the world."

Her words slowed, drifting. "There is so much beyond the stars... it would take an eternity to teach you. Some say..."

Her voice trailed off.

Drake lifted a finger gently to her lips. "Shh. Let us sleep."

He kissed the top of her head. Within minutes, his breathing deepened.

He just interrupted me, she thought. Who does this man think he is? And did he truly kiss my forehead?

Her stomach fluttered.

She felt safe. He had been there for her while she mourned, a place to rest her head, a steady presence beside her grief.

Softly, she whispered, "You have been nothing but kind to me, and I have been such a shrew. You care for me, do you? Truly? I still love Mikel, but I feel something for you. Perhaps because of your willingness to help. You have a heart of gold. Thank you for this night."

She rolled onto her back, one hand pressed to her forehead.

"Mother Earth, what am I doing?" she thought. "My father will never understand. He will not believe I was taken. He will blame me and marry me off more quickly. I cannot forgive him. He knew Mikel since boyhood. Loyal. Faithful. And he beheaded him like he was sacrificing a chicken."

Her thoughts drifted back to the first time she met him. The way he would tease her thin frame, mocking her protests whenever she refused to be treated as frail. She remembered her first kiss with him, soft and uncertain, and then the day he no longer appeared at warrior training. No longer at the camp.

Night after night, she recalled sitting on the steps, waiting, watching the road for his return.

They all knew of his demise.
Yet no one told me. Not even Iney.

She lay still now, listening to Drake's steady breathing, studying his face in the firelight. His beard had grown fuller since she met him. His mouth open as he slept.

She brushed her fingers lightly through his jet-black hair.

"I have never touched a western man's hair before," she whispered. "Tis full."

Her gaze drifted to his chest. "So strong."

Then to his legs, his calves carved as though by a sculptor.

She looked at his lips again.

"What am I doing? Mikel, forgive me."

Slowly, she leaned in and kissed Drake.

She pulled back with a faint smile, then kissed him again. When she withdrew, the quiet sound of their lips parting lingered between them. She scooted closer, draping her arm across his stomach. Within minutes, sleep claimed her.

Drake had felt it all.

Though she believed him asleep, he was awake. He opened his eyes, smiling faintly in the firelight.

She stole a kiss.

He had heard her whispers. Every one of them.

She feels something. For me?

Grief, he reasoned. Mourning does strange things to the heart.

"I cannae fall in love," he murmured silently. "I need tae get home."

He drew her closer, held her tighter than before, closed his eyes, and finally slept.

Morning Rain and the Shack

Morning arrived with thunder.

Rain hammered the roof of the hut, a steady downpour that rattled the earth and stirred them from sleep. Drake turned onto his side at the same moment Nzingha opened her eyes. They met each other's gaze without a word, the silence thick but unbroken.

"Are you hale?" he asked quietly.

She nodded once. "Yes."

Drake studied her in the dim light, the rain casting shadows across her face. Her light brown eyes were clear, unguarded. Too innocent for the world she had been dragged into. She looked unbearably beautiful in the morning, her hair loose, her expression soft with sleep.

He shifted closer, propping himself on one arm. His head rested in his hand as his other fingers caught a loose strand of her hair, winding it gently. She smiled at him, slow and shy.

"I wish our circumstances were not as such," he said,

"What do you mean?"

"I believe in faith," he replied. "Faith led me tae this wee isle. Faith had you find me. Life is strange that way. If I were tae leave and go home, I could not leave you here alone. Not knowing if you would be forced tae fend for yourself. Not knowing if some bastard might come ashore and try tae take you again."

His hand lifted to her face, his thumb brushing her cheek. "Ye are special. Not because ye are a princess. But because ye have courage. Spirit."

He bent and kissed her brow.

"And you are special because you listened to my hurt," Nzingha said. "You did not dismiss it. My tongue can be sharp, yet it does not trouble you. I like that. You are easy to speak with."

Drake smiled, mischief flickering in his eyes. "Yer sharp tongue doesnae frighten me. I've sailed through worse storms."

She gasped, her mouth falling open as he rose and stretched. Turning back toward her, he offered his hand. "I have news."

"Oh?"

"Aye. I meant tae tell you last night, but after Iney's passing, it did not feel right."

Her posture straightened. "What is it? Did you find a village?"

"Well. Sort of." Drake crossed to the clay pot of water and drank deeply before moving to the hut's opening. Rain spilled inside, heavy and relentless. He squinted. "My, it is coming down."

"DRAKE!"

He grinned, enjoying her impatience. "I found a small shack. Looks like the folk who lived there were shipwrecked. They left behind supplies. Useful ones."

Her fist struck his arm. "Truly? Why did you not say so sooner?"

He laughed softly, rubbing the spot. "Remember when I told you we were not alone on this island?"

She nodded.

"Those people live not far from the shack."

Her gaze sharpened. "Truly? So is it safe to live?"

"Aye, it is. So long as we keep well clear of them. They live atop the mountain, so it shouldnae be a problem. The shack will serve us better than this hut, fewer blood-suckin' insects, for one. There's a bed and a barrel of food, though I didnae have time tae search properly before nightfall."

"It is sad that the people who lived there have passed," she said, then smiled. "But I am relieved. We must leave once the storm breaks. Where is the boat?"

"I tucked it away nearby. We can leave this morn."

For the first time since Iney's death, Nzingha felt something loosen in her chest. Her spirit lifted. She believed, truly believed, that Iney was at peace now.

The Afternoon Brought Sun

The storm cleared as swiftly as it had arrived, leaving the island steaming beneath the heat. Drake rowed steadily, his head wrapped in his blouse to shield himself from the sun. His back flexed with each stroke, strong and sure.

Nzingha sat in the stern, watching him without realizing she was staring.

"How far until we reach the shoreline?" she asked.

"'Tis just around the bend."

Her thoughts turned sour. Blast Iney for leaving me. Trapping me here with this man. Does he even see me as pretty? She leaned forward, elbow to knees. He calls me bonnie. Perhaps all Scottish men do. Once his men find him, he will leave. And I will be here alone.

Her gaze stayed on his back, the steady pull of muscle beneath skin. The thought slipped out before she could stop it.

"The view is nice," she said, "I could look at your back all day."

He turned. "Did ye say somethin'?"

"Only that I am so hungry I could eat hay." She turned her head.

He chuckled as he turned back to the oars.

"For a princess," he said, "ye amaze me."

She quickly scowled again, hiding slight attraction.

"Here we are." He pointed to dense bush.

"I do not see anything."

"That path," he pointed ahead. "It will lead us there. Come."

He reached for her hand as she stepped into the water, then lifted her fully into his arms as though she weighed nothing.

"What are you doing?" She laughed.

"Treatin' ye like the princess ye are. This is yer island. Yer kingdom, and I'm here tae serve ye."

"Until you leave."

"Nae... Until we both leave," he said, winking.

Her breath caught. Why does he do that?

In his arms, she felt like the heroines from her childhood stories. "When foreigners came to our kingdom, they brought books. My father ordered them burned once they left."

"Let me guess," he said, "You stole them."

"Yes, I did. One book spoke of a knight who rescued a woman from a tower. That is how I felt just now. As though you rescued me."

"Well then," he said lightly, "ye are in luck. I was knighted by our king. Drake is my sea name. But I am Sir Andrew Barton."

"Sir Andrew Barton," she repeated, tasting the name. "Not Drake?" She smiled faintly. "It is a nice name. But what does knighted mean?"

"It is when a king honors ye for yer service," he said, smiling back.

"I see." Her eyes sparkled. "And you rescued many lassies from towers?" she teased, mimicking his accent badly.

He laughed. "Are ye the jester now?"

He set her gently onto the sand. They walked in companionable silence until the shack came into view.

"There ye have it," he said, gesturing ahead. "Her ladyship's shelter."

"Is there water?"

"Aye. About two miles from here."

He pushed open the driftwood door. Nzingha gasped, excitement lighting her eyes.

"Oh my... they made it comfortable. It is not my father's castle, but it will keep us dry."

He gestured toward a crate by the wall. "There may be supplies inside."

She knelt and pried it open, smiling. "You said you like whiskey?"

"Well, aye. I'd give my right arm for a dram."

She lifted an unopened bottle of Irish whiskey.

Within seconds, he was beside her, sniffing it. "You jest." He took a cautious taste, then grinned. "'Tis potent. These folk were Irish, I'd wager, shipwrecked, most like. What else is there?"

"Four jugs of red wine," she said, peering inside, "and a few pieces of cloth."

Drake grinned, near giddy, like a child at Yule. "I dinnae know whether tae have a drink or dance a jig."

"There are no cups," she teased. "For now, we'll use coconut shells."

The second crate revealed parchment. She lifted it carefully. "There is a map. Have a look."

He studied it, his brow furrowing. "Hmm... Las Tortugas. If I recall rightly, my men and I were no far from here." He tapped the edge with his finger. "If this map is true, we're in the North Atlantic."

"How far from your home?" she asked. "Scotland."

"Three tae four moons by a large ship," he said, "Eight by a smaller one."

"Christ above." He paced, drinking deeply from the bottle. "I must leave this damned island. My brother needs me. He doesnae handle loss well."

"Well," she said evenly, "that may be possible."

He froze. "Why would ye say that?"

She held up a journal. "I may not have the language correct, but it speaks of an English settlement."

He took it from her, scanning the page. "You have got tae be bloody jesting. There's a trading port, less than a week's travel by ship."

She stepped outside as he stared at the words, breath caught between disbelief and hope.

What Grief Allowed

Night settled over the island without Drake marking the moment it arrived. The candle beside him had burned low, while the journal lay open across his knees, forgotten lines blurring together as his eyes strained. When he finally looked up, it was the silence that struck him first.

Nzingha had not spoken in some time.

There had been no sharp remark from the far side of the hut, no impatient pacing, no sigh heavy with irritation. The absence of her presence pressed in on him, uneasy and wrong.

He scanned the small space and found it empty.

"Shit," he muttered, pushing himself to his feet. He dragged a hand down his face, the weight of the evening crashing over him all at once. "What the hell have I done? Night's already upon us, and I've spent the entire evening buried in a bloody book instead of seein' tae what matters."

He shook his head, exhaling sharply. "I dinnae need her temper aimed at me tonight."

He crossed the hut and swung the door open.

The scent reached him immediately, rich and unmistakable, heavy enough to stop him short. Meat was roasting somewhere nearby, its warmth cutting through the night air. His stomach tightened with sudden hunger.

Beneath the scent came another sound, softer but no less distinct, water splashing gently, accompanied by a woman's voice, low and melodic, carried on the steam-thick air.

Drake followed the sound around the back of the hut.

A wooden tub sat nestled near the trees, candles burning low on a rough stand beside it, their flames trembling in the faint breeze. Steam rose steadily from the water, curling upward in slow, drifting coils.

Nzingha sat immersed in the bath, the water stopping at her waist.

She was naked, wholly unguarded, and utterly unashamed.

Her breasts were bare, full and glistening in the candlelight, dark curls spilling forward over her skin as she leaned back against the tub. Her posture was loose, her shoulders relaxed in a way he had not yet seen from her. She sang softly, eyes closed, her voice unburdened, almost tender.

Drake stopped where he stood.

She finished the tune with a faint smile, as though savoring the last note, then reached for a cup resting near the rim of the tub. She took a slow sip before setting it aside, her teeth catching her lower lip as she resumed humming. Steam fogged the air around her, clinging to her skin and making it glow.

"God help me."

He moved closer before he realized he had taken a step.

Her eyes remained closed, but her lips curved knowingly.

"This is becoming a habit, Captain. You do enjoy interrupting my baths."

His mouth tilted, slow and dangerous. "And you enjoy temptin' me."

He studied her in the candlelight, desire tightening low in his gut.

"Suppose I were a man without honor and chose tae ravage ye where ye sit."

She smiled, still not looking at him.

"If you wished to ravage me, you would have tried the first time you saw me naked at the falls."

She opened her eyes then and sat up just enough to remind him of every inch of her.

"Besides, I do not believe you are brave enough unless you wished to lose a limb."

She reached for the soap, sitting beside her golden-handled dagger, the gesture deliberate.

"Wash my back."

The invitation hung between them, heavy and unmistakable.

Drake swallowed before stepping closer. "As ye command, Your Highness."

"While you played scholar, this princess hunted supper and kept us alive. If books filled bellies, you should have kept reading."

A smile tugged at his mouth as he shook his head. It had only been a matter of time before her tongue drew blood.

"My thanks. I smelt the pig from inside. How did ye manage tae bring such a beast here alone?"

"One learns quickly when hunger is the alternative," she said simply.

"I cannot believe I was reading that long. I found out some interesting things about this isle."

"Truly?"

"Aye. Turns out the people that built the shack were from Ireland. They were on a mission to deliver silver and supplies to the new world. They were set upon by pirates, whom they were able to outrun, which landed them on this island. They made friends with the natives until some of the crewmen got forward and raped one of the daughters from the tribe. The tribesmen ambushed their camp, capturing all but letting him and his wife go. Twenty of his crewmen were burned alive. The natives took his ship; it is docked at a cave's entrance, which is on the other side of this island. If we can manage to steal the ship or convince the natives we come in peace, I can get you home and make it back home to Scotland."

He massaged the soap onto her back as he spoke, his gaze drifting upward toward the darkening sky. "It is a daft idea that might get us killed, but we must converse on a plan." Without pausing, he continued to work the soap across her shoulders, his thumbs pressing deeper as he rubbed the knots from her neck.

She breathed, her head tilting slightly. "Mmm, that feels very good."

The sound she made, soft and unguarded, went straight through him.

He leaned closer, drawn by instinct rather than thought, his nose brushing her neck. Her scent filled him; it was warm and intoxicating.

His voice roughened. "God help me, you smell incredible."

His lips touched her skin before restraint could catch up.

She startled, breath catching sharply. "Drake, what are you doing?"

"Lass, I cannae help it, every joint in my body screams ye."

He winked. "Besides, I was returning the kiss ye stole last eve."

She turned slowly in the tub, water lapping against her skin as she faced him. Their eyes met, desire flashing bright and unguarded between them.

The urge was hungry. She reached for him.

Her arms slid around his neck, drawing him down into a kiss that allowed no hesitation. Her mouth opened beneath his, a soft sound escaping her lips that made his breath stutter as he kissed her deeply, his hands moving with intent, learning her, claiming only what she willingly offered. Her fingers threaded into his hair, tugging just enough to pull a low groan from his chest.

"Drake… we mustn't," she whispered, her voice breaking even as she held him.

His breath caught against her lips. "I've been wantin' ye, lass," he said softly. "Dinnae deny it. Ye feel everything. Dinnae deny it."

He pressed his mouth to hers again, and she opened for him, their tongues finding a slow, unhurried rhythm, unexhausted, inevitable. His fingers slowed beneath the water, the change in pace sending a shiver through her as she leaned back against him, surrendering to the heat of his body and the surety of his touch. His hands explored her with reverence and hunger, and she allowed it, her breathing growing uneven as she pressed into him.

"You're doing this on purpose," she breathed, eyes closed, her voice labored.

"Aye," he murmured, his mouth near her ear. "Because I want ye tae feel what tortures me every time I look at ye."

Her breath broke into gasps as sensation overtook her, her hands clutching at him, her body arching back as she cried his name. "Drake."

"That's it, lass," he whispered. "Let go. Dinnae hold yourself back."

She released, heavily, her breath laboring as the moment crested and passed. When it ended, she sagged against him, breath ragged, her chest rising and falling as though she had run a great distance.

And then she broke.

The weight of what had passed came down upon her swift and merciless. She folded inward, turning away as tears spilled freely, sobs tearing from her chest as shame took hold.

Drake froze.

"God… what have I done? Nzingha," he said, panic threading his voice. "Look at me. I swear I never meant…"

She whispered, broken, "Leave me be. My father was right. I am a harlot."

His chest tightened painfully. He stripped off his shirt and wrapped it around her, lifting her gently from the bath and carrying her into the hut as she cried softly against him. He laid her in the bed and curled behind her, holding her as though she might shatter beneath his touch.

"I am so sorry. I never meant tae dishonor ye."

After a time, he rose and left the hut, slamming the door behind him.

Outside, he kicked a bucket and paced beneath the stars, cursing himself, guilt burning hotter than desire ever had.

"Son of a whore… What the hell did I just do? I have taken advantage of a woman whose lover was recently executed, while her friend and bodyguard just died last eve. I need to get the hell off this God-forsaken island."

Drake kicked the bucket again and walked over to the pig that was roasting. "For Christ's sake, the royal lass hunted and killed an entire pig while I sat inside on my arse and read a bloody journal."

He took the roasted pig to the area of the yard used as a kitchen, where a stone hearth sat surrounded by rusted pots. Placing the roast on a long banana leaf, he carved the meat. Drake added a few pieces of fruit Nzingha had stored, then went back inside.

"Nzingha?" He walked closer to the bed. "Nzingha," he called softly.

She did not answer.

He rested the food on the table and studied her small frame in the bed. Seeing that she slept, he sat on the bench, ate in silence, and took a long swig of the Irish spirit.

Noticing the kerosene lantern hanging unlit on the wall, he muttered, "Damnation," then stepped outside to light it. Undressing, he returned to the tub, using the water from Nzingha's earlier bath, which was still warm.

After bathing, he went back inside. Nzingha still slept. He crawled into the box bed behind her, placing his arms over her carefully, and drifted into sleep.

Chapter 8

The Ones Who Came Before

"Zingha."

Nzingha stirred at the sound of her name, the syllables spoken with a familiarity that reached beyond waking. She opened her eyes to the dim interior of the shack and saw Drake beside her in the box bed, his hair damp, his body slack with sleep.

He must have bathed and fallen asleep after I did, she thought.

She rose quietly, careful not to wake him, and crossed the small space to the door. When she opened it, a cool breeze slipped inside, brushing her skin and raising a shiver despite the heat of the night. She shut the door again, the latch settling softly.

"Zingha."

Her breath caught.

"Mikel?" she whispered. "Oh, the Gods… is that you?"

She turned, and he was there.

She ran to him without thinking, throwing her arms around him as she had so many times before, her face pressed to his chest. Relief broke through her like rain after drought.

"Mikel, I have been searching everywhere for you," she said, her words tumbling over one another. "What are you doing here?"

His arms did not fully close around her.

"I cannot stay long," he said gently. "I came to tell you goodbye."

Her head snapped back. "Goodbye? You have just found me. What do you mean, goodbye?"

"Nzingha," he said softly, "I am no longer of this world."

She reached up, touching his face, needing the reassurance of flesh beneath her fingers. Her hand passed through him.

The air left her lungs.

"Oh, Mikel," she cried, her voice breaking. "It is all my fault. Everything that has happened is all my fault. You, Asha… then Iney."

"Hush now," he said, lifting a hand that glowed faintly in the dark. "We cannot question the laws of karma. When we passed on, it was our time to leave this earth. All is well." His gaze drifted past her. "I know this man will love you and take care of you, until the end."

She turned, following his line of sight, and saw Drake asleep in the box bed. She faced Mikel again, her brows drawn tight.

"Mikel, what is it you speak of? You and only you will always have my heart. Please understand, I accept that I am a disgrace. I betrayed you tonight. Please… forgive me."

She tried once more to touch him. Again, her hand fell through.

"No," he said firmly. "Do not say such things. It is fine for you to move on. We are worlds apart now." His voice softened. "I knew the risk of loving you, and I was prepared to risk it all. As will you with this man."

A tear formed in his eye, shimmering, then breaking into colors like a fractured rainbow before fading into nothing.

"I died with a smile on my face," he continued, "because I knew my death would bring you freedom. Most of all, happiness. I had the honor of loving a courageous woman. Though we were passing soulmates, our time together on this earth was all I needed."

She swallowed hard. "But what about death being too far away?"

His spirit reached for her, and when his glowing hand brushed her face, chills swept through her body. She closed her eyes as tears slipped free, placing her hand over his. It felt warm. Alive.

"Cease this crying," he said, "Our love will never be too far away. You will always carry me in your heart."

Another voice spoke.

"He is right, you know."

Nzingha turned.

"Iney," she breathed.

Iney stood behind her, whole and smiling. Nzingha clutched her stomach and shook her head slowly, the weight of grief crashing down on her all at once.

"I saw your mother," Iney said. "Queen Tafaria. She is as beautiful as ever. I asked the Mother to allow me to thank you in person." Her expression turned knowing. "She said to name your daughter Destiny. This entire ordeal has brought you to your destiny."

"Daughter?" Nzingha scoffed weakly. "Iney, what are you on about? You were always the jester."

The air shifted.

Queen Tafaria appeared, regal and radiant, and Nzingha dropped to her knees.

"Mother," she sobbed.

Beside the queen paced Asha, her great lioness, tail swaying, eyes steady and watchful. Nzingha reached for her, smoothing her hand over familiar fur, burying her face against Asha's neck. The lioness licked her cheek and pressed closer, a low sound of comfort vibrating through her chest.

"I am so sorry, girl," Nzingha whispered. "I will forever love and miss you."

She kissed Asha once more, then bowed her head.

"Mother, I miss you as well. It has been so long since you visited. Are you here to tell me to return to Mbemba Kingdom?" Her voice cracked. "You must understand, I cannot go back to Father. Why did you refuse treatment? Why did you choose to leave us so soon? You left me with a selfish and unreasonable man."

Queen Tafaria bent and kissed her forehead.

"My baby girl," she said tenderly. "Death has no sorrow that love cannot heal."

"There was no way I would allow your father to marry you to a rival kingdom," the queen continued. "To a man who would mistreat you, or cast you aside when he tired of you. Our kingdom will not endure as it once was. Foreigners will come. They will seize our lands, capture our people, and scatter our children across distant shores."

Nzingha's chest tightened.

"Many kings will betray their own," her mother said. "They will sell their people instead of standing to fight. Warriors will die for freedom. Others will be stolen away."

"Can our deities stop this?" Nzingha asked, clutching Asha.

"They cannot interfere with all paths of life," the queen replied. "Beliefs will be forced to change. Our deities will be buried with the ancestors. The elders have prayed for storms to destroy the ships that carry Africa's children away. The goddess Yemaya will take many into her arms beneath the sea rather than allow them to live in chains."

The queen turned to Mikel and Iney. "My daughter and I need privacy."

They bowed and vanished. Before he disappeared, Mikel pressed a hand to his chest.

"Remember, Zingha," he said, "You are free to love."

Queen Tafaria looked upon her daughter with pride.

"I asked the Mother to send this man to you," she said, "I knew Iney's time was short. I asked that both Iney and Sir Andrew protect you. His ship was closest, so the Mother created a storm."

Nzingha's heart pounded.

"You will give life to a noblewoman," her mother continued. "She will be raised in other lands. She will learn other ways. Yet she will know she is a princess through her father. Our bloodline will rest in distant soil. The world is changing."

Tears streamed down Nzingha's face. "What about me, Mother?"

"There will come a time when you sacrifice one life for another but know this. We will be waiting when the mother calls you home."

"Nzingha!"

She gasped, waking with a stare as though she was in another realm.

Waking With Guilt

She woke with a sharp intake of breath, her chest tight, the remnants of the dream still clinging to her like mist. Her mother's voice lingered in her ears, and for a moment she could almost feel the warmth of Asha's body pressed against her once more.

Then the world returned.

The low fire.
The hush of the small home.
Drake beside her.

"Lass," he said softly. "What ails ye? Ye were cryin' in yer sleep."

She turned her face away, embarrassed by the tears on her cheeks. His hand lifted and brushed them away with care, then stilled, as though he feared even that might be too much. He withdrew it slowly, giving her space.

"I need ye tae hear me," he said quietly. "Truly. I am sorry. I never meant tae hurt ye, nor tae dishonor ye. I would never force a woman. Nae ever."

She turned back toward him then, meeting his eyes.

"It is not you, Drake. Not you."

Her voice wavered as she lay staring up at the thatched roof, the shadows moving gently above them.

"I woke feeling ashamed, as though I had betrayed Mikel. When you kissed me, when you touched me, I forgot about him... And, when I realized it, fear took hold of me."

Drake did not interrupt her. He did not reach for her. He remained still, listening, letting her words find their way out.

She drew a slow breath and turned her head toward him again.

"But I am no longer afraid. He came to me. He released me. I am free from him now."

Her gaze held steady on his.

"And I want you."

The words were deliberate, spoken without haste or uncertainty.

She leaned toward him and kissed him, slow and sure, closing the space herself. There was no confusion in the kiss, no searching. Her lips parted willingly, her body following the choice already made.

Drake answered her for a moment, then pulled back just enough to look at her.

"Are ye certain this is what ye want?" he asked. "I will stop now if ye ask it."

"Yes," she said, without hesitation.

He paused, nerves taking hold as he studied her face carefully. "Is this yer first time with a man? You and Mikel never...?"

"I told you before, no."

"Do ye still love him?"

"Yes."

His brow furrowed. "Then how do ye ken this is right?"

She did not look away.

"I do not know if it is right or if it is wrong. I only know that, in this very moment, I wish to be with you. You have seen my pain and carried grief that was never meant to be yours to bear, and I am grateful that I found you."

She touched his face.

"What we share can remain here, on this island, when it is time for you to leave. I may never be with another man. I do not know how I will return to my kingdom, or if I will be taken again. If I do return, my father will force me to wed a tyrant who will care nothing for my body or my will. But you do see me. I have seen the way you look at me, the care with which you desire me, and that is what I choose to give to you freely."

Drake let out a slow breath.

"I do not ken if this is right either. But I ken what I want."

His gaze held hers. "If ye choose me, I will no' pretend I dinnae want ye."

She did not smile. Her breath deepened, her chest rising as though her body had already answered.

And with that, the choice was made.

The Night Chosen

Andrew gave her a soft peck to her lips. A test, to see her comfort.
Did she really wish to go through with this?
He went in for another. This time he held it longer, unmoving, their breaths intertwined from the closeness.
She opened her mouth for him, and then the kissing grew stronger.

Not gently.
Not hurried.

His mouth covered hers with intent, silencing the breath she had been holding, stealing it outright.

She startled against him, not from fear, but from the sudden awareness of what lay before her. In her life, she had faced battles of blood and will, yet this was the one that unsettled her most. To yield herself to a man, to allow him entry into her body, awakened a vulnerability she had never learned how to fight.

Drake felt the tension at once. He stilled above her, his hand coming up to smooth her cheek, grounding her where she lay. When he kissed her again, it was slower this time, softer, meant to reassure rather than claim. His lips parted, coaxing hers open, drawing her into the kiss until her body eased beneath him.

Her resistance softened. Her breath deepened.

He kissed along her jaw, down the curve of her neck, then to her breast where he lingered, tasting each nipple, before returning to her mouth, reminding her with each touch that he was there, that he was attentive. His hand slid along her side, firm and sure, drawing her closer, anchoring her beneath him as her body finally relaxed into his.

When his mouth left hers, it traced a deliberate path down to her sex. He was unhurried, slow and deliberate. He kissed her there until her breath broke entirely. She gasped as sensation overtook her, her body arching instinctively, writhing beneath his attention, every lick, every suckle. Just as she neared release, he stilled, withdrawing with intention, leaving her painfully aware of how much she wanted more.

She spoke softly. "No, what are you doing? Please. Do not stop." Breathy, she pleaded for more attention, her hips still writhing against him. She wanted more of his mouth.

Before she could crave any further, in one careful motion, he entered her fully.
She gasped, eyes closing at the sudden intensity, her fingers clutching at his shoulders as sharp sensation stole her breath.

His voice deep and low, he murmured atop her. "Easy lass. Look at me."

She forced her eyes open, meeting his gaze as discomfort flared, stealing her words. His mouth found hers again at once, softer now, coaxing rather than taking.

"Let me feel ye answer with yer body." His eyes claimed hers. He stared, deep and intense. His looks alone sent heat through her.

Her breath broke as his kiss deepened, slower, more deliberate, until the sharpness dulled, until heat replaced it and her body began to respond instead of resist.

His forehead rested briefly against hers.

"Listen tae me. I'll guide ye. Ye tell me if I go too far."

"Yes," she breathed, the word barely a sound.

He kissed her again before moving, as though he would not take another step without reminding her of his mouth, his presence, his control.

His voice lowered as he pushed forward.

"More?"

"Yes."

"Deeper?"

"Mm. Hmm." She nodded.

The further he stretched her, the more she held her breath.

"Lass, I need ye to breathe." He deepened the kiss, releasing her breath.

She gasped against his lips, the sound swallowed by the kiss as her body tightened around the unfamiliar sensation.

Her hands flew to his shoulders, unsure of pushing him away, or to embrace him.

He broke the kiss only long enough to ask quietly, "Do ye wish me tae stop?"

She shook her head at once, breathless, desperate, her mouth finding his again in answer.

He broke their kiss. "Say it. Tell me ye wish me to stop."
"No, please, do not stop."

Drake carried a rhythmic motion.

Back and forth.
In and out.

He moved with intention, desire, and hunger.
His voice broke. "Christ, Nzingha… ye are so beautiful."

His chest tightened, looking at her beauty in the candlelight. This was more than any one night, more than a tavern fling. His heart felt something shift. She carried no hardened scowl like she normally did. Her face was softened, delicate, like a goddess. Her eyes filled to the brim with water. It was passion, infused with delicate desire.

He kissed her hard then, deeper, holding her there as he continued slowly, deliberately, giving her time even as he claimed her.

When discomfort flared again, sharp and startling, she gasped into his mouth, her body instinctively pulling back.
"Sh, stay with me. I've got ye," he whispered, kissing her through it.

He remained close, his mouth never leaving hers for long, kissing her until the tension softened, until her body adjusted, until the sharpness gave way entirely to heat.

He murmured against her lips. "Aye. That's my lass. Move with me."

She pressed into him without thinking, seeking his mouth again, answering the kiss with hunger now, her breath heavy and uneven.

The pace moved faster. He lifted his chest to match the movement of his waist, his arms flexed muscle over her.

His breath was unsteady, his control thinned. Drake was on edge. He claimed her ear, his mouth close, his voice low and urgent.

"Stay with me," he whispered. "Let me protect ye."

His heart grew weak with the force of it.

"Let me be the one who holds ye," he said, the words breaking, stuttering with his movement. "Lass, can ye feel me… because I dinnae ken if I can hold on much longer."

She cried out, her fingernails sinking into his back. "Uhhh, Drake."

That was his cue.

Andrew Barton roared, spilling fully within her walls.

Breathless, he dropped atop her. Before he could speak, his chest heaved. Then he smiled, breath finally returning.

"Are you well?"

She nodded, uncertain of what to say, uncertain of what to do.

Drake held her, kissed her forehead, and within minutes, he was asleep.

Claim Denied

Nzingha slipped from the bed while he slept.

Of course you sleep.

Drake lay sprawled on his back, breathing deep and easy, one arm flung wide as though he had conquered something worth keeping. His chest rose and fell with the untroubled confidence of a man who believed the world bent easily to him. The sight pulled a scowl across her face before she could stop it.

"Oh, look at you," she muttered under her breath. "Snoring like a satisfied ox."

Pain followed her as she straightened, a dull, persistent ache low in her body that made her pause and grit her teeth. She steadied herself against the edge of the bed, waiting for the worst of it to pass. When she finally stood, warmth slid down her leg, unmistakable and unwelcome.

Blood.

She hissed softly between her teeth. "Wonderful."

Gathering the cloth, she stepped outside the hut, the night air cool against her bare skin. It brushed over her like a reprimand, sharp enough to wake her fully. She crouched near the basin and began to wash herself, careful at first, movements measured and controlled. But irritation simmered beneath the surface, and before long her motions grew rougher, less patient.

The water bloomed red.

Her jaw tightened. "So now I'm yours," she whispered sharply as she scrubbed. "*Ye are mine.*" She scoffed, bitterness curling her lip. "Listen to him. One night and suddenly he is king of the bloody world."

She squeezed the cloth between her thighs and winced, breath catching despite her effort to remain composed.

"Protect me? Hold me?" Her mouth twisted. "Arrogant foreigner. Just because I let you touch me does not mean you get to decide where I belong."

Her hands began to tremble. She forced them still, breathing through the sting until it dulled to something she could bear.

She had chosen him. *Chosen.* That mattered. What did not matter was whatever foolish notion had lodged itself in his head while he lay panting and possessive, whispering like a man who thought desire was a contract and pleasure a binding oath.

She snorted softly. "Men. Give them a moment and they think they've conquered an empire."

Straightening slowly, pain flaring again as a reminder she could not ignore, she muttered under her breath, "You are a stubborn, infuriating, broad-shouldered mistake."

The words did not land the way she meant them to.

Her throat tightened.

"I am not your wife," she said quietly to the dark. "I am not your prize. And I am certainly not yours to take home. What do you take me for? A pet?"

She exhaled, long and steady, forcing the tension from her shoulders.

Beneath the anger, beneath the sharpened tongue and the rigid spine, something softer pulsed, aching and inconvenient. She hated that part of herself most of all.

Mikel had seen it.

This man had not.

Nzingha lingered outside the sheltered home, the night pressing close around her like a living thing. She lifted her face toward the moon, bright and unblinking above the treetops, and folded her arms across her chest.

"Mother Earth," she murmured, "you have a cruel sense of humor."

She paced a few steps, the grass cool beneath her bare feet, thoughts still bristling and unsettled. The island lay too quiet around her, the kind of silence that raised the hairs along her arms. Then, from somewhere beyond the trees, a low pounding rose, distant but deliberate. Drums. Slow and steady, measured enough to pull her full attention toward the sound.

Her head lifted, eyes narrowing as every sense sharpened.

Then, just as suddenly, it stopped.

Her brow furrowed. "What is that?" she whispered.

Silence closed in again, thick and watchful, pressing from all sides. Nzingha stood very still now, breath shallow, listening. She wondered if her mind had betrayed her, if the night itself was playing tricks.

She drew a slow breath and let it out.

That was when she heard it, the faint rustle of leaves.

Her body stiffened, pulse kicking hard as instinct took over. She reached for her dagger.

Her hand met nothing.

Her breath caught. She reached again, higher on her hip, fingers searching in disbelief.

Still nothing.

"Shiiit," she whispered.

The bushes stirred once more.

That was enough.

She bolted.

"Draake!"

He was already awake.

She burst through the door to find him seated at the small table, eating. He spat out his food and shot to his feet, chair scraping hard across the floor.

"WHAT THE DEVIL?" he shouted. "Did ye see a ghost?"

Nzingha stood just inside the doorway, eyes wide, chest heaving, one hand braced against the frame.

"Hh… hh…" She swallowed air. "Someone was… someone was following me."

Drake was already moving. He wrapped his kilt around his waist, snatched up his sword, bare feet thumping across the floorboards. "Where the devil did ye go?"

"I stepped out to take care of my needs," she said between breaths. "Afterward, I walked for a bit. Then the drums started, out of nowhere. Curiosity got the better of me, and I followed the sound. That is when the bushes began to move. Footsteps came next."

She swallowed hard. "I was unarmed. So I ran."

Drake peered through the opening near the door, eyes sharp, posture coiled. "Well, whoever it is," he muttered, "I'll be waitin'."

He crossed back to the table, grabbed the jug of wine, and pressed it into her hands.

"My thanks," she said, taking a long drink, then another.

He studied her for a moment, then lifted his hand and smoothed her cheek with his thumb. "Is all well, bonnie princess?"

She mocked his tone with a quick wink. "Aye."

He huffed a laugh. "Ah ha. I see I'm startin' to have an effect on ye." He leaned in and kissed her quickly.

Nzingha moved back to the door and peeked outside once more. The night showed nothing. When she turned, her gaze fell to the bed.

The linens were fresh.

She stopped short.

"Aye," Drake said, following her look. "I changed them. I thought ye went out for privacy when I awoke."

Her head dipped. Embarrassment crept in despite herself.

"There's no need for shame," he added gently. "It happens to all women their first time."

"My mother died when I was twelve summers," she said quietly. "I heard the village women speak, but no one mentioned that part. Mikel only ever kissed me. He was afraid to do more. He did not wish to risk getting me with child."

Drake hesitated. "You do know… there is a chance you may conceive."

Her mouth tightened at once. She looked away, jaw setting as irritation flared hot and sudden in her chest.

He pressed on, unaware he was nearing the edge. "If that's so, then we'd best think about what comes after. About startin' a life together. I would take you back to Scotland with me."

That did it.

The last of her softness drained from her face. Her spine straightened, chin lifting as though a crown had settled back into place.

"You look as though that troubles you," he said cautiously.

She crossed to the window, turning her back to him before her temper could fully break loose. "I do not wish to go to Scotland with you."

He stared. "What? Why not?"

"Scotland is your home, not mine. Your people do not look like me. We do not share beliefs."

"But I thought..."

"You thought what?" Her restraint cracked at last. "That I would go quietly to a land that may never accept me?"

He pressed on, stubborn now. "But what about us? Ye could be carryin' my bairn."

She turned, eyes sharp. "Yes. Well. You should have thought of that before we took it to this level of intimacy. You could have spilled outside."

Drake frowned. *Spilled outside?* How much did she ken?

She did not turn back to face him. Her voice, when it came, was calm, reserved, and utterly unforgiving.

"There is no realm, dark or otherwise, in which I would go anywhere with you. When your men find you, we part ways."

She turned then, hands clasped before her, back straight, face perfectly composed.

"I thank you for the intimacy of this night. It does not bind me to you."

In that moment, Drake felt the coldest winter settle in his chest, even as his face burned with anger.

"Are ye daft?" he demanded. "There's no chance I'm leavin' ye… Nzingha. Look at me."

"I SAID NO!" she shouted. "I am not your property!"

She wrenched free.

Fury flashed across his face. He grabbed his shirt and boots, dressing in sharp, angry motions, sheathing his sword and dagger before storming past her and slamming the door without another word.

The Cost of the Night

Nzingha slipped from the bed while he slept.
Of course you sleep.

Drake lay sprawled on his back, breathing deep and easy, one arm flung wide as though he had conquered something worth keeping. His chest rose and fell with the untroubled confidence of a man who believed the world bent easily beneath him. The sight pulled a scowl across her face before she could stop it.

"Oh, look at you," she muttered under her breath. "Snoring like a satisfied ox."

Pain followed her as she straightened, a dull, persistent ache low in her body that made her pause and grit her teeth. She steadied herself against the edge of the bed, waiting for the worst of it to pass. When she finally stood, warmth slid down her leg, unmistakable and unwelcome.

Blood.

She hissed softly between her teeth. "Wonderful."

Gathering the cloth, she stepped outside the hut, the night air cool against her bare skin. It brushed over her like a reprimand, sharp enough to wake her fully. She crouched near the basin and began to wash herself, careful at first, movements measured and controlled. But irritation simmered beneath the surface, and before long her motions grew rougher, less patient.

The water bloomed red.

Her jaw tightened. "So now I'm yours," she whispered sharply as she scrubbed. "Ye are mine." She scoffed, bitterness curling her lip. "Listen to him. One night and suddenly he is king of the bloody world."

She squeezed the cloth between her thighs and winced, breath catching despite her effort to remain composed.

"Protect me? Claim me?" Her mouth twisted. "Arrogant foreigner. Just because I let you touch me does not mean you get to decide where I belong."

Her hands began to tremble. She forced them still, breathing through the sting until it dulled to something she could bear.

She had chosen him. Chosen. That mattered. What did not matter was whatever foolish notion had lodged itself in his head while he lay panting and possessive, whispering like a man who thought desire was a contract and pleasure a binding oath.

She snorted softly. "Men. Give them a moment and they think they've conquered an empire."

Straightening slowly, pain flaring again as a reminder she could not ignore, she muttered under her breath, "You are a stubborn, infuriating, broad-shouldered mistake."

The words did not land the way she meant them to.

Her throat tightened.

"I am not your wife," she said quietly to the dark. "I am not your prize. And I am certainly not yours to take home. What do you take me for? A pet?"

She exhaled, long and steady, forcing the tension from her shoulders.

Beneath the anger, beneath the sharpened tongue and the rigid spine, something softer pulsed, aching and inconvenient. She hated that part of herself most of all.

Mikel had seen it.
This man had not.

Nzingha lingered outside the sheltered home, the night pressing close around her like a living thing. She lifted her face toward the moon, bright and unblinking above the treetops, and folded her arms across her chest.

"Mother Earth," she murmured, "you have a cruel sense of humor."

She paced a few steps, the grass cool beneath her bare feet, thoughts still bristling and unsettled. The island lay too quiet around her, the kind of silence that raised the hairs along her arms. Then, from somewhere beyond the trees, a low pounding rose, distant but deliberate. Drums. Slow and steady, measured enough to pull her full attention toward the sound.

Her head lifted, eyes narrowing as every sense sharpened.

Then, just as suddenly, it stopped.

Her brow furrowed. "What is that?" she whispered.

Silence closed in again, thick and watchful, pressing from all sides. Nzingha stood very still now, breath shallow, listening. She wondered if her mind had betrayed her, if the night itself was playing tricks.

She drew a slow breath and let it out.

That was when she heard it, the faint rustle of leaves.

Her body stiffened, pulse kicking hard as instinct took over. She reached for her dagger.

Her hand met nothing.

Her breath caught. She reached again, higher on her hip, fingers searching in disbelief.

Still nothing.

"Shiiit," she whispered.

The bushes stirred once more.

That was enough.

She bolted.

"Draake!"

He was already awake.

She burst through the door to find him seated at the small table, eating. He spat out his food and shot to his feet, chair scraping hard across the floor.

"WHAT THE DEVIL?" he shouted. "Did ye see a ghost?"

Nzingha stood just inside the doorway, eyes wide, chest heaving, one hand braced against the frame.

"Hh… hh…" She swallowed air. "Someone was… someone was following me."

Drake was already moving. He wrapped his kilt around his waist, snatched up his sword, bare feet thumping across the floorboards. "Where the devil did ye go?"

"I stepped out to take care of my needs," she said between breaths. "Afterward, I walked for a bit. Then the drums started, out of nowhere. Curiosity got the better of me, and I followed the sound. That is when the bushes began to move. Footsteps came next."

She swallowed hard. "I was unarmed. So I ran."

Drake peered through the opening near the door, eyes sharp, posture coiled. "Well, whoever it is," he muttered, "I'll be waitin'."

He crossed back to the table, grabbed the jug of wine, and pressed it into her hands.

"My thanks," she said, taking a long drink, then another.

He studied her for a moment, then lifted his hand and smoothed her cheek with his thumb. "Is all well, bonnie princess?"

She mocked his tone with a quick wink. "Aye."

He huffed a laugh. "Ah ha. I see I'm startin' to have an effect on ye." He leaned in and kissed her quickly.

Nzingha moved back to the door and peeked outside once more. The night showed nothing. When she turned, her gaze fell to the bed.

The linens were fresh.

She stopped short.

"Aye," Drake said, following her look. "I changed them. I thought ye went out for privacy when I awoke."

Her head dipped. Embarrassment crept in despite herself.

"There's no need for shame," he added gently. "It happens to all women their first time."

"My mother died when I was twelve summers," she said quietly. "I heard the village women speak, but no one mentioned that part. Mikel only ever kissed me. He was afraid to do more. He did not wish to risk getting me with child."

Drake hesitated. "You do know… there is a chance you may conceive."

Her mouth tightened at once. She looked away, jaw setting as irritation flared hot and sudden in her chest.

He pressed on, unaware he was nearing the edge. "If that's so, then we'd best think about what comes after. About startin' a life together. I would take you back to Scotland with me."

That did it.

The last of her softness drained from her face. Her spine straightened, chin lifting as though a crown had settled back into place.

"You look as though that troubles you," he said cautiously.

She crossed to the window, turning her back to him before her temper could fully break loose. "I do not wish to go to Scotland with you."

He stared. "What? Why not?"

"Scotland is your home, not mine. Your people do not look like me. We do not share beliefs."

"But I thought..."

"You thought what?" Her restraint cracked at last. "That I would go quietly to a land that may never accept me?"

He pressed on, stubborn now. "But what about us? Ye could be carryin' my bairn."

She turned, eyes sharp. "Yes. Well. You should have thought of that before we took it to this level of intimacy. You could have spilled outside."

Drake frowned. Spilled outside? How much did she ken?

She did not turn back to face him. Her voice, when it came, was calm, reserved, and utterly unforgiving.

"There is no realm, dark or otherwise, in which I would go anywhere with you. When your men find you, we part ways."

She turned then, hands clasped before her, back straight, face perfectly composed.

"I thank you for the intimacy of this night. It does not bind me to you."

In that moment, Drake felt the coldest winter settle in his chest, even as his face burned with anger.

"Are ye daft?" he demanded. "There's no chance I'm leavin' ye… Nzingha. Look at me."

"I SAID NO!" she shouted. "I am not your property!"

She wrenched free.

Fury flashed across his face. He grabbed his shirt and boots, dressing in sharp, angry motions, sheathing his sword and dagger before storming past her and slamming the door without another word.

Chapter 9

Hot Metal and Skin

*N*zingha nodded, though her hands betrayed her, trembling despite her resolve as she forced herself to remain still.

Drake had Haemish pinned by the arms, his grip locked and unyielding, boots braced wide against the floor. The small shelter felt too tight for the strain in his body, for the force he was holding back, and when he spoke, his voice cut through the hut, sharp with urgency.

"Hurry, lass."

Nzingha tipped the bottle and poured the whisky onto Haemish's arm.

The liquid struck torn flesh, and Haemish roared, his body bucking hard against Drake's grip as his back arched on instinct and the pain ripped the breath from his chest in a raw, broken cry.

"Ahh! Son of a whore. That hurts!"

Nzingha drew in a steady breath before she answered, and when she spoke, her voice did not rise.

"It could have been worse."

Drake shot her a warning look and tightened his hold as Haemish thrashed again, muscles straining as though pain alone might free him.

She moved quickly then, climbing onto Haemish's legs and straddling them to keep him from kicking loose. She poured again, this time over the open wounds on his thigh, and Haemish bellowed beneath her, bucking wildly as pain stripped away what little restraint he had left.

Drake pressed the knife into her hand.

The blade smoked faintly, heat shimmering along its edge.

Nzingha swallowed and lifted the hilt to her mouth, biting down hard to anchor herself. With both hands she pinched the torn flesh together, her fingers slick with blood, her focus narrowing until there was nothing but the wound beneath her grip.

Haemish surged upward.

"What in God's bloody hell are ye doin'? Get the hell off me!"

"Hold him," Nzingha ordered around the hilt, her voice steady even as chaos erupted beneath her.

Drake leaned in, bringing his full weight down to keep Haemish pinned.

Nzingha did not hesitate.

She pressed the heated blade into the wound.

The flesh hissed, the sound sharp and unforgiving, and the smell followed at once, burned and acrid, clinging to the air as Haemish screamed and kicked, buckling beneath them, fighting like a man half-mad with agony.

One massive leg tore free.

The heel struck Nzingha square in the face.

The blow was brutal and unmeasured.

Nzingha was thrown backward, her body lifting from atop him, before she struck the floor hard and slid to stillness.

Drake did not move at first.

For a moment, the hut seemed to hold its breath with him.

Then he saw her lying there.

Something in his chest broke loose.

He turned.

Haemish was barely aware of what was coming.

Drake drove his fist into Haemish's jaw, all the force he had left behind it. The impact snapped Haemish's head sideways, and his body went slack at once, crumpling back onto the bed without a sound.

Drake stood there only long enough to be sure he was down.

He grabbed the linen, his hands shaking as he wrapped and tied Haemish's wounds, pulling the cloth tight enough to hold, tight enough to stop the bleeding.

Only then did he leave him.

Drake crossed the hut quickly, dropped to his knees, and gathered Nzingha into his arms.

"Nzingha."

She did not move.

"Nzingha," he said again, fear roughening his voice as he gathered her into his arms.

Blood filled her mouth, warm and metallic, and his heart sank as he parted her lips carefully, checking for broken teeth or bone. Her teeth were intact, but blood slicked her mouth, and anger burned low and dangerous in his gut as he held her.

She was so small.

"Mmm… ouch."

Her lashes fluttered. She groaned softly as she stirred.

Drake was already there, close enough that she could feel his breath.

"Lass," he murmured. "Are ye hale? Christ, ye took a hard blow. That was brave. Bloody brave."

She lifted a hand to her face and winced. "My face hurts."

He caught her wrist gently before she could press too hard, easing her hand away.

"Easy. Easy now."

His mouth curved into a faint smile that did not quite hold.

"Ye're so fine to me. My Zing."

Her breath hitched. Tears gathered, not falling yet.

She whimpered, the sound small, almost childlike.

"I tried… but he… but he was too strong."

Drake leaned in until his forehead rested against hers.

"Shh. I ken."

His thumb brushed her cheek, careful of the swelling.

"Ye did well. Better than most men would."

He set her upright against the wall, fetched water and a coconut shell, then knelt before her again.

"Drink."

She sipped.

"Spit."

She did, and he cleaned the blood from her lips with slow, careful strokes, each one deliberate, grounding them both.

"How is he?" she asked.

Drake glanced toward the box bed. "Haemish? He'll sleep now. I had to knock him senseless to finish bandaging him. He's a big bastard. I'm shocked he didnae break yer nose. I was fit to kill him when he kicked ye."

"How did you knock him out?"

Drake lifted his fist and gave it a small shake. "With this."

Despite herself, her mouth twitched.

He leaned in and kissed her gently, careful of the swelling.

"That hurts," she murmured.

"Och. Forgive me." He pressed the cool cloth to her mouth again.

"What now?" she asked. "If his wound is not kept clean, he could die. Like Iney."

Drake stared into the fire, jaw tight.

"Aye. I ken. We need some sort of healer. We must get to that ship."

"I have a plan. I can climb the mountain and present myself as someone washed ashore. If I tell them I escaped a slave ship, they may listen."

"It's not all a lie," Drake said quietly. "You did escape."

He pulled her into his arms and looked into her light brown eyes.

"I cannae hog-tie you and drag you home with me, but if ye're with child… I want to be there. I want to raise the bairn. Origin, titles, and crowns mean nothing to me. My people will come to know you, as I have. And if any man ever dares lay a hand on you, I'll answer for it myself."

She opened her mouth, but he kissed her brow before she could answer.

"Think on it. Help me get Haemish well. Let us rest."

 She nodded and said nothing. As she lay beside him, his closeness set her heart racing, her skin burning without reason\. An unwanted desire crept in, and instead of reacting, she let herself drift into sleep.

Beneath the Box Bed

Morning crept into the hut in pale bands of light, slipping through the narrow window and tracing the rough wood of the walls. Beneath the low roof, Drake lay awake, listening to the uneven rise and fall of Haemish's breathing from the box bed above. The man had crawled through hell to reach this island, and the sound of his breath told the tale better than words ever could.

Drake turned his gaze to Nzingha sleeping beside him.

Her face was bruised now, darkened along her cheek and mouth, and the sight stirred anger in him again, slow and controlled. Pain did not excuse cruelty. Haemish should have held himself better. Drake could not rid himself of the question that had lodged deep in his chest since the night before. Had the kick been instinct, or had it been carelessness born of pain?

He brushed his fingers lightly along her cheek, then let his hand rest at her stomach, feeling the steady rise and fall beneath his palm. Heat stirred in him, quiet and unbidden. He glanced toward the bed above. Haemish did not stir.

Carefully, Drake lifted Nzingha's skirts, his hand sliding along her thigh. She blinked awake, eyes unfocused at first, then found him.

"Good morrow, beautiful princess," he whispered, a crooked smile tugging at his mouth.

"What are you doing?" she murmured, still half lost to sleep as she reached for her dress.

He caught her wrist gently and held it there. "Trust me."

"This is not proper," she whispered, her voice low. "Your man lies above us."

He kissed her before the protest could take hold, slow and reassuring, until the tension in her body softened. His hand slipped between her thighs, touching her where she was already warm.

A wide smile came to his face as he felt her sex.

"I've never seen a woman so bare," he murmured. "How do ye do it?"

"In my homeland, the paste is made from lotus leaves, honey, and the fat of a hippo. It is prepared over fire and taught to us by the elder women."

His brows lifted. "Hippo fat?"

"Yes. It protects the skin. It is what we have."

"And here?"

"Here I must make do. I drain oil from coconuts and mix it with honey. It does not work as well, but it holds once it cools."

"So it's wax."

"It is enough to serve its purpose."

"For cleanliness?"

"For care," she corrected. "It is something we are taught long before desire is ever part of it."

"Fascinatin'."

He freed her breast and kissed her there, slow and reverent, hushing her softly when her breath broke. His thumb slid slick with her heat and she shifted beneath him, her body answering before her thoughts could catch up. He turned her onto her side, close and careful.

"You can enter like this?" she whispered.

"Aye. Shh."

He entered her slowly from behind, giving her time to take him in. She gasped.

"Christ, Nzingha," he breathed. "So wet. So tight."

He moved with care at first, then deeper, lifting her thigh as his rhythm built, unhurried and sure.

"God above… ye feel like Heaven."

He rolled her gently beneath him, bracing his weight, steady and contained.

"Drake," she whispered. "Stop. I cannot breathe."

He stilled at once. "I'm sorry."

He kissed her, then entered her again face to face, moving slow and certain, breath uneven now as the rhythm quickened and his heart pounded against her chest.

"I cannae hold on."

His release came strong, drawing a long breath from his chest as she met him, her body trembling as they came together, breathless and shaking, the world narrowing to the space between them.

He pressed his forehead to hers. "Zing… I need ye. Since my parents passed, ye're the only one that's brought light back tae my chest. I feel bound tae ye. Be my wife."

She slipped from beneath him, drawing her dress back into place.

"Drake," she said firmly. "You barely know me. Please, do not ask again."

Above them, the box bed creaked.

"Laird Barton?"

The cough dragged from Haemish's chest as Drake rose at once, tying his kilt while crossing the hut.

"Aye. How do ye feel?"

"Like I've been hauled from the sea and beaten for it. Thirst. I need water."

Before Drake could move, Nzingha was already at the pitcher. She poured into a coconut shell and returned, lifting Haemish just enough for him to drink. He swallowed greedily at first, then slower.

"My thanks."

His gaze lingered on her a moment too long.

Nzingha felt it. She straightened. "Eh-Em, I will tend to my needs." She left before either man could speak.

Haemish watched her go, then looked back at Drake. "Well… she's nae from Scotland."

"Nae. She isn't. Princess Nzingha of Mbemba Kingdom. Taken by Portuguese pirates from her father's lands. She escaped them. Ended up here."

"So I heard ye ask for her hand."

Drake said nothing.

"Are ye daft?" Haemish went on. "If ye stay here, Alex will take it hard. Back to drink and whores for him. Comin' home would give the lad hope again."

"I'm no stayin'. Ye ken that."

Haemish grinned. "So she yer woman now? For a man not stayin', ye made a fair bit o' noise. Floor was thumpin' like boots on timber."

Drake let out a rough breath and shook his head.

"God's wounds, Haemish, shut yer gob. She's no wench. She's royalty."

He moved to the far end of the bed and sat, elbows braced on his knees, his voice steady now.

"She saved my life. Fed me. Tended my wounds. I owe her more than ye ken." Drake lifted his head. "Enough about her. What happened to the men?"

Haemish leaned back. "A few drowned. Three of us stayed afloat on a bit of wood for days. When we swam for land, the sharks came. Two were taken under."

"Aye." Haemish swallowed before going on. "Benjamin the young ship runner was with us. When I saw the shark comin', I shouted for him to swim, but the lad froze with fear. The next thing I knew, I was swimmin' through his blood."

"Christ above," Drake muttered.

"Aye, it was a sight. I started swimmin' like hell made chase. Then I saw it… another fin." Haemish went on, voice tightening as the memory took hold.
"It clamped onto my arm and shook me like a rag doll. I stabbed it with my dirk, then another came in and took a piece from my thigh. I struck that one too, and swam for shore bleedin', half tae death."

He drew a breath, steadying himself. "When I reached land, the natives saw the blood and left me there. I wandered for two days after that, cleanin' the wounds with saltwater. Fever near took me in the mountains."

His voice softened as the memory shifted. "That's when I saw her. I tried to call out, but I must've scared the saint out of her."

Drake crossed the hut and set the food within reach. "I need ye to eat."

He came back to the bed and lifted the map. "I found this last eve. We're here." He tapped the parchment once. "Las Tortugas, in the West Indies."

He lowered the map and raised the journal instead. "There's word in here of a ship, but we dinnae ken her exact location yet. Ye need to rest and get stronger. Once we find that ship, we can make our way home."

Haemish studied him for a long moment before asking quietly, "And what about the lass?"

"I offered her home. She refused." Drake's jaw tightened as he spoke. "I cannae leave her."

"Ye think she's carryin'?"

Drake shrugged, uneasy. "I dinnae ken. We just…"

"Andrew!"

Haemish cut in, his patience thinning. "Ye're soundin' like a laddie who's just lost his virginity and fallen headlong in love. Just like yer daft brother Alex. If the lass doesnae wish tae go, then ye leave her be."

Drake shook his head once. "Nae. What if she is carryin'?"

Haemish let out a long, measured breath. "Then ye have a bairn somewhere in the world."

Andrew shot him a hard look.

Haemish went on, the absurdity of it settling in his tone. "And then ye'll have those old farts tae answer tae. Aye. The clan elders."

Drake was already moving when he said it. "If they dinnae accept her, then they dinnae accept me."

"Andrew," Haemish pressed, his voice sharpening, "I've kent ye since ye were five years old. I'll drag yer arse back across the clouds if I must. That lass doesnae share yer colour, and half the fold will swear she's put some witchcraft on ye."

Drake stopped short and turned back on him.

"Christ, Andrew," Haemish continued, words tumbling now, "think. If there is a bairn, do ye truly believe it would be safe? A child with African blood? Wake up, lad. Ye're thinkin' with yer cock instead of yer mind."

"I am not leavin' her here alone," Drake said, his voice ironed flat. "And that's final."

He stormed out of the hut, slamming the door so hard it tore free from its hinges.

Outside, he passed Nzingha without seeing her, standing just beyond the doorway.

She had heard every word.

The heat rose fast in her chest, sharp and burning, her heart pounding as her hand slid instinctively to the hilt of her dagger. Her jaw tightened, eyes hardening as she stepped back into the hut.

Haemish sat propped against the bedding, skin slick with sweat, fever still clinging to him. He looked up when she entered.

"Good morn," he attempted a grin that did not quite settle on his face.

Nzingha stopped just inside the doorway. Her voice was flat, edged like stone.

"Who said it was?"

Haemish let out a short laugh that ended in a wince. "From the sounds beneath the floor, I'd say,"

The dagger struck the wall beside his head with a sharp crack.

Before the echo faded, she was on him.

She climbed onto the bed, pinning his arms with her knees, the blade pressed firm to his throat. A thin line of blood welled where steel kissed skin. Haemish froze, breath hitching as his eyes finally sharpened with understanding.

She spoke calmly. "Listen to me, you mountain of rhinoceros shit."

His grin vanished.

"You know nothing about me," she went on, the blade never wavering. "While you lie in this place, under this roof, you will show me respect. Or I will carve you for the fish and let the sea decide what remains."

She held his gaze another heartbeat, long enough for the lesson to sink in.

Then she rose, withdrew the blade, and walked out without saying another word.

The Lion and the Sheep

At the shore, Drake tore at the traps with bare hands, fury burning itself out in sharp, violent motions. Nzingha watched from a short distance, arms folded, her face unreadable.

He turned and checked the fish traps with more force than necessary, hauling one basket up only to fling it back into the sea. For a moment he glanced over his shoulder at Nzingha, then turned away again, jaw set, shoulders rigid.

She watched him quietly. After a beat, she smiled.

"You know, in my land, it is better to live one day as a lion than a hundred as a sheep."

Drake snorted and hurled another basket back into the water without looking at her.

"What does that even mean?"

She stepped closer, unbothered by his tone.

"You should not let other people's stupid opinions disturb your peace of mind, nor your ability to remain calm."

He said nothing, still working, listening despite himself.

"In the safari," she continued, "when a lion is cast from his pride, he does not weep or beg to be taken back. He goes out and makes his own pride. And if he cannot, then he learns to fend for himself."

She placed her hand at her waist.

"But a sheep, when separated from the herd, becomes frightened and lost. More than that, it becomes prey. Sheep are lower on the food chain. They survive only when surrounded by others who think and move as they do."

Drake slowed.

Nzingha watched him now, her voice steady, deliberate.

"You need to be more like the lion, stand for what you believe in, and do not worry about the opinions of those who stand in fields chewing grass and gossiping all day, making baaah noises at one another."

A corner of Drake's mouth twitched despite himself.

"A sheep cannot stand alone," she finished. "They are not strong enough. They need approval. They need numbers. But you…" She tilted her head, studying him. "You are a leader. You already know how to survive on your own. You have the ability to build your own pride."

She stepped closer until they stood side by side at the water's edge.

"When I had Asha, my lioness, people feared her. They did not understand why she would not allow anyone near me. Only Mikel."

Drake glanced at her now.

"To Asha," Nzingha said, "Mikel and I were her pride. She was doing her duty as protector. She never allowed anyone close enough to harm me." She turned to him fully. "I see that in you."

She lifted her hand and rested it against his cheek.

"You have the heart of a lion, you are a protector."

Drake exhaled, some of the tension finally leaving his shoulders. He smiled, leaned down, and kissed her gently.

"My thanks," he murmured. "You are a very wise woman indeed."

She bent, picked up a small stone, and tossed it into the surf.

"I think Haemish will learn to respect me while you are still here," she said, smiling.

Drake chuckled, then grew serious again as he took her hands in his.

"Have you given any thought to what I asked you this morning?"

She met his gaze.

"My heart has grown fond of you, you are… remarkable. If you do not wish to return to your father's lands, then let me take care of you. No one will question what we have growing between us."

She withdrew her hands and paced for a moment, thinking. Then she stopped and placed them at her waist.

"If I am with child, I will consider it, but if I am not, I must return home and face my father's wrath. I believe he will understand. If they have found Asha's body, they will know something is wrong."

She looked back at him. "I do not wish to lose you, Drake. But those are the only two paths I can see."

Drake smiled, slow and sincere.

She inhaled, then spoke again, already planning.

"I will go into the natives' village this night, I will make it seem as though I was savagely beaten. Haemish's large footprint upon my face should convince them."

"Nae," Drake said at once. "Do not call him that just now. I am no' pleased with him."

She smiled, unbothered.

"If he wishes to leave this island, he will change."

Drake's eyes widened. "You heard our conversation?"

"As I said," she replied evenly, "do not worry. I shall leave this eve."

Drake paced once, then stopped in front of her.

"I dinnae like it, It feels like walkin' into a death trap. Are ye certain this is what ye wish tae do?"

She nodded.

His voice softened. "Once ye uncover the ship, come back tae me at once. I cannae bear the thought of anything happenin' to ye."

He exhaled slowly. "If I go with ye, they may burn us all alive. So, we do this apart."

They sat together on the sand, the sky stretching wide above them.

"I shall sneak away from their village whenever I can to see you," she said, laying her head against his chest.

Drake wrapped an arm around her and whispered,

"You better."

Chapter 10

The Natives in the Mountains

Dusk settled over the island as Drake and Nzingha left the hut and followed the narrow path toward the mountain's north side, the light thinning as the trees pressed closer and the ground began its gradual rise.

Drake said little as they walked, keeping his attention fixed ahead, measuring where the path narrowed and where stone broke through the soil, committing each turn and incline to memory.

When they reached the place where the climb began in earnest, he stopped. His hand came to her waist, firm and deliberate, and he drew her close before pressing his mouth to hers. The kiss held urgency without indulgence, restraint bound tightly to need, the kind exchanged when a moment is understood to be finite.

Even as he held her, unease settled in his chest. The certainty had been with him since she first proposed the plan, a quiet warning that once set in motion, some things could not be reclaimed.

"Please," he said against her brow, his voice low. "Have a care."

She nodded once and stepped back, offering no argument and no comfort to ease his doubt. Turning, she continued on until the brush swallowed her, leaving Drake standing alone on the path, watching the place she vanished. He remained there longer than he should have, drawing a breath only when she was fully gone, sending a prayer after her and hoping the mountain did not take more than it was owed.

Useless Plea

Nzingha reached the upper ridge by endurance alone.

The climb punished her hands and arms, bark tearing through skin, and the stones bruised her bone as she hauled herself upward. Cuts opened across her palms, stinging sharply each time she found a new hold, but she did not slow. When she made the final pull and dragged herself onto the mountain's edge, her breathing had turned labored, her muscles burning with strain.

She lay still for a moment, chest rising and falling as she listened past her own breath.

Creeping forward, she looked down and found no sign of the shack or its firelight anywhere below. The brush was thick enough to swallow both smoke and sound, and relief settled quietly in her chest. At least they had been unseen.

She pushed herself upright and turned.

Two native men stood only paces away, bows drawn, arrows leveled squarely at her chest. Their stance was steady and practiced, their eyes fixed on her without hesitation.

She did not scream.

Moving with care, she pointed toward the east side of the mountain, away from Drake and Haemish, then motioned with her arms as if cutting through water. Crossing her wrists together, she lowered herself to her knees.

"Captured," she said, shaping the word clearly before lifting her gaze. "Help."

The men studied her in silence. Then, without warning, they laughed.

One stepped closer and lifted a lock of her hair, smelling it as though judging something unfamiliar. Nzingha turned her head slightly, allowing the hair to fall from his fingers without flinching. The second man joined him, touching the fabric of her dress and the jewelry she still wore as they spoke rapidly in their language, amusement threading their voices.

Her stomach tightened, but she held her expression carefully, letting desperation show where calculation might have been more honest. She needed them to believe she was vulnerable.

Instead, one seized her wrist and pulled her to her feet while the other shoved her forward, forcing her pace as the forest closed around them. Branches clawed at her sleeves and skirt as they moved deeper into the trees, and through it all one thought remained sharp and steady in her mind.

Was she being welcomed, or led to fire?

The forest opened at last into a clearing.

Triangular huts stood scattered across the camp, children running barefoot through the dirt until their laughter slowed and faded at the sight of her. Women paused in their work and stared without blinking. A goat turned slowly on a spit over open flame while another hung upside down from a tree, already split and being carved open. Nearby, two men shaped a hollowed log into a canoe as others loosed arrows into trees with practiced ease.

As Nzingha was led through the camp, movement stilled. Conversations fell away, and every eye followed her.

Her stomach weakened under the weight of it, the certainty settling in her mind even as she kept walking. This was a bad idea.

They approached an enormous tent at the center of the camp, and the moment she crossed its threshold, whatever discussion had been underway died. Elders sat around a fire, their attention turning as one to the strangers entering, the air thick with smoke and the sour scent of bodies long accustomed to heat and confinement. The smell struck her hard, and she lifted her hands briefly to cover her nose and mouth before schooling her expression and lowering them again.

She did not allow herself to look small.

Instead, she lifted her chin and surveyed the space with measured calm, as though standing in her father's court rather than bound and escorted. Authority was familiar to her, and she recognized it here. This tent belonged to their chief.

The elders spoke among themselves for a time, their language harsh to her ear, voices rising and falling until one elder turned his scowl fully upon her. He shouted an order and motioned sharply with his hand.

The men stepped forward and bound her wrists with rope, the fibers biting into her skin as the knots were pulled tight.

Shock rose swift and hot. "Wait," she pleaded, struggling just enough to make her meaning clear. "Please. I was captured. Taken from my home."

The elder raised his hand and spoke again, halting them. Another command followed, slower, deliberate.

One of the escorts left the tent and returned moments later with a young woman whose skin was pale and whose hair burned red as flame. Her eyes were heavy with sorrow, and she looked close to Nzingha's age, perhaps younger, no more than eighteen summers.

The elder addressed her, and she nodded before turning to Nzingha.

"Hello, miss," she said carefully. "He wants to know why you disgrace yourself and arrive here with a creamy-skinned man. He says they are evil people."

The words struck hard.

"I beg your pardon?" Nzingha said, the question escaping before she could temper it.

The young woman continued as the elder spoke. "They saw you with a creamy-skinned man before you climbed the mountain. They know you arrived on a boat together. They have scouts in the trees. They watch for ships." She hesitated, then added quietly, "They did not bother you because you did not carry metal fire. He means muskets."

Urgency threaded Nzingha's voice as she spoke again. "Miss, please. Tell them I am Princess Nzingha of Mbemba Kingdom. I was captured by Portuguese pirates and placed onto a slave ship."

The young woman translated as Nzingha continued without pause.

"My guard was also captured. We arrived on the west side of the island. During our time here, my guard died from infection. I never met the captain until he came six moons after we did. Please, we only wish to return home."

At the words return home, the young woman's gaze dropped, her expression tightening with something unspoken.

Nzingha noticed, but did not press it yet.

"Please," she continued evenly. "We are on the same side. You protect your land from invaders. I was stolen from mine. They invaded my land as well. Will you help me?"

When the translation finished, Nzingha offered the young woman a brief smile. "Thank you."

The woman nodded faintly in return.

The chief rose and stepped closer, looming as he spoke, his tone tightening the space around them. The young woman's voice strained as she translated. "How can we trust you when you lie with such evil? My scouts saw you together inside the hut. Did he send you here?"

"No," Nzingha answered, the word clean and sharp. "I came on my own looking for help. I heard there is a ship. Is this true?"

Laughter spread through the tent when the words were interpreted.

The chief spoke at length, anger woven through his voice. "Do you think you are leaving this place? We do not wish for ships to come here. White men come to this land and take us. Every year we hide deeper into the mountains. We trust no one."

Nzingha straightened despite the rope biting into her wrists. "If you do not wish to help me, then I shall be on my way."

She turned and began to walk calmly toward the tent opening, her hands still bound, her posture deliberate. It was not escape yet, but declaration.

She meant what she said,

The Flight and the Reckoning

Nzingha had taken no more than a single step toward the tent opening when a man surged in from behind and seized her arm, hauling her backward toward the fire as though strength alone might drag her into submission. The rope binding her wrists snapped tight as her balance shifted, biting hard into her skin, but instead of resisting the pull, she let it carry her.

She swung both bound hands up and over his head in one fluid motion, slipping out of his reach as the rope slid across his throat. Before he could understand what had happened, she twisted her body and pulled hard, drawing the rope tight against his neck and locking her weight forward.

He staggered, bare feet skidding in the dust as his breath broke apart beneath the sudden pressure. His hands clawed uselessly at the rope and at her arms, his strength draining as the struggle faltered. She held him there, unyielding, until his body went slack against her, the fight leaving him all at once.

Before she could fully release him, another islander rushed her from the side and slammed into her shoulder, jolting pain through her arm and forcing her a step forward. She struck backward on instinct, her heel connecting hard with bone, and felt the man falter. In the same breath, she reached out and caught the red-haired girl by the wrist, pulling her into motion before fear could root her to the ground.

They burst from the tent into the clearing as shouts erupted behind them.

The camp exploded into movement. Men surged forward, voices raised in fury, arrows loosed without care for aim or consequence. One arrow struck the ground close enough to spray dirt against Nzingha's leg. Another splintered wood near her shoulder. She did not look back. She ran with her grip locked tight around the girl's wrist, forcing her forward as the ground shifted beneath their feet and the trees closed in ahead.

The girl faltered, breath breaking as panic caught hold of her legs.

"Please. I cannot. I am weakened."

Nzingha tightened her grip and kept them moving, her pull firm enough to leave no room for collapse. "You move or you die."

They entered the forest with effort rather than speed, the brush closing around them and resisting every step as the ground began its steady rise. Nzingha adjusted her pace to the uneven drag between them, refusing to let go.

"I cannot breathe. My legs will not..."

"They will." Nzingha's voice came through the strain of movement. "Slow your breath. Match mine."

The girl stumbled again, nearly pulling them both down. Nzingha stopped just long enough to steady her, hands firm at her shoulders, forcing her to look up.

"Look at me. You are not running from them. You are choosing to live."

"But... I am afraid."
The words barely held together, her breath catching as the last light drained from the trees.

"So am I." She did not slow, did not turn, and the truth of it steadied them both.

"Fear is not command. Move."

They pressed on together, the sounds of pursuit carrying through the forest behind them, close enough that the girl flinched whenever branches cracked or breath followed too near.

"They are near."

"I know. Do not listen for them. Listen for me."

The ground steepened beneath their feet, the wind shifting as the forest thinned ahead. When the edge came into view, the girl froze, staring into the darkness beyond.

"I cannot," her voice breaking as she stared into the darkness ahead. "There is nothing there, nothing at all. What do we do now. They are almost upon us."

Nzingha was already reaching for the vines. "There is. You will trust me."

A stone exploded nearby as an arrow struck rock.

The young woman cried out as panic overtook her. "They will kill us. I do not want to die."

"Only if you stop."

She drew the girl close, foreheads nearly touching, her grip firm enough to steady both of them as the sounds of pursuit tightened through the trees.

"When I tell you, you will cut the rope. Not before. Not after. Do you understand me."

"Yes."

"Say it."

"Yes."

She nodded once. "Good. Now breathe."

Nzingha shifted her stance, gathering the vines in her hands as the drop opened at her back, the rough fibers biting into her palms.

"Now.!"

The girl's hands shook as she slipped the dagger beneath the hem of Nzingha's dress and worked it carefully against the rope at her wrists. The fibers resisted at first, fraying slowly beneath the blade while the forest behind them filled with voices and the pounding of feet drawing closer. When the rope finally gave way and fell loose, Nzingha did not stop to rub the raw skin or catch her breath. She closed her freed hands around the vines, tested their strength with a single hard pull, and then turned her body so her back faced the cliff.

"Climb onto me," she said, leaving no room for refusal. "Hold tight."

The girl climbed onto her arms locking around Nzingha's shoulders, weight heavier than Nzingha had allowed herself to calculate.

She eased them over the edge and began the descent, lowering them inch by inch. The vines stretched under strain, rough fibers burning against her palms as her shoulders trembled from the effort. Above them, arrows hissed past, and she could feel the air move with each one, close enough to steal breath.

The girl shifted with panic, clinging tighter.

"Do not move," Nzingha warned through her teeth, fighting to keep them steady. "Do not..."

They were close now, close enough that she could see the ground clearly below.

Six feet.

Then the vines snapped.

The world dropped out from beneath her.

They hit hard, the impact driving the breath clean from Nzingha's lungs. The girl landed on top of her with crushing weight, forcing pain through her ribs and stomach until her body refused air. For a moment, Nzingha could not even gasp. White stars burst behind her eyes, bright and merciless, the world ringing as though the island itself had struck her.

"Miss," the girl whispered, voice shaking. "Miss, are you hale."

Nzingha blinked through the stars and forced herself to move. She rolled the girl off her and tried to rise, only for pain to tear through her ankle the moment she placed weight upon it. The joint had twisted in the fall, and it screamed protest with every attempt to stand. Still, she stood. She would not lie there and wait.

"Come, we must move," she managed with a thin breath. "They are coming down."

The girl clutched her arm. "I hear them. What do we do."

Nzingha swallowed against the pain burning through her ankle and pointed toward a boulder half-swallowed by brush, its shadow thick enough to hide a body if one stayed very still.

"Hide there." She guided the girl with one hand, her other arm extended for balance as the ground tilted beneath her. "Do not move. Do not come out until I tell you."

"But..."

"Go!"

There was no room for argument in her voice. The girl ran, stumbling low and fast, reaching the boulder just as movement broke through the trees.

Three islanders burst into the clearing, spreading instinctively as they closed, feet light on the ground, cutting off retreat before it could form.

Nzingha reached for her blade and swung as they advanced, but her body was slower now, the injury in her ankle stealing speed and certainty from every step. She struck one with the flat of her dagger and turned sharply, forcing the others to stay in front of her, narrowing the fight to something she might survive.

A stone lay half-buried near her foot.

She snatched it up and hurled it with everything she had left.

It struck one man squarely in the forehead. He dropped without a sound.

The remaining two did not slow.

Pain exploded across her back as a wooden club slammed into her from behind, the force driving her forward and tearing a gasp from her lungs. Fire raced up her spine as she staggered, fighting to stay upright, fighting to turn, to lift her blade again.

Another body collided with her.

Hands locked around her arms, crushing them tight against her sides. She twisted and struck blindly, breath coming hard as she tried to wrench free, but the injured ankle folded beneath her weight. She went down hard, the earth knocking the air from her chest.

The dagger slipped from her grasp.

One man pinned her shoulders to the ground, his weight pressing the breath from her lungs. The other stepped back, deliberate now, lifting a spear. Its sharpened point caught the dim light as he leveled it at her chest, steady and unhurried, as though this part required no haste at all.

Time slowed.

Nzingha's breath came shallow and tight, every inhale scraping against pain. Her limbs were trapped, her weapon gone, her body aching everywhere it had been struck. She understood, with a strange and terrible clarity, that the spear did not require her to struggle for it to kill her.

So, she stilled.

She fixed her gaze on the dark space above the branches, jaw clenched and waited.

The blow never came.

Instead, a violent jolt tore through the man above her, followed by a choking sound that rose and cut off all at once.

Nzingha's eyes flew open.

A sword drove through the man from behind, punching clean through his body and bursting out beneath his ribs, dark with blood.

His arms froze mid-motion, mouth opening in shock as red spilled down his lips. The spear slipped from his hands and struck the ground uselessly as his weight collapsed away from her.

Drake stood behind him, both hands locked on the hilt.

He wrenched the sword free and turned as the last islander lunged, club raised in blind fury.

Drake did not retreat.

He stepped into the attack, steel flashing as he sliced deep across the man's flank, stopping the charge cold. Before the islander could recover, Drake drove the blade up and through his neck, ending the fight with swift, final force.

The body fell.

Silence rushed in.

Nzingha lay where she had landed, chest heaving, the taste of dirt and blood sharp on her tongue as the world rang around her. The ground felt cold and solid beneath her back, real in a way she had not expected to feel again.

Drake turned.

The hardness in him fractured the instant he saw her there, sprawled where they had nearly taken her.

He was beside her in the next breath.

Leaving the Ashes Behind

Drake stayed close to Nzingha as the forest finally stilled, one hand firm at her back while she tested her weight and drew a breath she clearly did not wish to take.

"My ankle is twisted," she said at length, her voice steady despite the tightness at its edge. "My back and neck ache as well. I will walk, but I will not do it prettily."

He looked down at her properly then, taking in the way she favored one leg and the stiffness she tried to hide. His jaw set, and when he spoke, it was low and edged with more than anger.

"I telt ye this was a bad notion, marchin' into a village alone, thinkin' clever words would keep steel at bay."

She lifted her chin, refusing to yield ground even now. "They did. For a time."

"Aye, and near carried ye into the earth for it."

The dark beyond the trees pulled at his attention, but his hand did not leave her back. "You'll no walk fast. And if you fall again, I'll not be kind about it."

She followed his gaze and nodded toward the boulder. "She is still hiding there. I told her not to move unless I called her out."

"Aye," he said more quietly. "I ken who she is. That's Lady Annabella McKinny of Ireland."

At his words, Annabella stepped from behind the stone, hesitant at first, then straighter as recognition settled. Her voice trembled, but she did not look away.

"You… know me?"

Drake held her gaze. "I dinnae know you, lass, but I know your name. I read your father's words, his journal. I found it in the hut."

Her breath caught. "Then you know what became of him."

Drake's mouth tightened. He shook his head once, the answer given before the words could soften it.

"He didna survive."

Annabella went very still.

"I found him," Drake continued, quieter now, the honesty plain. "I buried him myself. There were other graves near him, folk he'd already laid to rest, but your father… your father was mine to bury."

Annabella stood very still, as though bracing against a wave. "May I see them?" she asked quietly. "Just for a moment."

He rested a hand at her shoulder. "Aye. But we cannae linger."

They moved toward the small clearing where the graves lay. Nzingha followed several paces behind, the limp no longer hidden. Drake noticed.

"You're hurt more than you're sayin'."

She answered dryly. "Indeed, Gravity and vines were unkind."

He stopped without warning, turned, and before she could protest, lifted her clean off the ground and slung her over his shoulder.

"Put me down," she demanded, striking his back. "I can manage my own limbs."

He smacked her backside without ceremony. "Let me do the managing before ye complicate matters."

She cursed him in two languages. Annabella stared, startled, then covered her mouth to hide a laugh.

At the graves, Drake set Nzingha down and stepped away, giving Annabella privacy. He said nothing of the state in which he had found her father. Annabella knelt, tears sliding silently as she removed a crest from her pocket and buried it. From her hair she drew a silver comb and placed it beside the marker.

"Did you bury them both?" she asked, not looking up, her voice careful.

"Nae," Drake said gently. "Just yer father. Your mother was already laid to rest by the time we came ashore. I didna ken the place of her grave."

Annabella's fingers curled into the earth. "She always said this island would keep its own secrets."

"Aye," Drake said. "It has."

She bowed her head. "Thank you… for not leaving him alone. Mother… Father… rest now. We shall all be together again someday."

Drake cleared his throat. "We must go. They'll be huntin' us."

They hurried back to the shelter where Haemish lay sprawled across the box bed, his shirt clinging to him, his skin slick with sweat as though the fever had decided to finish what the island had begun. His breathing was shallow, uneven, and when Drake stepped close, the heat rolling off him was unmistakable.

"Haemish," Drake said, laying a firm hand against his shoulder. "We must leave. Now. Can ye walk, or will ye force me to drag ye?"

Haemish squinted one eye open, then the other, as though the hut itself had offended him.

"What?" he rasped. "Aye… I mean… I can manage."

He shifted, grimacing. "But why in God's name are we leavin'? And why do ye look as though ye've just crawled out of purgatory itself?"

Drake had already turned away, digging through their things for the map and the journal.

"No time for idle questions. I'll explain once we're clear of this place."

Haemish pushed himself up on one elbow. "Then answer me this... did ye manage to get the ship?"

Drake did not look at him. "Nae."

Haemish let out a long, suffering groan and collapsed back onto the bed.

"Then this day is truly cursed beyond redemption."

The door creaked open.

His eyes drifted toward it just as Nzingha limped inside, Annabella at her side.

Haemish froze.

Firelight caught Annabella's hair, turning it copper bright. Her face was drawn with exhaustion yet unmistakably composed. Even here, even now, she looked as though she belonged to a different world entirely. Haemish forgot to breathe. "Well, I withdraw my complaint."

He squinted, then relaxed, letting the sight settle. "Either the fever has finally claimed me, or the saints have decided I've suffered enough."

He swallowed. "If this is a dream, I beg you... do not wake me."

A step sounded beside her.

Nzingha came fully into view, her limp unmistakable, her expression already sharp with impatience.

Haemish's shoulders sagged.

"Nae, I am awake," he muttered. "And truly cursed. For every blessing on this island arrives tethered to the she-devil who delights in my misery."

Nzingha scowled. "Speak again, and I will test how long a fevered man can crawl."

Haemish huffed a weak laugh. "There she is. Balance restored."

He forced himself upright, pain cutting through him, though his eyes returned... helplessly... to Annabella.

He asked, smoothing his tone. "And who, might this radiant miracle be, standing so calmly beside my impending death?"

Drake turned sharply. "Haemish. Mind your tongue. Ye stand before a princess and a lady."

Haemish inclined his head, as much as his condition allowed. "Then my apologies, illness has rendered me foolish."

Behind Drake's back, Nzingha stuck her tongue out at him, quick, shameless, victorious.

Haemish saw it and bit back a grin.

"She's beautiful, aye," he muttered, "but that temper,"

Nzingha leaned in just enough. "Finish that thought and you will not need the fever to excuse your suffering."

"Point taken," he said quickly.

As he tried to stand, his legs faltered. Nzingha seized a length of driftwood and shoved it into his hand.

"Use this. If you fall, I will not catch you."

"My thanks," he muttered, leaning heavily on it.

"There's no time," Nzingha said, turning to Drake. "We take what we can."

"Aye." Drake reached for a crate.

Nzingha stared. "Wine and whisky?"

"Bollocks to linens," he said, "Good drink should never be abandoned."

She shook her head, half disbelief, half acceptance, then handed Annabella linens and a lantern. She gathered what food remained and hoisted a crate atop her head as though pain were merely a suggestion.

They moved together toward the shore and limped, sweating, burdened.

As they reached the water, the night opened before them. Behind them, the small hut flared suddenly, flames climbing fast, devouring the place that had been shelter and illusion both.

Somewhere across the water, a shout carried faintly, then faded.

The fire took hold quickly, brightening the shoreline in hard orange light against the black sky.

Annabella stopped, staring back.

Nzingha did not.

Drake set the skiff into the water and steadied Haemish as they climbed in. The heat from the flames lingered on their backs as the hut collapsed inward, sparks lifting and vanishing into the dark.

They rowed on.

Chapter 11

Recovery, History, and the Quiet Rebalancing

Nearly three moons had passed.

Haemish was on his feet again. By day, he and Drake sparred until sweat soaked their clothes and their arms trembled with familiar strain. By night, they hunted along the tree line or took the skiff out to fish, baiting the water with scraps of boar meat to draw in larger catch. When the sea lay quiet, they rowed farther from shore, speared fish, and gathered shellfish and sea snails before turning back.

His limp had lessened enough that most days he no longer noticed it, except when exhaustion crept in.

Three moons earlier, he had nearly died.

When they first brought him back to the hut, fever had taken him hard. His body burned, his thoughts wandered, his strength left him in waves. Nzingha stayed. She cleaned his wounds while Lady Annabella kept watch, both women rising through the night to cool his skin with damp cloths and coax medicine between his lips with a folded banana leaf. At times he did not know where he was. At times he spoke to ghosts.

Nzingha had not liked him, and she made no attempt to pretend otherwise. Still, she remained.

She brought remedies she knew well. Bitter vines steeped into sharp tea. Fever grass boiled until the hut smelled clean and green. Seaweed warmed and pressed into poultices for the deeper wounds. When the bite marks closed and began to scar, she rubbed aloe into the healing flesh. Coconut oil followed, easing the itch that came with new skin. Her hands were firm, practiced, without tenderness or cruelty. It was simply what needed doing.

Even after his strength returned, she did not stop.

One afternoon, as she worked oil into the pale ridges along his shoulder, Haemish spoke without looking at her.

"I never said thank you."

Her hand paused.

She glanced at him, clearly expecting something else. "Oh. Um. You are welcome."

"You brought me back to half the man I was."

She resumed her work. "My thanks."

"I see why Drake cares for you."

Her fingers stilled again. "Is that so?"

"Aye… ye stayed, even when I was an arse tae ye. Ye make a person feel… accounted for."

She exhaled through her nose. "Lady Annabella helped as well. She sat with you through the worst of it. She spoke to you when your thoughts ran astray."

Haemish lifted his water skin, swallowed, and choked. "Truly?"

"Yes. You should thank her."

Nzingha saw the way his attention shifted then, unguarded. She recognized it immediately.

She had seen that look once before, the first time she had lifted her head from the salt water and found Drake watching her as if he had forgotten how to breathe. The sea had still been clinging to her skin then, her senses sharp with brine and sun, her body bare of defenses. He had not looked away. He had not known what the feeling was yet, only that it had struck him without warning.

Drake had never learned to hide such things. Even now, she caught him staring when he thought her unaware, his gaze too honest to be anything but telling. The memory stirred something small and unwelcome in her chest, a reminder of how quickly attention could turn into weight.

"I have seen how you look at her," she said, still rubbing oil into his skin. "I have also seen you watching her bathe. Is that a custom where you are from?"

"Um… ah, nae." Embarrassed by what Nzingha had said, he began to scratch at his scars.

She smacked his hand away. "Ah-ah. Your fingernails are filthy. You'll have your cuts putrid again."

Nzingha laughed. "We have a saying where I am from. Let your love be like misty rain. It comes softly, but it falls enough to flood a river. If you care for Bella, tell her first. Then show her."

"And just how do I do that?"

"By letting her know," she said simply. "Drake watched me the same way. He never once looked away. Hence… this predicament."

Drake walked over and kissed Nzingha's forehead. He turned to Haemish.

"Do you have a moment?"

"Aye."

"Good. Grab your sword. Let us spar."

As the men moved away, Lady Annabella came into view, shaking pine needles from the bedding they gathered from the small hut, the island carrying on around them as it always did.

Plans, Bonds, and Fracture

The men had been sparring for some time when Nzingha beckoned Annabella to her side. Their blades met and slid, met again, the sound no longer sharp but familiar.

Drake pressed forward, testing him, forcing Haemish to turn and recover, to trust his footing rather than think through each step. The effort showed in Haemish's breathing and in the way he set his jaw, but he held his ground. Whatever the sea had taken from him, it had not taken his will.

Nzingha motioned her hand after watching the men. "Bella, come. Sit."

Annabella joined her, brushing pine needles from her skirts. For a time, they watched without speaking, eyes following the men as they circled, the rhythm of their bodies settling into something steady.

"He moves more easily now," Annabella said at last. "Still… wounds like that do not forget."

Nzingha inclined her head. "Drake would not drive him so hard if Haemish's body could not answer. Men push where they believe strength has returned."

She watched Annabella quietly, taking in her posture, the ease with which she observed the men at practice. "When I first saw you among the natives, you spoke their language as though it were your own. Might I ask how long you have been here?"

"It has been years," Annabella said. "Long enough that the language no longer feels borrowed from my mouth."

She watched the men as she spoke, the steady ring of steel grounding her. "I was still young when my father brought me across the water.

He believed the journey would widen me, teach me what lay beyond the edges of home. He was not careless. He was curious."

She drew a slow breath. "We did not mean to land here. We hid the ship in a cove, tucked it away from pirates who had been dogging us for days. It was meant to be brief. One night on shore. Long enough for the sea to forget us."

Her hands folded together. "By morning, everything had shifted."

Nzingha did not interrupt.

"The islanders took me with the men. Not in haste. Not in cruelty, at first. I was placed among women. They touched my hair. Spoke to me. Showed me how words shaped themselves in their mouths." She exhaled. "It would have been easy to mistake it for kindness."

"What changed?" Nzingha asked.

"A girl," Annabella said simply. "She did not live. And grief demands payment."

"How did they know? That it was your people."

"They did not guess. They found what was left behind." She lifted her eyes again. "Blood speaks, no matter the tongue."

The sound of steel cut the air more sharply. Haemish stripped off his shirt, scars catching the light as he turned.

Annabella drew in a breath. "It looks as though something tried very hard to claim him."

"It nearly did," Nzingha said. "Twice."

"And yet he stands strong from fighting against death."

"He did not do so alone."

Annabella glanced at her. "No."

Nzingha allowed herself the faintest smile. "A man can mend more easily when he believes someone remains."

Annabella looked up and met Haemish's gaze without meaning to. The pause was brief, but Drake saw it. He struck harder than before, catching Haemish off balance and sending him stumbling.

Annabella rose without thinking, which drew a brief laugh from Nzingha.

"There is no need to worry," she said calmly, guiding her back down. "They do not spare one another."

Annabella sat again, warmth rising in her cheeks. After a moment, as if to move away from her embarrassment, she asked, "Do you miss where you came from?"

Nzingha's gaze moved past the men and out toward the trees. She considered the question, the weight of it, before answering. "In short… yes and no."

Annabella waited.

"What I miss no longer exists as it did," Nzingha said. "Returning does not restore it."

"And Drake?" Annabella asked carefully. "Would you return with him?"

"Nae."

Annabella noticed the slight change in Nzingha's posture at once. She had begun to lean forward without thinking, her hand settling against her side.

"Do you have pain?" Annabella asked.

"Only a little," Nzingha replied. "My courses draw near. It is never easy at the beginning."

Annabella nodded, the explanation settling easily between them. "That explains it. I suffer the same at times." She glanced toward the trees. "I shall make tea later. But first, the waterfalls. The cool water may help."

"Yes," Nzingha said.

They rose together and walked away at an unhurried pace, their voices fading as they followed the path toward the falls.

Drake's attention strayed, his eyes following Nzingha as she moved away with Annabella. A smile touched his mouth before he could stop it. Haemish caught it at once and wasted no time, driving the flat of his boot hard into Drake's stomach and dropping him to his knees in the dirt.

"There you go again with that bloody giant of a boot," Drake groaned, bracing himself with one hand. "Ye kick like ye mean tae kill."

"Aye, and ye look like ye were beggin' for it," Haemish said without apology. "If ye're goin' tae lose yer wits every time a woman walks by, I'd rather knock 'em back into ye before someone else does."

He offered his hand and hauled Drake upright, giving him a sharp look to make the lesson clear. "Eyes on the fight, not the view."

The sparring ended there. Both men moved beneath the tree where Nzingha and Annabella had been sitting moments earlier, the ground still pressed flat from their weight. Drake lifted his water skin, took a long swallow, and spat it out before drawing a breath, the effort of the morning settling into his shoulders.

"It is time for us tae leave this place," he said at last.

Haemish studied him. "That's no small thought tae be droppin' between breaths. Ye finally got a plan, or is this another of yer grand notions?"

"Aye," Drake replied. "At first light, we make for the eastern side of the isle. The land tightens there. Fewer places for them tae circle us."

"And then?" Haemish asked, already suspicious.

"Then there's no other way but ambush," Drake said. "Once we're close enough, we strike hard and fast."

"The two of us?" Haemish asked, incredulous. "Against how many men, exactly? Or are ye countin' on frightenin' them tae death with yer glare?"

"Aye," Drake said evenly, "the two of us, and Nzingha."

Haemish stopped short and stared at him. "Ye jest. The princess?" He shook his head. "Christ, Drake, are ye daft or just hopin' I am?"

Drake took another sip of water and spat again. "Laugh if ye like, but trust me. She can hold her own. Better than most men I've known. The plan is tae set the camp afire. Once chaos rises, we take them one by one."

Haemish folded his arms, unimpressed. "And Annabella?"

"She'll sneak aboard the ship," Drake said. "Unhinge a few of the sails."

Haemish let out a sharp breath through his nose. "Aye. Of course she will."

Haemish did not like that idea one bit. He straightened and set his hands on his hips. "Now I ken ye're daft. Annabella is nae built like Nzingha. She's delicate, and those cursed knots will fight her like a drunken sailor."

Drake began to pace beneath the tree, boots grinding into the dirt as he worked the thought through aloud. "We only need the ship shifted from the shallows into deeper water. Once she drifts free, the rest will follow."

Haemish stared at him as though he'd lost his wits entirely. "That is the daftest plan I've heard since a lad tried tae wrestle a boar with his breeches down. If she cuts the lines, how in God's name are we meant tae ken there's more rope aboard? Ye plannin' tae wish it there?"

"'Tis a chance we'll have tae take," Drake said, stubborn as stone.

"A chance?" Haemish echoed, shaking his head. "That's no a chance. That's hopin' the sea suddenly takes pity on fools."

Drake stopped pacing and clapped a hand hard against Haemish's back. "I think we can do it. We must. Or we die here and rot polite-like in the sand."

"This is risky, Drake," Haemish said. "I nae like it. I dinnae trust plans that rely on luck and prayers."

"Aye, I ken," Drake replied. "But ye and I both want off this cursed island and back tae Scotland. And if Alex has had free run of the castle this long, I fear he's turned the place into a brothel with better drapes."

That did it. Haemish barked a laugh before he could stop himself. "God help us all. I miss a proper tavern, a warm fire, and a busty lass findin' her hands up my kilt without askin' permission."

Drake laughed with him then, the sound rough and familiar, easing the weight for the briefest moment.

The scream tore through the trees, sharp and unmistakable.

The laughter fell away, leaving only the sound of their breathing.

Drake met Haemish's eyes for a brief moment, and then they were moving, running hard toward the waterfalls.

A Plan Gone Wrong

Returning from the waterfalls, Annabella carried a small bouquet of dandelions clasped carefully in her hands. She turned as she walked and smiled at Nzingha, her expression open and unguarded.

"Who would have thought," she said lightly, "that I would find a princess from the far east to be my savior, and now my friend." She offered her hand without hesitation.

Nzingha took it, her grip warm and steady.

"Do you sing?" Annabella asked as they walked.

"I do," Nzingha replied, smiling. "It brings me joy."

Annabella spun once, skirts lifting. "I miss a proper céilí. Dancing all night until one forgets one's own feet. Things will be different when I return to my father's castle in Ireland. I suspect my uncle believes us long perished by now."

Nzingha slowed, her attention shifting to the brush. "That is possible," she said evenly, her hand settling closer to the dagger at her hip.

Annabella, still speaking, did not notice the change. "Do you have dances where you are from? I love a good dancer."

"We do," Nzingha answered. "We call them tribal dances."

"Will you teach me?"

"Yes," Nzingha said, meeting her eyes. "Of course."

The boar burst from the brush without warning.

Annabella screamed as the animal charged, its weight and speed knocking her backward. She fell hard, skirts tangling beneath her as she tried to scramble away. In the same breath, Nzingha drew her blade and flung it with deadly precision. The knife struck the boar squarely in the forehead, stopping it mid-charge. The animal squealed, still thrashing, and Nzingha was upon it at once, retrieving her blade and cutting its throat cleanly.

She turned and dropped to Annabella's side.

"Are you hale, Bella?"

"My leg," Annabella sobbed. "It hurts."

Nzingha lifted the fabric carefully and saw the wound at once, a deep gash along her calf where the boar's hoof had torn her skin.

"My lady," she said quietly. "You are injured."

She pulled the scarf from her hair, her dark locks falling loose, and pressed the cloth firmly to the wound, binding it tight to slow the bleeding.

"Oh God… it hurts," Annabella cried, leaning into her shoulder.

"The pain will ebb," Nzingha murmured, holding her steady. "I promise. Can you stand?"

"No," Annabella said through tears. "I cannot."

They heard shouting then, Drake's voice carrying through the trees.

"NZINGHA! ANNABELLA!"

"Here," Nzingha called back, calm as she wiped Annabella's tears. "You are safe. They are coming."

The men burst through the brush moments later and stopped short. Annabella lay on the ground, her leg bound, blood seeping through the cloth. Nearby, the boar lay dead.

Haemish surged forward at once. "Jesus, what's this?" he demanded. "Did ye take this poor lassie huntin'?"

Nzingha shot him a sharp look. "No, you big buffoon. A wild boar charged her from the brush."

Drake dropped to one knee and examined the wound, his fingers hovering just short of the torn flesh as he gauged the damage. He glanced up at Nzingha. "Is it deep? Did it cut near a vein?"

"It did not," she said, already answering the question in the way she had bound it, the cloth pulled tight and deliberate. "It is an open wound. I secured it as firmly as I could."

Haemish knelt beside Annabella then, his voice softening as he took in the pain etched across her face. "My lady," he asked gently, "can ye stand?"

She tried, failed, and shook her head instead. "No. It hurts too much."

"Then I'll carry ye," he said, as though there were no other choice worth discussing.

He lifted her with care, steady and sure, holding her as if she were something easily broken. Annabella flushed, uncertain whether the heat rising to her cheeks came from the pain in her leg or from the way his gaze never left her face.

"Thank you," she murmured, her voice barely above the sound of her breath.

Drake slung the boar over his shoulder, and they started back toward camp.

Nzingha walked beside him and wrinkled her nose. "That animal smells dreadful."

Drake barked a laugh. "Aye, likely rolled in its own shite." He glanced at her. "Are ye hale?"

"I am," she answered. "But I am concerned for Lady Annabella."

Drake exhaled as they walked. "I do not wish to sound arrogant, but my plan was for us to leave at first light and take the ship. Annabella was part of that plan."

Nzingha stopped.

She turned fully to him, her voice even. "What do you mean, Annabella was part of the plan?"

"We set the camp afire. Create chaos. While that happens, Annabella boards the ship and loosens the sails."

"Drake, Annabella cannot fight. She is not built for that."

"I never said she will. Her duty will be to cut rope."

"You expect her to climb. In darkness. Onto a guarded ship."

"Christ," he snapped, "now ye sound like Haemish."

That was enough. She snapped.

"Andrew Barton. This is not your keep, nor is it your ship, and I am not your soldier. You do not make plans that endanger her life without speaking to her, or to me. Do you understand me?"

Drake lost his temper. "Woman, haud your wheesht! Must ye tear down every plan I make?"

The air went still.

Nzingha stepped closer, eyes blazing. "Pardon me, Captain?"

She jabbed a finger into his chest. "Before you came to this island, I had peace. I had order. You did not rescue me. I rescued you."

She struck his chest again. "I did not ask to leave this place. You want me to. You wish to leave so badly that you would risk Annabella's life to satisfy that desire."

Drake grabbed her wrist. "Enough..."

SLAP.

The sound rang out so loud it sent birds scattering from the trees.

Rage tore from her. "Remove your hand from my person."

He froze, shock written across his face.

"Now. Get out of my way."

Annabella gasped.

Drake staggered back, stunned. "Nzingha... I didnae..."

Haemish let out a low, almost amused breath. "No offence, my laird, but I did warn ye. That was a daft notion."

Drake stood silent, cheek burning, finally grasping the depth of his mistake.

Nzingha turned and walked away.

Not hurried.
Not shaken.
Walking as one who expected the world to move aside.

Vexing to Euphoria

Annabella rested against the pallet, her injured leg elevated and wrapped tight, the cloth already darkening where blood pressed through.

Haemish knelt beside her, careful hands hovering before he spoke. "My lady, would ye have me tend that again, or will ye wait for the princess?"

Annabella shook her head, wincing but composed. "I shall wait for Zing. She should be the one."

"Aye," Haemish said, rising. "That sounds right."

Outside, Drake stood at the edge of the shore, sleeves rolled, rinsing the boar clean in the shallows. He worked harder than necessary, scrubbing until his knuckles burned. His cheek still throbbed, not from pain alone, but from the shock of it. He had known Nzingha to be fierce, but did not expect to be reminded so clearly of it.

Haemish approached and leaned against a rock, watching him for a time.

"She caught ye fair," he said at last. "Did she knock that ridiculous plan clean out o' yer senses?"

Drake let out a breath through his teeth.

"Piss off, Haemish."

Haemish tilted his head. "For what it's worth, when I first met her, I was grateful. Bein' dragged from a shark's mouth tends tae soften a man's judgment." He huffed a breath. "That boot I put in her face? Accident. I didnae ken she was listenin' when ye and I were speakin'. Thought it was just soldier's talk."

Drake shot him a look. "Are ye finished lecturin', or is there more salt ye'd like tae rub in?"

Haemish snorted, tugging at his beard as if the answer might be tangled in it.

"Aye, well... she threatened my life. Called me a rhinoceros shite. I still dinnae ken what kind o' beast that's meant tae be, but I took offence all the same. My feelin's toward her were... dark."

Drake let out a sharp breath. "Christ."

Haemish's tone shifted then, the humor falling away. "But then I watched her nurse me when I was nearer death than breath. No fear. No fuss. Just hands that kent what tae do. And I've watched her with Annabella, how she looks at the lass, how she puts herself between her and danger without thinkin' twice."

Drake said nothing, jaw tight.

"Her duty, Andrew, was never just tae fight. She was raised tae keep her people safe. That was her charge as a princess." His eyes hardened. "And today, ye threatened that. Not with a blade, but with a plan that treats a person she cares for as expendable."

Drake swallowed, anger giving way to something heavier.

"She's every right tae be offended," Haemish said quietly. "And if we leave this island, it'll be because of her judgment as much as her strength. Ye need her clear-headed. Not furious."

Drake dragged a hand through his hair. "Aye... damn ye."

"Then go find her," Haemish said. "And dinnae go as a captain. Go as a man who kens he crossed a line."

Drake washed the blood from his hands, stripped off his shirt, and plunged into the sea, scrubbing himself clean. When he rose, the sun was already sinking. He dressed and went looking.

The cliffs were empty. The cove where they hid the skiff lay still. The pool beneath the falls held only drifting leaves.

At last, he followed the narrow path beyond the water.

Nzingha lay beneath a tree on her back, one hand tucked under her head, the other resting upon her stomach, ankles crossed. Her face was serious, as though lost deep in thought. She heard his footsteps as he came closer.

"I do not wish tae be bothered," she said calmly. "Please leave."

"I ken," Drake said, stopping short. "But I came tae apologize. I was a complete fool layin' my hand on ye like that. I dinnae ken what took hold of me. I've been laird of my keep and captain of my ship so long now, I'm used tae no one questionin' my judgment." He swallowed. "I was bein' an arse. Plain and simple. Will ye forgive me?"

Nzingha lay in silence, staring up at the evening sky as it shifted through purples, reds, and silver. Tall trees framed the horizon, their dark silhouettes unmoving. She did not answer him, her gaze fixed on the world above.

At last, Drake lowered himself beside her without a word. After a long moment, he spoke.

"This place is bonnie."

Nzingha said nothing.

"It reminds me of Scotland in the summertime," he went on softly. "We've waterfalls like these back home. Folks say the fae live among them, wee spirits with powers for healing, love, and fortune."

"What are the fae?" Nzingha asked.

"Small spirits, they say," Drake replied. "Guardians o' the forest. Bringers of luck, if ye believe."

She frowned. "Where I am from, we call that obeah. Any form of magic is obeah. That is what my father taught."

"Truly?" Drake shifted onto his side, propping his head on his hand. "Is obeah akin tae witchcraft, then?"

"Yes. It is."

Drake smirked faintly. "Back home, anyone caught practisin' such things would be burned alive for it."

"But your people believe in small spirits that wield magic," she said, shaking her head. "Seems a bit foolish to me."

Drake grinned and edged closer, resting his hand gently upon her stomach as he whispered, "Ziiing... I truly am sorry. Will ye forgive me?"

Butterflies formed in her stomach. She scooted away.

"You reminded me of my father," she said quietly. "He always reprimanded me for having an opinion, for thinking for myself. He made me feel powerless... small. I have despised that feeling my entire life. For months, I have been free of him, but today was the first time I felt it again."

She swallowed and stared at the darkening sky.
"When I was fifteen summers, he was furious because the cook reported that Asha, my pet lioness, had been hunting the goats. He ordered me to lock her in a chamber and forbade her from roaming without a rope. He said either that, or he would skin her and wear her teeth as a necklace and her fur as a cloak."

Her jaw tightened.
"I grew angry and answered him back. I never thought my father would strike me, but he did. Twice. Then he locked me in my chambers for a fortnight." She exhaled slowly. "During my confinement, I snuck out to see Asha. She was tied and nearly starved. So weak she could no longer hunt. I had to kill prey myself and feed it to her."

She turned toward Drake then, her eyes steady.
"I do not do well with dominance. I despise a man who takes advantage of a woman because she is smaller or weaker. That is why

I train. That is why I fight with every fiber of my being, so I am never subjected to that again."

Drake shifted closer and lowered himself, resting his head against her chest.

"But Zing," he murmured, voice rougher now, "I am nae your father. I couldnae, wouldnae, ever raise a hand tae ye. I lost myself today. Got tangled in a daft notion and let my temper lead me."

"It was not all bad," she said after a moment. "Just do not involve Bella. She is too fragile."

"Aye. I ken."

"We can place her on the ship after the ambush. Hide her until the fighting is done."

"Aye," he said quietly. "Do ye truly think we can still make the attempt come mornin', with her in such a state?"

"I think so. According to Bella, her father's ship holds many supplies. We could tend her wound better there. The natives do not know what most of it is. Bella once snuck away and found the ship, no one aboard. They camp around it, guarding it, unaware the captain is long gone."

He edged closer still. "Bella needs ye, Zing. Will ye come back tae the shelter and tend her wounds?"

"Of course. I must apologize for leaving so abruptly. She is a good friend. And very brave."

Drake looked at her then, hunger plain as daylight in his eyes.

"But first... give me a few moments more with ye. We've nae had a moment tae ourselves these three moons, and I miss ye somethin' fierce."

Nzingha's heart raced as she caught the look in his eyes, focused, intent, like a male lion on the hunt.

"What if the others search for us?"

"Nae," he murmured. "Haemish willnae leave Annabella. She's safe."

As Nzingha lay back, he leaned in and kissed her softly, his weight braced on his hands above her. She slid her fingers into his dark hair, drawing him closer. The kiss deepened, unhurried at first, then hungry. Drake shifted and drew her up onto him, his hands gliding from her shoulders down the length of her back. He squeezed her firmly, a low sound leaving his throat.

"God help me," he murmured, rough with want. "I've missed ye somethin' fierce. I dinnae think I've a minute's restraint left in me."

She laughed breathlessly and sat up, pinching her nose. "I am sorry, but you still smell of boar. Truly, you reek of it. Come. Let me bathe you."

Drake grimaced. "Nae. The sun's droppin', and the water'll be cold as sin."

She rose without another word and let her dress slip from her shoulders, the fabric falling to the ground at her feet. She stood before him, unashamed, wholly bare.

Drake pushed himself upright at once and dragged his shirt over his head, any protest forgotten as his gaze traced her slowly. He reached for her thighs, but she brushed his hands aside and turned toward the water. He smiled, followed her to his feet, and let his kilt fall away.

She dove in first, arms stretched forward, toes pointed, her body cutting clean through the water. Drake followed moments later, the chill drawing a sharp breath from his lungs as he surfaced near her.

They moved beneath the falls where the water softened and broke, mist clinging to skin. Nzingha reached for the coconut shell she had left there earlier, its contents still intact from her bath with Annabella. Inside, crushed hibiscus leaves, jasmine blossoms, and ground coconut had mingled into a fragrant paste.

She dipped her fingers into the scented paste and traced it slowly along his jaw, down the column of his neck. Her touch lingered there, thumb pressing lightly at his pulse as she drew closer.

Her hand closed at his neck, not tight, but certain, guiding him to her as she claimed his mouth. The kiss deepened at once, slow and insistent, stirring a sharp, unmistakable want in him.

The friction of their tongues moved with intense desire, causing heat to surge between the two.

In this very moment, a secluded paradise was created. There was nothing else, no danger, no plans, only the two. Drake grabbed her by the arse, wrapping her legs around him.

Teasing, she pulled away. "Ah... ah... ah. I am not done."

She gathered more of the sweet-smelling paste and worked it over his shoulders, her hands firm and unhurried as they moved down his chest and across his stomach, washing away the grit of the day.

"Lift your arms," she said,

He obeyed at once.

Nzingha scrubbed along his arms and beneath them, working the paste into skin still sore from sparring and stained from cleaning the boar. Her touch was thorough, purposeful.

"Turn around." He turned.

Taking a handful of the paste, she rubbed his back down to his buttocks.

Walking in front of him, she gave him a mischievous grin.

"Now, here comes the fun part."

She submerged her full body underwater, cleaning his male area. Drake scooped water into his hands and washed his face, smiling despite himself.

"God help me... ye're mad."

Then he jerked with a look of surprise, his eyes opening in shock. "Christ, woman, what are ye doin'?"

His heart betrayed him, it was racing fast. Nzingha took him fully inside her mouth.
That did it.
He almost came.

He snatched her arms, bringing her above water. "Christ, woman... ye need to breathe." He grinned.
"But... I want to bring you pleasure," she protested.
"And that, you will."

He lifted her and drew her legs around his waist, the sudden closeness stealing her breath as he pressed into her without warning. She jerked and gasped, feeling his invasion. Her facial expression showed pain and pleasure all at once.

Drake walked with her behind the veil of the falls, his footing sure as he stepped onto the flat stone hidden there. Beyond the curtain of water, a narrow opening revealed itself. He took her inside and eased her down against the cool rock. Spray from the waterfall splashed over them, misting their skin like rain trapped within the cave.

Once Nzingha's back lay flat, he thrust into her uncontrollably.
"Jesus Christ... ye feel like heaven."
He leaned in with a lingering kiss that stole her breath, then moved

to her breast.

She arched her back and moaned. "Oh, the Gods, Drake... take me to your heaven."

In one swift move, he rolled to his back, placing her atop him.

She hesitated, eyes flicking to his as though unsure what came next.

Drake leaned closer and whispered, "Just follow the motion o' my hands."

Grabbing a handful of her buttocks, he moved her hips back and forth.

She grabbed onto his chest and created a rhythm that became fast and steady as she rode him.

Nzingha shouted in ecstasy. "Oh, the gods. Yes!"

Drake's toes curled. He was about to release. "Shite," he drew away, forcing himself to slow, unwilling to let the urgency steal the moment from them. "Nae, not yet. I am not done yet."

Shock moved through Nzingha when he seated her onto his face, devouring her as if she were a feast at Yule.

She made loud noises that echoed through the small cave as she cheered him on. "Oh, yes... yes... Drake."

He sucked and nibbled until the sensation carried her away as if the ground had vanished beneath her feet. Euphoria flooded her, sharp and luminous, dissolving thought until only feeling remained. She gripped his head with a back-and-forth motion. She then touched herself, riding the waves of ecstasy, a feeling she never truly understood before.

Drake gripped her hips tightly, his mouth too full to speak. Jolting, she experienced the greatest climax there ever was. She collapsed, weakened, breathless, but he was not done.

She gave a look as if to question whether there was more. "Aye, lass," he said, "There's more."

He guided her onto all fours, then entered her from behind. He thrust his waist against her bottom, the sensation striking hard. A euphoria echoed through her like applause that would not fade, each beat louder than the last. The cave filled with the sound of them.

He slowed his tempo and watched himself as he disappeared and appeared from her secret place. In and out, he sank deeper, spreading her buttocks apart to make an imprint against her inner walls. The beauty of their skin tones reminded him of pouring milk into his tea. The warmth of her flower swallowed him whole. Drake rolled his eyes back each time he pulled out and went back in.

He stood, lifting her into the air and cuffing her thighs over his muscular arms. Nzingha's legs spread like the wings of a falcon. Walking with her, Drake placed her back against the stone wall. He pounded and pounded. His legs began to weaken.

Drake roared, as if a cannon went off. "Christ, Nzingha!"

At last, they slid down together onto the wet stone floor, limbs tangled, bodies still trembling as the water whispered around them. Drake drew her close, wrapping her against his chest, and Nzingha rested her head there, listening to the rapid thrum of his heart beneath her ear.

When she spoke, her voice came soft and unguarded, carried on heavy breath.

"On this day," she said, "you allowed me to know true passion between a man and a woman." She lifted her head and pressed a kiss to his chest. "You have my thanks."

Drake laughed quietly, breathless still, a sound full of wonder. For a fleeting moment, he felt the absurd urge to rise and beat his chest like a victorious fool. Never in his life had he gone so far with any lass, never felt his heart so unsteady afterward. He kissed the crown of her head, his breath still racing.

"I couldnae speak before," he murmured, a crooked smile in his voice. "My mouth was otherwise occupied. But aye, ye are mine." He winked.

With his thumb, he brushed away a bead of sweat from his brow.

"That was finer than any sparrin' session I've ever had."

They laughed together, the sound easy now.

When she tried to rise, her legs betrayed her, buckling beneath her weight. She caught herself on a sharp breath as the ache set in, joints protesting the exertion.

Drake was on his feet at once, steadying her. "Easy now, my love."

She stilled at the words, fingers tightening in his shirt. Fear and warmth stirred together in her chest.

Lightly, she said, "Who would have thought that pleasuring one another could leave a body so weak?"

"Aye," he agreed with a grin, shifting his weight as he winced. "A bonnie place for it, but the stones show nae mercy."

Nzingha stepped back beneath the falls, letting the water spill over her, washing away sweat and the sting of scraped skin. Drake followed, joining her as the cascade showered them both. He leaned in and kissed her gently, water sliding down their faces.

"I cannae get enough of ye," he said softly. Then, as if the thought could no longer be held back, the words came in a rush. "When we leave this place, will ye take my hand in marriage? I want ye, Nzingha. No... I need ye as my wife. I dinnae wish to leave ye behind. I wouldnae be the same man if I did."

He sank to one knee and kissed her stomach, reverent. "Please, Zing. Let me have happiness."

She looked down at him, her expression tender and conflicted, and slowly shook her head. Her fingers slid into his hair, holding him there for a moment before he rose again.

"I love you," he said simply. "With all I have."

She drew breath to answer. "But I still love Mik..."

He placed a finger gently to her lips. "Shh. Dinnae fret." He cupped her face in both hands. "With child or not, what we shared tonight is not something I'd ever give to another. Ye have my heart."

He dove back into the water with a grin. "Are ye comin'?"

She followed him without hesitation.

Drake drew her close again, holding her as they moved together toward the riverbank. When they reached the shore, he carried her from the water and laid her down gently upon the grass. His movements slowed then, unhurried, deliberate, as though the world had narrowed to just the two of them.

"In this short time," he said, meeting her gaze, "I've fallen madly in love with ye. Truly."

She threaded her hands through his hair, her voice steady and sure. "And I am madly in love with you also."

He smiled and kissed her deeply, sealing the promise between them.

They remained there by the river's edge until the sky surrendered fully to night, the water murmuring its quiet witness as the world around them fell away.

Chapter 12

The Pull of the East

Morning came softly, and Drake was the first to wake.

He turned onto his side and looked at Nzingha, still wrapped in his plaid, breathing slowly and even. A smile tugged at his mouth before he could stop it. He shook his head once, quietly, thoughts drifting back to the night before. What they had shared had been unlike anything he had known. Not hurried. Not timid. Nzingha had given herself without shame, without apology, her passion unguarded and fierce.

She was nothing like the timid virgins he had known before.

With Nzingha, everything was different. She was bold. Carefree. Unafraid to bare not only her body, but her spirit. The bond between them had formed as though it had always been meant to exist, as natural as breath. Husband and wife, if only for the night. If he were a man who wrote songs, he thought, this one would be sung for years to come. An almond-skinned lass from the far east who had undone him without trying. The moment Sir Drake had met her; his heart had known the truth.

The sky beyond the trees had begun to pale, first light breaking through the canopy.

Drake shifted and brushed his knuckles gently against her arm.

"My love," he murmured. "Zingha… 'tis time we head back tae the shelter."

She stirred, stretching slowly, a soft moan leaving her lips.

"Mmm," she said sleepily. "I wish we could stay here forever. It is so peaceful."

"Aye," he agreed. "It is. But we must see tae Lady Annabella."

Nzingha rose, gathering her dress and pulling it over her head before wrapping her hair. She smiled faintly as she turned toward the waterfall, memories of the night pressing warmly against her thoughts. As she watched the water tumble over stone, something else surfaced in her mind.

The cave. Long. Narrow. Echoing.

She remembered how voices carried strangely through it. And then Annabella's words returned to her, the ship, on the east side of the island, near a cave.

She stilled, eyes fixed on the falling water.

"Drake?"

"Hm?"

"When you traveled tae the south side on the skiff," she asked, "did you see any caves?"

He finished tying his plaid. "Nae."

"And the west?"

"Nae. Nae caves at all."

Without another word, she untied her hair, shed her dress, and ran straight into the lake.

Drake froze just long enough to hear the splash. He planted one hand on his hip and waved the other.

"Now what in the devil are ye doin'?" he called. "Zingha!"

She did not answer.

Something about the way she moved unsettled him. He stripped off his plaid and followed.

Nzingha climbed the stones behind the waterfall, water streaming down her skin as she slipped into the darkened mouth of the cave. Drake caught up quickly, laying a hand on her shoulder.

"And just what do ye think ye're about?" he whispered.

She turned to him, eyes bright with certainty.

"This cave leads tae the east side of the island."

He took her hand. "Lass, it's too dark. There's nae opening on the other side. We've nae torch, and I dinnae like the look of it."

"Listen tae me," she said firmly. "Annabella said the ship was near a cave on the east side. What other caves have you seen on this island?" She met his gaze. "You said nae. Every time. This one leads there. I know it."

Drake sighed. "Are ye sure?"

"Yes," she said without hesitation. "Trust me."

They moved deeper into the cave, hands grazing stone as they felt their way forward. The air grew thick and stifling, heat pressing in from all sides. Sweat slicked their skin as they walked, the darkness swallowing sound and sense alike.

"This had better nae be a waste of our bloody time," Drake muttered.

Then, after what felt like miles, cool air brushed across their skin.

Nzingha stopped short. "Do you feel that?"

"Aye," Drake said, breath sharp with sudden awareness. "There's a breeze… comin' from ahead."

They moved faster now. The breeze strengthened. A faint glow appeared in the distance. The sound of waves reached them, rough and unmistakable.

"I think we've reached the end," Nzingha said.

They broke into a hurried walk, emerging at the cave's edge. Both froze.

"Well, I'll be a daft highlander," Drake breathed.

Below them sat a great galleon, proud and whole, anchored in clear view. Beyond it, along the forest's edge, fires burned where the native islanders' camp.

Nzingha turned to Drake, breathless.

"We did it. We found the ship."

Escaping Paradise

By the time they reached the shelter, the island had gone strangely still, the sun standing at its highest point.

Before stepping inside the hut, Drake lifted his voice. "Haemish!"

No answer came.

"Haemish!"

"Aye, Laird?" Haemish finally called back. "I see ye've found yer way back. Is all well between the princess and yerself?"

As Drake and Nzingha passed through the entrance, they noticed Lady Annabella lying on her side as though she was still sleeping. Haemish stood nearby, adjusting his attire.

Drake smirked, nodding once.

Nzingha immediately scowled, her jaw tightening. Something was afoot. "What are you about, Haemish? Lady Annabella… are ye hale?"

Annabella shifted, her face flushed crimson from embarrassment. She turned from her side and smiled faintly. "Ah… yes. I am well." Her eyes slipped away. "The pain in my leg worsened through the night. We waited for you to return, but it grew so grave I could not bear it. I was awake half the night. Haemish cleaned the wound and used part of his blouse as a bandage. He also used the herbs you gathered so it would not become putrid." She hesitated, then added softly, "He was most honorable."

Drake chuckled. "Honorable my arse."

Nzingha knelt beside Annabella and examined the wound carefully. It was clean. Exceptionally well-tended. She smiled.

"Bella," she said gently, "we found your father's galleon."

Annabella's eyes widened. "Truly? How did you? When?"

"The waterfall," Nzingha explained. "The cave behind it leads directly to the east side of the island. Drake and I found it this morning."

"Oh, my lady," Annabella breathed. "When you did not return, I feared you were captured. We waited all night."

"Nae," Drake said firmly. "We are here. And ye can finally go home, my lady."

"Oh, Princess, this is exceptional news…" Annabella's gaze immediately shifted to Haemish, a silent question lingering there.

In an instant, the moment shattered.

THACK!

An arrow struck the hut with a violent crack.

"Get down!" Drake shouted.

Another arrow slammed into a post as smoke began to creep into the shelter. Drake peered through a narrow opening, his expression darkening as he saw painted faces closing in.

"We were followed," he said grimly. "'Tis the natives. They've tracked us all the way here. Bloody stubborn bastards."

Nzingha looked at him. "How do we get out of this?"

Drake's hand closed around his sword. "I'll pull them away. Ye dinnae hesitate. Run!"

"Nae!" Nzingha cried. "I cannot risk you dying. I will not."

He gripped her shoulders, forcing her to meet his gaze as shouts rose outside the shelter and smoke thickened the air.

"There's nae other way," he said, low and urgent, his words pushed between breaths. "If we run together, one of us falls. Nzingha, look at me." His brow pressed briefly to hers. "Trust me."

She nodded once.

Before he could draw another breath, she wrenched free, seized her staff, and burst from the hut.

"Bloody daft princess!" Drake shouted, already moving.

He spun on his heel, voice cutting through the chaos. "Haemish! Take Lady Bella tae the waterfall. Behind it is a cave that leads east. Dinnae stop. Wait for us there. Now go!"

"Aye, Laird Barton!"

Haemish scooped Annabella into his arms and ran, her gasp swallowed by the roar of flame and shouting as arrows struck the shelter behind them.

At the same moment, Drake charged from the burning hut.

The first attacker rushed him headlong. Drake met him with steel, driving his sword clean through the man's chest without slowing. He wrenched the blade free as a second closed in, pivoting hard and cutting him down in a single brutal arc.

A third came too close.

Drake turned and split him nearly in two.

Across the clearing, Nzingha fought with her long blade, her movements sharp and relentless, feet sure even as the ground churned beneath her. She struck without hesitation, driving back one attacker, then another, her body moving on instinct alone.

She did not look for Drake.

She trusted him.

An islander charged Drake with an axe. He ducked, slicing the man's flank.

Ahead of him, Nzingha spotted an archer raising his bow toward Drake. She ran, aimed, and hurled her staff with such force it tore through the man's chest and pinned him to a tree.

Drake barked a laugh. "Saints preserve me, lass."

More natives poured from the brush.

"HOLY SHITE!" Drake barked.

"Nzingha!" he shouted, his voice cutting through the clash of steel. "We must leave! We're outnumbered. Fall back tae the cave behind the falls!"

They kept coming.

Men poured from the tree line, one after another, relentless. Another native rushed Drake. He met the charge head-on, steel biting hard as he drove the man back.

"Nzingha, haste!"

She cut down one attacker and ran.

The sound of pursuit thundered behind her as her sandals tore through the dirt. She glanced back.

Drake was no longer there.

Her chest seized. Fear hit sharp and sudden, threatening to steal her footing.

Then his voice broke through, strong and unbroken.

"Keep runnin' lass! Dinnae stop!"

She looked up and saw him moving fast along the high ridge, drawing them away, every stride deliberate. Relief surged through her like fire.

"The snares!" she yelled. "I have an idea!"

She veered hard toward the outer edge of the camp, angling for the narrow path she had cleared days before. Her feet found the familiar rise of packed earth beneath the brush, the ground firm where she had tamped it down by hand.

The men followed without slowing.

She ducked low and burst through the first wall of tangled vines.

Behind her, a foot struck the hidden line.

The trap snapped tight.

A scream ripped through the air as a man was wrenched backward, the rope hauling him up by the ankle. His body slammed into the branches overhead, limbs flailing as the line cinched and held.

She did not stop.

She ran again, lungs burning, legs pumping as another man closed the distance.

He took two more steps…

The second trap snapped shut with a brutal crack, the rope biting hard as it jerked him off his feet and dragged him sideways into undergrowth.

She broke through the last stand of trees and skidded to a halt, chest heaving.

Silence pressed in.

Only one set of footsteps remained.

He was fast.

Too fast.

She stopped. "Come at me."

He charged with his axe.

Nzingha did not think. She moved.

She slipped to the side and drove her heel into his face. Bone cracked beneath her foot. He staggered back, swearing in his own tongue, spitting blood into the dirt.

She did not wait.

Her feet stayed light, ready, her body coiled as he came at her again with a roar. She ducked the swing, drove her fist into his jaw, felt the shock of impact ripple up her arm, and when he stepped in too close, she took her chance.

She leapt.

Her arms locked around his neck, forearm crushing tight beneath his chin. She squeezed with everything she had, legs clamping hard around his waist as the world narrowed to breath and pressure.

There you go, Nzingha.

Mikel's voice cut through the roar in her ears, calm and steady, as though he stood beside her.

Hold on tight. Do not let go.

The man thrashed, choking, clawing at her arms as his breath rasped thin and desperate. She tightened her grip, teeth bared, muscles screaming as she held fast.

Then he slammed her backward into a tree.

Pain exploded through her spine.

"Dammit... resist!" she screamed, refusing to release him, tightening her arms until her vision sparked white.

He rammed her again, harder.

The breath tore from her chest, but she did not let go.

Before he could strike a third time, she wrenched one hand free, drew her blade, and drove it deep into the side of his neck. There was a wet tear of flesh, a sound she felt more than heard, as the steel ripped through him. It made her stomach churn.

She fell away as he collapsed, choking, blood spilling hot across the ground. She landed hard on her hands and knees, chest heaving, throat burning as she dragged air back into her lungs.

He reached for her.

The movement was weak. Dying.

That was what undid her.

Sorrow struck swift and crushing, stealing the strength from her legs as she watched the life leave him. She had not wished this. She had not come to his land seeking blood. She had been driven to it, pressed into survival by fear and fire and pursuit.

Yet as she looked at him, something shifted.

This man had charged her to defend his ground. His land. His people.

The same way she would have died for hers in Mbemba.

The same fury she had seen in the eyes of men who rose against invaders on her shores. The same desperation that drove warriors to their feet when foreign boots crushed familiar soil.

For a breath, the jungle fell away.

She saw her father's banners. The dust of marching feet. The cries of villages burned in the name of conquest and protection alike. She saw men like him, fighting not for cruelty, but for home.

And she knew, with a sickening clarity, what she had become in this moment.

The outsider.

Her hands trembled as she stared at them, slick with blood not unlike that which stained her own soil back home. Somewhere nearby, the clang of Drake's sword rang sharp and distant, echoing through her skull as memory and reality collapsed into one.

She rose unsteadily and began to walk toward the falls, head bowed, steps slow and hollow.

"Nzingha!" Drake called.

She did not answer.

When he reached her, his voice dropped, urgent and afraid. "Zingha… are ye hale?"

She bent sharply at the waist.

The sickness tore through her without warning.

Nzingha doubled over and retched uncontrollably, her body heaving as though trying to purge more than bile. Her stomach clenched and twisted, the taste of blood and salt burning her throat as the violence of it left her shaking.

Drake was there instantly, catching her hair and pulling it back, one hand steady at her shoulder as her body betrayed her.

"Christ," he muttered. "Easy, lass. Easy."

She gasped, the world swimming as another wave seized her. She retched again, knees buckling, the sound raw and broken.

"We must hide," Drake said tightly, pulling her closer as shouts and footsteps thundered nearby.

He guided her into the brush, crouching low as bodies rushed past, unseen in the smoke and shadow. She clutched at the earth, breath shallow, heart pounding as the jungle swallowed them whole.

When the sounds finally faded, Drake helped her to her feet, her hands still trembling as he led her uphill, away from the clearing.

They found Haemish and Annabella tucked among the trees, both frozen with fear.

"My laird," Haemish whispered. "We are here."

Drake nodded once, jaw set. "They'll nae stop," he said quietly. "They'll hunt us till we're gone, or dead."

Nzingha said nothing.

Her stomach churned again, and she knew, deep in her bones, that this was only the beginning.

"There's no way through the cave now," he added. "We take the skiff north and swim to the galleon at nightfall."

They dragged the skiff downhill, sweat pouring from them. They reached the sea and rowed hard.

Nzingha retched again.

"Lass," Drake said, watching her closely, "ye nae look well."

"My stomach turned after battling my last attacker," she said softly. "Seeing the fear in his eyes placed guilt in my heart."

She washed the blood from her hands with saltwater.

Annabella reached over and rubbed her back. "Do not worry, Zing. You protected us. This will soon be over."

The Galleon

It took the better part of the day to reach the entrance of the cave. They moved carefully, often stopping to listen for pursuit, resting only long enough for breath to steady and fear to settle. Afterward, they stayed to the water, rowing for hours along the bay.

From the shelter of the rocks, they watched the galleon.

It sat at anchor just beyond the curve of the cove, dark against the water, its masts cutting into the sky. The shore nearby was quiet, though Nzingha could see movement farther back among the trees, shapes, watchful and patient.

They waited.

Only when the light softened and the air cooled did Drake finally speak, his voice barely more than breath.

"We'll swim tae the galleon," he whispered. "Quiet as the tide. Any sound carries here." He glanced toward Annabella. "I'll climb aboard first and lower a rope. It'll take nae time at all."

He hesitated, then turned fully to her.

"Lady Annabella," he said gently but firmly, "ye'll need tae ride upon Haemish's back. I ken it's nae proper, but ye're wounded, and there's nae other way. Whatever pain ye feel, ye must bear it in silence."

Annabella nodded, her face pale but resolute.

They slipped into the water together.

At first, they waded, and the sea cooled against their legs. Then the ground fell away, and they began to swim, strokes slow and measured, keeping close to one another as the water deepened.

The galleon loomed above them.

Drake reached it first.

He drew his daggers and drove them into the hull, one after the other, using the dirks as handholds as he hauled himself up. When he reached the deck, he stayed low, eyes sweeping the shadows.

What he saw made his jaw tighten.

A basket of swords sat near the rail. A table held muskets and powder. Another crate overflowed with bows and arrows.

"The captain left the weapons aboard," Drake muttered under his breath. "Smart but daft. Thought it'd keep the peace. Cost him his life."

He found a coil of rope. "Thanks be tae Christ," he muttered, tossing it over the side.

Nzingha climbed first, arms burning as she hauled herself over the rail and rolled onto the deck. The wood was slick beneath her palms, her breath ragged as she turned back.

Haemish followed, Annabella clutched tightly to his back, her fingers knotted in his shirt as he reached for the rope.

Drake leaned over the rail, reaching down. "I've got ye..."

Their hands met.

Then slipped.

For a heartbeat, the world seemed to hold its breath.

Annabella's grip tore free.

She fell backward.

Her screams tore loose as she dropped the length of the ship, ten feet of open air before she struck the water below with a brutal splash.

"BELLA!"

Haemish did not think. He dove.

The bay exploded into sound.

Shouts rose from the shore as men poured from the rocks. Arrows screamed through the air, thudding into the hull, skipping across the water, splintering against wood.

Drake spun, already moving.

He seized a musket, rammed powder and ball home with practiced speed, and fired.

CRACK!

A body pitched backward from the rocks.

Nzingha grabbed a bow, knocked an arrow, and drew. Her arms shook as she loosed.

Missed.

The arrow struck water and vanished.

She drew again. Missed- wide this time, the arrow clattering harmlessly against the ship's side.

"Nzingha!" Drake barked. "What in Christ's name are ye doin'? Ye shootin' ants? Fire!"

She tried again.

Her stomach twisted violently, bile rising as the deck seemed to tilt beneath her. Her vision swam. The arrow flew, and missed.

Below, Haemish fought the water, Annabella clinging to him as arrows struck close enough to spray them both.

"Haemish!" Drake roared, rage tearing through his voice. "Move yer arse!"

"Aye!" Haemish shouted back, coughing. "I am! The bloody dress weighs a ton!"

At last, Haemish reached the rope and began to climb, muscles straining, Annabella pressed tight against him as the water churned below.

This time, Drake leaned far over the rail and caught Annabella beneath her arms, hauling her up with a grunt as though she were a child. He dragged her onto the deck and shoved her clear.

More figures splashed into the bay.

"They're swimmin'!" Drake shouted. "Cut the bloody anchor!"

"Aye!" Haemish yelled.

He seized Drake's great sword and hacked at the line. Once. Twice.

The rope snapped.

Drake ran for the wheel. "I'll steer! Haemish, get the sails loose! Let the wind take us!"

"I'll help!" Nzingha called, forcing herself forward.

They climbed the posts together, hands slipping as they hacked and sawed at stiffened ropes. Muskets thundered behind them.

CRACK!
CRACK!

With each blast, Nzingha flinched, knowing a man fell with every shot.

A native clambered over the rail.

Drake turned and fired.

CRACK!

The man screamed and vanished into the dark water below.

At last, the final rope gave way.

The sail caught the evening wind.

The ship lurched, then moved.

Slowly at first. Then with growing certainty as the current pulled them free of the bay.

Smoke drifted across the deck. The island fell back into shadow.

Drake leaned heavily against the rail, chest heaving, blood streaking his sleeve. He stared out over the dark water and allowed himself one breath.

"Finally," he said hoarsely. "We're goin' home."

Chapter 13

The Open Sea

Drake could not believe they had made it. It had been an entire

moon on the open seas. He was grateful. Thank God for Lady Annabella. Without her knowledge of the ship, they still would have been stuck on that bloody island.

Day and night while the ship sailed, the captain and Haemish ran it as a two-man show, taking extreme measures to ensure there were no further casualties on the voyage home. Storm clouds were watched without pause. The first night aboard, they checked the supplies. The ship's kitchen was fully stocked with food, with plenty of herbs and water stored, enough to survive on the open waters for three months or more, until their arrival home. Though the galleon had sat on the water for over three years, it sailed smoothly.

Drake and Haemish rotated shifts for sailing at night. On the nights Drake sailed, he sat beside the wheel, thinking of how distant

Nzingha had grown since their departure. He saw how sick she had become, losing so much weight she was little more than skin and bones. The sickness had plagued her from the day they escaped and boarded the ship. Drake had no idea how to make her better. He wished to hurry home so she could see a healer.

Blast, if she would just let me get closer tae her. Stubborn Princess.

Dawn came.

Haemish walked up the stairs to the upper deck. He strolled over to Drake, sipping a hot cup of cider.

"From the way ye're steer'n the ship off course," Haemish said, "it must be somethin' grave."

Drake snapped out of his trance and looked at the quadrant. He then focused the compass and shifted the hourglass.

Haemish stared at the captain. "What ails ye? Yer body's here, but yer mind's someplace else."

Drake sighed. "'Tis Nzingha. I dinnae ken if she wants me near her. For near a moon now, she willnae look at me. If I try tae speak tae her, she answers short. I think she wants tae go home, but doesnae wish tae disappoint me."

Haemish stepped in front of the wheel. He drew in a deep breath of fresh air, then let it out slow, knowing what he was about to say might be hard for Drake tae hear.

"I've grown respect for Nzingha," he said, "She's tough, caring, quick-witted. The Princess is a wonderful person. But as I've said before, Laird Barton, takin' her home is reckless. Do ye think she's miserable now? Wait until she arrives in an unknown land where folk will judge her, maybe even mistreat her. I'm nae sayin' that will happen. But when we reach Scotland, she may resent ye for the rest of her life. Make certain this is a decision she wants, and no just you. Some folk in our country are nae as open-minded as ye."

Drake walked to the ship's rails and leaned over, staring at the sky as dawn broke. He clasped his hands together, lost in thought. Puffs of cloud stretched across the horizon, streaked with reds, blues, and greys.

Drake sighed. "The thought of our clan's reaction is in the back of my mind every day. Maybe I can speak tae the clan, have them understand why I love her. Let them know she saved my life. Ask them not tae judge her, but give her a chance."

"Andrew, ye may have tae keep her hidden. If word reaches the king's court that ye've brought a lass from Africa, there could be trouble. And ye ken the gossipin' crofters and their wives. How will ye manage her at the castle with servants everywhere?" Haemish chuckled. "Dinnae get me started on the lasses ye've bedded. They're all waitin' for ye tae come home."

"I ken. But I willnae know until we arrive home. Right now, somethin' ails her, and I intend tae find out what it is."

Haemish turned back to the quadrant. "Aye. In the meantime, I'll hold the fort."

Drake turned and climbed the stairs toward the captain's quarters. He opened the door to the sound of soft groans from the bed. Nzingha lay on her side, curled into a ball.

When he pulled her hair back, her skin burned beneath his hand. Sweat drenched the bed, her body trembling, her lips chattering as if she were freezing.

"Christ," Drake murmured. "Ye're fevered."

He went to the washstand and took up a cloth, returning to her side as he loosened her garments.

She stilled his hand with a weak groan. "No…"

"Zing, I must cool yer body," he said softly. "Yer skin is afire."

He wiped her face and shoulders with the damp cloth, but the chill only worsened her trembling. Another cloth was laid across her brow, and when that failed to still her shaking, Drake rose and left the cabin at once.

Annabella's door was not far. He knocked, breath unsteadily.

"My Lady, 'tis Laird Barton."

"One moment, please."

She opened the door, concern already written across her face. "Good eve, Laird Barton. Is all well?"

"It is Nzingha. She is gravely ill. I went tae see if she had improved, but she has worsened. She is soaked in sweat and shakes uncontrollably. Please, I need help." His hand dragged through his hair, helpless.

Annabella did not hesitate. "Have you taken any herbs from the kitchen?"

"Nae. I am no healer, My Lady."

"There should be willow bark and peppermint below. I will fetch them, along with a kettle of hot water."

"My thanks."

When Drake returned to the cabin, he stood watching Nzingha, fear settling deep in his chest. It was the first time in two years he had known it so sharply. His thoughts went to his parents, taken by the sweat not long past. A ship offered little mercy to the ill, and there was so little he could do.

He dabbed her skin again. "Do ye still feel chilled, my love?"

"Yes… yes," she whispered, trembling, her eyes fluttering as if she struggled to stay present.

Annabella came in quietly, already setting the kettle aside as she went to Nzingha's bedside. "We must cool her body. Though she shakes, her heat is far too high. Fill the wooden tub with cold water."

"There is only seawater, My Lady."

"That will do."

Drake filled the tub and lifted Nzingha with care, easing her into the water. She gasped at the shock, breath racing, but Annabella watched closely and nodded when it had been long enough.

"That is enough."

He lifted her out and dried her, wrapping her in the shift Annabella handed him.

"Her skin is cooler," he said quietly.

Annabella steeped the willow bark and brought the cup to Nzingha's lips. "I shall give this to her slowly."

At the first spoonful, Nzingha gagged and retched, bringing up only bitter bile. Annabella steadied her, rubbing her back.

"Shh… it is all right, Princess. Try the peppermint. It will ease your stomach."

Nzingha managed a few sips before sinking back against the pillows.

"When her stomach settles, she must eat," Annabella said gently. "Haemish's soup will help."

"No… no soup," Nzingha protested faintly.

Drake sat beside her. "My love, ye may be stricken with the sea. Try a little when ye can. It will give ye strength."

Her eyes closed. Exhaustion claimed her, and within moments she slept.

Drake walked Annabella to the door. "Do ye think she will be hale?"

"I cannot say," Annabella replied. "I will sit with her tonight. You must rest, you have the morning watch."

He nodded, reluctant but grateful.

As he turned to leave, Annabella asked quietly, "How long until we reach home?"

"If the winds hold, another month," Drake said. "Let us pray she survives."

Annabella inclined her head. "Aye.

A Fragile Calm

Four months passed, and Nzingha was no longer fevered. She ate little, barely enough, and scarcely resembled herself, her frame thinned to fragility. Each day, Drake prayed they would reach home without further loss. She needed a healer, and soon.

Every day, Drake spooned food into her mouth, determined to keep her from wasting away as they sailed on. Some days she kept the food down. Other days, she retched uncontrollably, the motion of the galleon turning her stomach. Because of this, she rarely left the captain's quarters.

One morning, Lady Annabella knocked and entered Nzingha's chambers. She presented a bowl that had steam coming out of it.

"Good mornin', Princess."

Nzingha nodded; her voice was raspy. "Good morning."

Smiling, she placed the tray on a table next to Nzingha.

"I brought ye your mornin' meal. I made porridge."

"My thanks, Bella, but I am not hungry."

Before closing the door, the soft-spoken Irish lady spun around.

"I went through all this trouble to be sure you had a warm bite to break your fast. I even burned my hand."

She held up her hand, showing the bandage wrapped around it.

"I'm not the finest cook, but I promise it'll help ye feel better."

Nzingha smiled. "I shall eat when my stomach allows it."

Nzingha got up and walked over to a tiny window in the captain's chambers. She sat down at the table, then placed a hand atop her head as if the head pains were back.

"Does your head still ail you?"

Nzingha nodded.

Lady Annabella smiled and walked over to Nzingha.

"Come now, maybe if you had a bath, it would ease. There's fresh rainwater Andrew gathered an' stored for you."

Annabella poured the water from a pail into a small wooden tub that sat in the corner of the captain's quarters. She walked over to Nzingha. As she helped her undress, she gathered the dirty clothing. She realized every other day she helped Nzingha with a bath for the past four months, but she never saw her use any cloths for her menses. Annabella thought to herself, I had my courses all four months while aboard. But Nzingha… never?

Picking up the clothing and afraid to look at Nzingha, she asked, "Um… Nzingha?"

Nzingha answered with a strained, softened voice. "Yes, Bella?"

"May I be forward and ask a personal question?"

"Come on, it is me. Ask away."

"I have been assisting you for quite some time since we came aboard. I have helped with your baths, washed your clothes, and helped you dress and undress. Yet, Zingha, I have never once heard you ask for cloths, nor have I seen you use them for your courses. Are you well? Have your courses come at all since you took ill?"

Nzingha went from smiling to a serious, unimpressionable face. She stared off as if in a trance and blinked. She then sat up straight from laying back in the wooden tub. The water made a pouring sound as it slid from her breast.

"No. No, I have not had them. I was so ill, I did not notice their absence. I have never been this sick before, never fevered in my life."

She started counting her fingers, stopping at four. Nzingha furrowed her brows and bit her lip. Immediately she began biting her nails.

"Have you and Laird Barton… ah… well, you know. Had relations?"

Nzingha had a look of worry on her face.

Her eyes turned into two round coins.

"Oh, the gods. Yes. Yes, we have."

"Then do you think you might be?"

"It has been in the back of my mind. But I do not wish to be. I cannot be." She shook her head, voice tightening. "I want to go home. Please, do not tell Drake. I must return to my kingdom. I cannot go to this… this Scotland… I miss my country. Even hiding from my father would be better than living in another man's land."

She held Annabella's face and spoke softly.

"If he knows, he will not let me leave. He will try to keep me here, perhaps even keep the child. I cannot risk that." Her voice faltered. "I would rather go without his knowing than be trapped by it. Please, Annabella. Say nothing. I beg you. I cannot let this turn into something I cannot flee."

Bella frowned with confusion.

"But what if he… um…"

Nzingha whispered and glanced toward the door.

"Please keep your voice down."

Bella whispered, "But what if he finds out? You cannot leave so easily if you are with child. He wishes to wed you. Do you truly want a child born with only one parent?"

"I grew up with just my insane father of a King and turned out fine. Besides, it does not matter to me. When we dock, I will go into hiding. I shall pay a captain to take me back home."

Bella raised her voice.

"Back to eastern Africa? Are you mad? Anything could happen. You could be taken, sold, or far worse."

Nzingha placed a finger to her lip.

"Shh."

"Zing, how will you pay for this? If you ask Andrew for silver or gold, he'll ask the reason."

"I plan on selling my jewelry; this should be more than enough to get me home."

"Nzingha, no. They are memories of your mother and Mikel. You cannot just trade or sell them."

A knock came at the door.

"Zing, can I come in?" It was Andrew.

Nzingha looked at Bella, eyes wide with fear.

"You are my good friend. Promise me, not a word."

Bella pressed her lips together, saying nothing.

"Bella, promise," Nzingha pleaded, gripping her arms.

For the first time, Lady Annabella pulled free, her voice steady.

"It is open, Andrew. Come in."

Drake opened the door and smiled as Nzingha was putting on a nightgown.

"Good mornin', Lady Bella."

Bella nodded once and slipped from the chamber.

"Bella, is all well?" Andrew called after her.

The door closed hard behind her.

Andrew turned back to Nzingha, his voice low as he crossed the room and pressed a kiss to her brow.

"Did I interrupt somethin'?"

"No. We had a small misunderstanding."

"A misunderstanding with Bella?" He frowned. "She's nae one tae take offence lightly. Ye must've ruffled her feathers."

"Indeed, I did," Nzingha said faintly. "She was upset that I would… uh… not eat her porridge."

"Och, Zing." He gave a small shake of his head. "Come now. Ye must eat."

He retrieved the bowl from the stand. As he drew near, the scent of cinnamon and apples turned her stomach. Even the familiar musk of his clothing made her ill. She stepped away.

"Zing, why do ye draw back each time I come near? Do ye no wish me close?"

"No. My head, it aches."

Sorrow crossed Andrew's face.

Nzingha leaned in and pressed a brief kiss to Andrew's cheek. The closeness turned her stomach. When she drew back, he kissed her in return, his arm already circling her waist, lifting her before she could find the words to stop him.

The motion tipped her fully into nausea.

"Put me down," she said, breath breaking. "Please, I beg you."

He lowered her at once. She barely made it to the chamber pot before retching violently, her body folding in on itself as the sickness took hold. Andrew moved toward her in alarm, but she lifted a hand, stopping him.

He stood there helplessly, fists clenched, watching her shake.

"Is there aught I can do, my love?" he asked softly. "I hate seein' ye suffer so."

"No, Andrew," she said, still breathless. "Allow me to rest."

He lingered, torn. "D'ye wish me tae fetch Lady Annabella?"

"No. I only need rest."

For a long moment he did not move. Then, reluctantly, he nodded.

"Then I'll leave ye be."

She nodded once in return, too spent to say more.

Andrew stepped out of the cabin and onto the upper deck, drawing in a breath of cold sea air as though it might steady him. Haemish stood at the chart table, chalk marking the map as he adjusted the quadrant and turned the hourglass.

"How are we lookin'?" Andrew asked.

"The wind's risen sharp," Haemish replied. "We may need tae reef a sail, else she'll pull us off course."

"I'll climb an' tie it."

Haemish glanced up. "Are ye sure, Andrew? 'Tis hard work for one man."

"I need ye steadyin' the wheel. We cannae drift."

Haemish nodded. "Then have a care. Dinnae break yer neck. We need ye whole."

Andrew climbed the rigging, the cold biting hard into his hands, his thoughts no less sharp than the wind. When the task was finished, he paused, gripping the ropes, staring out across the endless stretch of sea.

Until something broke the horizon.

"Mary, mother o' all that's holy," he breathed. Then, louder, "Haemish!"

"Aye, Laird?"

"Land, mate… land. Is the quadrant true north?"

Haemish checked. "Aye. North holds."

Andrew's chest tightened. "I ken where we are. That's Carrauntoohil. County Kerry."

"What d'ye say?" Haemish asked carefully. "Pull in there first, then sail on tae Scotland?"

Andrew shook his head. "Nae. We go straight on. Nzingha needs a healer, and I ken none here."

"But are there healers in Ireland?"

"Aye, but my keep lies in Scotland," Andrew said. "And I trust no other hands."

His jaw set, resolve hardening into place. "I'll tell Lady Annabella. She'll be glad o' the news."

He hurried below and knocked at Annabella's cabin door.

"My Lady, 'tis me."

"Enter."

He stepped inside and stopped short. She was crying.

"My Lady," he said quietly, "what ails you? Be honest with me. I saw you troubled this morning."

She wiped at her eyes. "I cannot say. Nzingha made me promise."

Annabella pressed her lips together, breathing hard. Tears spilled freely, streaking her cheeks as her shoulders shook. Her nose ran, and she scrubbed at her face, failing to stop any of it.

This was bad. Drake could see it at once. She was holding something back, and it was tearing her apart.

So he tried another way.

It was how he'd always done business. Let folk think they knew more than they did. Let them talk.

Drake sat beside her and smiled.

"There now," he said lightly. "Dinnae cry. I've come down with good news."

She sniffed. "Did… did Nzingha tell you?"

There it was. The slip.

His brow lifted before he could stop it. Then he smiled wider, all teeth.

"Well, aye. Aye, she did."

Relief flowed from her like a breeze. "Oh, Drake… congratulations on the bairn. When did she tell you? She made me swear not to say a word. Did you know she meant to leave as soon as we reached land. I'm so glad you talked her out of it."

The smile dropped from his face.

"I'm a Da?" he said quietly.

He stood, already turning for the door.

Annabella darted in front of him. "Oh, curses." She planted herself against the door. "Wait, Drake. She did not tell you. You used trickery."

She swallowed, panic rising fast. "Please, do not let her know you found out. She will never forgive me. I wanted to tell you, but she begged me not to. Now that you know, it makes me feel better than before."

Drake stared at her with a blank expression.

Then he roared.

"SHE PLANNED ON BLOODY LEAVIN' ME?"

"Aye," she said quickly, shaken by his anger. "She… she meant to sell her jewelry to buy passage. I… I told her she was daft. The seas are full of monsters and worse. I do not know how she thought she would survive it."

Drake didn't answer.

He turned and slammed his fist into the oak wall. A sickening crack echoed through the cabin, followed by a rush of blood and the pale gleam of exposed bone.

Annabella squealed from shock.

"Drake! Your hand!" she gasped. "You've broken it."

She rushed for cloths.

He stood, thoughtless, the news leaving him defeated. "I'm… I'm sorry. Sorry if I frightened ye. I lost my temper."

She nodded, still shaken, and set the bone as best she could, using a spoon for a splint. Drake barely noticed the pain.

"I understand," she said quietly. "I was upset too, when she told me."

He breathed once, steadying himself.

"We are near Ireland, and I ken ye wish tae go home. But I must take Nzingha tae a healer at once. I'll write yer family. In the meantime, keep Nzingha company."

He turned to leave.

"Laird Barton? Now that you know, what will you do now?"

Drake paused.

He shrugged and left, without saying a word.

TAKEN | Kera C. Munnings | Page - 345

"Laird Barton? Now that you know, what will you do now?"

Drake paused.

He shrugged and left, without saying a word.

Chapter 14

The Straw that Broke the Donkey's Back

Drake lay awake in Haemish's quarters, staring at the low beams above him as the ship creaked and groaned around them.

The sound of the sea had once lulled him. Now it only reminded him that there was nowhere to run.

Sleep had abandoned him days ago.

It was easier to pretend he was busy. Easier to claim exhaustion. Easier than turning his face toward the woman who had broken him without meaning to.

Every message Annabella carried to him felt like a knife dragged slowly across his chest.

Nzingha is asking for you.

Tell her I am busy.

She awaits to see you.

Tell her nae tonight.

Nzingha is worried.

Tell her I'm nae feeling well.

Each excuse tasted fouler than the last.

He hated the messages. Hated the pity in Annabella's eyes. Hated himself most of all for letting the distance stretch until it became something cruel.

She had planned to leave him.

The thought sat heavy and unmoving in his chest. Raw. Unresolved. He could not look at her without feeling foolish. Betrayed. Afraid.

He rolled on his side. "'Tis why I never fall in love with a woman... It hurts."

Drake could not sleep. He tossed and turned the entire night. Hearing the door creak open, he spoke.

"Haemish, is it morn already? I barely got a wink of sleep."

A soft female African accent whispered, "No. It is not Haemish, and no, it is not morning."

Drake sat up.

"Zing, what are ye doin' out o' yer quarters? Are ye no ill?"

He lay back down, turning his back to her.

"I have not seen you for an entire fortnight. Are you upset with me?"

Hurt, yet annoyed, he answered,

"I assumed ye wanted tae be alone. After all, ye cannae stomach bein' near me."

Drake gave involuntary hints that he knew she was with child, and that she had planned to leave him.

"I am doing much better. I miss you, my love."

He turned, facing her. "Truly? Miss me? Huh... I need time tae myself. Maybe ye should go back tae bed. I dinnae want ye gettin' ill."

Nzingha frowned. "What demon has taken hold of you, Sir Andrew? Is there something you wish to speak of?"

"Oh, aye? Hmm... I should be the one askin' ye that question." He turned his back to her once more.

And at that very moment, Nzingha knew that Drake had found out she was with child. She balled her fist and whispered in rage,

"BELLA!"

Nzingha stormed from Haemish's chambers and marched straight to Lady Annabella's door. She flung it open and slammed it shut behind her.

"How dare you," she said, her voice shaking. "I trusted you."

Annabella startled, fear flashing across her face. "My Lady, please, it is not what you think. He used trickery. He twisted the conversation and made me speak."

Nzingha clasped her hands together, knuckles whitening as hurt bled into her voice. "No. You told him. You had to. He gave me hints... cold ones... and then told me to leave him be. You are my only friend." Her voice cracked. "I trusted you to keep this in silence."

Annabella's voice trembled, panic rising. "No, Nzingha, you must believe me. Drake came to my chambers speakin' of good news. God help me... I thought he meant you being with child. I asked him if you had told him. He smiled and said aye." Her breath hitched. "I congratulated him on the bairn before I realized what I had done."

She wiped at her tears. "That is when his temper broke. He struck the wall and shattered his hand. Only later did I learn the truth, that the news he meant to share was that we were sailing near Ireland, close to his home."

Annabella fell into sobs. "Please do not hate me. I cannot bear for you to be angry with me."

Nzingha's voice sharpened, demanding, "How long has he known?"

Bella swallowed hard, her words trembling out. "A... a fortnight."

Nzingha stamped her foot, fury spilling free. "Dammit, Bella! And you... you said nothing? Not even by accident?" She began pacing the room, breath ragged. "I thought you were my friend."

Annabella dropped to her knees. "Please, Nzingha. I was afraid." Her voice broke. "I love you, not only as a friend, but as a sister. I would never betray you."

Nzingha drew in a slow breath and let it out. She crossed the room and rested a gentle hand on Bella's back. She had forgotten how delicate Annabella could be, soft as an egg, easily cracked if handled without care.

"Shh," Nzingha murmured. "This is not your fault. Drake is clever. He sensed something amiss long before words were spoken." She brushed Bella's hair back. "Do not cry, pretty Bella."

She pulled her into a brief embrace. "I am not angry with you. I shall return to my quarters. All this rocking from the ship, it unsettles my stomach."

She patted Annabella's back once more, then scowled. "But first, I need to vent."

Nzingha straightened and left the cabin. Yet instead of turning toward her own quarters, she changed course.

She headed back to Haemish's cabin.

Opening the door slightly, she paused, then listened.

Soft snores drifted from the box bed. Drake was asleep.

A mean scowl curved her mouth. She crossed to the washstand, seized the water pitcher, then turned back toward the bed.

Without hesitation, she tipped the pitcher and dumped the entire contents onto his face.

Drake jolted awake with a violent gasp, twisting in the bed as water streamed down his face and chest.

"What the..."

She flung the pitcher against the wall. The crash rang through the cabin, ceramic exploding into jagged shards that skittered across the floor.

She stood rigid, eyes blazing, breath sharp with fury.

"I am Princess Nzingha Mbemba of the Mbemba Kingdom," she hissed. "I am of royal blood, and I will not have you speak to me as if I am daft."

Drake surged upright, water dripping from his hair, rage flashing white hot across his face.

"JESUS CHRIST, WOMAN... WHAT IN THE DEVIL IS WRONG WITH YE?"

The shouting began at once.

"YOU KNEW!" Nzingha screamed, the sound tearing through the cabin.
"You knew I carried your child and still you turned from me. I gave you my body, my love, my loyalty, and you cast me aside like refuse? DAMN YOU!"

Drake let out a sharp, humorless laugh, wiping water from his eyes.

He snapped. "Loyalty? Hm... Ye're one tae speak o' that. Now I ken ye truly are daft."

He stood slowly, every movement tight with restraint. He grabbed a cloth, scrubbed his face, then flung it aside. He yanked off his soaked shirt and tossed it to the floor. With a growl, he ripped the wet linens from the box bed and hurled them away, dragging another blanket into place.

Nzingha watched him, chest heaving, as his anger finally broke through the surface. He would not look at her.

"You decide tae leave me after I ask ye tae marry me. After I ask ye tae be my wife. After I tell ye, again and again, that I love ye. I stood there with my heart bared like a daft laddie."

He turned then, eyes blazing.

"Aye! Circumstance forced ye tae stay on that cursed island. But now that we're free... now that ye carry my child... ye decide tae flee? Tae leave with my babe still inside ye?"

His hand curled into a fist.

"Ye ken I love ye. Ye ken I'd die for ye. And yet ye chose tae betray me, tae keep our child secret, tae plan yer escape as if I were nothing."

He kicked the chair in a burst of rage. The leg snapped clean off, skidding across the floor.

"DAMN IT, NZINGHA! I GET NAE SAY IN THIS? NONE AT ALL? WHY MUST YE BE SO BLOODY SELFISH?"

Nzingha's pregnancy hormones were raging. She walked straight up to Drake.

"Yet you found out and chose to stay away from me for an entire fortnight?" she demanded. "Whatever happened to talking? Or asking me why I chose to leave?"

She jabbed her index finger into his chest.

"You are a coward, Andrew Barton," she pressed. "So, when we get to Scotland, you will let me leave? If that is the case... take me home."

Nzingha screamed, "TAKE ME HOME. RIGHT NOW!"

Drake was so angry he grabbed her wrist and backed her against the wall. He shook her once.

"What the devil has gotten into ye?" he snapped. "Calm yerself. Ye're actin' daft. Ye're clearly pickin' a quarrel tae make an excuse tae leave me."

He did not let go. "So now ye're the victim? That's my babe too. Why in God's name would I let ye leave?"

His voice dropped, still hard.

"Maybe... just maybe... I wasnae ready tae talk tae ye. Findin' out ye wanted tae leave me broke me."

He stared at her.

"Nzingha, ye broke my heart. I couldnae face ye because I wanted tae strangle ye for it. But I would never harm the woman I love."

"But I could never hurt the woman I love."

Nzingha answered him with her forehead.

She head-butted him hard enough to snap his teeth together.

"Och, Christ!" Drake cursed. "Have ye lost yer senses, woman?"

"Let me go!" she shouted, fighting him again, striking his chest, clawing for space. "Let me go!"

"That's enough," he growled.

Before she could strike him again, Drake caught her under the arms and lifted her clear off her feet. She kicked and twisted, furious, breathless, pounding at his shoulders.

"Put me down!" she screamed. "Let me go!"

"Nzingha," he snapped, carrying her across the cabin, "calm yerself."

She fought harder, wild and desperate, but her strength failed her. Drake laid her firmly onto the bed. Not gently. Not cruelly. Decisively. When she tried to rise, he caught her wrists and pressed her back down.

"Stay," he ordered. "I willnae chase ye through this cabin like animals."

She bucked against him, sobbing now, rage collapsing into fear.

"Why?" he demanded. "Why are ye so afraid ye'd tear us both apart?"

Her resistance broke.

"I am afraid," she cried. "I heard what you and Haemish said. I know how your people speak. I know what they will see when they look at our child." Her voice shook. "I have been taken before. Decided for. I will not raise my child where she is judged before she ever breathes."

Her chest heaved. "All I know is how to survive. And survival means going home."

A knock struck the door.

"My Lady?" Annabella called, fear sharp in her voice. "Is everything hale?"

Drake did not take his eyes from Nzingha. "Aye," he answered. "We are fine. Go back tae bed."

A pause. Then retreating footsteps.

The cabin fell quiet.

Drake loosened his grip. Slowly. He did not release her completely, only enough for her to breathe without fighting.

"You are not alone," he said, "Ye never were."

She went still beneath him.

"We are in this together," he continued. "No runnin'. No hidin'."

He crawled between her legs and raised her night rail.

"Wait, what? What are you doing? No. Remove yourself off of me."

He held her gaze, unwavering, his voice low and certain.

"Shhhh... let me love you."

He then pried her legs open with his shoulders and began to devour her with his mouth.

Nzingha thrashed her head from side to side, feeling completely powerless. All her life, she had given orders and commands. Power had always been hers to wield. She had never known the ache, the fear, of yielding it to another.

"No. Cease this." The more she said no, the more Drake licked and suckled her feminine nub.

Finally, Nzingha did the one thing she had never done in her entire life. She gave in.

Holding onto his head, she writhed beneath him with an intense motion. The overwhelming feeling of want took over her body. Drake placed two fingers inside her. The intensity of her passion made her move her hips faster. Moaning loudly, Nzingha raised her hips off the bed as the euphoria left her body.

When she was done, Drake lay next to her.

"Nzingha," he said, his voice low and unyielding, "ye are mine. As long as there is breath in my body, I will take control of our love."

He held her hand.

"I will fight for us. The only time I will not... that is if ye tell me, plainly, that ye no longer love me, and that ye dinnae wish tae be with me. Then, and only then, will I escort ye back tae Mbemba Kingdom myself, tae be certain ye are safe. But right now... this very moment... I ken ye love me. Ye carry my bairn inside ye. We are a family now. Ye are my wife, my love, my everything."

He tore a strip from his plaid and bound it around her wrist, tying the other end firmly to his own.

"You are part o' my clan now," he said, "Part o' me."

Drake rolled onto his side and reached beneath his pillow, drawing out his dagger. Without ceremony, he pricked his finger. Then, taking Nzingha's hand, he pricked hers as well.

He pressed their bleeding fingers together, rubbing them until their blood mingled.

"And now," he said quietly, "ye are blood o' my blood."

"From this night on, we are husband and wife."

His mouth curved, just slightly.

"If ye ever leave me," he added, voice dry, "I will search the oceans tae find ye."

Then, with a wicked glint,

"And when I do, I'll strangle ye."

He said it in jest, the kind that carried truth beneath the humor.

They lay together in the quiet that followed, neither speaking for a long moment. At last, Nzingha broke the silence.

"Drake," she said softly, "I am afraid. Truly, I am scared. And I do not know if I can do this."

He drew her closer, steady and sure. "Ye will be fine, I promise. I will see tae it."

"When we reach the castle, ye will want for nothin'. I will make certain ye and the bairn are safe. Ye have my solemn vow."

"My family may not be rich in gold as your father's," he added, "but ye will never lack. Ye are a princess, and I will treat ye as such. This will be your new home. I will see that ye and the bairn have the finest."

He kissed her hair. "Nae worry, Zing."

She rested her head upon his chest. "Please," she whispered, "do not leave my side when we arrive."

"I will not," he promised. "And if I must run an errand, Haemish will be your guard."

"Drake?"

"Hmm?"

"I am sorry for acting daft," she said, "Fear took hold of me. I thought you wanted nothing to do with me after you learned of the babe. I see now that you love me. Will you forgive me?"

"Aye," he said easily. "Of course."

Then, with a crooked smile, "Though I ken now not tae cross ye. That head-butt truly hurt." He gestured to the scratches on his chest. "I thought ye a wildcat."

"And you," she said with a laugh, kissing him, "are my lion. Grrr."

Drake chuckled. "Now I'm a lion? I thought I was a big mandrill. By the way, what in hell is a bloody mandrill?"

She covered her mouth, laughing. "An enormous monkey."

They spoke and laughed, their voices low as the ship rocked gently beneath them. And as the night wore on, they found their way back to each other, bound by promise, comfort, and the quiet certainty that neither would run again.

Land Home

Drake shot up from his sleep the next morning as someone pounded on the cabin door.

"Andrew!" Haemish yelled.

Rubbing the sleep from his eyes, he turned over to see Nzingha lying beside him, her naked breasts exposed. Looking at her made him hard in an instant. He grabbed his groin as the morning stiffness tempted him to ignore Haemish's knocking.

The knocking came again.

"Aye, Haemish!"

"We are docked at Tantallon."

"I will be right out."

He crawled out of bed, fully naked. He stretched, then donned his clothing. Looking over at Nzingha sprawled across the bed, he saw she was in a deep sleep, worn out from the festivities of the night before. He smiled at the woman he loved. Nzingha was still malnourished and thin, but he noticed something else.

Is that a small bump from my bairn? That is my bairn growing. I cannae believe I am a Da.

When he finished dressing, he looked down at his clothing and shook his head. Everything he wore was torn and disheveled. The previous shipmate's clothes did not fit. His beard had grown to his chest, and his hair was so long he tied it into a bun atop his head. He was growing tired of looking like a vagabond. He could not wait to return home, back to civilization, back to a hot bath, and most importantly, back to his enormous four poster bed.

He opened the door and stepped onto the ship's lower deck. Haemish leaned against a post, arms folded, wearing a smirk.

"Last night must've been a wild one. From the looks of that big bruise on your forehead, I can tell ye and the lass had a tussle."

Haemish pointed at Drake's forehead, where Nzingha had head butted him. A large bruise had formed.

"First, I heard yelling and screaming as if ye were at war. Then I heard loud moaning and passion from below. I need tae try me an exotic lass. Seems Nzingha keeps ye on yer toes. No one should ever confront her. She'd carve them into pieces. She's a feisty one, that one."

Haemish chuckled.

Drake smiled, rubbing his forehead. "Aye, she definitely is. She is nae ordinary lass. Her temper's bigger than Hades himself. But we resolved our differences, for Nzingha is with child."

Haemish slapped him on the back. "Congratulations, Laird!"

He felt excitement swell. "We handfasted last eve and plan tae wed as soon as I return home."

"'Tis excellent news, my Laird. I'm happy it took a foreign lass tae get ye tae settle down. Now if Alex can do the same."

Drake laughed. "Dinnae get me started on that rogue."

Both men walked to the upper deck and stared out at Tantallon Castle as the wind picked up, their hair twisting in the gale. Drake raised his spyglass.

"How shall we get tae shore? We dinnae have any skiffs."

Haemish scanned the deck. "We can use wood from a bench."

"But we cannae leave the women alone aboard. Nor risk Nzingha rowing in these waters."

"Agreed," Drake said. "I'll go. Alex and a handful of men can bring a skiff, an anchor, and ropes to secure the ship. This was Lady Annabella's father's vessel. Best we see her settled proper."

"Remain aboard and guard the women. I shall return anon."

"Aye, my Laird."

Drake returned to the cabin. Nzingha still slept, curled on her side, her breath soft and even. He pressed his palm to her brow, warm, but no fever. Relief loosened his chest.

"Zing," he murmured, brushing his thumb along her temple. "Ye must wake now, my love."

"Mmm..." She stirred, eyes barely opening. "I am so fatigued."

"I ken." His voice softened. "But we've reached my homeland. I must swim ashore to fetch a skiff so ye and Lady Annabella may land safe."

He bent and kissed her brow, lingering. "Welcome home, my love."

Her hand caught his sleeve. "Drake?"

"Aye?"

"Do not leave my side when we reach shore."

"I shan't." His answer came without hesitation.

Laird Andrew Barton was finally home.

The water was merciless, black, bitter, alive with cold. Waves battered him as he swam, muscles burning, breath tearing from his lungs.

When his boots struck sand, ten guards rushed forward, swords flashing.

"Halt! Before I split yer arse in two."

Andrew rasped, "Do that and Alex will shove that blade so far up yer arse ye'll taste steel."

A heartbeat of silence.

His long time friend Rory stepped forward. "Saint Peter's Cross. Andrew!... ye live."

Cloaks were thrown over his shoulders, hands steadying him.

"Where is my brother?"

"In the great hall," Rory answered.

"And what is this day?"

Rory's face gave concern. "It is the fifth of October, the year of our Lord, 1622."

Andrew looked around the familiar stone walls, the damp air, the gathered faces.

"A year," he muttered. "Only a bloody year." He exhaled sharply. "Christ... it feels like an eternity lived."

The swim had drained what strength remained in his limbs, the cold still biting deep into muscle and bone. Yet the scent of the Highlands filled his chest with peat, stone, and wind. For the first time since the wreck, something inside him settled.

A guard brought forward a stallion. Drake mounted and urged the horse toward the keep.

At the castle gates, voices rose all at once.

"Laird Andrew!"

"He has returned!"

"Sir Andrew, you live!"

Amelia's voice cut through the clamor. "My Laird! Sir Andrew!" She hurried forward, eyes bright, cheeks flushed. "You are alive."

Andrew turned his head away as she approached. "Shit!"

He already knew the trouble she would bring. *I must keep her from my chambers... and from Nzingha*, he thought grimly.

Amelia beamed, pressing closer. "I prayed every night for your return," she said breathlessly. "Is there anything I can do for you? Anything at all? Shall I help you with your bath?" She winked, arching herself toward him.

"I dinnae need help with a bath," Andrew said curtly. "But I do need the eastern guest chambers prepared at once. Have extra drying cloths brought to my rooms. Hot water. And fetch my mother's trunk from storage."

Amelia faltered. "Your mother's trunk, my Laird? Are there guests?"

"Dinnae concern yourself with it," he said flatly. "Do as ye're told. Now haste."

"Aye, my Laird."

Andrew took the steps two at a time and pushed through the great doors.

Inside, Alex stood mid argument with one of the elders, parchment in hand. When he looked up and saw Andrew, the color left his face.

"Brother?"

The papers fell forgotten as Alex crossed the hall. They collided, gripping each other like boys returned from war.

"Praise be to God," Alex said hoarsely. "I thought you lost. I thought I was alone."

Andrew huffed a tired breath. "I wasnae about tae let ye turn the keep into a tavern."

Alex laughed, the sound breaking as tears welled. "When some of the men returned without you, I feared the worst. Denton told us what happened. The storm, the wreck. They even searched for ye, Andrew. For days... days... but supplies ran dry."

"What about the orders for the Kirk and Court?" he asked quietly.

Alex exhaled slowly. "Most of the crown's cargo was lost. But it matters little, Andrew. Goods can be replaced. Lives cannot." He hesitated, the weight of it settling heavy in his chest. "Haemish and ten men never returned."

A faint smile touched Andrew's mouth. "Haemish lives."

Alex stilled. "Lives?"

"Aye. And two lasses besides. We were stranded on an island." Andrew paused, choosing his words. "I met a princess there."

Alex stared at him, then gave a slow, knowing smile. "A... princess?"

Andrew huffed softly. "Shortly after I arrived, I found her stranded as well. She saw the state I was in, near starved, half mad with thirst, and she took me in. Tended tae me. Fed me." His voice lowered. "She saved my life."

Alex's smile turned thoughtful. "Hmm. Oh? Is that so?"

"Nae," Andrew said sharply, cutting the thought off before it formed. "Get your mind out o' the trenches." He drew a breath. "Not long after, we came upon Haemish. The poor bastard had been torn open by a shark, hoverin' on the edge of death." Andrew's gaze hardened. "The princess saved him too. And the Irish lass... she was held prisoner by natives. The princess freed her."

He shook his head. "It is... much, brother. Too much for a hall full of ears."

Alex swore under his breath. "Yeezus. What an ordeal." He studied Andrew closely. "That journey would have broken lesser men."

"Aye," Andrew said quietly. "Overwhelming." Then, softer still, "And a blessing."

He turned toward the doors. "Come. Let us fetch the skiff."

The Bartons Keep

Within moments, Andrew, his brother, and five guards were riding back to the shores of Tantallon.

Andrew and Alex took the skiff out to the ship, where Haemish waited aboard with the ladies.

Alex greeted him at once. "Haemish, ye and Andrew cheated death." He embraced him with a Highland warrior handshake. "Glad tae see ye."

Haemish laughed. "Alex, it's good tae see ye as well. I've been graced with yer bonnie face again." He slapped Alex's back after jesting.

Lady Annabella of Ireland and Princess Nzingha of the Mbemba Kingdom stood side by side. Nzingha wore a yellow day dress that had once been Annabella's mother's, her long locks twisted into a bun that softened her small, rounded face. Annabella, dressed in green, stood just as striking beside her, her red hair loose in the wind, the color drawing out the brightness of her green eyes.

Andrew and Alex turned toward the women.

Alex stepped forward on instinct, lifted Annabella's hand, and pressed a courteous kiss to it.

"Princess, it's a pleasure tae grace yer presence."

Annabella's smile faltered. "Ah... I am not..." She hesitated, uncertainty creasing her brow.

Nzingha's eyes lifted, and then she laughed, soft at first, then freely, as the moment unfolded exactly as she had predicted.

"Did I say a jest?" Alex asked, genuinely confused, his gaze shifting between the two women.

Andrew crossed the space and slipped an arm around Nzingha's waist, the motion easy, unguarded.

"Nae, Alex. She is Lady Annabella of Ireland."

He turned slightly, drawing Nzingha closer, his voice calm.

"And this is Nzingha, Princess tae eastern and western Africa."

He gestured lightly with his hand. "Nzingha, my elder brother, Alex."

Nzingha inclined her head in greeting, a slow, composed nod. Still amused by the moment before, she smiled.

"It is a pleasure to meet his Lairdship."

Alex cleared his throat. "Oh... eh-em." He straightened, gathering himself.

"The pleasure is mine. Truly."

Alex jested, "It's nae every day a man meets a princess who's crossed oceans and survived half the world just tae end up here."

Nzingha's smile widened, bright and knowing.

Andrew stepped in beside her, took her hand, and kissed it without ceremony.

Shock flooded Alex. His gaze dropped to their joined hands. Then to the strip of Barton cloth bound around her wrist.

His mouth opened. Closed again.

"Now wait just a..." He stopped himself, swallowing.

What in God's name... have they handfasted?

Andrew looked down at her with an ease that said more than explanation. "Nzingha needs a healer. She's been ill and requires assistance forthwith."

Her elbow met his ribs.

"Ugh..."

"No, I do not," Nzingha said at once, smiling sweetly at the ring of gawking men. "It was only a little sea sickness. That is all. Is that not so, Annabella?"

"Aye, she's right. She's been ill since we escaped the island."

Andrew motioned for Nzingha and Lady Annabella to exit the galleon.

"Come. We must haste. A gale's comin'."

Alex studied Andrew's and Nzingha's body language as he hopped down into the skiff and assisted the ladies to sit. Once aboard, Andrew handed both Nzingha and Lady Annabella a cloak as the temperature dropped. Nzingha trembled as she settled in.

"Is it cold like this every day?"

Andrew smiled. "Aye. Through winter and fall, sometimes spring as well. I'll keep ye warm, my love."

He wrapped his arms around her, rubbing warmth back into her chilled limbs.

Alex turned at the sound of it. "My love? Is Andrew hale? Did he just say my love?"

Alex could scarcely believe what he was seeing or hearing. Andrew had always consorted freely, grown friendly with foreign women as easily as breathing, but to bring one home? And not just any woman. Someone from the far east.

.

From the corner of his eye, he stole another glance at the couple snuggling into each other.

"Is that better?" Andrew asked.

Nzingha nodded. "Indeed. Much better."

After watching his brother a moment longer, Alex turned his attention to Lady Annabella. The lass was stunning, and he took her hand to steady her seat, flashed a saucy grin, and kissed her atop the knuckles.

"Ye're verra beautiful."

Annabella bowed her head politely. "Oh, my thanks."

Haemish had been watching from the corner of his eye, his expression darkening by the second. Alex Barton had always been a rogue, too free with his smiles, too comfortable where he did not belong.

Already lowering himself into the seat beside the redhead, Alex shifted, only for Haemish to appear out of nowhere and drop into the space first, crowding it with a thump that sent Alex stumbling aside.

"Sorry, my Laird," Haemish said, not looking at him. "Didnae see ye there."

Annabella laughed before she could stop herself, then covered her mouth.

Haemish turned to her at once, the edge gone from him. "My Lady, would ye like me tae keep ye warm?"

"Oh, my thanks," Bella said readily. "I am so cold."

He drew her in, easy as breathing.

Alex stood there a moment longer than necessary, frowning as the meaning caught up with him.

Haemish glanced his way only once.

That was enough. *Keep away.*

Finally, they reached the shore. Nzingha and Andrew rode a horse together, while Annabella and Haemish sat on separate horses. As they rode through the villages, the stares and whispers began.

"Look at her. Where is she from?"

"Oh my, I never seen a woman with brown skin."

"She is beautiful. Look at her eyes, almost wolf-like."

"But what is she doing all the way in Scotland?"

"Look at her jewelry."

"Is that real?"

"Why is she on the same horse as Laird Andrew?"

Nzingha studied everyone's demeanor. Some seemed confused. Others whispered. Some frowned. Some pointed.

"Is it so uncommon here, to see a woman like me?"

Andrew glanced toward the village before answering. "Aye. It is."

He exhaled softly. "They've nae seen the like before. It'll take time. Scots can be a wee bit superstitious."

"Is Alex similar? More open-minded?"

"Aye," Andrew said readily. "Though he's nae half as careful as I am when it comes tae women. He can be a rake."

"What is a rake?"

"He rakes through women the way a pitchfork rakes straw," Andrew said dryly.

Nzingha chuckled. "He sounds like my father."

She glanced at Alex, then at Haemish's deadly stare.

"Well, I do not have to worry about protecting Annabella's innocence."

Andrew laughed under his breath.

"My people will learn," he said, "Someday. And ye'll be their first lesson."

"I shall never leave my chambers," she said quietly.

"Aye," he replied, gentle now. "Give them time."

Finally, they reached the keep. Andrew turned to Alex.

"Have the servants show Annabella to her chambers. And Alex?"

"Aye, brother?"

"Stay away from her."

Alex huffed. "Aye, aye." He waved a hand. "I'll let you and your princess get settled. But I expect ye in the solar at half past the hour."

Andrew nodded, took Nzingha's hand, and walked her through the castle.

As they climbed, she whispered, "You were called Drake at sea."

He answered quietly, "Aye. That name is not to be spoken in these lands."

She nodded once, understanding.

Drake nodded, took Nzingha's hand, and walked her through the castle.

Her gaze lifted at once to the great hall. She did not take it in all at once.

First, her eyes went to the tapestries that hung high along the stone walls. They were old, their colors darkened with time, not bright or gilded like the hangings in her father's halls. They showed scenes of hunts and battles, men on horseback, weapons raised, blood implied rather than shown. Among them were saints, their faces stern and unyielding, watching over the hall as if they were meant to remind all who entered where authority lay.

Between the tapestries, swords and shields were fixed to the walls in careful order. The steel caught the firelight as it flickered, flashing briefly before turning dull again, cold against the warmth of the flames. The air smelled of smoke and iron, of cooked meat and damp wool, the scent heavy and unfamiliar, clinging to the stone itself.

Beyond a long table set upon a raised platform stood suits of metal armor. They were tall and rigid, empty inside, lined up as though waiting for the men who would one day wear them again.

"Is this where the Laird eats?" she asked, lifting her hand to point.

"Aye," Drake answered. "'Tis called a dais. This is the great hall. Folk come here tae dine."

Her brows lifted slightly. "Oh. We call my father's table a paduak. But we never dine with nobles or commoners, only as the royal family."

The Warmth Inside his Chambers

As they climbed, her gaze moved to the walls. There were paintings of horses running across open land, their legs stretched mid-stride. Past those were portraits of men in kilts, arranged one after another, their faces changing with the years but their posture much the same.

She slowed without meaning to.

There, among them, was a family portrait.

A man with fair hair and sharp eyes stood beside a woman whose hair was dark as raven's wing, her expression proud, watchful, unmistakably strong. Two young boys stood between them. One favored the father in height and build, fair-haired like him, already carrying a confident set to his shoulders. The other bore the mother's coloring instead, dark hair framing blue eyes that seemed too serious for so young a face.

Her gaze lingered.

"That is you," she said quietly, touching the air near the frame. "And Alex."

Drake nodded.

She smiled at the boy who could not have been more than five summers. "I hope our child has your eyes," she murmured. "You were very adorable."

He did not answer, but his hand tightened around hers.

They continued upward. On the fourth landing, Drake reached for a candle from the wall and led her down a dim corridor. There, set apart from the rest, hung another painting.

Drake alone now older, standing tall in his kilt, one boot braced upon a footstool, sword at his side. One hand rested near the hilt, the other tugged lightly at the lining of his coat. His gaze was fierce, unyielding.

She recognized him at once. This was how his people saw him.

She studied it longer than the others.

At last, he stopped before a single door.

"Your quarters?"

"Mm-hmm."

He nodded, then lifted her without warning and carried her across the threshold. She laughed, surprised, the sound light in the quiet hall.

"Welcome to your chambers, Your Grace," he said, setting her down and kissing her briefly.

Warmth greeted her at once.

A massive four poster bed draped in thick fur dominated the room, its size and weight reminding her of her own great bed in Mbemba. A wooden tub stood near the hearth, steam faintly curling from its rim. A desk cluttered with parchment occupied one corner, ink and candle close at hand.

And then she saw it.

Books.

Her expression shifted before she was aware of it.

She took another step into the room, then another. Her eyes moved, widening slightly as they settled on the shelves, the bed, the fire. A moment passed, just long enough for her to realize she was smiling.

It was not a smile she gave often.

The fire crackled softly behind her, and the cold she had carried in with her began to ease, slipping away a little at a time. She turned, slowly now, as though afraid the room might change if she moved too quickly, taking it in from one end to the other, the comfort of it registering in small, quiet ways.

Drake watched her.

When she looked back at him, his mouth curved in response, not wide, not for show, but enough to bare his teeth for a brief moment, pleased in a way he did not bother to hide.

He showed her the privy, then the trunk at the foot of the bed.

"My mother's," he said, "There's nae clothing for ye yet, but ye may choose from here until the seamstress comes."

"I could never wear Mbemba clothing here," she said, shaking her head lightly. "I would freeze."

Drake laughed. "Aye, and draw more attention than ye'd care for."

The day caught up with her then. She yawned, the effort small but unmistakable.

"I shan't be leaving your chambers this evening."

"Very well."

He helped her into the bath, the hot water drawing a long, contented sigh from her lips.

"No more saltwater," he murmured. "Only fresh well water from here on."

Later, when he left her with a book and a fire, she did not read at once.

She warmed her hands first, then let herself wander, slow and unhurried, twisting her hair absently as she moved about the chamber. It felt different being alone here, in a man's private space, and she found herself noticing small things without meaning to. The desk with its scattered parchments, his handwriting careful and disciplined, the order of his belongings. There was nothing excessive, nothing carelessly kept, as though every object had earned its place.

Her attention drifted, unplanned, to the sword resting nearby.

Curiosity drew her closer. She reached out, fingers closing around the hilt, and lifted it before she quite understood what she was doing. The weight pulled her arm down at once. The blade dipped and struck the floor with a solid clang, sharp enough to make her inhale in surprise. She laughed softly to herself as she set it back, rubbing her wrist, a new respect settling in.

"So, that is how you build those muscles," she murmured, amused.

She moved to the bed then and eased herself down onto the thick furs. Warmth rose beneath her, unexpected and comforting. She stretched out slowly, letting her hand trail across the pelts, sinking into the softness, different from the open heat of home yet sheltering in its own way.

Her hand found her stomach and rested there, unthinking, natural.

A small smile touched her lips.

"So, this is our new life."

Chapter 15

Still on His Skin

Andrew stepped into the solar with his shoulders already tight.

He knew what this was.

The door closed behind him, too quickly, too final, and before anyone spoke, his eyes moved, counting without meaning to.

All of them.

Elders. Factors. Men who had never once bled beside him, never clung to wreckage in the dark, yet now sat straight-backed and solemn as if they held his life between their palms.

Christ, he thought. Could ye no even let me wash my arse first?

A year swallowed whole by the sea, and here he was, hauled straight from the yard and set before judgment like a half-trained hound.

He was still rank with salt and iron. He could feel it in the seams of his clothes, in his hair, in the scrape of his beard against his collar. Travel-worn. Sea-worn. Not fit for a laird returned from the dead.

Let them look, he told himself, jaw setting. Let them choke on it.

Andrew's gaze slid, unbidden, to Uncle Graham.

Graham sat exactly as he always had, solid and unmovable, broad hands folded on the table as if they had been carved there. His mouth was set in that familiar line Andrew had known since boyhood, not approval, not judgment, but watchfulness. Measuring. The look of a man who did not rush to speak because he did not need to. Something in Andrew's chest eased at the sight of him, small but real. If this room turned against him, Graham would not be among them.

Across the table sat Alex.

His brother's face was composed, too composed, giving nothing away to the men around him. But Andrew had grown up reading that face, and he saw the truth of it easily enough, in the way Alex's fingers lay flat against the wood instead of laced together, in the tightness held at the corner of his jaw. Alex was not surprised by this meeting. He had been expecting it. Listening already. Choosing his moment.

An elder rose at last.

"Laird Andrew," he said, solemn as a sermon and twice as rehearsed. "Praise be to God. We feared ye lost to the deep. Yet His mercy endures."

"Amen," came the reply, neat and unified, as if spoken from habit rather than relief.

Andrew inclined his head because the moment demanded it, because this was how such things were done.

"Aye," he said,

"Come. Sit. Let us speak."

He crossed the room, boots echoing too loudly in the hush, and took the seat offered at the far end of the table, beside Uncle Graham. Graham glanced at him then, only once, and gave the faintest nod. It was enough. There was no need for words between them.

Alex spoke not long after.

"Denton told me what he kent before ye reached the gates," he said, his voice measured. "Of the storm. Of the men."

Andrew let out a slow breath through his nose.

"Aye."

"That only you and Haemish returned."

"That is so."

The truth of it settled over the table, heavy and unadorned. Andrew did not attempt to soften it. He did not dramatize what had been bad enough already. He spoke of cards and whisky, of a wind that turned without warning, of a ship tearing itself apart beneath their feet as though it had tired of holding together. He spoke of the rope, of the wave that came over the side like judgment itself, of the dark that followed.

"When I woke," he said quietly, "I lay on a foreign shore. Burned. Fevered. Near dead."

Only then did he lift his head.

"That is when Nzingha found me."

Her name passed through the room like a breath taken too deep and too fast, subtle but felt all the same. Andrew sensed the shift in it, the easing of posture, the turn of faces, curiosity thinning and tightening until it edged toward suspicion.

He spoke of her then without ornament or flourish, because she did not require it. He told them how she had found him broken on a foreign shore and tended him without question, how she fought when she needed to, how she took in Haemish and Annabella when she owed them nothing at all. He spoke of the way she stood, back straight, gaze level, as one who had never bowed without reason and would not begin now.

His admiration crept into his voice despite himself.

"She took us in," he said, "Asked for nothing. Gave everything."

Only then did he notice the looks that had begun to pass between them, the glances exchanged and quickly masked, mouths tightening as if they had tasted sour ale and found it wanting.

It was Alex who finally gave voice to what the room had already decided to weigh.

"Andrew, are ye courtin' the foreign woman?"

Heat flared in Andrew's chest, sudden and bright, burning away the last of his patience.

"She is no woman to be weighed by yer tongues," he snapped. "Nor a curiosity for this table."

Silence fell, heavy and abrupt.

"Nzingha is a princess of Mbemba Kingdom," he went on, slower now, each word set with care, his voice edged with iron.
"She's Royal born. Trained. Disciplined. She was taken by slavers after defyin' her father, and she near paid for it with her life..."

An elder cleared his throat, stiff with unease.

"Eh-em. And will she be returnin' tae her lands?"

Andrew rose.

The scrape of his chair against stone rang louder than any voice. He poured himself a tot of whisky without asking, drank it down in one hard swallow, felt the burn cut clean through him, then set the glass on the table with enough force to make it rattle.

"Nae."

Murmurs broke loose at once.

Alex stood with them, his voice firm and controlled.

"This must not reach the court. If word of her presence spreads, if Edinburgh hears of it, questions will follow."

Andrew rounded on them then, restraint finally stripped away.

"Questions?" he barked. "From men who've never crossed the bloody sea? Who've never watched good men die and lived to tell it?"

Another elder spoke, stiff-backed and pale.

"She cannot remain in the castle."

That was it.

Andrew leaned forward, hands braced hard on the table, eyes bright with fury.

"This is my father's hall, ye sanctimonious bastards, not a kirk pew for yer delicate sensibilities. If any man here finds himself offended by her presence, he's welcome tae take his arse elsewhere and swear fealty tae another clan."

No one spoke.

"She crossed oceans and bled for her life," Andrew said, his voice low and unyielding. "She will eat at my table and drink from my cup. That is my word."

He turned to Alex.

"Meet me in the study. Now!"

He looked back at the rest of them, his voice broad and unforgiving.

"And if a single one of ye breathes her name toward Edinburgh, I'll see ye cursed so deep yer grandchildren will feel it."

He left the solar without another glance.

Between Brothers

Andrew did not slow until he reached the study. He shut the door behind him and crossed toward the hearth, his hands already in his hair, dragging back salt-stiff strands as if he could pull the day out of himself by force alone. His breath came too fast, too sharp, and he hated that they had done that to him.

"Bastards," he muttered. "Every last sanctimonious, silk-arsed bastard."

The word barely left his mouth before his hand struck the mantel, not in rage so much as need, the quick pain grounding him where thought would not. He stood there a moment after, shoulders tight, jaw locked, until the pressure in his chest eased enough to breathe again.

The door opened quietly.

Alex came in without ceremony and closed it behind him, sealing the solar away. He did not interrupt. He poured whisky as he always had, the sound familiar, unremarkable, and set one glass within Andrew's reach before taking the other for himself.

Andrew did not look at him at first.

"They sit there... safe, fat, and untouched, and think they ken a thing about survival. As if a life can be weighed like a ledger entry." He let out a short, bitter laugh. "Christ, Alex. They looked at her like she was a danger just for drawin' breath."

He drained the whisky and turned at last, anger still bright in his eyes.

"They're judging her for her skin," he said flatly. "Say it plain. That's what this is."

Alex did not deny it. He took a slow breath before answering.

"Aye. Some of them are."

Andrew let out a harsh breath, equal parts fury and relief. "At least you've the stones to admit it."

"That's why it cannae reach Edinburgh," Alex said, steady as ever.

Andrew stiffened. "They'll whisper."

"They always do," Alex said. "But if the court hears even a breath o' this, the questions willnae stop. Nae about her, and nae about you. They'll ask why a Scottish lad came home with nae sign o' the supplies he was sent for, yet somehow returned with a great Irish galleon under his feet. They'll ask how a man the sea was said tae have swallowed whole turned up again at all, and what bargains might explain it. And once folk start tellin' the tale that way, they'll wonder what else was brought back with him, and at what cost."

Andrew's jaw worked. "What? That I bought a slave? What sort o' horse shite is that?"

Alex's mouth twitched. "Aye... well. Gossip in these lands grows taller than Edinburgh Castle if ye leave it long enough. Christ, they once said I was keepin' a French widow in the wine cellar and feedin' her on nothin' but figs and scandal."

Andrew barked a laugh and nearly choked on his whisky, coughing hard as he bent forward. "A French widow?" he wheezed. "You?"

"Aye," Alex said mildly. "Apparently, she taught me wicked habits and drained the coffers besides. I've yet tae meet the woman, but I hear she was devastatin'."

The laugh that tore from him surprised Alex, rough and unguarded, and with it something in his chest finally loosened. He took another swallow, slower this time, then looked back at his brother.

"So," he said, voice steadier now, "what say ye, brother? Do I take her back to her home, with me beside her?"

Alex shook his head at once. "Nae, arseling. That's no the answer."

He met Andrew's gaze, all humor gone, but no warmth lost.

"You're to protect her."

Andrew turned away again, not pacing so much as holding himself still, his voice lowering despite him.

"She kent this would happen. Warned me. Begged me tae take her home. Said she wouldnae have our bairn growin' up under looks like theirs."

He swallowed.

"I'm the one who asked her tae stay. I told her she'd be safe."

Shock hit Alex. Whisky sprayed everywhere.

"Bairn? Andrew, what in hell's name..."

"Aye," Andrew said dryly. "Ye heard me."

Alex stared at him a long moment, then barked a laugh and stepped closer.

"Christ alive. And they called me the daft brother."

He clapped Andrew's back.

"Christ, a princess lettin' ye loose arrows inside her and nae pull way. Aye, that's trust beyond reason."

Andrew nodded once, his throat tight.

"She trusted me with her life. With our child. I cannae fail her now. I willnae."

Alex's hand came to his shoulder, firm and sure.

"You will not," he said quietly. "Not while I draw breath."

Andrew looked at his brother and felt something inside him finally ease. He stood a moment longer, staring into the fire as if it might answer him. Then he said, quieter, more settled.

"We'll be leavin' in a week, maybe less. I'll take her tae Mother's dowager house in Leith. Fewer eyes there. Quieter. I promised her safety. I mean tae keep it, even if it costs me half the clan."

Alex did not answer at once. He nodded instead, already turning it over in his head, weighing who could be trusted and who could not. "I'll send servants ahead, three. Folk I ken well."

They fell quiet then, not in discomfort, but in the rare ease of men who had nearly lost each other and knew it. The fire cracked softly between them.

"I worried about ye. Thought ye'd turn the place into a tavern and drown yourself in whores."

Alex snorted. "You wound me."

"I mean it," Andrew said, the edge gone now. "I feared I'd come home and find ye gone too."

Something unguarded crossed Alex's face. "When ye vanished, I put the bottle down. Someone had tae stand. I reckoned it should be me."

Andrew clapped his brother's shoulder. "I'm glad of it."

They stood like that a moment longer before Alex cleared his throat. "There's one more thing."

"Go on."

"I saw Amelia earlier. She's askin' questions."

Andrew's mouth tightened. "Keep her away from my chambers. From Nzingha. From all of it. For her own sake."

Alex nodded once. "Dinnae fret. I'll keep her busy."

Andrew let out a long breath and looked back to the fire, thinking of dark skin warmed by its glow, of steady eyes that had never once looked at him with judgment.

"A week, then we go."

Alex inclined his head. "And when the world catches up to ye, it'll have tae answer to both of us."

Andrew smiled, not wide, not easy, but real.

Where He Is Andrew

Andrew went back to his chambers and knocked. The corridor lay dark and quiet; the castle settled into its night hush. When no answer came, he knocked again, harder this time. Only then did the bar slide free and the door open.

Nzingha stood there, her hair neatly done, her body wrapped only in her drying cloth. He frowned at her at once.

"Why are ye not dressed? Do ye wish tae catch yer death?"

Cold air swept in behind him as he stepped over the threshold, and she shivered.

"I fell asleep while reading," she said, rubbing her arms. "I still cannot believe how cold this place becomes."

He crossed the room without another word, lifted a fur from the bed, and wrapped it around her shoulders, tucking it close as if she were something precious and easily lost. She trembled beneath the sudden warmth, then softened, leaning into him without thinking.

"This castle was built tae keep enemies out," he muttered. "Nae tae keep folk warm."

She smiled against his chest. "In my home, stone holds the heat. Here, it feels as though the walls breathe winter."

That gave him his opening.

"I was thinkin'," he said carefully, "it might be a grand idea if we moved tae my mother's dowager house. It's smaller. Warmer. And it would be a better place tae raise our child without the whole clan stickin' their noses where they dinnae belong."

Her face lit at once, the worry of the day loosening.

"That is the best news I have heard all day. Will we have servants?"

"Aye," he said, "Three. Well paid. Good ones."

She considered this, head tilting. "I would only wish for one. Someone to help me with the babe."

He nodded. "That can be arranged."

"How soon do we leave?"

"In a week."

"A week?" Her eyes widened. "Why the wait?"

He exhaled, dragging a hand through his hair, the weight of it slipping free at last.

"There's business tae settle with my brother. I need tae ken if Alex has spoken with the King or the kirk. We may owe debt tae the Cross for the loss of their merchandise." He grimaced. "Two galleons came back battered. Sailin' again will take time. We may have tae sell land tae make it right."

As he spoke, he began to undress, setting his things aside, already half-thinking of the bath.

Nzingha watched him in silence, then said softly,

"In my father's kingdom, gold is like earth beneath one's feet."

She reached up and removed her necklace, the heavy chain cool against her fingers, the sapphire catching the candlelight as she stepped closer.

"Drake," she said gently.

"Aye?" He was still wrestling with his boots, not yet looking.

She held the necklace out.

"Take this. See if it will help."

He turned, saw it, and immediately pushed her hand away.

"Nae," he said firmly. "I cannae accept that. It's yours." He leaned in and kissed her quickly, as if to soften the refusal. "I appreciate the offer, truly, but my pride would die a screaming death."

She smiled at that, even as he turned away, his thoughts flicking briefly to other means, to gold tucked away where no one would ever think to look.

After a moment, another thought struck him.

"Nzingha," he said more quietly. "I have a favor tae ask."

"Anything, my love."

"When we're nae alone, ye must nae call me Drake. That name belongs tae the sea only. Never land." He grimaced. "It's known as a pirate name. Sea Dogs and other such nonsense."

She nodded at once. "Of course. I would never wish you trouble, though I may forget at first."

He met her eyes, all humor gone.

"Two years past, my brother and I near lost our lives tae the English Navy. We were almost strung up by our cods. Only a royal pardon spared us." His voice lowered. "The King of Scotland claimed the gold on our ship as his own. Said it was a gift from France. He helped us because we serve him."

He took her hands.

"So in public, it's Laird Barton, or Andrew. If ye slip and call me Drake, and the wrong ears hear it... piracy means death."

She tilted her head, studying him.

"So," she said thoughtfully, "are you a pirate?"

He winked, kissed her cheek, and tugged his beard with a grin.

"Do I look like one?"

She laughed. "You are impossible. Yes, to looking like one. And yes, I understand." Then she hesitated. "But when we first met... why did you not allow me the right to call your birth name?"

"For protection," he said simply. "I didnae ken what island I was on, or who you were." He pointed toward the basin. "Can ye fetch my shavers?"

"Of course."

He smiled at her. "Does Her Majesty ken how tae give a shave?"

She smiled back. "I think I can manage."

He lowered himself into the bath she'd used earlier and sighed as the warm water closed around him.

"Ahh..."

She knelt beside the tub, kissed him deeply, then lathered his face before settling behind him with the razor. Tilting his head back, she drew the blade along his jaw in slow, careful strokes.

"I cannot believe I have never seen you without your beard," she murmured. "It feels as though I am getting a new man."

He laughed, his Adam's apple bobbing, and she froze, blade hovering.

"I cannot finish if you laugh like a hyena."

He pulled a stiff grin. "My apologies. Then dinnae make me laugh."

He went still beneath her hands.

"What, the devil, is a hyena?"

She resumed shaving. "An exceptionally large canine from my homeland. They laugh uncontrollably, but they are not friendly. They will eat you."

He blinked. "Strange creatures your lands breed."

"Just a different part of the world," she said lightly.

When she finished, she stepped around him and studied his face.

"Oh my," she breathed. "So this is the real you."

He smiled, dimples deep, teeth bright, and without the beard he looked every inch a laird, sun-browned and changed just enough to make her fall for him all over again.

She cupped his face and kissed him.

"Now I see why you go by Drake. No one would ever know."

He rubbed her stomach gently. "We'll have a fine life, you, me, and our bairn. Have ye thought of names?"

As she washed his chest and shoulders, her smile turned distant.

"Do you remember our first night together?"

He grinned. "Do ye mean the night we got high off cannabis?"

"Nae!" She punched his arm.

"Ouch. So feisty," he laughed. "Of course I remember."

"I had a dream that night," she said softly. "My mother came to me. She told me I would bear a little girl. She gave me her name, but it slipped away when I woke." Her smile returned. "She said our daughter's beauty would be rare."

She handed him the drying cloth.

He rose from the bath and wrapped the towel about his waist. She did not look away. There was no modesty in her gaze now, only appreciation, heat stirring low and slow.

While he dried his face, she leaned close and murmured, "How does it fit?"

He laughed. "What was that?"

"Nothing," she said quickly, turning away, smiling all the same.

They climbed into bed together at last.

"I cannae believe it," he murmured, drawing her close. "That I'll sleep beside the woman I love, in my own bed."

She lay quiet against him for a long moment, listening to his heart, fingers tracing slow circles against his chest.

"Andrew," she said at last, careful now.

"Mm?"

"I have been thinking."

He smiled into her hair. "That usually means trouble."

She frowned faintly. "I am serious."

"Aye. I ken."

She hesitated, then lifted her head just enough to look at him.

"Will it hurt the babe?"

He blinked. "Will what hurt the babe?"

She gestured vaguely between them. "You."

A beat passed.

Then Andrew laughed. Not politely. Not gently. It burst out of him before he could stop it, warm and startled and entirely unguarded.

"Christ, Zing..." He cut himself off, still smiling. "That's... no."

She pulled back at once, eyes wide. "No?"

"No," he said, still grinning. "I promise ye, I'm no a battering ram."

She studied his face, unconvinced. "But you are... very large."

That did it. He laughed again, harder this time, pressing his forehead to hers.

"God help me," he murmured. "You're killin' me."

"Andrew, I am not jesting."

He sobered then, not fully, but enough, cupping her cheek.

"Listen tae me," he said softly. "I love how careful ye are. Truly. But it will nae harm the bairn. Women have lain with their husbands while carryin' children longer than either of us have drawn breath."

She still looked unsure.

"Perhaps I should speak to a healer," she said,

He smiled, slower now, affectionate, touched clean through.

"If that's what ye need tae feel safe, then aye. We'll do that."

She relaxed at last, settling back against him.

"You are laughing at me."

"Nae..." he said, kissing her hair. "I'm laughin' because I love ye... and... because ye've the purest mind of any woman I've ever shared a bed with."

She smiled then, pleased despite herself.

"So... we should not be intimate?"

He chuckled. "If ye wish tae wait, we'll wait."

His hand slid, teasing but unhurried.

"But there are other ways tae make a man feel loved."

"Andrew."

"Aye?"

"You are impossible."

He grinned. "And yet, here ye are."

She kissed him, laughing, and any thoughts of harm to the babe were well and truly forgotten before the candles burned low.

Among Women

The morning came gently.

Nzingha woke with her eyes still closed and rolled toward Andrew out of habit, seeking his warmth. Her hand met parchment instead. She smiled before she even opened her eyes.

Good morning, my love,
Our counsel summoned me early. I hate leaving you alone. Your breakfast waits on my desk.
Haemish is guarding the door. I have sent for Annabella. Take care of our babe.

I love you.
Andrew.

There was a knock at the door.

Nzingha straightened when she heard Haemish's voice.

"My lady. Lady Annabella is here."

She reached for Andrew's plaid on the bed and pulled it around herself before opening the door.

"Good morning, Haemish. Thank you."

She turned to Annabella with a small smile. "Come in, pretty Bella."

Annabella smiled at Haemish. "Thank you, Haemish."

She pressed the parchment to her lips, still smiling when the knock came.

"My lady," Haemish said through the door, his voice pitched just a touch too formally. "Lady Annabella is here."

Nzingha wrapped Andrew's plaid around herself before opening the door.

"Good morning, Haemish," she said warmly.

He bowed deeply and very deliberately kept his eyes anywhere but on her bare shoulders. His gaze flicked instead to Annabella, who stood just behind him, bundled against the cold and pink-cheeked from more than the morning air. He smiled at her, awkward and fleeting.

"Good... morning," he said, clearing his throat.

Annabella slipped past him at once. Haemish straightened, fixed his eyes on the opposite wall, and might as well have been carved from stone for all the movement he allowed himself.

The door shut.

Nzingha turned slowly, one brow lifting.

Annabella exhaled like she had been holding it since the corridor. "He is impossible."

Nzingha laughed, a soft, delighted sound. "Oh no. He is terrified."

"That is not funny."

"For a man that size, it is a little funny," Nzingha said, grinning.

Annabella dropped onto the edge of the bed with a groan. "If I so much as breathe too loudly, he looks like he's about to confess to a crime."

Nzingha crossed the room and tugged open the trunk. "Come. Help me dress. These clothes belonged to Andrew's mother, and I am convinced she despised women."

Annabella laughed and produced the stays like contraband.

Nzingha recoiled at once. "Absolutely not."

Annabella gave a wide smile. "But they support..."

"Annabella. I am with child. I will not be trussed like a roast bird," Nzingha said, grinning.

Annabella smiled, unsurprised. "I thought you might say that."

They settled for softer layers instead. Annabella worked the laces while Nzingha shifted, then shifted again.

"Not tight. I enjoy breathing."

"I am not trying to kill you," frustration spewed from Annabella.

"You are considering it," Nzingha said.

Annabella snorted. There was a pause, followed by a laugh she tried and failed to swallow.

Nzingha watched her for a long moment, head tilted, amusement gathering rather than bursting.

"You grow very quiet when he is near," she said mildly, pointing at her friend's face. "And very pink."

Annabella froze, hands still tangled in fabric.

Nzingha studied her, then burst into laughter, pointing. "Oh... you like Haemish."

"And what makes you think that?" Annabella asked too quickly.

"You turn red when he clears his throat."

"That is not true."

Nzingha's gaze slid to her face. "You are red now."

Annabella groaned and collapsed onto the bed. "You are unbearable."

"And yet," Nzingha said pleasantly, "you have not denied it."

Annabella pressed a finger to her lips and seized Nzingha by the hand, dragging her toward the far side of the chamber as if the walls themselves might be listening.

"Must you say it so loudly?"

Nzingha laughed outright. "It is no secret. He already knows."

"No, he does not."

"He absolutely does."

Annabella covered her face with both hands. "Fine. Yes. I like him."

Nzingha hummed, deeply satisfied.

"And before you say anything," Annabella added quickly, "no... I did not give him my innocence."

"I was not going to ask that," Nzingha said.

Annabella peeked between her fingers. "You weren't?"

"No. I was going to ask why you are sitting like someone who has just survived a storm."

That broke her.

Annabella laughed, sharp and helpless, the sound spilling out before she could stop it.

Outside the door, Haemish caught it and failed, just barely, to hide the crooked smirk that tugged at his mouth.

"On the island, we would speak for hours," Annabella said once she could breathe again. "I would tell him about Ireland. He would speak on his clan and how he despises porridge."

"Oh, everyone despises porridge," Nzingha said gravely.

"And then he kissed me."

Nzingha's brows lifted. "Mm."

"And then he stopped."

"Oh, gods."

"He said he did not wish to ruin me."

Nzingha snorted. "Men become philosophers when they are frightened."

"I thought perhaps he found me plain."

Nzingha crossed the room at once and lifted Annabella's face in her hands. "Look at me. You are beautiful. You are kind. And you make him forget how to speak."

Annabella smiled, small and shaky. "He said that."

"Of course he did. And then?"

Annabella leaned closer, voice dropping despite herself. "He said there were other ways."

Nzingha's grin spread slowly. "Hahaha. Of course he did."

"And then," Annabella whispered, "he used his mouth."

Nzingha laughed outright, clapping a hand over her own lips. "Oh, absolutely."

Annabella flushed. "Is that... normal?"

"In my homeland," Nzingha said easily, "it is encouraged."

"Encouraged?"

"Yes. Especially if a man wishes to remain alive."

Annabella laughed so hard she had to brace herself. "I nearly fainted."

"And did you?"

"No," she admitted. "But I forgot my own name."

Their laughter spilled together then, bright, unchecked, the sort that comes only once the worst secrets have already been spoken.

After a time, Annabella grew quiet.

"I think I love him."

Nzingha's smile softened. "That will complicate things."

"Yes."

"But love often does."

"My family will never allow it."

"Mine did not either."

Annabella looked up sharply.

"I loved Mikel," Nzingha said plainly. "And it was forbidden. He was killed for it."

Silence settled, heavier now, truer.

"I did not love Andrew at first," she went on. "I did not even like him. He was arrogant. Irritating. He spoke too much."

"And now?"

"He grew on me."

Annabella smiled, thoughtful. "Haemish is irritating."

"There you have it."

They finished dressing, fixed Annabella's hair with ribbons. When the door opened, Haemish straightened so quickly he nearly struck the lintel.

"Haemish," Nzingha said sweetly, "we are walking to the study. You may escort us."

He swallowed. "Aye. Gladly."

As they passed, Annabella brushed his arm.

"Haemish," Nzingha called.

"Aye, miss?"

"Do not forget our conversation. Remember... let it be like the flood."

Run Away

After Andrew's meeting, he stopped by the study to gather a few books for Nzingha. He recalled a conversation they'd shared when they first met, her fondness for stories about knights and damsels in distress, the sort of nonsense he'd never given much thought to.

Andrew shook his head to himself.

I'm a fierce sea captain, he thought, *and here I am huntin' for books on love and romance. Have ye ever seen such a thing?*

He located several volumes that had once belonged to his mother. Running his fingers along the spines, he read each title aloud, one by one.

"Let me see... hmm... *Romeo and Juliette... Macbeth...*" He paused, squinting. "Christopher Marlowe... *The Passionate Shepherd to His Love.* Hmph." He nodded to himself. "She should like that."

He heard the door open and close again.

Andrew turned, expecting to see someone between the shelves. There was no one.

Frowning, he stepped out into the open space of the study.

"Who goes there?"

A soft female voice answered from behind him.

"It is me, my Laird."

Andrew stiffened. "Amelia?" He turned fully now. "What are ye doin' in here? Have ye a message from Alex?"

"Nae." She smiled as she spoke, already loosening the ties of her gown. "I thought I should speak with you in private. I have not seen you since you arrived." Her voice dropped. "Do you not miss me, my Laird?"

"Amelia, don your clothing," Andrew snapped.

She giggled and moved closer. He stepped back and struck the edge of a table.

"My Laird," she murmured, pressing nearer. "I have missed you so much. I have gone months without your touch." She reached for him. "Take me on this table, as you have done once before."

She pressed her bare breast against his chest and kissed him, her tongue slipping boldly into his mouth.

Laughter and voices echoed in the corridor.

The study door opened, and Nzingha froze.

Haemish stood there with Annabella beside him, but Nzingha saw only one thing. A naked woman pressed against Andrew, his mouth still caught in a kiss that had not yet broken.

Andrew reacted instantly, shoving Amelia away from him. The room went dead still. Tears burned in Nzingha's eyes as she turned and fled the study without a word.

She took the stairs two at a time, heart pounding, reaching the fourth landing before bursting into the chamber. Her hands shook as she gathered what she could, her daggers, bracelets, necklace, and Andrew's mother's sealskin cloak.

Heavy boots thundered down the corridor.

Andrew.

She dropped to the floor and rolled beneath the bed just as the door flew open.

"NZINGHA!" Andrew's voice filled the room. "Nzingha, are ye in here? Shit!"

The door slammed shut.

She waited. Counted breaths.

Peeking out from beneath the bed, she listened.

Silence.

Nzingha crawled free and slipped into the hall. Seeing no one, she pulled the cloak's hood over her head and wrapped a scarf across her mouth and nose.

She moved quickly through the keep, reaching the great hall where guards and servants passed in loose clusters. She forced herself to walk calmly, head lowered, and slipped out through the main entry.

Outside, the cold air hit her full on.

She had no plan. No destination.

Only one thought mattered.

I must leave this place.

She made her way toward the stables, recognizing the path from their first arrival. Crouched behind a stone wall, she watched as guards mounted their horses and rode off in frantic directions, green plaids snapping sharply in the wind.

When the moment came, she moved.

Nzingha mounted an already saddled horse and swung into place.

A young boy shouted just as she turned the reins.

"Hey! That is nae your horse! Haemish will give me a wallop if he goes missin', please, dinnae take it!"

She tore the bracelet from her wrist and flung it toward him.

"Take this," she said sharply. "Tell Haemish I am sorry."

The boy froze, eyes fixed on the gold in his hand.

His fingers loosened.

Nzingha spurred the horse and rode hard into the forest.

Chapter 16

Ye Wee Devil

After Nzingha stormed out of the study, Andrew shoved Amelia away and turned on Haemish without a moment's pause. Annabella stood frozen near the doorway, witness to it all.

"Get a guard," he snapped at Haemish. "Lock her up till I decide what's tae be done."

Amelia cried out behind him. "My Laird, my apologies, I did not..."

"Haud your tongue," Andrew cut in sharply, not even turning. "Ye've caused enough trouble already. I told ye tae dress and leave, and instead ye flung yourself at me like a whore from a brothel. Ye'll answer for it."

He stepped out of the study and slammed the door behind him, the echo ringing through the corridor. His chest heaved as he dragged a hand through his hair.

"Damn it," he muttered. "I told Alex tae keep her well away from me."

He turned back to Haemish, lowering his voice as Annabella hovered nearby, pale and shaken.

"Escort Lady Annabella back tae her chambers," he said firmly. "Then find a guard tae see Amelia tae the servants' quarters. Post one at her door. I dinnae want any more tricks or temptations."

He wiped his mouth hard with his forearm where Amelia had kissed him.

Haemish hesitated, reading the anger still burning in Andrew's face. "The cellar, my Laird?"

Andrew exhaled sharply. "Nae. Too harsh. I spoke in fury. Lock her in her chambers instead. I'll deal with her later when I can think straight."

Without another word, Andrew took the stairs two at a time. Nzingha's temper could be fierce, and he braced himself for the worst as he reached their chamber door.

"Nzingha," he called, pushing it open. "Nzingha, are ye in here?"

The room was empty.

"Shit."

He slammed the door and thundered back down the stairwell, stopping short at the third landing, Alex's chamber. His brother had mentioned earlier he planned to lie down before checking the stocks.

Andrew flung the door open.

His whore of a brother lay flat on his back while a woman rode him like a stallion.

Andrew caught sight of her bare breast and turned sharply away. "A nap, my arse! Damn it, Alex, I need a word with ye now!"

He stepped back into the corridor and slammed the door.

Moments later, Alex emerged with nothing but his plaid wrapped low around his waist.

"What is it?" Alex demanded. "What's got ye tearing through the keep like a madman?"

"I cannae find Nzingha."

Alex's humor vanished. "Is she hale?"

"Nae." Andrew exhaled hard. "Amelia followed me into the study, stripped herself bare, and threw herself at me. I ordered her tae stop, but before I could blink, Haemish, Annabella, and Nzingha walked in. She saw everything."

Alex barked a laugh. "Ye've not been home a full day and ye're already knee-deep in shite, ye wee devil."

Andrew rounded on him. "Haud yer wheesht! I'm nae jestin', Alex. She's gone. Just help me find her."

Alex swore under his breath and vanished back into his chamber. A moment later, the woman slipped out, eyes downcast.

"Pardon me, my Laird," she muttered, fleeing down the hall.

Alex reappeared, tugging his shirt over his head. "We'll check the great hall first. Then the stables."

They moved fast. Servants, guards, even elders were questioned. Andrew's temper frayed with every answer.

"Christ," he swore. "She's the only dark-skinned woman in this bloody castle, and none of ye saw her?"

They reached the stables at last.

"Christopher," Alex called.

The stable boy peered out from behind a stall. "Aye, Laird Alex?"

Andrew stepped forward. "Did ye see the lass we arrived with pass through here?"

"The almond-colored lady?" the boy said. "Aye. She came through in a hurry and jumped on Haemish's black stallion. I told her it was nae hers tae take."

He swallowed and held something out. "She threw this at me and rode off."

Alex took the gold bracelet and turned it over in his hand. "Christ," he murmured. He scraped it with his dagger, no mark. Tried to bend it, nothing. "Andrew... this is real gold. This alone could cover half the debt tae the Crown."

Andrew snatched it from him. "It's Nzingha's. I'll nae use her like that."

He swung up onto his horse. "Are ye comin'?"

"Aye."

Andrew pointed sharply. "Check the forest. I'll ride toward Annabella's father's galleon. Meet back here in two hours. If we've nae found her by then, I'll raise a search party."

Stranger to These Lands

Deep in the forest, Nzingha rode without direction, the world around her vast and unfamiliar, closing in with every step the horse took beneath her. The trees rose taller than any she had known, their branches knitted thick with green that seemed to swallow light whole.

"Why did I not go to the ship?" she muttered, slowing the stallion as she stared about her in wonder. "I have never seen such green."

Life moved everywhere. Rabbits flashed through the brush and vanished as quickly as they appeared. Small birds, brighter than jewels, hovered over blossoms she had never seen, their wings humming like whispers. When she breathed, the air itself answered her, pale fog blooming before her mouth and disappearing again.

She laughed, breathless and delighted despite herself. "So cold," she murmured. "And so alive."

She followed the sound of water until the trees opened onto a narrow stream. Dismounting, she let the stallion drink while she stepped aside to tend to her own needs, the forest oddly quiet around her. She had only just straightened when movement caught her eye.

Three men stepped from the trees.

They were filthy. Clothes stiff with grime. Hair matted. Skin dark with sweat and rot. The smell reached her a moment later, thick enough to turn her stomach. She covered her nose briefly, then lowered her hand and smiled, careful and polite.

"Good day to you."

One of them laughed, low and ugly. "Well now. What have we here?" His gaze crawled over her. "A negro lass wanderin' alone in Scotland. Ye run from a ship, then?"

Nzingha laughed outright. "Absolutely not. The Laird brought me here to be his wife."

That gave them pause, only a moment. Another man's eyes dropped to her hand, to the diamond ring glinting there, and his smile sharpened.

"And which Laird might that be?"

She slipped her hands casually into her pockets, fingers brushing the familiar comfort of steel.

"Did the Laird nae warn ye?" one of them said softly, stepping closer. "There are reivers in these woods. Men who'll sell ye."

He rushed her.

There was no thought, no hesitation. Her body moved as it had been trained to move. Steel flashed, and his throat opened beneath her blade in a wet, startled sound.

"Richard!" one of the others screamed. "That bitch killed Richard!"

The remaining two charged together. Her cloak caught at her legs, heavy and cursed, dragging her just enough to steal her speed.

These clothes will kill me, she thought grimly.

She tore the cloak free and spun as one man lunged, slicing his arm as he reached for her.

"You black cunt," he snarled through his pain. "We'll take turns with ye, then sell what's left."

A voice cut through the forest like iron striking stone.

"Try it, and I'll hang ye from the nearest tree."

Nzingha turned, heart hammering. "Alex!"

The last man rushed her in blind fury, slamming her to the ground with his weight. Pain exploded through her shoulder as they rolled. She flung her dagger upward, caught it by instinct, and drove it into him again and again until his body finally went slack.

By the time she looked up, Alex stood over the carnage, wiping blood from his sword as though it were nothing more than rain.

Breathing hard, Nzingha pushed the body from her and staggered to the stream. She washed her hands and face, watching the water cloud red and clear again before she turned back to him.

"My thanks."

"Andrew's tearing Scotland apart lookin' for ye," Alex said.

"Well," she replied coldly, gripping the horse's reins, "let him."

"Ye cannae leave," Alex said, sharper now. "Not alone. These men were only the first."

"I'll take my chances."

She took one step, and the world tipped.

Her knees buckled.

Alex was off his horse in an instant. "My Lady, are ye hale?"

She grabbed the reins and swayed. Before he could reach her, she retched uncontrollably.

Nzingha's world went black.

Alex gathered her up at once and turned his horse back toward the keep, keeping the pace slow and steady with her draped across the saddle.

When she woke, Andrew's face filled her vision. She blinked once, twice, then Alex came into focus beside him, the world still blurred and swimming.

"Put me down," she murmured, trying to rise. "I must leave."

"Nae," Alex said firmly, holding her steady. "Ye took a nasty blow. Ye fainted. And if anything happens tae you, or the bairn, Andrew will kill me."

"Bairn?" she whispered, pain blooming behind her eyes. "You know?"

Alex snorted. "My brother keeps nae secrets from me."

Her head throbbed as the horse shifted beneath them. The forest slid past in green and shadow, and despite her will, darkness crept in again, pulling her under as they rode

I Wanted Blood

Haemish was already coming down the keep's stairs when Alex

reined in. He moved quickly, boots striking stones as he crossed the yard.

Alex carefully handed Nzingha's limp body over to him.

"She took a nasty hit to the head," Alex said, keeping his voice low. "I'm going tae fetch the castle's healer. Take her straight tae Andrew's chamber."

Haemish nodded once, his jaw tight, and adjusted his grip as though she might break if handled too roughly.

He lifted his voice just enough to be heard.

"Fetch Lady Annabella," he called to one of the guards. "Bring her tae Laird Andrew's chamber."

Nzingha woke slowly.

The first thing she saw was Annabella's face, pale and tight with worry. Beside her stood another woman, older, broad-shouldered, calm, her presence solid, a leather basket resting against her hip.

It took a moment longer for Nzingha to realize she was in Andrew's chambers.

"My Lady," the healer said gently, fingers pressing along the side of her head. "There's a lump here. It'll pain ye for a few days. I'd have given ye milk of the poppy, but Lady Annabella says ye're with child. I'll set a warm compress against the swelling instead."

"My thanks," Nzingha murmured, her voice rough. "But I wish only to sleep."

The healer began gathering her basket.

"Wait." Nzingha lifted her hand, weak but insistent.

"Aye, miss?"

Her breath caught before the words came. "Is... is all right with my babe?"

The healer straightened fully and smiled, calm and certain.

"Aye. The babe is perfectly fine."

The breath Nzingha released felt as though she had been holding it for hours.

"Can you tell how far along I am with this pregnancy?"

"I can check, if ye like."

Nzingha nodded. "Yes, please. I would like that."

The healer washed her hands at the washstand, then returned to the bed. She pulled the covers back carefully and lifted Nzingha's shift.

Her hands pressed, measured, waited.

The babe kicked once.

Then again.

Then a third time.

"Well now," the healer said softly. "All right. I'll check ye further."

She inserted two fingers, quick and practiced, then withdrew and washed her hands once more.

"From the looks of it, ye're in the fourth or fifth moon cycle. I'd say fifth, by the way the babe moves." She studied Nzingha closely. "Your stomach's small because ye're malnourished. If ye want the babe tae survive, ye must begin eating fruits, vegetables, and meat. Blood clots and bleeding are dangers otherwise. And if ye wish tae survive the birthing, greens especially are vital."

Nzingha laid a hand over her stomach. "My stomach will not allow me to eat."

The healer rummaged through her basket and produced a knotted piece of ginger root.

"Chew this, but dinnae swallow it. I'll have a servant bring a kettle tae keep by the hearth. Make tea from it. It'll help the sickness." She paused. "I'll also have them bring meat and vegetables. And no more horse riding until after the babe is born."

She moved toward the door, then turned back once more.

"I'll return in the morning tae check on ye."

"My thanks," Nzingha said.

When the healer exited, Annabella pulled a chair close and sat beside the bed.

"How do ye feel?" she asked quietly.

"Like I was struck in the head," Nzingha replied.

Annabella hesitated, then leaned in.

"Zingha... if I tell you something, will you hear me out?"

"Yes."

"It was nae Andrew's fault."

Nzingha looked at her and rolled her eyes faintly.

"I'm telling you the truth," Annabella insisted. "He went to the study to fetch you more books. The servant girl followed him. She undressed herself. He ordered her to stop, but she ignored him. After you left, he had her locked away for insubordination. From what Haemish says, she's being sent away so she causes no further trouble. Andrew never betrayed you."

"He does not need to send her away," Nzingha said quietly. "From what he told me earlier, we are leaving this castle regardless. We are moving to his mother's dowager house. I do not know where it is, but I trust it will be better than here."

Annabella smiled softly.

"So you forgive him? He's still out looking for you."

Nzingha sighed. "I forgive him. Now that I know what truly happened."

Annabella exhaled.

"From what Haemish says, it's a good thing you're leaving. Many women throw themselves at Laird Andrew. They've even brawled over him. He was a prized bachelor. Haemish says he'd rather you not kill anyone."

Nzingha chuckled and winced slightly, touching her head.

"Ah. Haemish knows me all too well."

Her voice softened. "Annabella... I was afraid today. Those men meant to ravage me, to sell me. I was slow, weak, trapped by a dress that weighed a ton. I nearly died. I could have lost my babe."

She swallowed.

"And everywhere I go here, people stare at me. As if I am filth. I should have asked Andrew to escort me home, but he was so determined that I come here before he knew I carried his child. Now he knows... there is no way he would let me leave. Only if I told him I did not love him. And that would be a lie. I love him too much."

Annabella reached for her hand.

"Give his people time. Dine with them. Speak with them. Show them you're human. Those men today were thugs. They deserved what they got. If not you, it would have been someone else. You cannot hide forever."

Nzingha squeezed her hand. "When I am better, I will join them for supper."

The chamber door opened. Andrew stood there, worry etched deep across his face.

"How is she?" he asked at once.

"I am fine," Nzingha said, gazing at him.

Annabella stood. "My Laird. I'll return in the morning when the healer comes back."

"My thanks," Nzingha said.

Andrew nodded as Annabella exited.

He crossed the room, boots heavy on the floor, and sat beside her. The bed dipped beneath his weight.

"How's the bairn?" he asked quietly.

"The babe is fine. I have been placed on bed rest. And ordered to eat more."

She tried to sit up. Andrew steadied her.

"My thanks," she said softly. "I want to apologize for running off the way I did. Seeing a naked woman with her hands all over you set a fire inside me. If I had stayed... someone would have died."

"And ye got yer wish in the woods," Andrew replied gently. "Alex told me what happened."

"Alex?"

"Aye. He said ye were punched in the head, but ye ran two men through before he reached ye. He was impressed."

"I thought I was going to die," she admitted. "My dress was so heavy. Thank God Alex came when he did."

Andrew closed his eyes and kissed her forehead.

"I should've sent Amelia away the moment we arrived."

"I know," Nzingha said. "We have women like her in Mbemba Kingdom as well."

"Nzingha," he murmured, pressing his lips to her stomach, "ye must ken my days of being a rake are long past. I care only for ye and our bairn."

"Your stomach is so tiny," he added softly.

"Yes. I am between four and five moons. The healer says I am malnourished."

Andrew's hand stilled.

"The babe kicked," he said quietly, awe softening his voice. "That's my bairn. Feisty. Just like her mother."

After murmuring at the child and resting his hand there, exhaustion finally claimed him. He snored softly.

Nzingha tapped his shoulder and spoke softly into the dim.

"Andrew?"

"Hm?" he answered, half asleep.

She laid a hand over her stomach.

"I am hungry."

Chapter 17

An Mbemba Princess.

*T*wo days passed since Nzingha had been placed on bed rest.

In those two days, restlessness crept into her bones.

The confinement of four stone walls plagued her. She longed for movement, for air, for the familiar ache of training beside her uncle Femi and Mikel, days when her body had been honed for war and purpose. She had lived and breathed as a warrior. That life had shaped her.

Now, as her hand drifted to the gentle swell of her stomach, she felt the life stirring within her.

Her world had changed.

But she did not yet know whether it had changed for the better... or simply changed forever.

Each morning, Andrew departed early for council meetings. Without fail, he returned afterward to spend his nooning with her, spending two full hours before leaving again to train in the lists. Annabella, meanwhile, had received word that her family would arrive within the sennight to escort her home. Knowing the strain, it would place upon them should she remain, Annabella accepted her fate and prepared to depart.

Servants moved steadily through the chambers in the days that followed, packing Andrew's and Nzingha's belongings in preparation for their journey to Leith.

When her strength finally returned, Nzingha chose to join the clan for the evening meal. Only two nights remained at Tantallon Castle.

Annabella helped her dress.

Earlier in the week, Andrew had summoned a seamstress to attend Nzingha personally. The woman had stared in wonder as Nzingha described the garments she wished made, colors bold, lines free, movement favored over restraint. The seamstress admitted she had never seen such designs, nor colors that so richly complemented a woman's skin.

That night, Nzingha wore a gown inspired by Mbemba tradition.

The amber satin, imported from France, caught the candlelight as though lit from within. The collar was cuffed. The skirt flowed freely, slit high for ease of movement. The bodice covered her bosom, though the neckline dipped lower than custom allowed in Scotland.

There were no stays. No petticoats.

Only her.

To soften the boldness, she had asked for a pleated cape to be sewn into the back, something she could draw around herself if needed.

Still, as the chill kissed her skin, doubt followed.

Her hair was drawn high into a ponytail; the ends curled into small pin loops. A strip of royal blue and amber cloth was braided and wrapped across her brow, a quiet mark of Mbemba heritage.

Andrew entered the chamber just as she polished her jewelry at his desk.

He stopped.

For a long moment, he simply stared.

Nzingha turned, nerves tightening. She presented herself fully.

Andrew tilted his head, one brow lifting.

Annabella rose at once.

"Good eve, my Laird. Do you see how beautiful Nzingha looks this night?"

Andrew folded one arm across his chest, rubbing his chin thoughtfully.

"I dinnae know whether to ravage ye or hide ye away," he said at last. Then his mouth curved. "But if ye are happy, then I am happy. Ye look beautiful. My people will simply have to learn the woman I intend to marry."

Relief bloomed across Nzingha's face. Her smile struck him clean through the chest.

Annabella excused herself, leaving them alone.

Nzingha caught Andrew watching her again.

"What?" she asked softly. "You do not like my clothing?"

"Nae," he replied. "I'm reminded why I truly love ye."

She slipped her wrists into her gold tribal bracelets and lifted the necklace that rested in her palm, a heavy gold herringbone chain bearing a large garnet.

Andrew stepped closer.

"Allow me."

She hesitated.

"I do not know if I should continue wearing this."

A tear escaped her.

"Why would ye not?" he asked gently.

"There is a story behind this jewel."

"Then tell me. "He said, drawing her toward the hearth. "We have time."

They sat together as the fire crackled.

The Curse Behind the Jewels.

Before Mikel had ever spoken words of love, they traveled together on expeditions to Tafaria Island.

These journeys were not adventures, but vigilance. They were quiet patrols meant to intercept invaders who dared creep onto Tafaria's shores. Nzingha had trusted Mikel with her life long before she trusted him with her heart. He guarded her flank without question, learned her rhythm, matched her discipline.

One night, as they made camp near the cliffs of Tafaria, the elders' old stories surfaced again. They made whispers of the Fiery Caves, spoken only in low voices when the fire burned thin.

The elders said the caves belonged to Mpungu Tulendo, the fire-spirit of the deep earth, an aspect of Nkisi power that ruled flame and molten stone. The jewels within were not believed to be treasures, but offerings formed where the land itself bled. Gold ran through the rock in quiet veins, the gems shaped by heat far beneath the earth. They were beautiful, yes, but never spoken of without warning.

What Mpungu Tulendo created was not meant to be taken.

To remove a stone was to steal from the balance of the land, and when balance was broken, the earth demanded repayment.

Nzingha listened with interest, not fear.

She had grown up on such stories.

Later, as they watched the fire settle into embers, she spoke quietly, not as a princess, but as a warrior.

"My mother once told me that courage must be anchored. That a warrior must carry something that reminds her who she is when fear comes."

Mikel looked at her then, curious.

"The Queen wore a ring, not for beauty, but for remembrance. She said it steadied her hand."

Her gaze drifted toward the dark outline of the cliffs.

"I would like something like that. A piece of the earth itself. Not for ornament. But for strength."

Mikel gave her a look, steady and resolute. A plan had settled behind his eyes, unspoken and already decided.

After the warriors had fallen asleep, he woke Nzingha gently and took her hand.

"Follow me."

She blinked, still half asleep. "Where are you taking me?"

"To the caves," he said quietly. "I found a path, one that leads to an opening."

Without another word, she smiled and rose with him, her fingers tightening around his. Curiosity stirred within her as a childhood wish, one she had never truly believed would be fulfilled, began to take shape.

When they entered the Tafaria caves, the air thickened at once. Heat pressed against their skin. Steam clung to their lungs. Each step deeper felt like trespass. The stone walls glowed faintly, streaked with red and gold veins as though the earth itself bled fire.

They reached a vast chamber.

Before them, a lake spread of molten lava, slow and bright. Its light touched the cave walls, revealing gems trapped high in the stone. Gold ran through the rock in thin seams, catching the glow before disappearing again.

Nzingha's breath shortened, her chest burning as the heat pressed in around them. She knew then they had gone too far. Turning to Mikel, she said sharply, "We should leave, stubborn man."

She glanced back once more, her gaze drawn to the gems high in the stone. Their light flickered across the cave, and for a fleeting moment, temptation tugged at her, not for wealth or beauty, but for something solid to anchor courage against fear.

She exhaled slowly and lowered her gaze.

"No," she said at last, more to herself than to him. "That is not how courage is carried."

She turned toward Mikel. "My uncle used to tell me that bravery is not something you collect," she said, "It is not taken from the earth, or forged by fire, or worn around the neck so others may see it. It lives here." She pressed two fingers to her chest. "And it lives here." She touched her temple.

"If a warrior must rely on an object to remind her who she is, then she has already begun to forget."

Her eyes lifted once more to the ceiling of the cave, to the stones gleaming in the firelight.

"These belong to Mpungu Tulendo," she said softly. "They are not meant to steady our hands. They are meant to test them. I was wrong for wanting such a treasure."

She shook her head, a faint smile touching her mouth.

"I suppose courage must come from within."

That was when the heat overtook her.

She collapsed.

When Nzingha awoke, she was in her tent, cooled and wrapped in damp cloth. She sat up, then pushed herself to her feet and stepped outside.

The camp lay quiet near the riverbank, embers dimming in the fire pit. She followed the sound of water and found him at the river's edge, seated with his back slightly bent, both hands submerged in the current. His shoulders were drawn tight. At the sound of her approach, he went still.

"Mikel," she said sharply. "Do not turn away from me."

He exhaled slowly but did not look up.

"What did you do?" Her voice shook now, anger cutting through fear. "Tell me what you did."

"It is nothing," he said, "You fainted. I carried you out. That is all."

She stepped closer. "Lift your hands."

He hesitated.

"Mikel."

Slowly, he drew them from the water.

Her breath caught.

Blisters crawled across his skin, raw and angry. Burns streaked his forearms and crept beneath the edge of his warrior cloth. Her eyes lifted to his chest, where the cloth was darkened and torn.

"Why did you not listen, fool? You went back," she whispered.

He said nothing.

"After everything the elders warned us about. After I told you to leave?"

"I could not," he said quietly.

She struck his shoulder, not hard enough to wound, but hard enough to be felt. "You are reckless. Mad. Do you have no respect for the land? For Mpungu Tulendo?"

He finally looked at her then.

"I have respect for you."

She laughed bitterly. "That is not respect. That is foolish pride."

"No," he said, "That is devotion."

She turned away and paced a few steps before stopping.

"I heard stones fall before I collapsed. I heard them break loose. You climbed where you should not have."

"Yes, I did."

She looked back at him, waiting.

"The stone beneath my foot shifted," he explained quietly. "I had already started up the wall. When it gave way, the loose rock fell into the lava below. I could not stop it."

"And the fire?" she asked.

"When the gravel struck the lava, it splashed upward. Not far, just enough to reach me."

She took that in, her brow tightening. "Enough to burn you."

"Yes."

She turned again, pacing slowly now, her voice steady but strained.

"And after that happened, after you saw what the cave could do, you still went on."

"I did."

"Why?" she asked, stopping and facing him fully. "Why would you keep climbing after that?"

He stepped closer and gently pressed it into her hand before she could refuse.

"It is not for beauty," he said, "You know that. It is for courage."

Her fingers closed around the stone without intention. It was still warm.

"When fear comes, you remember who you are."

She stared at him, understanding settling slowly.

She stared at him, her chest tightening, her heartbeat loud in her ears. "You would steal from Mpungu Tulendo? You would risk his wrath for this?"

"I would walk into the fire itself, if it meant you never doubted your strength."

Tears gathered in her eyes. "You will die for this one day," she said, her voice breaking despite herself. "Do you understand that?"

He smiled then, not with pride, not with foolish bravado, but with a quiet gentleness that undid her.

"If that day comes, then I will have lived knowing I loved you without fear."

Silence settled between them, heavy and unbroken, as though the land itself listened.

That was the night he confessed his love.

And it was the night Nzingha learned that courage, once shared, could be just as dangerous as fear.

Years later, he would die because he loved her. She was the jewel, one he was never meant to claim. Long before him, her mother had walked into the same fire and never returned.

The Great Hall

When the doors to the great hall opened, warmth rolled toward Nzingha at once, thick with firelight and the scent of roasted meat. Voices carried across stone walls, softened by the long tables already set for the evening meal. Steak and tatties lay steaming on trenchers, carrots glazed with butter, bread torn by hand and passed from place to place.

Conversation did not stop, but it changed.

She felt it in the way heads turned. In the pause before cups were lifted again. In the quiet stretch where people took her in without meaning to stare.

Andrew's hand rested firmly at her waist.

"Stay close," he murmured. "They mean nae harm. They're only curious."

At the dais, Alex rose first. His face broke into an easy smile as he stepped forward.

"Well," he said warmly, glancing between them, "I see my brother was telling the truth for once."

A ripple of laughter followed, easing the tension.

Andrew leaned closer to her ear. "Breathe," he whispered. "Ye're among friends."

They were seated, and food was set before her. She ate sparingly at first, aware of her movements, of the quiet attention that followed her. Questions came gently, about where she was from, about her journey, about the way she spoke.

One of the elders studied her openly.

"Ye are… striking," he said, not unkindly. "Do all yer people share the same skin? And your eyes are sharp. Like a she-wolf."

Nzingha met his gaze calmly.

"There are many shades among my people," she said, "Dark brown, light brown, even some nearly white. Scholars in my father's court believed the sun shapes us, just as the cold shapes you."

A murmur of interest followed.

A small boy at the dais leaned forward. "What is it like where you come from?"

She smiled at him.

"Very hot. There is no snow in the part of Africa where I am from. It is summer all year."

One of the aldermen's wives laughed softly. "I cannot imagine such a place. Summer all year? Take me with you."

Another woman leaned forward, curious. "Is English the tongue of your people?"

"No," Nzingha replied gently. "We speak what is called the language of the Swahili coast, the traders' tongue. It is spoken along the shores and in the ports where many peoples meet."

A man across the table nodded. "Aye. Our folk speak Gaelic. How did ye come tae ken English so well?"

"As a king's daughter," Nzingha said, "I was taught many languages by scholars who came from across Africa and from distant lands. It was required at court. Trade demands understanding."

She paused, then added, "I was also taught numbers, alchemy, and the reading of maps."

Alex's brows lifted. "And your homeland, there is war, aye?"

"Yes," she answered, her tone sobering. "Men, women, and even children are forced to fight. Many nations come for our gold and our people. Some to trade. Others to steal."

Before she could continue, Graham's voice cut in.

"Aye," he said, leaning back in his chair. "I've heard of it. Slaves taken by the thousands. Shipped to the New World to work the fields," he said, "Sugar, tobacco, cotton. It's said to be a profitable trade."

The table went still.

Nzingha's hand tightened around her cutlery. Before she could speak, Andrew's chair scraped back.

"Enough," he said, his voice firm, controlled. "There is a difference between honest labor and chains. Between work and cruelty. I've seen those ships with my own eyes. We've broken them open. Pulled people from holds meant for cattle."

Alex stood beside him. "We did," he said quietly. "And we'll do it again."

Andrew turned back to Graham. "So mind your tongue, Uncle."

Graham lowered his gaze, the tension easing from his face. After a moment, he rose from his chair and stepped toward her, bowing slightly as he took her hand with practiced courtesy.

"My apologies, my lady," he said evenly. "I spoke without weighin' my words. That was ill done o' me."

Nzingha inclined her head. "No offence taken."

He released her hand slowly. His eyes drifted, not to her face this time, but to the ring at her finger, then higher, to the necklace resting at her throat. His interest appeared idle, almost thoughtful.

"That is a fine stone," he said, "Fit for a queen, if ever I saw one. It suits you well. Was it brought from your homeland?"

"It belonged to my mother," Nzingha replied. "It was passed to me when she died."

"A family piece, then," Graham said, nodding as though the thought pleased him. "Those are always the ones that carry the most weight."

His gaze lingered a moment longer before lifting again, polite and curious.

"And the jewel itself," he went on lightly. "Such stones are not common. Where would one come by something like that?"

"There are caves," Nzingha said calmly. "Places where the earth yields them."

"Caves," he repeated, tasting the word. "Aye. I've heard tell of such places. Lands where the ground itself keeps its treasures."

She hesitated then, just enough to feel it.

"They say," she continued after a breath, "that such places are not meant to be disturbed. That stones taken from them come at a cost."

Graham tilted his head, his expression open, inviting.

"Forgive me," he said gently. "You were saying?"

"The legends say," Nzingha finished quietly, "that those who remove stones from the caves do not live long."

For a moment, the space between them held.

Graham nodded slowly.

"A sobering belief," he said at last. "Your people hold deep respect for the land."

"Yes," she replied. "We do."

She drew in a steady breath and rose. "You must excuse me for a moment."

Andrew was on his feet before she had fully pushed back her chair.

"I'll go with ye," he said, already offering his hand.

Andrew guided her from the great hall at an unhurried pace, his hand resting lightly at the small of her back. The warmth followed them into the kitchens, where servants moved in steady rhythm, tending pots and platters, their voices low and purposeful. The air smelled of bread and roasted meat, of herbs crushed beneath fingers.

As they passed, a few servants glanced up. One smiled. Another murmured something about her gown. Nzingha kept her gaze forward, grateful when the sound of the hall faded behind them.

Once they reached the stair, she slowed, her breath easing.

"I am glad to leave," she said quietly. "They were kind, but I felt as though I was on display. Watched. Measured. Even their curiosity has weight."

Andrew nodded as they began the climb. "Aye. Curiosity can be heavier than judgment. Folk here are unused tae seein' someone so different. They mean nae harm, but they dinnae always ken when tae look away."

She glanced at him. "Do they ever?"

"Eventually," he said with a faint smile. "When the new becomes familiar."

They climbed in silence for a few steps, the stone cool beneath their feet. Torches cast long shadows along the walls. Guards straightened as Andrew passed, and he acknowledged them with a quiet nod.

"My uncle," he said after a moment, lowering his voice. "Ye must forgive him. He has a habit o' listenin' harder than he speaks. Ye never truly ken what's turnin' in his mind."

"I noticed," she replied. "He did not sound cruel. But he was… searching."

Andrew glanced back at her. "That's exactly it."

They emerged onto the ramparts, and the wind greeted them at once, sharp and clean. Andrew adjusted the tartan around her shoulders as she drew a breath and shivered.

"It is cold," she said, half laughing. "I do not know how you live in such a place. Stone everywhere. Even kindness feels as though it has walls."

Andrew turned to face her fully. "Ye wouldnae be trapped here," he said gently. "Walls can shelter as well as confine. What matters is whether ye have space tae breathe."

She nodded, considering his words.

A faint touch brushed her cheek.

She frowned and held out her hand. "Rain? It is already cold."

Something pale settled against her palm.

She stared.

"It does not fall like rain," she said slowly. "It is lighter. Like dust." She watched as it vanished against her skin. "It melts."

Andrew smiled at her wonder. "Nae. That's snow."

"Snow," she repeated, eyes widening. "I have only read of it. In books."

Another flake drifted down, resting briefly on her almond skin before disappearing.

She laughed, delight breaking through her composure. "It is beautiful," she said, "Cold, but beautiful."

Andrew watched her as the snow continued to fall, soft and silent around them.

"Aye," he said quietly. "It is."

Chapter 18

Scotland Winter

Morning came slowly, light filtering through the chamber before either of them stirred.

Andrew woke first. He lay watching her for a time, the steady rise and fall of her breath, the loose curl of her fingers against the linen. When he finally reached for her, his thumb brushed her cheek until her lashes fluttered.

"Good mornin', my wife."

She smiled before her eyes fully opened. "You are awake far too early. That usually means you are planning something."

"Aye. I might be. And before ye protest, I think it best ye dress."

She pushed herself up on one elbow, studying him with amused suspicion. "That is not an explanation. That is an order."

"A suggestion," he corrected, already moving toward his mother's old trunk. He lifted the lid and drew out a woolen gown, folded with care. "I ken ye'll dislike this, but ye'll dislike the cold far more."

She sighed, though the sound carried more humor than complaint, and allowed him to help her dress. "You Scots have an impressive faith in wool. I am beginning to believe you think it cures all things."

"It cures most." He handed her the cloak, then the mittens, then the scarf. "And before ye object, aye, every piece o' this is necessary."

"You are enjoying this far too much."

"I am enjoyin' the part where ye listen."

They walked together through the corridor, her arm resting easily in his. Just before the great hall, he stopped and lifted a cloth.

"I do not like that expression."

"Ye like me well enough."

"I like you best when I can see you. This feels suspicious."

"Trust me. I wouldna lead ye astray, especially so early in the day."

Cold air brushed her skin the moment they stepped outside.

"It is extremely cold. I do not understand how you live in such a place without complaint."

He laughed quietly. "We complain plenty. We just dress it up and pretend it's poetry."

Inside the carriage, she reached for him without thinking, her fingers finding his sleeve as he pulled her close beneath his cloak.

"You are enjoying my confusion."

"I am enjoyin' your curiosity. It suits ye."

By the time the carriage stopped, she was shivering despite the layers. "How much farther? If this involves another hill, I will not be pleased."

"All right. Stand there."

"I am trusting you entirely now."

The cloth was untied.

For a moment, she said nothing.

Then a soft laugh escaped her, blooming into wonder. "Oh, Andrew. This is snow."

White stretched before her as far as she could see. Trees stood softened beneath it. Stones vanished. The world felt quieter, gentler, as though it had been remade overnight.

"I have read about this in books and travelers' journals," she went on, words flowing freely now. "I always imagined it harsher, more unforgiving. But this is almost gentle."

She knelt and gathered a handful, watching it slip through her mittens. "It disappears. It does not wish to be held."

Her gaze lifted, bright and curious. "Does it always fall like this?"

"Sometimes. Sometimes it comes hard. Sometimes it takes the whole night tae settle."

"I think I would like to see all of it."

A small handful struck her shoulder.

She gasped, then laughed. "You did that deliberately."

"Of course I did."

She tried to return it, her throw clumsy and wide. "I will require instruction."

He crossed the distance between them and lifted her easily, turning once before setting her back on her feet.

"I wanted this for ye. Somethin' that belonged only tae this day. Only tae us."

She touched his face, her smile unguarded. "All the stories I have ever read feel nearer now. As though I have stepped inside them."

Snow continued to fall as he kissed her, slow and warm, sealing the moment in quiet joy.

A Gift for You

Four months had passed since Andrew and Nzingha arrived at Leith. Shortly after, they were wed in a small ceremony, quiet and unadorned, with only Alex, Haemish, and Annabella standing as witnesses. It was enough for them. Later, for the sake of Andrew's family and their customs, Nzingha agreed to a traditional ceremony as well.

When Nzingha's pregnancy reached its seventh month, Andrew stopped traveling across the seas, unwilling to be far from her so close to the babe's arrival. On occasion, he still rode to Tantallon to assist Alex with clan business, but he always returned the same day.

Even so, during those brief absences, Nzingha felt the loneliness keenly. Shortly after the ceremony, Annabella's family arrived and escorted her back to Ireland. That had been more than four months ago, leaving Nzingha without the support of another woman as her body changed in ways she did not yet fully understand.

She was not accustomed to a life of idleness. The dowager house felt hollow, its rooms too still. To pass the hours, she read whatever books she could find and wandered the grounds, yet there was nothing that truly needed her. She felt useless. In her former life as a princess, her days had been filled with purpose, with tending to those who relied on her. Here, in this unfamiliar land, she was unsure where she belonged, afraid to act or to move beyond what was expected of her. At times, she wondered whether love was worth the cost of leaving her title behind. She kept those thoughts to herself, unwilling to seem ungrateful, knowing that Andrew's love was steadfast and without limit.

She made an effort to form friendly relationships with the two servants who had come with them, one of whom served as a nursemaid. She relied on them to teach her needlework, something she had never learned in her homeland, where such tasks had not been expected of her as a princess.

Still, restlessness crept in. She painted portraits and studied plants used for healing. She even tended a small garden of herbs and vegetables with her own hands. Yet despite filling her days, a sense of emptiness lingered, as though she were merely passing time rather than living it.

When Nzingha lived in Kongo, her days had been filled with movement. She trained to fight, went on missions, and helped protect villages. She had never imagined herself as a domestic spouse, sitting idle and waiting for her husband to return.

As the later months of her pregnancy set in, her body slowed despite her will. She wondered at times whether she carried two babes, for her belly had grown enormous. The healer placed her on bed rest, but she ignored it whenever she could, continuing to move about simply to feel useful.

One afternoon, Nzingha sat on a blanket in the garden of the dowager property, eating from a bowl of apples and grapes. The sun was warm, the breeze gentle. Spring had finally begun to fade, and she welcomed the quiet comfort of being outdoors.

Andrew had an errand to run and went in search of his wife. Stepping out of the house, he spotted her at once, lying on her side in the garden with a book open in her hands. She took a generous bite of her apple, utterly absorbed in the pages before her.

As he approached, he called out to her, a smile already in his voice.

"Will ye save me an apple?"

Nzingha lowered the book and tried to sit up, rocking gently from side to side as her body resisted the movement. Her belly had grown so large that finding her footing had become an effort of its own. When Andrew reached her and laughed, she scowled and swatted him with the book.

"Oh, you laugh. You think I'm a whale?"

"Nae, lass. Ye're bonnie. That's our wee bairn growin' inside ye."

He stretched out his hand and helped her up.

"My poor wife. If the bairn grows any bigger, ye'll nae be walkin' at all."

Nzingha took a drink of water.

"I am ready for this to be over."

Andrew gave her a peck on the cheek.

"I came tae tell ye I'm leavin' tae run an errand for Father McPherson. I should be back before the evenin' meal."

Nzingha frowned.

"Fine. I shall take a nap until then."

As Andrew escorted Nzingha to the house, she bent over, clutching her side as sudden pain struck.

"OUCH!"

"My wife, are ye hale? Is there pain?"

She stood straight and began to take deep breaths.

"I am fine. I just need to lie down."

They continued toward the house. As soon as they reached the paving stones, Nzingha's water burst, splashing loudly against the rubble beneath her feet. She stood frozen and lifted her skirts.

Nzingha looked down, then up at Andrew as though something were terribly wrong. Andrew frowned in confusion.

"What's the matter? Did ye piss yerself?"

Nzingha breathed heavily, irritation flashing across her face.

"Do not be such an ass. I think the babe is coming."

Andrew's eyes widened in fear. He scooped her into his arms and carried her through the doors, calling out to the servant.

"Miriam, ride out and fetch the healer this instant. Let her ken Lady Barton's water has shown."

"Aye, Laird Barton."

Andrew took the stairs two at a time with Nzingha in his arms. She breathed heavily, groaning with each contraction.

At last, he reached their chamber. As soon as he laid her upon the bed, she twisted from side to side in discomfort. A knock came at the door.

"Laird Barton, 'tis me, Haemish. Are ye ready tae visit Father McPherson?"

Andrew stepped toward the door, but Nzingha tugged his hand.

"I need a moment with Haemish."

"Certainly, my love."

Andrew opened the door and stepped into the hall, his hands folded.

"It's Nzingha. She's in labour, but she wishes tae speak with ye."

"Me? What does she want with me?"

Haemish drew a steady breath, entered the chamber, and bowed.

"Nzingha, is all well? Ye wished tae see me?"

"Yes. Have a seat."

Haemish sat in the chair beside the bed.

Nzingha paced her breathing as another labor pain came.

"There is a woman who loves and cherishes you. She is sad because she wishes for you to feel the same."

Another contraction struck.

"Ohhh… ohhh… ohhh…"

She grasped Haemish's hand. Fear crossed his face as she struggled to speak.

"She… she waits for you to offer your hand in marriage. But something blocks that path. Your station in life, only being a guard. Do you love Annabella?"

Haemish drew a deep breath.

"Aye. Aye, I do."

"Then will you give me your word you will marry her?"

"But how? How can I marry a baroness?"

Nzingha lifted the garnet necklace and her two gold bracelets.

"Buy a ship. A large one. Hire men. Trade with Europe. Use everything you learned from Laird Barton. With your profits, purchase land and become a laird. I will speak to Andrew about helping you."

"My lady, I cannot accept this."

"Haemish."

She took his hand.

"A gift from a friend. A gift in the name of love. I no longer need this, for I have found happiness."

She looked to Andrew and smiled.

Haemish's eyes widened. He looked at Nzingha, then at Andrew.

"I am not sure the lady will approve of me. I have secrets."

"Whatever they are," Andrew said, "I'm sure Annabella will see past them, for she loves ye deeply."

"Aye," Nzingha said softly.

Haemish hesitated, clearly weighed down by more than gratitude. Andrew nodded for him to accept the gift.

"My thanks, Princess."

Nzingha squeezed his hand.

"One more thing. I would like you to be the baby's godfather. If anything ever happens to Andrew or me, I entrust you with our child's life."

Haemish stood and kissed her cheek.

"I would be honored."

Destiny

Eight hours passed, marked by the sound of screams coming from the top of the stairs. Andrew and Haemish sat in the drawing room with glasses of whisky untouched in their hands. The healer had arrived more than four hours earlier. Fear kept Andrew from remaining still. He paced the length of the room, folding his arms, then dropping them again. When that was not enough, he began to bite at his fingernails without realizing it.

Nzingha screamed, as the healer yelled.
"Push, My Lady, I can see the head."

"AHHHHHHHH."
Nzingha was out of breath and tired.
"Andrew, I want Andrew."

"Laird Barton is right outside; he can hear you. I need one more push."

Nzingha screamed.
"ANDREW… ANDREEEEWWW."

The door flew open, and Andrew answered,
"Aye, my love?"

The amount of blood on the bedcovers made Andrew's stomach churn. Then he saw the baby's head, emerging from a place he had once cherished. The sight hit him all at once, sharp and disorienting, and he knew he was going to be sick.

Andrew swallowed and took a deep breath to gain his composure.
"I'm here Love. Is the bairn stuck?"

He scooted in the bed next to her.
"I'm here, my love."

Nzingha cried.

"My love, I cannot push, I cannot!"

Another contraction came. Nzingha screamed and moaned.

"Zing, listen tae me. Ye're strong. Ye're the strongest woman I ken."

The healer leaned in close, her voice cutting through the chaos of the room, urgent and unyielding, rising over the sound of Nzingha's breathing and the wet rustle of the sheets.

"Come on, lass, give it one more enormous push."

Nzingha shook her head weakly, sweat slicking her skin until it clung to the sheets beneath her. Her hair was plastered to her temples, her chest heaving as she fought for air. Tears slipped freely down her face, not from pain alone, but from the crushing weight of exhaustion that had settled deep into her bones.

"I cannot, I am too tired. Help... I am not going to make it."

Andrew climbed onto the bed behind her, moving with urgency born of fear rather than instruction. There was no ceremony in it, no hesitation. He pressed himself close so she could feel him there, solid and immovable.

"I shall help."

He lifted her thighs, bracing them hard against her chest, anchoring her body when it no longer seemed to belong to her. His grip was firm, almost desperate, as though letting go for even a moment might cause her to slip away from him entirely.

"We must see our bairn. NOW PUSH."

The command was not anger. It was terror sharpened into resolve.

Nzingha clenched her jaw, every muscle in her body drawing tight at once. Her teeth ground together as she bore down, the effort shaking her from the inside out. Her arms trembled. Her legs quivered against his hold. The sound that tore from her throat was raw and unrestrained.

"ERRRR."

It was not a cry. It was everything she had left.

In seconds, the baby slipped free.

She was fair-skinned, her hair thick and black, her arrival sudden enough to draw a sharp breath from everyone in the room. The sound that followed was immediate. The baby yelped, then cried out, strong and unmistakably alive.

After hours of pushing, Nzingha's strength gave way. Her body slackened against the bed, exhaustion overtaking her all at once.

Andrew shifted from behind her, moving carefully now, trying to see the baby clearly.

The healer's voice lifted, bright with relief.

"'Tis a girl, oh my goodness, 'tis a girl. She is beautiful. Well done, well done."

Nzingha drew in a breath. Then another. Her chest rose and fell, unsteady but present. Sweat coated her skin. Blood stained the sheets and her nightgown. She turned her head toward the sound of the crying child and smiled.

Andrew watched her closely.

Then her eyes rolled back.

Her head slipped to the side.

The change was so quick it barely made a sound.

Fear struck him in an instant. He leaned toward her, his voice catching as he spoke her name.

"Nzingha? Zingha."

No answer. Her body was limp, and her skin looked pale and clammy. This was the nightmare Andrew feared. He shook her body for a response. It was as if she collapsed. He tapped her face.

"Nae, nae. Zing, come on, love. Wake up."

The healer opened one of Nzingha's eyes. She then looked between her legs. Nzingha bled uncontrollably.
"Laird Barton, I need ye tae step oot for a minute. I have tae get the bleedin' under control, for she's losin' far too much blood. We've work tae do."

Andrew pushed back as the healer made him exit the chamber. He peaked around the healer's shoulders.

"My Laird, please. The longer I take, the more at risk she is."

He took another look at Nzingha and went down the stairs with his new baby girl in his arms.

Haemish grinned.
"Goodness, the babe is two minutes old and already she looks just like ye."

Andrew pulled back the babe's blanket exposing her face. The small babe had her wee thumb placed in her mouth; she was sucking away at it. He took the babe into the drawing room and sat behind his desk.

Haemish followed him into the drawing room, the weight of what had just happened still hanging thick in the air. Andrew stood rigid, the newborn held carefully in his arms, afraid that any movement might somehow undo her presence.

"How is Nzingha doing?"

Andrew did not look up at first. His eyes remained fixed on the small bundle against his chest, the rise and fall so faint it barely seemed real.

"Not too good. She passed out from the amount o' blood lost. I believe the healer is stitchin' her tae stanch the bleedin'. I am feared she willnae make it, for her eyes rolled back as if she'd died."

The words came out uneven, scraped raw by fear he had not yet shaken.

Haemish waved his hand, trying to bring some steadiness back into the room.

"Och, Nzingha's a fighter. She'd never roll over and die. She's too much tae live for."

He stepped closer, his attention drawn to the child. The tension in his shoulders eased as he looked down at her.

Haemish walked over to the babe and smiled.

"It's amazin', us men. We fight wars. We wield swords for hours. We lift heavy logs as if they're sacks o' tatties. But it disnae come close tae what a woman can do."

He extended his finger slowly, carefully, letting the infant curl her tiny hand around it. The grip was firm, instinctive.

Haemish smiled wider.

"Oh, the wee lassie's strong, just like her mother."

Andrew finally allowed himself a breath. His mouth curved into something that almost resembled a smile.

"I still cannae believe she's here. She's perfect."

As if responding to his voice, the babe opened her eyes. She blinked slowly, unfocused, then stilled.

"Oh my, look at this. Ye've hazel eyes."

The knock at the door made Andrew stiffen again.

The healer entered, her movements calmer now, her expression tired but composed.

"My Laird, Nzingha is fine. She sleeps. We were able tae stop the bleedin'. I shall place the bairn on the Lady's breast."

Relief hit him so suddenly his knees threatened to give way.

The healer reached for the child, and Andrew released her reluctantly, his hands lingering for a moment longer than necessary.

"Ye can come. We've changed the sheets and cleaned her up."

Andrew followed her up the stairs, every step lighter than the last. The chamber was quieter now, the air no longer sharp with urgency. Nzingha lay pale against the pillows, eyes half-lidded, her breathing slow and even.

"How are you feeling, my love?"

She huffed weakly.

"Like I pushed out a sack of flour."

Andrew let out a soft laugh, the sound breaking through him at last.

"Ye did a fine job."

The healer settled the babe gently against Nzingha's chest.

"Here, time for her feeding. Guide her mouth tae the nipple and make sure her head is supported. Ye're doin' a wonderful job."

The infant rooted instinctively, then latched on, suckling with surprising strength.

Nzingha watched her, awe crossing her tired features. She looked up at Andrew, her expression thoughtful, overwhelmed.

"I never seen a woman give birth or feed a babe. This is all new to me. I was only ever told that women in my country give birth within the ocean, a method that allows the birthing process to be calm, and less painful. This on the other hand," she shook her head, "my body almost lost the battle. I never fought this hard. I do not know if I wish for more children. Tis painful."

Andrew smiled, softer now, careful with the moment.

"Och, ye'll get used tae it my love. Ye're strong. I'll always be here when ye do give birth."

He looked at her, emotion tightening his chest.

"Thank ye."

She frowned slightly, confused.

"Why do you thank me?"

"She's a perfect gift. Ye did a wonderful job bringin' her into this world. I love ye even more. Our bairn is bonnie, just like ye."

Nzingha studied the child closely, her expression turning serious.

"Nae, she does not. Look closely. She looks just like you, but she has my mother's hazel eyes."

She traced a finger gently through the baby's hair.

"Her hair is black and curly, like yours. But her skin is almost as pale as yours also. I do not care of her features. She is healthy and beautiful."

Andrew watched them both, the sight settling deep into him.

"What shall we name her?"

Nzingha looked over at the book that rested upon the table, next to the bed. She then recalled the name from the dream she had with her mother. Suddenly it all made sense. Nzingha stared at the book for quite some time. It was the very first book she read when she arrived. Shakespeare.

Nzingha smiled.
"I read in a book that some are born great, some achieve greatness, and some have greatness thrust upon them. But it is not in the stars to hold our destiny, but in ourselves. We know what we are but know not what we may be. When I read those words of wisdom, immediately I thought about us. It was by faith that we met, but

destiny allowed us to hold on to each other. I wish for her name to be Destiny. What was your mother's name?"

"It was Andrea, hence I got my name Andrew. We shall name her Destiny Andrea Barton."

Andrew smiled.
"'Tis a fine name."

Chapter 19

Family Betrayal

Six months passed as baby Destiny continued to grow into a fine,

healthy baby girl.
She truly resembled her Da.

Dessie, Nzingha called her, had Laird Andrew's curly dark hair and his perfectly arched eyebrows. Nzingha could never get enough of her. Andrew always jested, saying the babe carried Nzingha's temperament; sweet, happy, but when she grew hungry, her cries were fierce.

Andrew stayed close to Nzingha during the first four months after Destiny's birth. He delayed leaving when he could, remaining at the manor longer than was usual for a man whose life had once belonged entirely to the sea.

There had been a time when Andrew would have said the sea was his wife. It claimed his hours and his patience, demanded loyalty, and left little room for anything else. He had spoken of it lightly once, as if it were simply the shape his life had taken.

That truth no longer held.

Nzingha was there now, and their child. Time could no longer be given without thought. It had to be chosen.

He had never imagined himself a husband. The idea had once seemed unnecessary, even impractical. Yet with Nzingha, the notion of staying and belonging to a life beyond the tides no longer felt like loss.

Still, the orders came. Large shipments that could not be ignored. Andrew and Alex returned to their work, restoring what had been taken by storm and wreck. Together, they repaid the debt owed to the crown and the church, settling accounts until no man could speak against them.

Trade resumed steadily after that. Their ships called at Venice and other ports along the Mediterranean, then sailed farther still, into routes that reached the Orient.

Andrew left home on his current voyage, and in the days that followed, the manor returned to its usual pace.

The manor felt too quiet to him, too reliant on routine rather than presence. Nzingha accepted his departure without protest, but that did little to settle him. He told himself she was safe, that the walls were strong, that servants and guards filled the space he left behind, but the thought did not sit easily.

It was Haemish who insisted on remaining, along with four other guards. He spoke of it as a matter of sense, not loyalty, and Andrew did not argue. The Lady and the child would not be left unattended.

One afternoon, Nzingha sat in the garden, a canvas propped before her as she painted a portrait of Destiny, now six months old. Miriam and Elinor remained nearby despite being given the day free, lingering more out of habit than obligation. Miriam, the child's wet nurse, held Destiny securely on her lap while the little girl gnawed contentedly on a strawberry, its juice streaking her chubby cheeks and fingers alike.

"My Lady?" Miriam asked.

"Yes, Miriam?" Nzingha answered, tilting her head as she stroked her brush.

"What are the men like where ye're from?"

Nzingha paused her strokes. Peeking from behind the canvas, she gave Miriam an inquiring look. The men of Mbemba and Tafaria? Why does she ask such a thing?

"Miriam, what do you mean?"

"Do they ken romance? My husband was never gentle with me. He was always braw and rough, and I never cared for it."

Nzingha burst into laughter, tears filling her eyes. She placed a hand to her chest.

"My apologies. I did not mean to laugh at your question. It was only unexpected."

As her laughter eased, her hand remained pressed there.

"Yes," she said evenly, "men where I am from are gentle as they are stern. They are taught that strength does not excuse harshness. They are expected to respect women, as does Laird Andrew."

"Fancy me having a man from your country."

Nzingha laughed. "Miriam, the distance alone would make that impossible. I do not see that happening."

"Are the men clever like you?" Elinor asked.

"They are educated," Nzingha replied. "Many fight as warriors not because they wish to, but because they must. Land must be protected. Because of this, they carry a sense of responsibility toward all who live there. For the most part, they are drawn to learning, astrology, healing arts, medicine. Some invest their wealth so that it may grow."

Miriam's curiosity did not wane. "If the Laird were tae ask for yer hand back home, would yer father accept him?"

Nzingha continued painting as she spoke. "Honestly, no. As you know, my father is a king, a very wealthy and powerful man. Think of him as similar to your own. Your king would never allow his daughter to marry a ship's captain. My father's intentions were always to bind our family to wealth and power. His plans were for me to marry a man like himself."

"But Laird Barton is wealthy, is he not?" Elinor asked.

Nzingha smiled. "Here in Scotland, yes. He has land, a castle, even houses. But none of it compares to the lands my father rules, gold mines, caves of jewels, wealth beyond counting. My father has so many houses, I have visited only five of them. I have not even spoken of the farms and crops."

Her smile remained, faint but knowing.

"If Laird Barton were ever to meet my father, let us pray he walked away with his head intact."

Miriam's eyes widened. "Oh my! Yer family's extraordinarily wealthy. Ye must truly love Laird Barton, tae leave all that behind."

Nzingha met Miriam's gaze, her expression steady. "I do. But true wealth does not come from material possessions. It comes from knowledge and discernment, from the people who love you, from being alive and whole."

She continued without raising her voice. "With great wealth come greater burdens. Wars are waged. People are placed into bondage. Lives are lost. Families are broken, and relationships are destroyed."

Nzingha's strokes grew sharper, the bristles scraping the canvas with quiet insistence as her thoughts drifted where she did not invite them.

Her father's face rose before her without warning, the moment she had spoken Mikel's name. The crack of his hand across her cheek before the question had fully left her mouth. The command that followed was colder still. *Leave my sight.* She had gone, her skin burning, her pride shattered, already understanding that love had no standing before power.

Another memory pressed in behind it. Smoke on the horizon. The hurried retreat. Nobles ushered into hiding while her father stood firm, negotiating lives like currency to keep blood from spilling where it would cost him most. Power preserved. Loss calculated.

Heat flared in her chest, sharp and familiar, and she let it travel through her hand instead.

She did not pause as she spoke.

"When a man aches for wealth, he aches for power. His ego grows larger than his heart. He will step over those who loved him when he had nothing, destroy them, if it serves his gain. Wealth such as that hardens the spirit. It turns the heart cold."

Her brush slowed. Her voice did not.

"Emotional and intellectual wealth allow us to live well. They give us peace. Remember that."

A small smile followed, measured and deliberate.

After a moment, Elinor asked quietly, "Do you wish to go home? To see your people. Your father?"

Nzingha kept her thoughts to herself. Her father would never accept her back if he knew everything. She had married a foreigner, a man without royal blood. She had borne his child. In her father's eyes, that alone would mark her as ruined.

A faint smile touched her mouth and faded just as quickly. He would say she had tainted his bloodline, disgraced his dynasty. He might even order her death.

Her gaze drifted to Destiny, content and unaware in Miriam's arms. That child would never be accepted. Of that, she was certain.

Nzingha said nothing more. Servants listened even when they appeared not to, and she had learned long ago which thoughts were best kept her own.

She smiled and spoke aloud. "No... it is too far."

The sound of horses reached her moments later.

Nzingha paused her painting and listened as Haemish greeted Andrew's uncle, Graham, near the entryway to the manor.

"Graham," Haemish called out, his voice carrying easily across the grounds. "What brings ye here? Ye ken Andrew and Alex are still away. They'll no' return for another sennight."

"Aye," Graham replied, "but I wished tae see my grand-niece."

Nzingha frowned. Graham had never written. No word of congratulations. No notice of a visit.

She motioned quietly to the servants. "Take Destiny inside."

Remaining near the trees, she listened.

"The Lady didnae mention a visit," Haemish said. "Did ye write ahead tae let her know ye were comin'?"

"Nae. I was in Leith and thought I'd stop by." Graham shifted and drew a parcel from his satchel. "See? I came bearing gifts."

Haemish glanced aside and noticed Nzingha standing just beyond him. He turned slightly, as if waiting for instruction. She gave a small nod.

She moved toward the gate as Graham dismounted and followed Haemish inside the entry.

As Nzingha walked toward them, she greeted Andrew's uncle with a courteous smile.

"Good day, Graham. It is good to see you."

"A good day indeed," he replied, returning the smile easily enough.

For a moment, nothing seemed amiss.

Haemish stepped aside to lead him through the gate. The sound of boots on stone echoed softly in the entryway. Nzingha was already turning, preparing to follow.

That was when the blow came for Haemish, unseen and from behind.

The hilt of Graham's sword struck Haemish low and hard at the base of the skull. He collapsed without a sound, his body hitting the ground with a heavy thud that carried farther than the strike itself.

Nzingha froze for half a breath.

Then she ran.

"Guards!" Her voice tore free of her. "Guards—intruders!"

No one answered.

She stopped short. Two of the guards lay sprawled near the wall, blood already pooling beneath them. The sight drove the air from her lungs. She turned and ran for the house, slammed the door shut, and drove the bolt home.

"Miriam!" she screamed. "Take Destiny and hide!"

The door burst inward before she could move again.

Graham caught her by the hair and yanked her back, the edge of a knife pressing cold and firm against her throat.

"What do you want?" she demanded, her voice tight but steady. "Why would you betray your own nephews?"

Graham did not flinch at her question.

The knife remained steady at her throat, its edge pressing just enough to remind her how little the distance separated her breath from blood. His grip in her hair tightened slightly, not in anger, but in adjustment, as though she were an object that needed positioning.

"Well now, it's simple enough."

His tone was calm, almost conversational, the voice of a man already counting his winnings.

"Ye told me a story once. A small thing, really. About a cave on Tafari Island." He leaned closer, his breath warm against her cheek. "Jewels hidden away where no crown could lay claim. Wealth enough tae change a man's fortunes entire."

The corner of his mouth lifted.

"At first, I thought tae take something smaller," he said calmly. "A keepsake."

His gaze settled on the chain at her throat.

"I even considered cuttin' yer throat and takin' that sapphire from around yer pretty little neck, and bein' done with ye."

The knife shifted then, just enough for the edge tae rest against her skin.

"But then I thought, why settle for one piece, when there's a whole chest waitin' tae be claimed?"

A low chuckle followed, soft and pleased, as though he were sharing a joke meant only for himself.

Nzingha did not lower her eyes.

"Are you mad?" she said, "I am not going anywhere with you."

Graham's smile did not fade. If anything, it deepened.

"Oh, I think ye will. Or we'll begin with the servants. One by one, if need be."

He paused, letting the words settle. "Then I'll take yer babe."

He held her there, letting the silence stretch until it pressed against her ears.

"I'll sell ye both. Like stock. Like flesh meant for profit." His mouth twisted. "Ye'll never lay eyes on her again."

His grip tightened, forcing her chin higher.

"And Andrew, he'll search for ye until it breaks him. And he'll find nothin'. No wife. No child. Just emptiness."

He leaned closer, his breath hot with it. "That's what ye've earned."

Nzingha spat.

The saliva struck his cheek and slid down toward his scarf.

"Andrew will kill you," she said,

Graham released her hair just long enough to remove the scarf from his neck. He wiped his face slowly, methodically, as though cleaning an inconvenience rather than an insult. Then he folded the cloth and tucked it away.

He did not look at her when he spoke.

"Show her."

The movement happened beside her.

A mercenary seized Elinor by the arm. She barely had time to draw breath before the blade crossed her throat. The sound was quick. Wet. Final.

Elinor collapsed at once, her body striking the floor with a dull, hollow thud.

Miriam screamed.

The sound tore through the room, raw and uncontrolled. Destiny answered at once, her wails sharp, a fear instinctively rising to meet the terror around her.

Graham turned back to Nzingha and smiled.

"Well now," he said calmly. "We shall leave for that island. You may say goodbye to your child."

Nzingha moved.

She drove her knee upward, hard and precise, straight into Graham's groin. The blow landed deep. His breath tore from him in a broken sound as his body folded, both hands dropping instinctively as the pain overtook him.

That instant was enough.

She twisted into him, tore the knife from his hand, and flung it without hesitation. The blade struck the man who had killed Elinor square in the chest. He staggered back, shock flashing across his face just before his knees buckled and his body collapsed, lifeless.

Another mercenary came at her from the side.

She slid past him, low and fast, her shoulder brushing his hip as she moved. Her hand closed around the dagger at his belt as she turned. She dropped her weight, swept his legs from under him, and went down with him. The first stab caught him beneath the ribs. The second drove deeper. The third ended it. His body slackened beneath her as the fight left him.

Pain exploded across her face as a fist struck her cheek. Her vision flashed white, but she stayed upright.

She struck back immediately, once, twice, then gathered her skirts in both hands and kicked. Her foot connected with bone. Then teeth. Then chest. The man was flung backward into a table. Wood cracked and split as he slammed into it, the structure giving way under the force of his body.

"Miriam!" Nzingha shouted. "Run! Take Destiny. Get a horse and go—go to Tantallon. Now!"

She saw Miriam clutch the child to her chest and flee.

Nzingha tried to follow.

Her skirts tangled around her legs, heavy and unforgiving. She dragged at the fabric, fighting it as another man lunged toward her. She turned, but too late.

A table leg slammed into the backs of her knees. She pitched forward, the impact driving the air from her lungs. Before she could rise, something heavy struck the side of her head.

The floor rushed up.

Sound vanished.

Darkness followed.

No Mercy Promised

Andrew was glad to be homeward bound.

The journey back had felt longer than it should have, not for want of fair wind or steady seas, but because each day away from home pressed harder than the last. More than once, he caught himself wishing he had never left at all. The work had been necessary, the contracts unavoidable, but none of it quieted the ache of missing his wife and child.

At nearly every port, he wandered the markets before returning to the ship. He paused at stalls meant for women and children rather than sailors, fingering small dresses, carved toys, bits of ribbon. He bought a doll at one port, another dress at the next, tucking each purchase carefully into his satchel. They were small things, but he imagined Destiny's hands closing around them, her laugh rising in delight.

On their final stop in Venice, while overseeing the loading of cargo, he found himself standing in a jeweler's shop before he fully realized how he had come there. The sapphire ring caught the light at once. He bought it without hesitation, wrapping it carefully before slipping it into his pocket, already picturing it on Nzingha's hand.

That morning, as the ship made for home, Andrew sat on his bunk turning the doll over in his hands, a quiet smile tugging at his mouth.

"Drop anchor!"

Alex's shout cut across the deck as the ship eased toward shore. He stretched, hands settling on his hips as the familiar rise of land came into view.

"Finally," he said, "I can get off this bloody ship, away from bollocks and beards, and find myself a nice, buxom woman tae bury myself into."

Andrew barely registered the words. He was already moving, already reaching for his things, the thought of home tightening something in his chest.

"Ye comin' tae the castle?" Alex asked, glancing back.

"Aye. Briefly," Andrew replied. "I'll be back tae Leith come morn."

They reached Tantallon late that morning.

Andrew saw Haemish before he took in anything else, before the yard, before the open gate, before the quiet that felt wrong in a place that should have been alive. Haemish stood outside the keep, waiting. Not at the manor. The sight slowed Andrew for a half step, confusion flickering, then irritation took hold and his stride hardened, boots grinding into the gravel as he closed the distance.

"Haemish," he called sharply. "What the hell are ye doin' here?"

Haemish turned, surprise flashing across his face.

Andrew didn't wait for an answer. "Why are ye no' with my wife and my bairn? That's where ye were left."

"Andrew, ye're back early…"

"I left ye there tae guard them," Andrew pressed, anger already rising. "So start explainin' why ye're standin' here instead."

Haemish held his ground. "Andrew. Hear me. It's the Lady."

That stopped him.

Andrew's voice came out tight. "What about her?"

Haemish hesitated just long enough for the pause to mean something. "She's been taken."

Andrew stared at him. The words slid past his ears without sense, as though spoken in another tongue.

"Taken?" he said,

"Your uncle," Haemish replied. "Graham."

His satchel slipped from his hand, hitting the stone at his feet with a dull thud. He didn't look down.

"Destiny," he said, "Where is my bairn?"

"Inside the keep. With Miriam. She's safe."

A breath tore from Andrew's chest, not relief, not rage, but something caught between. "Then tell me what happened."

Haemish drew a breath and spoke, the words coming out low and steady, as though he were holding them in place by force.

"He came tae the manor yesterday, said he'd been in Leith. Claimed he'd come tae see the wee lass. I didnae trust it, not fully, but the Lady… she motioned him inside."

Andrew's jaw tightened, but he said nothing.

"As we crossed the threshold, he struck me from behind, hard enough tae drop me. He'd hired men, mercenaries. They were already inside the walls by then." His voice roughened. "They killed the guards. Elinor too. Cut her down where she stood."

Andrew's hands curled slowly into fists.

"When I came round, the house was torn apart. Looked like a battle had ripped through the foyer. Three of the men Graham brought with him were dead, sprawled across the floor."

He drew a breath through his teeth. "The Lady fought them. Long enough tae give Miriam time tae take the bairn and run. She shouted for her tae go, tae ride for the castle, and Miriam did."

His jaw worked once. "I should've been on my feet. I should've stopped it. I'm sorry I couldnae help her."

His voice dropped. "Damn yer uncle."

Haemish fell silent then.

Andrew didn't interrupt.

By the time Haemish finished, his hands were clenched so tight the knuckles had gone white, his breathing slow and measured, the kind that came only when restraint was being forced into place.

"Did the bastard say what he meant tae do with her?" Andrew demanded. "Where the hell did he take her?"

Haemish answered before anyone else could. "It was for gold. Jewels. He spoke of a cave, Tafaria Island."

Andrew swore under his breath and kicked his fallen satchel aside. "Take me tae my bairn. I want tae see her with my own eyes. Then we leave. At once."

Alex stepped into his path. "Andrew, wait. We just docked. We need supplies."

"Fuck the supplies," Andrew snapped, the restraint tearing loose. "That's my wife. If Graham so much as lays a finger on her, if he touches one strand o' her hair, he'd best be prayin' tae whatever God'll hear him, because I will kill him."

He turned away and strode for the great hall.

Miriam sat on the floor with Destiny and two other weans, bits of toys scattered about them. Destiny laughed, bright and untroubled, as though the world had not already cracked open.

Andrew stopped short.

He crossed the room in a few strides and dropped tae his knees, lifting his daughter into his arms. He kissed her brow, her cheeks, her wee hands, holding her like she might slip away if he loosened his grip.

"Oh, my wee lass," he murmured. "I'll bring yer mother home. I swear it."

Miriam's composure broke then. She bowed her head, shoulders trembling.

Andrew looked at her. "I'm sorry, Miriam, about Elinor."

She sobbed, "She was only nineteen summers. She didnae deserve it. She was kind. Always kind." She wiped at her face, anger breaking through the grief. "That man is the devil himself."

Andrew said nothing. He rested a hand on Miriam's shoulder; it was firm and brief.

After a moment, she found her breath. "The Lady told me tae run. She shouted it, ordered me tae take the bairn and flee. I did as she said,"

"Aye. Ye did well."

He kissed Destiny, then handed her back to the wet nurse. "Ye saved her life. For that, I owe ye more than coin."

The small bag was already in her hand.

"Ye'll go tae Ireland. Today. I'll send four guards with ye. Take the bairn tae Baroness Annabella McKinney. She's her godmother. She'll keep her safe until we return."

"When do we leave?" Miriam stared at him.

"Now. Pack what ye can. I'll have my best mate Logan guard ye."

He brushed a finger along Destiny's cheek. She smiled.

"Protect her. Wi' yer life."

Miriam nodded, clutching the bairn close.

"Thank ye. For all of it."

He turned away.

Andrew, Alex, and Haemish went straight for the solar.

The doors were barely shut behind them before Andrew crossed the room and began tearing through the shelves and drawers, scattering papers, shoving books aside. He found what he was looking for at the back of the desk, a map, old and well-worn, the known world spread across it in careful ink.

He dragged it open across the desk and poured himself a measure of whisky without looking. One glance at the distance traced in black lines and he spat it back into the glass.

"Jesus Christ," he said hoarsely. "He's takin' her round the Cape. That's the long way, half the world away."

The room went still.

The glass left his hand and shattered against the far wall.

Andrew leaned over the desk, both palms braced against the wood, fingers digging into his beard as his eyes followed the coastlines and currents.

"If they sailed from Leith, we still have a chance. He has tae clear the Forth and round the mainland before he reaches open sea."

"And if he's already passed?" Alex asked.

Andrew straightened slowly. "Then we follow. And we take his ship."

Alex traced a line across the parchment. "Or we sail direct tae the island. Waiting for a ship tae pass is gambling with time."

"Aye," Haemish said. "Staying put's a risk."

Andrew nodded once. The decision settled. "Then we go straight for her."

"Rally the men. I want weeks o' water. I ken it's no' enough, but we'll pray for rain. Take every loaf Cook's baked this month. Make sure we have enough livestock and grain. Tell her it's an emergency departure. Alert Rory. Gather ten of our best fighters."

Haemish was already moving. "Aye, Captain."

His voice carried down the hall as orders were shouted and boots began to thunder.

Alex stepped closer and laid a hand on Andrew's shoulder. "We'll get her back."

Andrew slammed his palm into the desk. "What was he thinkin'?" Rage finally broke through, raw and unguarded. "My own blood. I kent he was greedy, but this?" His jaw tightened. "Takin' my wife."

Alex exhaled slowly. "While ye were gone, Graham ran himself deep into debt. Cards. Races. The wrong sort o' men. He owes more coin than he can pay. There's a bounty on his head, and every time he showed his face at court, he was humiliated. The King banned him outright. He was desperate."

Andrew straightened. "Desperate or not, he crossed the line."

He folded the map with care, a calm settling over him that had nothing to do with peace.

"Come, we've a ship tae ready."

The Threat That Waited

When Nzingha awoke, she was blindfolded in the back of a carriage, her hands and feet bound tight. The roll of wheels rocked her body, and somewhere nearby she heard the splash of waves against stone. Then Graham's raspy voice cut through the dark.

"We are here, Nzingha. I would remove the blindfold, but ye might try to fight. Seeing ye in action, ye are highly trained."

He gave a low chuckle. "I was impressed, the way ye kicked that mercenary across the foyer like he was a rag doll. I see now why Andrew is in love with ye. Ye are a brave, beautiful young woman. I have never met anyone like ye. For what it's worth, I hope ye can find it in yer heart to forgive me. If I do not pay my debts, I am a dead man."

Despite the ropes biting into her wrists and ankles, Nzingha sat straight, her posture unbroken. Her mouth was bound, denying him the satisfaction of a reply.

The carriage slowed, then lurched to a stop.

When Graham grabbed her arm and tried to haul her down, she shifted her weight, anchoring herself in place. He cursed under his breath.

"Come now," he said, "Do not be stubborn. We have three moons before we reach our destination. Perhaps ye'll warm to me by then."

A muffled cry tore from her throat as she shook her head violently. She did not want to leave her babe. Or her husband. She was so very tired of being taken.

"MMMMMM… MMMMMM."

Two men dragged her from the carriage despite her struggle. She cried out through the bonds as Graham seized her and slung her over his shoulder.

Each time she squirmed, trying to break free, he smacked her backside sharply.

"Still fighting," he laughed. "Tenacious, I'll give ye that."

"Enough now," he added with another laugh. "Stop this. Ye should be pleased to return home, back to yer homelands. I am doing ye a favor."

The boards beneath her shifted as they boarded the ship. A door opened. Then closed. Graham tossed her onto a bed, and her stomach roiled as the world tilted beneath her. Blind. Bound. Unable to speak.

For the second time in her life, fear found her.

"I am going to remove the blindfold and the cloth from yer mouth," Graham said quietly. "Nae screaming."

She nodded once.

When he freed her mouth, the words burst from her, raw and desperate. "How could ye do this to me? My babe is only six months old. She needs me."

"Sweetheart, I need ye more."

"Please," she begged. "I can get ye gold. We do not have to cross the world. My father has friends..."

"Nae." His smile hardened. "Gold is not all I want. I want gems. Diamonds. I want to be the richest man in Scotland, richer than the King himself. I want castles, lands, armies. I want a title. Most of all, I want to be respected... and feared."

"You are a greedy whoremonger," Nzingha spat. "I will never take ye there. So good luck finding it. It is men like you who give your people a bad name."

"People like me?" he echoed.

"Yes."

His voice sharpened. "That is a compliment. I was born in the slums. My mother was a servant who could not keep her legs closed. Andrew and Alex are not my blood. Their grandsire found me starving, took me in, and still I was nothing more than a tag-along, the one left to pick at scraps. When he died, I was left with nothing but the clothes on my back."

"I worked my fingers to bone for Andrew's father, first in, last out. When he passed, did he leave me anything? Did he see me as his adopted brother? Nae."

Graham lifted one finger. "Not one shilling."

Nzingha spat onto the floor. "So you let greed rule you. You are mad."

Graham laughed softly. "Mad? Nae. Let us say… an opportunist."

He lifted a flask. "When I first saw ye, I thought Andrew a fool for courting a Black lass. Then I noticed yer jewels. Ye were naive enough to tell me how to get them. I would have taken ye sooner, but ye were with child. See?" His smile thinned. "I do have a heart."

He drank.

Nzingha met his gaze without fear. "When I am unbound, I am going to kill you."

She turned her back to him.

What Graham did not know, what he never thought to look for, was how she had learned to survive.

The dagger rested high upon her thigh. A warrior always keeps a blade hidden.

Eyes on the Horizon

Within three hours, Andrew and his men were boarding his and Alex's ship, *The Lady Andrea*, named for their late mother. The deck creaked beneath his boots as he stepped aboard, a familiar sound that should have steadied him. It did not.

His jaw was tight, his thoughts restless. Somewhere beyond the horizon, Graham sailed with his wife.

Andrew did not linger. As soon as the lines were cast and the sails caught, he climbed for height, taking the crow's nest himself. He needed the sea laid bare before him. Every shadow, every ripple that might hide a sail. With the spyglass pressed to his eye, he swept the water from left to right, again and again, unwilling to trust a single glance.

Two men shared the nest with him, each watching a different quarter, silent and intent. The wind bit hard as the hours wore on. His feet burned. His back stiffened. Still, he refused to descend until the watch was changed by force of time rather than will.

When he finally climbed down, his muscles protested every rung.

He made his way to the captain's cabin, where the lamplight glowed warm against the dark. Alex and Haemish sat at the table, already into a meal, bread torn by hand, roast pork laid thick, cheese sliced without ceremony.

"Alex," Andrew said, his voice low but edged, "ye were right. Not a single ship in sight. It's a mercy we didnae linger, waitin' for those bastards tae pass us by."

Alex glanced up, untroubled, grease shining on his fingers as he held up a piece of pork. "Sit. Eat. Ye'll need yer strength."

Andrew shook his head, pacing instead. "Nae. I cannae stomach it." His hands flexed at his sides. "Only God knows what that traitor's done. Or what he means tae do."

Haemish tipped back his cup and drained it in one pull. He set it down with a solid thunk, then wiped his mouth with the back of his hand. "You ken as well as I do Andrew. Nzingha is nae some helpless lass. She can hold her own."

Andrew stopped pacing, but the tension did not leave his shoulders.

Haemish spoke in assurance. "If any fool thinks tae lay hands on her, e'll lose more than his pride. She'll cut off his bollocks and feed 'em tae the sea before he draws breath again."

Alex let out a quiet laugh. "Aye. I saw her fight. She's no fragile. She moves like the legends we heard as boys, like Scathach of Skye herself, from the old tales. Steel in her blood. Ye've nothing tae fear."

Andrew wanted to believe that.

The words eased something in his chest, but not enough. Pride warred with dread, neither willing to give ground. At last, he reached for the jug, poured himself a cup, then, on impulse, snatched the piece of pork from Alex's hand and took a rough bite.

Alex stared at him a moment, then shook his head with a faint smile and tossed a heel of bread at him. Haemish snorted into his cup.

The men ate on, the quiet camaraderie settling like a thin balm over Andrew's worry. But even as he chewed, his gaze drifted back toward the door, toward the sea beyond it.

Chapter 20

All Ships lead to Tafaria

*T*hree months passed, and Nzingha spent every one of them plotting her escape.

She watched the men closely, listening as they talked too freely among themselves, careless in their certainty. They were mad, every last one of them. They had no notion that this island lay under her uncle's military enforcement, that patrols moved through these lands day and night, unseen but ever present. The moment their boots touched shore, they would be outnumbered. Surrounded. Slaughtered.

She smirked at the thought.

Her only true dilemma was her uncle, Femi.

If he found her first, he would force her to return to Mbemba Kingdom. There would be no discussion. No mercy. No allowance for what she wanted. There was no world in which she went home willingly.

Blast Graham's greedy soul, she thought bitterly. I am going to kill him. This will be for Elinor… and for tearing me from my babe.

The pain came without warning.

A sharp ache shot through both breasts, sudden and fierce, swelling from deep within and moving from one nipple to the other. They felt heavy, tight beneath her skin, so full they throbbed with it. She sucked in a breath and straightened, pressing a hand to her chest.

"Ouch. Great God Nkondi, press this pain…"

She clenched her jaw and exposed her breast. She slid her palm lower and pressed firmly, the way she had learned to do. Warm relief followed at once, a thin release she welcomed even as it ached. She looked away as the milk spilled uselessly down, her breath shuddering as the pressure eased but did not fully relent.

It had been well over three months since she last nursed Destiny. Her body had not forgotten, no matter how far she had been taken from her child. Each day, without fail, she relieved the weight as best she could, letting it go where it could do no good. It was a quiet, private ritual, one that left her hollow every time.

"My baby needs me," she whispered, shaking her head.

A tear escaped before she could stop it. She wiped it away just as quickly. There was no room for weakness, not yet.

Her thoughts drifted to another escape, long ago, when she and Iney had fled the pirates and washed ashore on an island with no clear path home. She had not wanted to leave that fragile paradise. Yet her decision to stay had allowed the gods to send her Andrew.

Fate, she had learned, rarely moved in straight lines.

If I try to escape before we reach Tafaria, she thought, it would be foolish.

The sea would betray her. The men would catch her.

But once she was on African soil. On land she knew.

She could find her way home. Back to Destiny. Back to her husband.

Her plan was simple. Wait until the ship docked, then strike.

So she endured in silence for three long months, listening while Graham rattled on about the wealth that would soon be his. Day after day he spoke of gold and gems, of power and titles, of how Tafaria would be the making of him. He never tired of hearing himself speak.

She tired of it quickly.

One afternoon, as Graham's voice droned on yet again, Nzingha felt something inside her still. The patience she had hoarded for survival finally ran dry. She drew a slow breath, letting his words finish echoing in the small cabin, then spoke calmly, as though commenting on the weather.

"You are such a fool."

Graham stopped mid sentence.

Nzingha's gaze did not flicker. It did not rise to anger. That alone unsettled him.

"I have seen men like you," she said calmly. "Men who call their hunger destiny and their selfishness vision."

She shook her head once, slow and precise.

"Greed over blood. Greed over loyalty. Greed over two men who stood for you when you were already failing. And all for what… For what… A dream you were never strong enough to earn."

She leaned back.

"You will leave this world as you entered it, empty handed."

She gave a slow exhale. "'Tis a pity," she said at last. "You mistook appetite for legacy."

She crossed her legs with deliberate ease and began cleaning beneath her fingernails, as though the matter were settled.

Graham felt it then.

Not mockery.

Not defiance.

Threat.

These were not the words of a frightened woman grasping for bravado. They were measured. Certain. Spoken by someone who understood consequence and had already accepted it.

The realization struck him hard enough that his pride recoiled before his body did.

Anger churned in his chest. He stepped toward her, once… then again…

"LAND!"

The shout tore through the cabin.

Graham froze. A slow smile crept across his face as he turned sharply, flung open the door to the captain's quarters, and leaned out over the deck.

"What's the distance from shore?"

"Five kilometers, give or take!"

Graham nodded once. "Drop anchor. We'll take skiffs in."

The command rippled instantly through the ship. Chains rattled. Men shouted back confirmations. Skiffs were dragged into position as the deck erupted into motion.

Graham shut the door carefully behind him and turned back to her, his smile altered, thinner, edged with something colder.

"Now," he said, almost pleasantly, "what were ye sayin' about greed?"

Nzingha did not answer at once. She simply held his gaze, steady and unblinking.

He smirked. "Come along, then. We'll prepare tae cast off."

He reached for her.

She moved before he could finish, her heel driving into his leg hard enough to knock him off balance as her voice cut sharp and low.

"Get yer filthy hands off me, hear me well… Set foot on that island and you and every man with you will die before ye reach the shore."

The slap caught her mid-break.

"Shut yer mouth. I grow tired of yer speech."

Pain flashed white as the sound cracked through the cabin. Nzingha surged forward and drove her forehead into his face with everything she had. He staggered back, blood slicking his fingers as the chair behind him collapsed under his weight.

"Ah, ye wee bitch," he snarled, clutching his head, breath ragged. "Still feisty, are ye?"

He came at her then, full weight and fury, and they hit the floor hard. The air was crushed from her lungs as he forced her down, her body fighting on instinct. Claws, elbows, teeth, anything she could reach, but rage and size overwhelmed precision. The world tilted, a blow landed, and the dark took her whole.

Graham sat back on his heels, chest heaving as he looked down at her. His head throbbed where she'd struck him, the swelling already blooming beneath his hand.

A breath tore out of him.

"Hh. Hh… Tiny lass. Holy shite… she's a fighter."

He studied her face, the strength still written into its lines even in unconsciousness. A thought crossed his mind, unwelcome, dangerous.

He pushed it aside.

For all his bitterness, there were lines he would not cross. Andrew. Alex. Not blood, but close enough. That, at least, stayed his hand.

He was done being overlooked. Done being nothing.

This had to be done.

He slung her over his shoulder and carried her out onto the deck.

Men whistled as he passed.

"Aye, Graham," one called. "Looks like ye enjoyed yerself a slice o' almond pie."

"Shut yer gob," Graham snapped. "I'll not have ye disrespect a woman. She refused tae leave the ship, so this was necessary. While we're on this island, no one touches her. No one. Or ye'll answer tae me."

He lowered himself into the skiff as it bumped against the hull, and the jolt stirred her awake. Pain throbbed behind her eyes as she drew a breath, the air harsh with sulfur and scorched stone. The smell alone told her where they were.

They were close to shore.

The hull scraped against rock, and she opened her eyes enough to see the coastline. The land was blackened and torn, the ground scarred as if fire had swept through it. She scanned quickly for movement.

There were no guards.
No lookouts.
No fort along the rise.

That was wrong.

Fear tightened Nzingha's chest, but she forced it down. This was the moment. The skiff was already moving toward shore, close enough that the men had begun to relax. She drew a steady breath and let her shoulders sag.

She lifted herself upright and reached for the ties of her bodice, making a show of it.

The skiff shifted as several of the men turned toward her at once.

Graham's voice cut across the boat. "And just what in hell do ye think ye're doin'?"

She let her hand tremble slightly as she worked at the laces. "I am overheating," she said, her voice strained but controlled. "This air is nothing like Scotland. I will swoon if I do not rid myself of this wool."

She loosened the bodice and pulled it free, then reached beneath her gown and slid off her petticoats one by one. The men stared openly now, uncertain, confused, their eyes fixed on her as the layers fell away. When she was left in her shift, she lowered herself back onto the bench and fanned her face with her hand, breathing as though unwell.

No one spoke.

Then, without warning, she leaned back and slipped into the water.

The sea swallowed her whole.

Cold struck hard, stealing her breath as fabric dragged at her legs. She kicked downward at once, forcing herself deep, tearing free of the loosened garments as she sank. Above her, she heard shouting, then the splash of a body hitting the water.

One of Graham's men.

She did not look back.

The weight of his boots and kilt worked against him almost immediately. His strokes grew clumsy as the current pulled at him. He broke for the surface, coughing and gasping.

Nzingha kept moving.

Her lungs burned as she pressed on beneath the surface, letting the current carry her until rock rose ahead. She surfaced only long enough to draw breath, then pulled herself onto the stones and slid back into the water again, swimming low toward the mangroves. Their roots were thick and tangled, offering cover. She climbed onto a rock hidden deep within them and stayed still.

From the skiff, Graham's voice rang out. "Where the devil is she?"

"She went under," the man said between gulps of air. "I lost her."

Graham swore and scanned the shoreline. "You worthless fool. Swim tae shore. She'll have tae come up on land somewhere."

His gaze swept the coast, hard and calculating.

"That crafty bitch," he muttered. "She knows this island. And we do not."

Beyond the Shores

Nzingha watched from her hiding place as the men spread out, fanning through the brush in search of her. When their voices drifted farther away, she drew a steadying breath, rose, and ran.

From her time on missions on this island, she knew there was a village nearly five miles inland. The problem was the sun was already sinking. Darkness would come quickly.

Her breath grew ragged as she ran. She slowed, then stopped altogether, one hand flying to her stays. "I cannot breathe in this contraption," she muttered. "My goodness."

She drew her knife and sliced her garments straight down the front, tearing them away from her body. Tossing the ruined fabric into the brush, she started running again.

She covered nearly three miles before she saw it, an abandoned hut tucked deep within the jungle. The sky had darkened to dusk by the time she reached it. She paused, listening and scanning the trees. There was no sound of pursuit. The men had likely given up the search.

Inside, the hut was bare, the floor covered in dirt and rotting leaves. There was nothing of use. She stepped back outside and felt along the ground until her fingers closed around a stone. Returning inside, she gathered leaves and sticks into a small pile. She needed something to help the fire catch.

She stood still for a moment, hand resting at her waist, breathing slowly. A few loose locks of hair slipped free and fell against her side. She lifted one, studying it, then gave a small, rueful smile.

"I love my locs of hair," she murmured, "but I need this to survive the insects."

She cut the strand with her dagger and tucked it beneath the leaves and twigs. Taking her dagger, she struck it against the stone until sparks caught. The fire took quickly.

Nzingha smiled faintly. "What princess do you know who can survive like this?"

She lowered herself to the floor, drawing her knees to her chest, and stared into the flames. Tears slipped down her face as thoughts of her baby girl and her husband pressed in on her chest. She was too close to home. If anyone recognized her here, she would be returned to her father in the Mbemba Kingdom.

She bent forward, resting her forehead against her knees. "I have to get home to my daughter," she whispered. "No matter what it takes."

Sleep overtook her. Before it did fully, she gathered coconut leaves and spread them on the ground, curling atop them in a fetal position.

Morning came quickly.

Her legs ached when she sat up, sore and weak from the escape. The smell of burning lava still lingered in the air. She rose, stretched carefully, and tied her hair back before stepping outside. A narrow path led upward into the hills, and she followed it until the sound of waves reached her ears.

"I remember this place," she said quietly.

From the rise, she could see the village to the north. To the east, Graham's ship lay anchored offshore. She turned slowly, scanning the horizon.

To the south, a second ship cut across the water.

Nzingha squinted, her heart hammering. "A ship?"

She strained to see the banner, then sucked in a sharp breath. "Oh my God… is it Andrew?"

The crest was unmistakable as it snapped in the wind.

A rush of excitement surged through her, sharp enough to steal her breath. She forced herself still at once. Graham and his men were too

close. She would have to reach the southern shore without being
seen.

Too Late

Alex peered through the spyglass. "We're close, brother. Ten
kilometers off the coast."

"Good," Andrew said. "Do ye see Graham and his men?"

"Aye. Their ship's anchored to the far east."

Andrew took the spyglass and adjusted it. "We can come in along the
southern course instead. More importantly, we must stay clear of the
Tafaria military. From what Nzingha mentioned in the past, this
coast is heavily guarded."

Alex nodded once.

They lowered a skiff and began rowing toward shore.

Three miles out, Andrew lifted his spyglass again. Something caught
his eye, a lone figure on the rocks ahead. Dark-skinned. Barely
clothed.

He stiffened.

"What in God's name…" He squinted harder. "Is that… Nzingha?"

Alex snatched the glass from him. He stared, then let out a sharp breath. "Well, call me a daft Highlander. Aye. It's her."

Nzingha stood on a jagged outcrop above the water. She lifted her arms and waved.

Andrew's chest tightened. Relief hit him so hard he had to blink against it. She was alive. Alone. Unharmed.

Then a shape moved behind her.

Andrew opened his mouth to shout.

Too late.

A man lunged from the brush. Nzingha crumpled as he struck her from behind, her body dropping out of sight.

Hellfire ripped through Andrew.

"Row!" he roared.

The men drove the oars like madmen, muscles burning as they forced the skiff forward. After the first mile, they switched positions without slowing, sweat pouring as they pushed harder. In less than half an hour, they reached the rocks.

Andrew was out of the skiff before it settled.

A scrap of fabric clung to the stone, a torn piece of Nzingha's chemise. Beyond it, deep boot prints cut through sand and pine needles, leading inland.

They followed.

Haemish lifted his hand suddenly, signaling them to stop. He pressed a finger to his lips.

From somewhere beyond the trees, a voice carried, angry and unmistakable.

Graham.

The Ambush

Slap!

The sound split the brush, sharp and ringing, carrying through the trees as Graham's hand fell away.

"This is the final time I'm goin' tae ask," he said, his voice low and stripped of patience. "Where is the bloody cave?"

Nzingha said nothing.

His jaw tightened. "Tie her tae the tree," he ordered. "Bare her back. Since ye'll nae speak, I'll beat the truth out o' ye."

Hands seized her arms and hauled her forward. Bark scraped her skin as she was forced against the trunk, rope biting deep into her wrists as it was cinched tight. One of the men tore at her chemise, ripping it open and exposing her back to the morning air.

Graham stepped closer and studied her there, bound and silent, irritation tightening his mouth.

Graham paced back and forth in annoyance. He raked a hand through his salt-and-pepper-colored hair. Walking over to where she was bound against the tree, Graham grabbed her face and shook it.

"Lass, I cannae let ye interfere with my plans. Now, where… is… the… fucking… cave."

Nzingha said nothing. He shook his head in frustration.

He gave a short nod to one of his men. The man stood immediately, coiling the rope around his hands as he moved into position. The fibers creaked as he tested their weight, then he raised his arm and drew it back, ready to bring it down.

Nzingha shut her eyes.

But the whistle of the rope never came.

Instead, there was a wet, sickening sound, followed by a heavy thud. The man collapsed where he stood, the rope slipping from his hands as an arrow jutted clean through his eye. For a heartbeat, the camp froze in disbelief.

Then the air shattered.

Arrows tore through the clearing from all directions, striking men before they could move, before they could shout. Bodies fell hard into the dirt. Screams burst out and were cut short. The Tafari war cry exploded from the bushes, fierce and unrelenting, rolling through the camp like thunder.

A staff flew past Graham's head, close enough that he felt the rush of air. He ducked instinctively, spinning as chaos erupted around him.

"What in the seven fucking hells is this?" he roared.

He reached for his sword, but it was already too late.

Men surged from the tree line in numbers too great to count, Mbemba and Tafarian warriors moving together with brutal precision. Spears flashed. Blades struck. The clearing dissolved into violence.

Bound to the tree, Nzingha opened her eyes.

She smiled.

Graham looked around and saw the truth of it all at once. The numbers were too great.

"Retreat tae the ship!" he shouted. "We cannae fight over a hundred men. Retreat!"

The Crown Trumps Blood

Andrew, Haemish, and Alex watched from about a hundred feet away, concealed by brush and rock. When Andrew saw Graham strike Nzingha, something feral ignited in his chest.

"I'm goin' tae rip that son of a whore a new asshole," Andrew hissed.

He unsheathed his sword and surged forward.

Haemish caught him instantly, hauling him back and clamping a hand over his mouth. With his other hand, he pointed sharply toward the surrounding terrain. Andrew froze long enough to follow the gesture, and then he saw it.

Warriors everywhere.

Camouflaged bodies melted out of the land itself, crouched low, hidden among brush and stone, motionless until that instant. Andrew's eyes widened as the truth settled in.

Within moments, six Tafari warriors, tall, built like living fortresses, turned their heads in unison. One of them spotted the Scotsmen and straightened, muscles rolling beneath scarred skin.

"Move!" the warrior barked.

When Nzingha saw warriors from Mbemba fighting alongside the Tafari, disbelief washed over her. Joy and fear struck together, sharp and breathless. There was only one reason such forces would move as one.

Her uncle was here.

As the last of Graham's men faltered, the warriors closed ranks. Men and women alike dropped to one knee, heads bowed, while two fighters stepped forward and cut the ropes binding her wrists.

"My niece," Prince Femi said, his voice thick with emotion. "Thank the gods you yet live. After two years of searching, we have finally found you."

"Uncle Femi!"

Nzingha ran into his arms, the strength leaving her all at once as tears poured down her face.

Femi held her tightly, memories flooding back as he pressed his forehead to hers. For a moment, she was a child again, small enough for him to lift and spin. His voice shook as he spoke.

"Where have you been? We found Asha's remains near the beach, along with your arrows and longbow. We believed you had tried to flee. We feared the Portuguese had taken you and sold you." His expression darkened. "We could not find your guard, Iney. What happened?"

"Iney and I were taken by slavers," Nzingha said quietly. "But we escaped."

Femi searched her face. "Then how did you come to be held here on Tafaria by white men dressed for the cold? These are not Portuguese."

Nzingha managed a faint smile. "That is a story for another day."

He pulled her close again. "My brother, the King, has not been the same since you vanished. Sleeping sickness weakened him greatly. He mourns you daily. We will escort you home, and you will take your rightful place."

Movement rustled in the brush.

A group of warriors emerged with machetes in hand. When they saw Nzingha, they dropped to one knee at once.

"It is truly you, Princess?"

She nodded.

One of the men turned to Femi. "My lord, we found three men hiding in the bushes. What are your orders?"

Femi did not hesitate. "Kill them."

A few of the guards laughed darkly.

"One of them claims he is married to the princess," another said. "He claims to be the father of her child. I believe he speaks lies to avoid execution."

Nzingha spun.

"Wait!"

Her voice cut through the clearing. "Do not lay a finger on my husband."

Femi froze. "Your what?"

She was already running.

Andrew, Alex, and Haemish were on their knees, hands bound, blood marking their faces, positioned for execution. Nzingha reached Andrew first.

"My love."

She kissed him fiercely, her hands already working at the ropes. "You found me."

Andrew pulled her close the moment he was free. "I told you," he said hoarsely. "I would cross the world for you."

Femi stepped forward, fury burning in his eyes. "Remove your hands from my niece at once."

Nzingha turned and placed herself between them. "Uncle, all is well."

She faced him fully. "This is my husband, Laird Andrew of Scotland. He and his men crossed the sea to rescue me."

Femi's anger flared. "Are you mad?" he barked. "You expect me to believe you were taken, escaped slavery, and then married a white man? Did he force you? Did he dishonor you?" His voice hardened. "By the gods, I will…"

Nzingha raised her hand.

She spoke in the coastal tongue, her voice calm and commanding.

"Sitisha mashambulizi. Mimi bado ni binti wa kifalme wako. Cheo changu kiko juu kuliko chako. Utaonyesha heshima kwangu na kwa mume wangu."

The response was immediate.

Every warrior dropped to one knee.

The ropes binding Andrew, Alex, and Haemish were cut at once. The men bowed deeply.

"Forgive us, my Princess."

Nzingha lowered her hand. "Leave us. I will join you shortly."

They obeyed without question.

When the clearing emptied, Andrew looked at her in disbelief. "What did ye say tae them?"

"I reminded my uncle that I am still their princess," she replied evenly. "And that my rank stands above his. There will be no disrespect toward my husband."

She reached up and touched his face. Andrew wiped the blood from the corner of her lip.

"Are ye hale?" he asked quietly. "Did Graham harm ye on his ship?"

She nodded. "He struck me. He knocked me unconscious more than once. But he did not force himself upon me."

Andrew exhaled slowly.

"Is our baby well? Is Destiny safe?" she asked.

"Aye, she is safe. I sent her to Ireland, to Lady Annabella, until we return."

He kissed her forehead. "God, I love ye… ye're stronger than any warrior here."

Alex cleared his throat. "We should meet the men at the shore."

Femi's voice carried from behind them. "Take a small garrison of my men with you. I will not have you disappear with my niece."

Nzingha inclined her head. "Very well."

As they walked toward the shore, she waited until no one was close enough to hear. Then she leaned into Andrew's arm and whispered, low and urgent.

"My love, we must leave before nightfall. I do not trust my uncle. He may try to kill you and your men or take me back to my father's kingdom by force. He is furious."

Andrew stopped short. He glanced back at Nzingha's uncle, Femi. Femi's face was set in a hard scowl, his expression carved with intent rather than anger.

Andrew walked a step apart from Nzingha. He realized his formality was too grand for someone of her station in these lands. He cursed.

"Shite." He exhaled once, steadying himself. "I'll signal the men. Tell them to hide a skiff near the rocks and wait for us. There is no way you can return to Scotland without a fight."

The Threat Turned to a Promise

Before Andrew could think of a plan, a musket cracked.

The report split the air, sharp and violent, and an Mbemba warrior went down at once, the force of the shot throwing him backward into the dirt. Shouts rose from every direction as men burst from the brush, blades flashing, boots tearing through leaves and roots.

"AMBUSH!" Alex bellowed.

Steel came free in the same instant. Alex and Haemish surged forward, cutting into the mercenaries before they could regroup. Alex dropped the first man with a brutal slash, turned, and drove his sword through another before ripping it free again. Haemish moved beside him with cold precision, cutting down a third man, then a fourth, his blade never wasting a motion.

The clearing dissolved into chaos.

Femi charged into the fight without hesitation, his staff moving like an extension of his body. He struck one man across the throat, spun, and crushed another's skull before driving the end of the staff through a third. He did not slow. By the time he stepped back, six of Graham's men lay broken at his feet.

Graham saw it.

Men were falling too fast. The numbers were against him.

"Retreat!" he shouted. "Back to the skiffs!"

He turned and ran.

Andrew saw him break.

"GRAHAM!"

The name tore from Andrew's chest as he surged forward, shoving through bodies and brush, sword raised. Graham crashed through the undergrowth ahead of him, boots slipping in blood and mud as he fled toward the shore.

Andrew almost reached him.

Graham was too far ahead, boots tearing through brush and loose earth as he drove himself toward the skiffs. Andrew pushed harder, lungs burning, arm aching from the weight of his blade, but the distance held. Graham was going to make it.

Out of nowhere, Nzingha's quick feet carried her past Andrew.

She surged forward with quick, relentless strides, her focus fixed on Graham alone. Near the body of a fallen warrior, a staff lay abandoned in the dirt. She seized it without breaking her pace, drew her arm back, and hurled it with all her strength.

The staff drove straight through Graham's back.

He dropped instantly, the impact throwing him forward into the ground. His body struck hard, limbs going slack as the breath was torn from his lungs.

Nzingha reached him within seconds.

She planted her foot beside him and pulled the staff free. Graham rolled onto his side, gasping, blood pouring from his mouth in thick, bubbling breaths. His eyes found her face, wide with disbelief, struggling to focus as his chest hitched.

She looked down at him, unflinching.

"I said that I would kill you. Now this is where you die."

Graham laughed. It was wet and broken, blood spilling between his teeth as the sound rattled out of him.

"You win," he breathed.

His eyes stayed open as the last breath left his body.

Andrew stepped to Nzingha's side. She did not look away from the body.

"I'm sorry," she said softly. "But I had to."

Andrew nodded once. "I understand."

Femi approached them then, his face marked with a fresh scar, his expression unreadable. He looked down at the body and then at Andrew.

"Who is this man?"

Andrew hesitated. "He is my uncle," he said at last. "But I can explain."

Femi said nothing. He turned away and walked off, calling Nzingha to follow.

Alex came to Andrew's side and glanced at the corpse. "What do we do with him?" he asked. "Do we take his body back to Scotland?"

Andrew spat beside the body.

"Nae," he said coldly. "'Tis the birds for him."

He turned away, never looking back.

Chapter 21

Landscapes and Annoyance

*F*emi walked off in the direction of the village, speaking aloud as he went.

"You stubborn child. Do you ever learn? You must truly hate your father. Or perhaps you love watching your lovers meet their ends so quickly."

"Uncle, allow me to explain," Nzingha said, falling into step beside him.

Femi did not slow. He marched ahead at a hard pace, his anger driving him forward.

"Uncle, where are you taking me?" she asked.

"Back to Tafaria's castle."

"My mother's castle?" Nzingha said. "Why must we go there?"

Femi did not turn.

"Come now. You must let the commoner see who he has married." His tone remained even, dismissive by design. "Besides, we were already returning when we found you dragged about in rags. Have some dignity. As long as you stand on this land, you are a Princess, not a vagabond. You will bathe. You will eat. We will discuss what comes next once we reach the keep."

He paused, only briefly.

"Oh, and bring the commoner's allies."

Nzingha stopped. Her eyes widened. This was not a good sign. She inclined her head. "Very well."

Femi and his men walked single file along the terraced rise, while Nzingha, Andrew, Alex, and Haemish followed behind. When they reached the camp, Femi turned and explained why the horses had been left there.

They had been sent on a mission into the hot lands and did not wish for the animals to thirst or damage their hooves on scorched ground. Their plan had been to ambush the Portuguese as they slipped quietly into Tafaria, catching them unprepared. The mission had lasted more than a month. On their return toward base, two scouts witnessed

Nzingha being abused and carried the report back to her uncle at once.

As they entered the camp, Femi raised his voice and issued his commands.

"We will depart for Tafaria's keep. Of the one hundred and eighty men remaining, forty from the younger Mbemba regiment and forty from the Tafarian regiment will stay behind. Ensure we are not followed. Within a day, fresh and well-rested men will be sent to relieve you."

The younger men frowned and hissed through their teeth, muttering their displeasure at the general's decision. Femi turned to Nzingha and her guests.

"We lost men on this expedition," he said evenly. "You will ride their horses back into Tafaria lands."

The journey took six hours before they reached the edge of Tafaria territory. They passed through open safari and then two villages. Along the trail, Andrew found himself struck silently by the landscape. The land stretched wide and alive around them, beautiful in a way he had never seen before.

Nzingha was starving, and her breast ached. "Please," she said, "can we stop?"

Femi raised a hand, and the entire garrison came to a halt. Nzingha's face brightened at once. She dismounted and moved toward a stand of trees heavy with yellow fruit.

"Mangos!"

Andrew watched her in confusion. "Where are you going?"

She turned back with a wide smile. "Mangos." Then she continued toward the trees.

More men followed and began picking from the branches.

Andrew grew curious as well. He noticed a nearby river and smiled. The sun burned his skin, and dust clung to him from the long ride. He dismounted and walked toward the water, intending to wash his hands and face.

When Andrew knelt too close to the riverbank, Nzingha cried out, "No, wait!"

She seized a stone and hurled it into the water. The surface broke as a massive creature surged upward, its head rising above the river, a low growl rolling from its jaws.

Andrew took quick steps backward and landed hard on his backside.

Laughter rose from the garrison. From their reaction, he knew he had made a foolish mistake. He stood, brushed the dust from his trousers, and looked toward the water.

"What in the devil's name is that?"

Nzingha walked over, peeling a mango with her teeth. "Mamba."

Andrew followed her gaze back to the river.

"A crocodile," she added calmly.

She bit into the fruit without concern.

Femi joined them, his mouth full of sweet flesh. "Had you placed your hand in that river," he said, "you could kiss your precious Scotland goodbye." He pointed toward the water. "Look downriver."

Andrew saw logs upon logs of the great beasts floating along the water's surface. He narrowed his eyes, staring into the distance.

"Holy shite."

One of them dragged itself onto a narrow stretch of land near the lake's center. The creature's body stretched impossibly long, its massive snout lined with rows of sharp teeth.

Femi mounted his horse. "Come now. We must reach Tafaria lands before nightfall. You think these creatures frightening. Those that hunt after dark are faster and far more vicious."

Before they departed, Alex decided he wanted his share of the yellow fruit. Hunger pressed hard at him. As he walked toward the trees, his stomach betrayed him with a loud rumble. He had not eaten since the night before, when they were still aboard the ship.

He reached up, plucking fruit and tucking it into his satchel. As he worked, the brush beside him shifted.

Alex froze.

A towering form stood above him, legs stretching impossibly high. The creature lowered its head, chewing lazily, its mouth full of leaves. Alex jumped back as it stared down at him, unbothered by his presence. By his reckoning, the beast had to stand nearly one hundred feet tall.

"HAEMISH!" Alex shouted.

Haemish sat beneath a nearby tree, enjoying the sweet fruit at his leisure. He looked up toward the commotion. "What in the devil's name is that?" He rose at once, his hand settling on the hilt of his sword.

Nzingha laughed. "You great, frightening girls. It is only a giraffe." Her tone remained light. "Do not worry. They are harmless. They eat leaves and fruit. Just do not stand too close. They will trample."

She mounted her horse and urged it forward, riding to rejoin Andrew and Femi at the front.

Continuing their trail toward the castle, they rode past a herd of zebras. Alex pointed at once.

"Fascinating. They look like small white horses with stripes. Andrew, look at them. Horses with stripes, and wild besides."

Andrew laughed at his brother's reaction. It carried him back to their boyhood, to the days they hunted wild boar together, when Alex would shout his name at every new discovery, unable to contain his excitement.

They pressed on until a herd of elephants crossed their path. The ground trembled beneath their weight as they moved, the air filled with the sound of their low calls and the sweep of their trunks. The garrison guided their mounts away from the trail, giving the beasts a wide berth to avoid any chance of being trampled.

Farther along, they sighted a pride of lions resting high upon a distant cliff. Only two males lay among the lionesses, all of them stretched in the sun and fast asleep.

Nzingha lifted her hand and pointed. "There are only two male lions in that pride," she said, "The females hunt and provide. The males remain to ensure the strength of the pride."

Alex smiled. "Had Andrew not run off and married," he said lightly, "it might have been him and me, much like those lions. Though we would be in a tavern, surrounded by whores and whisky."

Laughter rose from the garrison, Andrew included.

Nzingha made a sour face at the jest. "Alex, at times you are such a pig." She urged her horse ahead of the others.

Alex only shrugged and laughed.

Another three hours passed before the castle came into view. The keep rose nearly six stories high, its walls vast and unyielding. Soldiers lined the ramparts, watching from above. The architecture left the Scots momentarily speechless. Alex's mouth fell open. It was the largest beige castle he had ever seen.

Alex and Haemish turned toward Nzingha. She avoided their eyes, her posture tightening. A brief moment of awkwardness followed.

"Nzingha," Haemish said with a grin, "you truly are high and mighty."

She narrowed her eyes and offered a strained smile that did little to hide her annoyance.

Introducing them to her former life as a princess unsettled her. She did not wish for her new Scottish family to see her as high and mighty, but simply as an ordinary woman. During her life in Africa, she had longed only for love and happiness. She had known that peace only while Mikel lived. When he went missing, Nzingha's world fell into disarray, and her ability to function unraveled. His absence drove her to flee in search of him.

She rode with her head held high. She preferred not being treated as royalty, for being treated as an equal gave her a sense of belonging. In her former life, no man or woman dared raise their voice to the Princess. No one challenged her authority. But Andrew had given her something different. With him, she had known ordinary life. That was why she had fallen in love.

As they drew nearer, the sound of the ocean waves grew steadily louder. When the castle finally came into full view, the tide crashed against a great wall that stood between the land and the sea.

Tafaria Castle

The Scots had never seen a castle built in such a manner. The design itself astonished them. The rooftops rose in teardrop shapes, each tapering upward toward the sky. What struck them most were the gold turrets that crowned the towers, gleaming against the light.

Each teardrop roof blended seamlessly into the structure beneath it, forming circular towers that rose into flat platforms where soldiers stood watch. There were five towers in total, one at the center and four set at the corners of the keep. The remaining sections of the castle were formed of high triangular arches joined with broad flat surfaces. Glass windows filled the walls, allowing sunlight to enter while sheltering the interior from rain.

White flags bearing a clawed lion hung from the parapets. The color and texture of the stone gave the impression that the castle itself had been shaped from the sand of the seashore.

As they approached the gates, a guard called out, "Open the gates." The gates were forged of solid metal and marked with the image of two gold lions facing one another in a fighting stance. As the company drew nearer, the gates began to open.

Riding through the castle gates, Femi's garrison broke away toward the soldiers' wing, while Femi remained behind to escort the Scots through the keep. As they entered the courtyard, the horses' hooves struck the cobblestones with a sharp, echoing sound.

When the nobles recognized Nzingha and Femi, they bowed without lifting their eyes. Upon reaching the court entrance, Nzingha froze. Femi dismounted without a word, deliberately avoiding her gaze.

Her attention fixed on the soldiers lined along the courtyard walls. Her breath quickened, fear tightening in her chest. She turned toward Femi and pressed a hand to her stomach.

He continued to look away. Something was not right.

"Femi," she called. He did not answer. "Femi." Still, he refused to look at her.

"Bastard."

Andrew had never seen such fear on Nzingha's face. Her hands trembled, her breath uneven, her eyes wide with dread. He stepped closer and spoke in a low voice. "What is wrong? You look as though you have seen a ghost."

With a shaking breath, she lifted her gaze to him. "My father, King Afonso. He is here."

Andrew stilled. "You jest. I thought these were your mother's lands."

"They are," she said, "He claimed them after they married." She shifted slightly, peering past Andrew. "Look around you. Those men are his personal guard. They wear Mbemba colors, not Tafarian. Their pins mark them as men of rank."

Alex and Haemish dismounted at once. Alex read the fear on Nzingha's face and motioned toward Andrew. Andrew answered with a subtle gesture of his own, forming the words silently.

Her father. The King.

Both men's eyes widened.

Femi handed his horse's bridle to a stable hand. As he removed his gloves, he spoke without turning. "Come. We must not linger. We have an audience with my brother, the King. He is aware of our arrival. I sent a missive this morning."

Nzingha turned sharply toward Andrew and grasped the plaid at his shoulder. "Quick. Give me your plaid."

He frowned. "What?"

"Your plaid. Quickly."

Andrew removed it at once.

She worked quickly, fashioning a makeshift dress by tying the cloth over one shoulder to conceal her disheveled undergarments. Andrew secured it in place by fastening his family crest at the fold.

She loosened her hair from the plaits that had been bound into a tail. It fell heavy and dark, reaching her hips. Hastily, she gathered a portion of it and tied it into a bun atop her head, the style softening her appearance and lending her a younger look.

She took Andrew by the hand and drew him toward the garden's waterfall nearby. There, she washed her hands and face, swift and deliberate. Andrew followed suit. The nobles gathered in the courtyard clutched their chests in shock, gasps rippling through them as whispers spread.

Femi waited at the court entrance. He cleared his throat.

"The King awaits."

Anger flared in Nzingha. She crossed the courtyard at once.

Grasping his wrist, she spoke under her breath. "Bastard. You knew he was here all along, and you said nothing."

"Zing," Femi replied quietly, "had I told you your father was here in Tafaria, you would have fled with this white man to God knows where."

"This man saved my life," she said, "He is my husband, and the father of my child."

"Come," Femi said with a thin smile. "We shall tell your father of his grandchild and his son-in-law."

Her stomach tightened. She pressed a hand against it. "Please. I beg you. Do not tell my father of my child or my marriage. My babe is eight months old. I was taken when she was only six months. If I am forced to remain here, at least let my husband return home to her. Please."

Femi studied her. "On one condition."

"Anything," she said at once. "What is it?"

"You must convince your father that you do not wish to be his heir. You will sign over all rights so that I may succeed him."

A short laugh escaped her. "I never wanted to be his heir. You are a fool. If this is what you desired, why bring me here at all? You should have let me leave."

Femi lifted his hands in frustration. "No. I could not. He has a son of twenty years, a boy who does not know the King is his father. If the truth comes out, I will be forced to fight for my place. I have built our forces against the foreigners. I have led our men through death and through victory. I have earned this."

"You have," Nzingha said steadily. "And I will stand by you. But do not coerce your own niece. I do not want this life. I love my husband. I want to return home with him. I want to see my daughter. She needs me."

Her voice softened. "Help us escape, Femi. You know my father's mind. Look at what became of Mikel. Please. This is my family."

Femi's heart faltered as understanding settled in him. Mikel had been one of his finest soldiers and his closest companion. He drew a slow breath and stepped forward, pulling her into an embrace.

"I am sorry, my niece," he said quietly. "I love you deeply. I grieve for Mikel. He was among my most skilled generals, and I knew you loved him. Now I see that you feel the same for this man." He paused, regret settling over him. "I allowed my own desire to blind me. It weighs on me that your father ignores all I have given to these lands."

He straightened, returning to his voice. "We will craft a tale. The Scots rescued you and Iney. They will remain here for several days, long enough to show good faith. When the time comes for their departure, we will speak again and set your escape in motion."

"He may kill you if you betray him, Femi," she said,

"He will not," Femi replied calmly. "He is my elder brother. Beneath all his hardness and discipline, he loves me."

King Afonso Mbema

Andrew, Alex, and Haemish stood together at the entryway. Nzingha turned toward them and lifted her hand, the gesture quiet but deliberate.

"It is time to meet my father, King Afonso," she said, "Make eye contact only when he addresses you and speak only if he asks. I ask that you show no arrogance. Femi and I have prepared a tale of how we came to meet. Do not speak of our marriage, and above all, do not speak of Destiny."

Andrew drew in a breath and nodded once.

Femi's gaze settled on Andrew and then shifted to Alex. "Do not present yourselves as Drake or Rowan. You and your men have been spoken of in councils across many nations. I know who you are and what you have done upon the seas. You and your crew, the sea dogs, Drake and Rowan, are hailed as white saviors." His tone hardened. "It is the only reason your heads still rest upon your shoulders."

Andrew allowed himself the faintest smile. "That is my sea name. I am Laird Andrew Barton."

Femi turned away. "Tell it to the King."

They paused at the threshold of the King's Hall, the chamber of the throne. A trumpet sounded, its note carrying through the stone. When it fell silent, a herald's voice followed.

"Introducing Princess Nzingha Tafarian Mbemba. Accompanying her, Laird Andrew Barton of Scotland, Laird Alex Barton of Scotland, and Haemish McTavish of Scotland, together with His Majesty's younger brother, Prince Femi Mbemba."

Tall metal doors, embossed with the same fighting lions that guarded the outer gates, were opened before them. Beyond the threshold, Nzingha's father stood waiting.

There was fear upon his face, and worry as well. She had never seen either upon him before.

When Nzingha saw him, something in her chest gave way despite herself. He looked older than she remembered. Silver threaded his hair, and his weight leaned heavily upon a cane as he began to walk toward her.

She took two steps forward, then stopped.

The memory of their last audience rose in her mind, unbidden. His rage. Her confinement. Mikel condemned to death for treason.

As the King continued toward her, his arm trembled slightly against the cane that supported him.

Nzingha kept her gaze lowered. The throne room seemed to fall silent around them. She listened to the slow rhythm of his approach, the tap of wood against stone echoing through the hall. Her breathing grew shallow, her heart pressing hard against her ribs as she stared down at her hands, which would not stop shaking.

King Afonso stopped before her.

"My daughter," he said, his voice deep and rough. "Nzingha. It is you."

She lifted her eyes then and saw the tears upon his face.

"My child," he continued, his voice uneven but controlled. "I believed you lost to the world. We did not know whether you lived or were dead. There was no trace of you." He drew a breath. "What I did was born of anger. It should not have happened." His gaze held hers. "Can you forgive me?"

Nzingha raised her chin and turned her face away. Tears slipped free despite her effort to hold them back. After a moment, she faced him again.

"Father, it is in the past. We must live for a new day. I do not question your judgment."

The King stepped back, nodding slowly. "Let me look at you. You bear your mother's likeness. Only two years have passed, yet life has shaped you. Are you hale? How is your health?"

"I am well, Father."

"I still struggle to believe you stand before me," he said, "My heart is glad, yet it aches with the knowledge of how deeply you despised me."

He turned then toward his brother and offered a small smile. "When I received your missive, I believed it a jest. Yet I waited for you with great unease."

His gaze finally settled upon the three Scottish men standing behind Nzingha.

Femi stepped forward and bowed, then placed his hand upon Andrew's shoulder.

"This is Laird Andrew Barton of Scotland. He rescued your daughter from a deserted island."

The King's expression eased, a smile spreading across his face. "You have the thanks of central, western, and eastern Africa."

Andrew bowed his head. "My thanks, Your Highness."

The King lifted his hand, signaling for the servants to step forward. "Come. We shall dine privately this evening, and tomorrow there will be a celebration."

Femi bowed in turn. "I will see our guests to their lodgings."

As the court began to move, a woman stepped to Nzingha's side. When Nzingha looked up, her breath caught for a moment. For an instant, she thought she saw Iney. She blinked, once, then again.

It was Iney's younger sister, Ifama.

Nzingha smiled and reached for her, drawing her into an embrace. Ifama did not return it. Slowly, Nzingha released her and lowered her head.

"Ifama," she said quietly. "I am sorry. Iney did everything she could to protect me. She was with me on the island." Her voice faltered, but she continued. "She fell ill there. I was able to lay her to rest with the Goddess Yemaya. Your family will be honored for her service."

She drew a breath. "I know you must hate me. Had I not escaped my chamber, Iney would be standing here beside me. I carry the blame for her death. I could not save her." Her voice softened further. "Please forgive me."

Ifama kept her eyes fixed ahead. When she spoke, her voice was even and controlled.

"Welcome back to Tafaria, Princess Nzingha." A brief pause followed. "I have been assigned as your guard."

Nzingha searched her face and understood at once. The resentment was settled there, unmoving. She remembered Ifama as a child, always following her and Iney, pleading to be included, only to be sent away.

Nzingha nodded. "Very well." She reached for the young soldier's hand. "Please know that I am truly sorry."

Ifama pulled her hand free and straightened, standing at attention without meeting her gaze.

Femi turned toward the Scots. "Come, gentlemen. You will be bathed and dressed before dining with the King."

The Bath Before the Tides

Femi led the men down a long corridor lined with flowers and carved figures.

Some of the statues were cast in bronze, others in gold, while tall stone forms depicted warriors frozen in quiet strength. The passage stretched on before them, cool and hushed.

At its end, he turned and guided them up a stairwell that opened into a broad foyer. Above them, glass panels covered the roof, and one window was propped open to allow a steady breeze to pass through. Sunlight poured in so freely that it felt as though they were standing outdoors.

The floor beneath their feet was marble, polished smooth, and the walls were adorned with paintings of African men dressed as scholars and noblemen. Some wore crowns, others bore sashes of cheetah skin or lions' mane across their shoulders, gold-plated necklaces resting against their chests.

Femi stopped and gestured toward three doors set side by side. "These chambers are joined within," he said, "You may lodge here."

He motioned again and turned away, leading them down another stair. This passage opened into a wide corridor supported by tall columns that rose to the ceiling above. At its center lay an expansive pool. Gold statues stood at its edge, water flowing steadily from their mouths into the basin below.

The pool drained through an open channel, the water moving continuously as it carried away its residue, leaving the surface clear and flowing.

Ever curious, Alex stood with his hands resting at his waist. After a moment, he knelt beside the pool, watching the murky residue slip away through the channel cut into the stone. When he rose again, he shook his head, a low sound of wonder leaving him.

"Well now, would ye look at that," he said, "Bloody clever." He motioned toward the flowing water. "They've drawn a source straight into the castle, then cut an exit for it to run out again. Clean water in. Filth away." He glanced over at Andrew. "I swear, I'll be doin' this at the castle."

Femi brought his hands together in a sharp clap.

At once, five women entered the bathing hall. They moved with practiced ease, their skin smooth and in different shades of dark, catching the light as they passed beneath the columns. Each wore the same patterned cloth, bound across the chest and tied at the neck, with skirts that fell to mid-thigh. Matching wraps covered their hair.

They carried baskets filled with rose petals, oils, sponges, and soap, the scent of them rising gently into the air as they approached.

Femi presented the women with a measured gesture of his hand. "These are the royal bathers and groomers. They attend to the cleansing of the body and the care of hair, as is our custom."

Alex regarded the women with open curiosity, his attention lingering on the baskets they carried.

"The care of hair," he repeated. "Ye mean the beard and head? Or is there more tae it than that."

Femi laughed softly.

"Let us say their service reaches places men rarely speak of."

Andrew was already familiar with the custom, having heard it explained by Nzingha in the past. Among her people, grooming was considered a matter of health and dignity, not merely appearance, and it reached further than what men of the north were accustomed to.

Alex's interest deepened. "I have never heard of such a thing before," he said, his tone thoughtful rather than crude. "I believe I would like to experience it."

One of the bathers stepped forward and bowed respectfully. "First, we will wash you. Afterward, we will prepare you."

Alex did not hesitate. He began removing his clothing without ceremony, treating the moment as a matter of curiosity rather than display. The bathers turned away with practiced discretion, murmuring softly among themselves as they prepared the pool.

The bather bowed in acknowledgment and stepped aside.

A different servant approached, holding a tray upon which rested finely crafted shaving tools and a small bowl of wax kept warm by glowing coals beneath it.

"Honored guest," she said, her voice calm and composed, "do you wish to be shaved, or do you wish to be groomed fully?"

Andrew considered the offer in silence. Life at sea, and the urgency that had driven him since leaving Scotland, had left little room for care beyond what was strictly necessary. Still, the warmth of the chamber and the practiced ease of the attendants gave him pause.

"Aye," he said at last. "I'll have a shave. Trim the beard and the hair, but leave it long enough. I've no wish tae look like a boy."

The servant bowed and stepped away to prepare the tools.

Haemish, Andrew, and Alex soon settled themselves into the bath, the warmth of the water easing the strain from their bodies. Each was handed a goblet of wine, which they accepted with quiet appreciation. The bathers scattered rose petals across the surface of the water, the petals clinging briefly to skin before drifting away as steam gathered beneath the high ceiling.

Another servant knelt at the pool's edge beside Alex and poured warm water slowly over his shoulders, her hands steady as she worked scented oil onto his skin with practiced ease. The touch was firm rather than indulgent, methodical in its purpose, as she worked the tension from his neck and back.

A woman approached Andrew with a sponge, her half-naked skin glistening in the steam. He raised a hand at once in refusal.

"I will see tae my own bath. My thanks," he said swiftly.

The last thing he needed was for word to get back to Nzingha. Her temper was one he never liked riling up, and as he rubbed his forehead, the memory of her last headbutt returned with painful clarity.

Alex's eyes remained closed as he yielded to the steady work of the bather's hands, every knot easing beneath the smooth, deliberate pressure. The tension he had carried for years seemed to unravel piece by piece.

When his eyes opened, he drew in a breath he had not known he was holding.

His brows knit together.

"Christ Almighty."

Time slowed.

A woman approached, barefoot and silent against the stone, her hips swaying gently from side to side with each measured step.

There was something uncommon about her, something that did not belong wholly to these lands. Her skin held the warm depth of dark almond bronze, smooth and even, catching the light without shine. Pale blond strands ran through her hair, fading into darker roots, as though the sun had once claimed it and never fully released its hold. Her eyes were a clear hazel touched with green, steady and observant beneath long lashes.

She met his gaze without hesitation.

"When you are ready," she said plainly, "we will begin the grooming process. It will sting, but it will pass."

Alex let out a short breath, half amusement and half anticipation. "I've endured worse than a bit of pain," he said, settling deeper into the water. "I'll no' flinch."

Haemish snorted softly into his goblet. "What a witless idiot."

When the groomer finally stepped away, Alex cracked his knuckles and looked between his brother and Haemish with a grin that promised trouble.

"Ya ken," he said thoughtfully, "this isnae such a bad idea tae have back at the castle."

Andrew smirked. "Except, I dinnae think ye'd be usin' it for bathin'."

Haemish barked out a laugh, and Andrew joined him. The sound of their laughter carried through the hall, echoing off stone and water.

"Bugger off, Andrew," Alex scowled.

Femi stood a short distance away, speaking in low tones with the same beauty Alex could not take his eyes off, as she prepared an area along the stone bench for waxing. It sounded suspiciously like a disagreement. When their exchange ended, Femi disrobed without ceremony, lifted his goblet, and stepped into the pool.

The man's body looked as though it had been carved rather than grown, and Alex glanced down without thinking before immediately spitting his wine across the bath. Andrew and Haemish followed his gaze a heartbeat later, both freezing in place as understanding struck.

Alex coughed violently as the wine went down the wrong way, wheezing,

"Great Saint Christopher Christ, do ye commit murder with that thing?"

Femi looked down at himself at last, genuinely puzzled, while the bathers burst into laughter, covering their mouths as they giggled at Alex's distress.

"What?" Femi asked, still utterly unaware of the cause.

Alex pointed. "Yer cock, man. If I carried a weapon like that, I'd have bairns runnin' all over Scotland. Ye look like ye could fell a tree with it."

Andrew groaned, pressing two fingers to his forehead. "Forgive my brother. He's an arse, and more often than not he dinnae ken when tae stop speakin'."

He jabbed Alex in the ribs with his elbow.

Femi laughed, unfazed. He glanced toward the waxer and spoke casually. "It is all right. My wives are quite pleased with my manhood. I have five children already. Another is on the way."

Alex stared. "Wives? Did ye say wives?"

"Yes," Femi replied. "Do you not take more than one wife in Scotland?"

"Absolutely not. The church would hang me by my stones, call it adultery, sacrilege, every holy crime they fancy." He gave a careless shrug. "Which is precisely why I'll never marry. I prefer options." His gaze slid toward Femi, eyes narrowing with curiosity rather than mockery. "And they dinnae grow jealous? Dinnae lose their senses the way most women do?"

Femi sipped his wine and set the goblet aside. "Of course they become jealous. When that happens, we share the bed. We settle frustration by mating." A faint smile touched his mouth. "They are sisters to one another. If one leaves, I take another wife. Their duty is to bear my sons and daughters." He tilted his head. "You do not wish for children?"

"NAE!" Alex said with confidence. "I've been very diligent with my withdrawal, thank ye kindly."

Andrew pinched the bridge of his nose. He had heard enough.

"There comes a time when a man must put aside rakish ways."

Femi studied him. "And you have done this?"

Andrew nodded, choosing his words with care. "Aye. I've found someone I love. I gave her my soul, and she gave me hers." He paused, his voice lowering without intent. "She gave me our daughter. For that, I will love her for as long as breath remains in me."

The bathers sighed in unison.

Femi's expression darkened for a breath as he glanced at the waxer preparing the bench. Then he looked back at Andrew and smiled thinly. "For as long as breath remains, yes?" he repeated.

Andrew nodded.

Femi provided him a look of assurance. "That day may come sooner than you think."

He laughed and lifted his wine.

Andrew narrowed his eyes. Was it a jest?

Alex shifted uncomfortably and rose from the pool. "Enough of this." He stepped out, drying himself. "I'm ready. Let us do this waxin' business."

He stretched out on the stone bench and flashed a grin at the royal groomer, his voice dropping into charm.

"Well then, bonnie lass," he said, "tell me exactly what this waxin' consists of."

The groomer spoke with calm assurance as she prepared her tools. "We remove the hair from your chest, under your arms, and from below."

Alex turned his head sharply. "My bollocks?" He barked a laugh. "I've never heard o' a man daein' such a foolish thing." He glanced down at himself, then back at her, lips twitching. "They've survived storms, sword fights, and bad wine. I see no reason tae trouble them now."

She smiled, unbothered, already reaching for a cloth. "It is our custom. It keeps the body clean and fresh. No smell lingers when one sweats." Her eyes dropped briefly, assessing him without shame. "It also helps a man appear more impressive."

Alex followed her gaze, then scoffed softly. "Appear, she says." He glanced toward Femi, who stood several paces away in conversation with Andrew, his attention elsewhere. Alex turned back to her with a slow grin. "Aye. Do whatever it is ye do. Give me your finest work. If I'm tae suffer, I may as well look legendary."

She reached for a small blade. "First, I must shave. Waxing too much hair will cause unnecessary pain." Her hand was steady as she began.

Alex leaned back, deliberately relaxing far more than was proper, his head tilting as he studied her face. He thought, not for the first time, that fate had a cruel sense of humor, placing a woman like this precisely where she could undo him. She was striking. Her lips were full, soft even at rest. Her nose was perfectly shaped, adorned with a delicate gold ring that carried a fine chain from nostril to ear. The ornament caught the light when she smiled, lending her an elegance that made her seem far removed from her task. Her face was round and warm, and when she smiled her teeth were straight and impossibly white. Her eyes held his longest. They were slanted, watchful, deep hazel, and they missed nothing.

"Ye ken, a woman as beautiful as ye has nae business spendin' her days waxin' men's cocks and pits." His mouth curved. "It feels like a cruel test set by the gods. Or a punishment. Hard tae tell."

She laughed freely, unashamed, her shoulders lifting as she did. "Only royalty I have worked with. Though you are my first who is not."

Alex frowned, offended in mock seriousness. "I am the laird o' my castle. Royal enough in my own lands, last I checked."

She looked at him then, unimpressed, and took hold of him without ceremony, continuing her work with practiced care.

Alex sucked in a sharp breath, then laughed under it. "Bold hands ye have, lass. If ye keep that up, I'll start thinkin' this is less groomin' and more courtship, and I was nae warned."

"And what is your name, lass?"

She leaned slightly over him as she worked, her breast brushing his shoulder. He caught her scent, rose petals and warm oil, sweet enough to unsettle him. His thoughts wandered shamelessly, imagining her hands employed in far more agreeable circumstances. He shifted, trying and failing to remain still.

"My name is Yvonne," she said, "But Evie, if you prefer."

"Aye," he murmured. "Evie." His smile turned slow and dangerous. "That name could get a man into trouble all on its own."

His body betrayed him. He stiffened, heat rushing in fast and undeniable. "Ah hell," he muttered, glancing heavenward as if betrayed by his own flesh. "I didnae mean tae. I just… my body's far too honest for its own good."

She smiled knowingly. "It is natural. The skin is sensitive, and my hands are warm." Her tone held no mockery, only quiet confidence. When she finished shaving, she straightened. "Now comes the interesting part."

Alex swallowed hard and thought that interesting was one word for it, though not the one forming in his head.

She lifted a small clay pot from above a candle, stirring the honeyed substance slowly until it glistened. "This will be warm. Tell me if it burns."

Alex nodded solemnly, as if accepting his fate. "If I scream, it's only because I value my future children."

As she spread the mixture, her body moved with practiced grace. Alex clenched his hands at his sides, breath shallow, already regretting every decision that led him to this chair.

When she looked at him again, her voice lowered, playful but composed. "Are you ready?"

"Oh God, aye," he breathed. "If this kills me, bury me facedown so the world remembers me fondly."

She counted calmly. "Moja. Mbili. Tatu."

The pull was swift and merciless.

Alex's shout rang out. "Bloody hell. Bollocks tae all the devils walkin' this earth. Jesus Christ, that hurt." He lurched forward, clutching himself, rocking in place. "I have survived cannon fire with more dignity than this."

Yvonne clapped a hand over her mouth, laughing despite herself. "Forgive me, honored guest, but I must finish." She raised her hands briefly, as if to placate him. "Shall we continue?"

He glared, eyes watering, pride in tatters. "Aye. Finish it. I'll no' be defeated by honey and spite."

She did, twice more, then stepped back to inspect her work. "There. You are done, Laird Alex."

He sat up carefully, squinting downward with grave concentration. "Be honest. I need tae ken if this suffering has purpose. Do I look bigger?"

She laughed openly. "Yes. Very much so."

Alex grinned. "Then I forgive ye everything."

Before he left, he caught her hand gently. She stiffened, surprise flickering across her face. His voice dropped, low and coaxing. "Come see me after the evenin' meal. Show me more o' this place. Preferably with fewer weapons involved."

She withdrew her hand at once. "I cannot meet a guest of honor alone. I would be punished. Permission would be required."

Alex only smiled and raised his voice. "Oh, Prince Femi. Might the groomer and a few o' her companions show me about this eve? 'Tis a beautiful land, and I would ken it better."

Femi turned sharply. His gaze went first to Alex, then to Yvonne. Something dark passed over his expression before he mastered it.

"Does the servant agree to attend?" he asked.

She shook her head at first, a small refusal meant to pass unnoticed. When Alex looked at her then, his expression softened into something almost boyish, wounded in a way that caught her off guard. The moment stretched, uncomfortable in its quiet. She felt the weight of it settle on her shoulders. Then Femi spoke again, his voice careless, dismissive, calling her a servant as though the word defined her place in the world. Something hardened inside her. Not alone, but resolve. She lifted her chin, her voice steady when she answered.

"I do. It will be pleasant."

Femi held her gaze a moment longer than necessary, his eyes narrowing with barely restrained fury, before he nodded once. "Very well."

As he turned away, Alex caught the tension that lingered between them. He smiled slowly at Yvonne, eyes bright with promise and trouble. "Then I'll see ye this eve."

He crossed toward the pool, still sore in both pride and body. When Haemish caught sight of him, he guffawed, and Andrew joined him without mercy.

Haemish eventually drew a breath, wiping at his eye before shaking his head. "Ye look like a laddie," he said, still amused.

"Shut your gob," Alex shot back. "It makes me look bigger."

He turned then, catching Yvonne's gaze across the steam. She had been watching him. When their eyes met, she smiled, just slightly, and he returned it without thinking.

The men dried themselves and made for their chambers, laughter still trailing behind them.

Risk It all

When Andrew entered his chambers, there was a female bending over, arranging clothing across the bed. He jumped because he was not expecting anyone to be there.
"Christ. Ye near took my heart clean out."

The young lady was extremely afraid. She spoke with a shaky voice.
"The Princess wished that I assist you with dressing. She requested

that I provide you with clothing until your clothes are cleaned and brought back to you."

Andrew nodded. He looked down on the bed.
"What kind o' clothes are these?"

He was expecting full-on ballroom attire, but what he saw was different.

"We call it our traditional dress." She handed him the undergarments and turned away as he dressed. When she returned, she gave him loose trousers of white cotton, threaded faintly with gold and secured at the waist with a simple tie.

Next came a blouse of the same cloth, white with gold designs across the chest. The collar was short and neatly structured, sitting close to the neck. When he looked at himself, he scarcely recognized the man reflected there. The attire made him look like a prince.

The servant asked, "Honored guest, can you sit on the bed? I must fit you for a pair of sandals."

"Aye."

When Andrew sat, she knelt before him and began measuring his feet, her movements careful and practiced. He watched with quiet curiosity. He had never exposed his feet in public before, and the attention felt oddly intimate, almost boyish in its novelty. After a moment, she nodded to herself, satisfied, and reached for a pair that would fit.

Before handing them to him, she paused and looked up. "Honored guest, I must groom your toenails."

Andrew nodded again, more amused now than surprised.

She took a small pair of shears and began clipping, steady and precise, then cleaned the edges of his cuticles with care. When she finished, she lifted her gaze and smiled warmly. "You have nice feet."

Andrew smiled back, a faint flush touching his face. "My thanks."

She slid the leather sandals onto his feet, the straps soft against his skin, leaving his toes exposed. When she stood, she looked him over from head to toe, clearly pleased with her work.

"You are all done, honored guest. It suits you very well."

She bowed and left the chamber quietly behind her.

Andrew walked to the looking glass and stopped short. He hardly recognized himself. The clothing was nothing like the stiff layers he wore at court, the heavy vest, the cravat pulled tight, the coat that weighed on his shoulders. This felt different, lighter, freer. He shifted his weight and turned slightly, watching how the cloth moved with him.

A thought crossed his mind, half serious and half amused. Maybe I need my sword.

He set one foot forward as if he were posing for a painter and placed both hands on his hips, studying the effect with a critical eye. "Traditional attire, they call it, aye? Though in Scotland this would be called a doublet with nae puffs."

He smirked and flexed his arms, unable to help himself. The cloth clung just enough to show the strength he had earned over years of labor and battle. He flexed again, slower this time, clearly pleased with what he saw. If nothing else, he thought, it was honest work finally being given its due. He wondered then if Nzingha might like a family painting dressed in her countrymen's finest, and whether she would laugh at him or admire him more for it.

All dressed, Andrew placed his sword belt at his waist; he felt naked without it. When he walked out of the chamber, he saw Alex and Haemish also dressed in their traditional garments. Alex wore blue, and Haemish wore red.

Alex smiled, clearly pleased with the sight of them all.
"We look like high-born princes," he said, lifting his chin as if daring anyone to argue.

Andrew glanced at Haemish and smiled.

"Ye cleaned up nice. I can finally see your face with all that hair gone."

Haemish huffed a quiet laugh, running a hand over his jaw.

"I wish Lady Annabella could see me like this. She'd no' ken what tae make o' me."

Before Andrew could answer, Femi stepped from his chambers, dressed in attire unlike the others. The cut was broader, the cloth flowing, the presence unmistakable.

Alex's brow lifted at once.

"And is yours called traditional attire as well?"

"It is," Femi replied calmly. "In the west, we call it agbada. In your tongue, it might be described as a wide-sleeved robe."

Alex let out a low whistle.

"Well then. Ye've made us look underdressed."

Haemish chuckled, and Andrew smiled as Femi motioned for them to follow.

He led them down the tower stairwell and into a grand hall. Two wide doors opened to reveal a dining chamber glowing with hundreds of candles. A long table stretched before them, already prepared with fruits and vegetables arranged in careful abundance. Servants bowed as they entered. One approached with a tray, offering each man a gold goblet filled with wine.

"Come," Femi said. "We must await the King."

They stood behind high-backed chairs cushioned in white velvet, the table laid with gold utensils that caught the candlelight. Then the doors opened again.

Andrew smiled as though it were his wedding day.

Nzingha entered, and the room seemed to brighten with her presence. She wore white, sleeveless, her shoulders and chest bare. Gold designs traced the fitted bodice, curving over her stomach and bosom. The skirt clung to her hips before flowing to the floor behind her as she walked.

Her hair was wrapped in white, her necklace resting between her breasts. Chandelier earrings framed her face, and a thin gold plait circled her upper arm, completing the look.

What undid Andrew entirely were her lips, painted red and full, and the dark liner that made her brown eyes luminous. She looked seductive. She was his.

She walked toward him, and he smiled, biting his lip before pressing his knuckles to his mouth. His thoughts were anything but polite. He wanted to find a room, hike her skirts, and throw her across the nearest table.

Haemish and Alex stared openly.

Alex's mouth hung ajar.
"Christ alive," he muttered. "That's no' fair on the rest o' us."

Haemish shook his head slowly.
"I dinnae think the room was ready for that."

Andrew did not hear them. His eyes never left her.

A voice bellowed, "Please remain standing for His Majesty, King Afonso Mbemba."

Nzingha's father's chair was at the head of the table. Her father smiled. "My daughter, I cannot believe how beautiful and mature you look."

"Aww, thank you, Father."

"Please call me Daddy, like you used to when you were a little girl. You were so innocent back then. That was the time when your mother scolded you and told you the proper way to address me was by calling me Father. Back when you would call me Daddy, my heart would melt."

Nzingha wanted to cry, but she held back her tears. She remembered there was a time when her father would walk the castle grounds with her uncle, Femi, at his side. She would play with the other children at court, but when it was time for them to go home, she would become saddened and run to her father. She would tug on his agbada, calling, "Daddy… Daddy… de other children cannot play with me anymore. Can you order them to come back to de castle and play?"

Her father would pick her up and laugh. "My little coco bean, it is late. They must go home to their mothers and fathers too. You shall see them tomorrow. I shall order them to play with you then." He would kiss her, and she would run off to find her mother.

When Nzingha remembered those days, it made her heart melt. She assisted her father with sitting, then kissed him on his cheek. When she wiped the red paint from his face, he held her hand and smiled. The King sat, and his other guests followed suit. It was a private dinner for the King, Femi, Nzingha, and the Scots.

The King raised his goblet and looked directly at Andrew. "I would like to make a toast to Laird Andrew Barton of Scotland. You are a brave man. Thank you for saving my daughter. Before you leave to go home, I would like to present you with a reward for bringing the Princess home."

Andrew bowed. "Your Majesty, thank you. You are most kind and gracious. Hear, hear." Everyone raised their goblets and drank to the King's toast.

The King smiled pleasantly. "Will you need an escort back to your ship? The reward is one hundred thousand pieces of gold."

Andrew froze, wine halfway to his mouth, then promptly spat it back into his goblet in a desperate attempt to save his dignity.

Alex was not so lucky.

He choked violently, coughing so hard he bent at the waist, while Haemish slapped his back with more enthusiasm than precision. The sound echoed through the hall, loud enough to turn heads.

The King narrowed his eyes, studying them with sudden suspicion. "Is your man hale?" he asked calmly. "We do test our food for poison."

Alex straightened just enough to bow, still wheezing. "Aye, Your Majesty," he rasped. "It's no' the wine. It's the number." He bowed. "Ahem… I am sorry, Your Majesty. I drank a wee bit too fast."

A servant clapped once, sharply, and the hall came alive with movement. Attendants entered in measured steps, carrying wide bowls and covered platters.

"For the first course," the servant announced, "we offer afang soup, slow cooked with smoked fish and tender cuts of meat, served with pounded afang leaf and ripe plantain. It is taken with fufu."

Bowls of warm water were placed before each guest, cloths folded neatly beside them.

The men exchanged uncertain glances. None of them moved.

Every pair of eyes shifted, almost in unison, toward Nzingha.

She noticed at once and suppressed a smile. With a small, discreet motion, she dipped her fingers into the water, dried them on the cloth, and nodded gently toward the bowls. They watched her, then the King and Femi, and quickly followed suit, fumbling only slightly in their haste to appear composed.

Andrew reached for the soup spoon out of habit, then paused. He watched as the King, Femi, and Nzingha instead picked up a small portion of the white substance that sat beside the bowl, rolling it smoothly in their palms. Andrew set the spoon down, lifted the same substance, and studied it with cautious interest.

"What is this called?" he asked.

"It is fufu," Femi replied. "Pounded yam."

Andrew nodded as if that explained everything. He mimicked their movements carefully, rolling it in his hand and dipping it into the soup before bringing it to his mouth.

The effect was immediate.

The spice hit him hard and fast. His ears flushed red, and his eyes widened before he could stop himself. He swallowed bravely, lips pressing together as he tried to maintain his dignity.

Across the table, Haemish was already on his second mouthful, smacking noisily and licking his fingers with unapologetic enthusiasm.

Alex had not come up for air once.

He leaned over his bowl, tearing into the food with alarming commitment, dipping and eating and dipping again, utterly unbothered by decorum or heat. A sheen of sweat formed at his brow, but his expression suggested only pleasure.

Andrew glanced between them, then back to his own bowl, nostrils flaring as the spice lingered. He frowned faintly at their table manners, though envy crept in despite himself.

Clearly, some men were built for battle. Others were built for fire.

The King spoke. "So, Laird Barton." Both brothers looked up at King Afonso. The King laughed. "Apologies, I meant Laird Andrew Barton. How did you come across my daughter, Nzingha?"

Before Andrew could speak, Nzingha chimed in. "Father. Iney and I were captured from our shores. We ran into Laird Barton as we were stranded on an island after we escaped from a slave ship."

Nzingha's father's face hardened. He shook his head. "I swear, we will kill every intruder that tries to enter our lands." Her father looked up. "Where is Iney? She was your childhood friend, then your guard. You both fought side by side together."

"Father, Iney was injured. The island we were stranded on had no medicines we were trained to use on our field missions. I could not treat her infection. Iney has passed on."

The King nodded. "So sad. She was so young. Did anyone hurt you? Did they beat you? Rape you? Are you still pure?"

Femi then chimed in. "Oh, brother, I am sorry to interrupt. Nzingha mentioned that she visited Laird Barton's country, Scotland, and she saw snow."

"It is all right, Femi. Here is not the time or place to discuss such personal and tragic events."

"It is all right, Father; I was not hurt in any way. I managed to escape before anything grave took place."

"I am so relieved. I have cried every night, praying to the gods to bring my daughter home." The King smiled. "Please tell me about the snow."

Nzingha giggled. "It is cold, colder than our waters during the chilly season. It turns into ice, and when you touch it, it melts in your hands."

She shook her head, amused by the memory. "We could never wear our clothing there. You can die from the cold. Men and women, especially the women, wear layers upon layers. They cover their hands with gloves and wrap itchy cloths about their necks."

She laughed again, softer this time. "It is most uncomfortable, though interesting. I had to wear something beneath my dress called stays."

Andrew and Haemish laughed, while Alex continued to feed his face.

Andrew spoke. "Aye, in my country the women arenae allowed to show their skin. They dress modestly for their husbands."

"So, you wore their attire, darling?" her father asked, curiosity edging his voice.

"Yes, it was most uncomfortable," Nzingha admitted with a small laugh. "But I got used to it." She glanced at Andrew and smiled, and he returned it warmly. The King noticed their exchange.

"Nzingha, now that you are back, we must match you with a royal tribe. We must continue our legacy. After I am gone, you will be Queen of the western and eastern lands of this continent."

Nzingha leaned back in her chair, sulking slightly. She could hardly believe her father was already speaking of marriage when she had barely returned.

Her father recognized that look at once. "Come now, do not slouch, and do not give me that face. You know this is our way."

Nzingha looked down at her hands, then sat up straighter and glanced at Femi, then at Andrew. "Father."

"Yes, my daughter?"

"What if you give the succession and crown to Femi? He has earned it. He has fought all our wars and has the scars to prove it. If he rules, then I will not have to marry. I do not wish to marry." She quickly peeked at Andrew from the corner of her eye before turning her gaze back to her father.

The King held his hand up. "Nzingha, that is enough. For generations, the rule says the King must pass the kingdom down to his first born. Your brother, Nsiah, is deceased. So, you must lead."

"But I am your second born. I do not wish to lead."

He barked at her. "Nzingha. Please. You are breaking my heart with this nonsense."

Nzingha rose so abruptly her chair scraped the floor. Her hand struck the table, hard enough to rattle the dishes.

"Father. Enough."

Her voice trembled, but she did not raise it. That restraint made it worse.

"I will marry for love. Not for succession. Not for crowns. Not for heirs." She drew a shallow breath. "You taught me to value truth, yet you refuse to see it when it stands before you. I choose love because it is the only thing that ever chose me."

She swallowed hard, one hand pressing briefly to her chest as if to steady her heart. "You took the only man who loved me for who I was, not for what I might inherit or rule. When he vanished, I went searching for him, believing he might still be alive." Her voice cracked. "I did not know you had already decided he was dead."

Her eyes filled, but she did not wipe them away, as if she no longer trusted her hands to do anything gentle.

"Mikel was my heart, not a weakness. Not a foolish dream. He was my heart." Her voice thinned, the words forced past something lodged deep inside her. "When you took him from me, you did not end a love. You took the part of me that still believed I was safe in this world."

She shook her head once, slowly, as though refusing what could not be undone. "Time has not eased it. It has only taught me how to carry the weight without falling." Her breath hitched. "I wake each day knowing he is gone, and I must keep living anyway."

Her gaze lifted then, steady through the tears. "He did not deserve to die. And I did not deserve to lose him."

The tears came then, silently at first.

"The night you locked me in my chambers, I escaped. I did not leave in defiance. I left in hope. I believed, foolishly, that if I could find him, we might still have a life. I dreamed of running away. Not from duty, but from a life where every choice is made for me."

Her voice rose, not in anger, but in pleading. "I wanted a place where I was not told where to go, who to be, who to love. I am not your puppet. I am not your pawn."

Her breath shook. "That night, I was willing to leave everything behind. I would have gone anywhere, Father, anywhere at all. I risked it all to find the man I loved."

She looked at him fully, no longer holding herself back.

"I was struck down, and I woke in the belly of a slave ship, chained, thrown into a goat's pen like something already forgotten. They starved us when it suited them, left us in filth, watched us as though we were already dead." Her mouth trembled, but she forced the words through it. "A man tried to rape me. I fought him. I killed him. I did what I had to do to keep my dignity, because there was no one coming to save me."

Her hand pressed to her chest, fingers curling into the fabric as if she could anchor herself there. "Iney died protecting me. She fought when I could not. She bled while they dragged me away, trusting me to keep her safe."

Her voice wavered, just once. "She should have come home."

The silence that followed pressed in on the table, thick and inescapable.

"That is what became of my hope," she went on, quieter now, steadier. "Not love. Not freedom. Chains, hunger, ash, and the knowledge that everything I believed in was taken from me." She swallowed, breath catching. "I risked everything that night. You. Iney. Asha. My name. My future. I risked it all for love."

When she spoke again, the anger was gone, replaced by something far worse.

"And still, you speak of marrying me away. Still, you speak of legacy, as though it is worth more than what it costs."

Her eyes never left him. "Mother never loved you. She married because she had no choice. I would rather kill myself, than to remain here with you."

She turned then and left the room, her sobs echoing down the corridor.

Andrew moved to follow, but Alex caught his thigh and shook his head once.

Across the table, Femi looked at King Afonso, his eyes glassed with grief.

He stood. "I will speak with her."

The King nodded, his face carved from stone.

Confessions From a Man in Love

When Femi left the room, King Afonso turned his attention to Andrew.

"Laird Andrew, I wish to have a word with you."

Andrew glanced at Haemish and then at his brother, Alex. He gave a small nod, and without question they left the chamber. The doors closed behind them, the sound final.

For a long moment, the King said nothing. He leaned forward, his elbow resting on the table, his fist pressed lightly to his lips, as though he were holding his thoughts there, weighing each one before allowing it voice. The lines at his brow deepened, not with anger, but with something older and heavier.

At last, he spoke.

"Laird Andrew, my daughter is in love with you. I see it in the way she looks at you." His gaze did not waver. "It is the same way she once looked at Mikel."

There was no accusation in his tone, only memory, and the ache that followed it.

"She has been away from home for nearly two years. I do not know what passed between the two of you during that time." His voice remained steady. "I only know this, if I allow my wrath to rule me now, I may lose her again."

He studied Andrew closely.

"Do you love my daughter?"

Andrew lowered his head, jaw tightening as his teeth ground together. His heart thundered in his chest. He knew, with absolute clarity, that this answer could grant him a life beside Nzingha or cost him his own.

"King Afonso, when I first met your daughter, I thought her mean, stubborn, arrogant, and pigheaded. She wouldnae listen tae a single word I said, even when her life hung in the balance."

Andrew lifted his gaze to King Afonso.

"She would rather throw herself into danger than let another bleed for her. She would place her life on the line tae save mine, or any other soul within reach, without a second thought."

The King's mouth curved for the briefest moment before settling again, his gaze steady and unreadable.

"There was a time when my guard Haemish, a Baroness of Ireland, and myself were stranded on that island with your daughter. Iney had already perished from her wounds. We were being hunted by the people who lived there. We had no proper shelter, no safe ground, and little hope.

"During one attack, I told Nzingha I would draw them off. I meant tae give my life if it meant the rest might escape. I told them all, on count o' three, tae run for the ship. I never reached three. Before I could finish the count, your daughter charged straight into battle. She didnae hesitate. She didnae look back. She went in with blade raised and fire in her eyes, as if death itself had dared her to blink."

A grin crossed the King's face, as though in quiet pride at her bravery. The King did not interrupt.

"She could not bear the thought of anyone dying or being left to suffer. It was as if once she had lost Iney, she would not allow the world to take another soul if she could stand against it.

"Another time, before we escaped the island, we found Haemish torn open by a shark. A piece of his flesh was gone, ripped clean away. He was fevered, half mad with pain, and cruel in his tongue. He was a complete arse tae her, King Afonso, and still she knelt beside him. She cleaned his wounds with her own hands, stayed through the night, watched his breathing, and wouldnae leave him even when exhaustion near claimed her. She would not rest until the fever broke, and she was certain the rot would not set in."

The King's brow lowered slightly, the line of his mouth firming. He did not interrupt.

"The night Iney died, your daughter made a vow. She said no one else would perish on that island if she had breath in her body. She meant it. From that moment on, she fought not just for herself, but for every soul stranded there.

"The more I spoke with her, the more she opened herself tae me. She told me about you, about Mikel, and about why she came tae hate being a princess."

King Afonso's gaze shifted once, then returned to Andrew.

"But more than any title or duty, it was your daughter that weighed on her the most. What troubled her, what brought her tae tears near every day, was the knowledge that you meant tae marry her off tae a stranger. A man she knew by reputation alone. A man spoken of as cruel, power hungry, and merciless.

"That fear lived in her, King Afonso. It never left.

"Before we ever left that island, Nzingha refused tae come with us. She didnae want tae return tae Mbemba. We argued over it more than once. She told me plain she would rather struggle alone than return tae your lands and have her life decided for her. She believed coming home meant losing herself."

The King sat back in his chair and drummed his fingers against the arm. His mouth tightened, his gaze lowering before lifting again. He did not speak.

"The only reason your daughter stands before you now is not because she chose tae return, but because she was taken. My uncle abducted her, driven by greed for jewels and power, and dragged her back here against her will."

The King sat upright in his chair, his hand still upon the arm. His expression set, sharp and cold. Andrew caught it and did not falter.

"Nzingha has taught me more than any battle ever did. She taught me how tae trust when there was every reason no' tae, and more than that, she taught me how tae survive without losing who I am."

Andrew lifted his eyes fully, his gaze meeting the King's.

"Do I love her? That word is far too small. She is the very air I breathe. Tae leave her here would drive me mad. It would break me, because I ken she never wished tae return."

His hands clenched once.

"If I leave without her, she will run again. She always does, because she has already learned what it is to choose her own life, and she will not surrender that again. She will risk everything for the two people she loves most, not because she is careless, but because love is the one thing she has never been willing to betray.

"She has already built the life she desires. She found solitude after losing Mikel. She found friendship after losing Asha and Iney.

"In her own kingdom, she once had that. And it was taken from her. Not by fate. Not by chance. But by one choice. One decision. Made by you.

"Nzingha now lives in a place where she can breathe and remain whole.

"What we share was not born of comfort or permission. It was forged in fear, loss, and choice. It is the one thing she claimed as her own, and it is the one thing I will not abandon her to lose.

"That bond reaches beyond you, beyond the crown, beyond any kingdom, because it was made where no one had power over her but herself."

He did not lower his gaze.

"What I am saying may sound like treason, but it is truth. Nzingha and I are bonded."

The King had been staring into the distance as Andrew spoke, his face unreadable. But at the word *bonded*, his gaze snapped back, sharp and cold.

"So," King Afonso said evenly, "you are telling me you have lain with my daughter."

Andrew did not look away. He drew in a deep breath, let it out slowly, and met the King's eyes without flinching.

"Aye," he said, "In my country, we are married. We made vows as husband and wife. She is flesh o' my flesh, blood o' my blood, bone o' my bone."

He took another breath, heavier this time. "We have a daughter. A wee lass named Destiny. Nzingha chose the name, for our paths crossed by destiny, whether we wished it or no'."

Andrew's voice softened. "I ask for your blessing tae leave this place with my wife. And if you cannae grant that, then grant me leave tae go tae my child. She bears no fault in this. She shouldnae grow without both her parents."

The King tapped his fingers slowly against the table once, then rested his chin against his hand. Silence stretched between them, thick and dangerous.

At last, King Afonso spoke.

"I cannot punish you, for you owe me no fealty. You kept my daughter alive. You are a laird of your own lands and, by your words, an honest man." His eyes narrowed slightly. "You spoke truth when lies would have served you better. I respect that."

He lifted his goblet and took a measured sip of wine, then washed his hands in the bowl of water before him. When he set the cloth aside, his voice was calm but layered with something older.

"Today was one of the happiest days of my life. When I saw my daughter again, standing before me, I cared little for the choices she made in my absence."

His gaze darkened. "Mikel was executed on principle. He broke an oath, and I could not allow such defiance to go unanswered."

The King lifted a finger, pointing it toward Andrew, the smallest shake accompanying the gesture.

"But you?" A breath of dry humor passed his lips. "If I were to bring you harm, who knows what my daughter might do. She might close my eyes for good. I taught her to be efficient."

The words were not a threat, but precise.

The King placed his head down; a tear came down his wrinkled face.

"I am an old man; I do not have long in this world. My only wish is to see my daughter happy. I became a king before I became a father, and because of that, Nzingha and I grew distant. I devoted myself to my family's traditions and the preservation of our legacy."

He took another sip of wine.

"When I met Nzingha's mother, she was only sixteen summers. My age exceeded her by five years. I knew she would never love me, but I did not care about love. All I wanted was a son. During our wedding night, I acted as though she wasn't a virgin, and I didn't care if she hated me.

"The union went on, and I bedded her three times a week, with no kissing, no passion, and no intimacy. I fucked her only to have my son. If she had not provided me with an heir, I would have married another. I told her this. But eventually my heart changed after my firstborn, Nsiah. My firstborn meant the world to me; we were indeed remarkably close.

"Two years later, Nzingha was born. She was perfect, the only child in the kingdom with the honey brown eyes of a lioness. My daughter stole my heart. What other king or nobleman would permit their child to keep a lion in their castle? I did. I am the King.

"We spoiled Nzingha beyond reason, without restraint. After Nsiah's death, she pulled away from me. She no longer called me Daddy, and she no longer followed me from place to place. After her mother's death, her attention turned to Mikel. I sensed something between them before I understood it, and then I saw them kiss with my own eyes.

"That sight lit a fire in me. I had placed all my trust in Mikel. I hired him to take her mind off the loss of her brother. When Nzingha wished to fight alongside the other female warriors, I allowed her to join missions. Never once did I believe Mikel would betray his word. I made it clear to him that my daughter was not to be touched. Yet he still went on.

"When I had his trial, Nzingha never knew of it. Breaking the King's trust was not something that could be answered with mercy. Judgment was passed swiftly. He was dead before he ever arrived."

The King took another sip of wine, continuing his calm conversation with Laird Andrew.

"The evening Nzingha confronted me was the same night she went missing. When she stood before me, I saw fire in her eyes, yet I never believed she wished to run away from home, to run away from me. That night, she acted like her mother. Queen Tafaria was as stubborn as Nzingha. Over the years, I grew to love and respect her because she bore me two children.

"During my union with her mother, I met another woman, one a bit older than the Queen. She satisfied my manly needs, as she was more experienced, more intimate. After many years of involvement, she bore me a son. In my culture, a man may take as many wives as he desires, yet I could not marry her. I loved the Queen very deeply. Not taking another wife was my way of showing Queen Tafaria that she alone would stand at my side.

"When the Queen became ill, I ended my relations with the other women I lay with, and there were many. I was able to tell my wife how deeply I loved her as she drew her final breath. But Nzingha was right; she never loved me. On the day she was dying, I knelt to kiss her, and she turned her head away from me and took her last breath. Do you know how much a person must hate you to use the last of their strength to turn away from you? My heart was broken."

"Deep within me, I do not wish that fate for Nzingha, but we have a kingdom to uphold and a bloodline to keep pure."

The King stood. "I will grant you this one favor, for the sake of my grandchild. Go home to your daughter, for I cannot bring harm to the man my daughter loves. As for Nzingha, I am sorry, but this child will have to live without her mother."

Drake stood, his heart dropping to his feet. "You cannot, King Afonso, please. I beg of you. She is your granddaughter. She needs her mother."

He dropped to his knees, bowing his head in honor. Even a tear slipped free.

The King lifted his hand. "Are you the King or Prince of Scotland?"

Keeping his head bowed, Andrew shook his head in defeat. His voice cracked. "Nae, King."

"Do you command armies of more than ten thousand men who would march upon Mbemba and Tafaria, the eastern and western lands I rule, and fight in the name of Princess Nzingha Tafaria Mbemba?"

Drake shook his head. "Nae."

"Then tell me this, can you meet her dowry, measured in gold by weight and land by decree, as befits a princess of my blood?" He stepped closer. "My son, your time with my daughter has come to an end. She may be wed in your lands, but here, judgment is mine. You will return to your homeland. Take good care of my grandchild."

The King turned to leave just as Femi burst through the doors of the dining hall.

"Brother, Nzingha has left the castle. She is not in her chambers, and she cannot be found anywhere on the grounds."

The King straightened abruptly, his composure hardening into command.

"What?" he demanded. "No. Not again. Seal the gates. Call every guard to the grounds. She will not vanish a second time under my roof. We move now."

The King took two steps toward the door, then halted, as though something had just occurred to him. He turned back to Andrew.

"You are not permitted to leave the castle. You may attempt to escape with my daughter." His voice rose, carrying across the hall. "Guards, escort our guest back to the west wing. I want my personal men stationed at the tower stairs and at the entrance to the bath hall. He is not to leave his quarters unless escorted."

His gaze settled on Andrew once more, steady and final.

"When my daughter returns, you are free to leave. Until then, you will remain a guest at Tafaria's Castle."

Chapter 22

Above Stairs

Andrew's blood burned the moment he heard that Nzingha had left the castle. The thought of her alone, moving through the dark, possibly making her way back toward his ship, set his teeth on edge. He muttered under his breath, "Daft princess," the words carrying more fear than irritation.

He was escorted alone up the marble stairs by the King's guards, his boots striking stone as his temper rose with every step. Andrew cursed freely as he climbed, the sharp roll of Scots spilling from him without restraint, the guards at his sides unable to understand his words.

"Daft wee lass," he growled under his breath. "What were ye thinkin'? Walkin' out again like the world hasna already tried tae swallow ye whole? One more foolish step and ye're gone forever."

His jaw clenched as he continued, the words tumbling out in a low, furious stream. "Why d'ye never bloody learn? God help our bairn if she inherits yer skull."

His thoughts remained fixed on his wife, on how easily she could vanish into the night if she chose to, and on how little power he had to stop it.

At the top of the stairs, the corridor opened toward the sleeping quarters. Alex and Haemish were already there, waiting near their chambers, their attention snapping to Andrew the moment he appeared between the guards.

Alex crossed the distance first, reaching for his brother's shoulder, the weight of his hand steady and grounding.

"Dinnae lose hope, brother," he said, his voice calm despite the tension pressing in on them. He followed the words with a wink and a faint smile, as though trying to hold the night together by sheer will.

As Alex turned, a subtle shift in the corridor caught his attention. Yvonne approached with unhurried composure, four women flanking her, their bearing polished and deliberate, their presence impossible to mistake. The tension in Alex's posture eased at once, interest replacing restraint as his expression warmed.

Yvonne inclined into a measured curtsy.

"Good evening, Laird Alex. Are you prepared to see Tafaria's Castle?"

Andrew faced his brother.

"I'm sorry, brother, but King Afonso has laid down strict orders. We are tae remain above stairs and move only under guard."

Yvonne's gaze moved briefly to Andrew before she curtsied again, untroubled.

"That will not be a difficulty. We have palm wine. We may remain above stairs, if it pleases Laird Alex."

Alex's mouth curved further as he turned toward his chamber.

"It pleases me well enough," he replied, already setting off. He glanced back once, his tone lighter than the hour permitted. "Dinnae fret, brother. Enjoy yer night."

Alex ushered the royal bathers and groomers into his chamber, Yvonne following last. Before crossing the threshold, her gaze lifted and fixed on Femi, who stood nearby, leaning against a post, his displeasure plain. They held each other's look only a moment before her expression cooled into unmistakable disdain. Without acknowledgment, she turned away and disappeared into Alex's chamber.

Femi remained where he was, his hands folded before him. After a moment, he shook his head once, slow and deliberate, as though sealing a private judgment, then turned and returned to his own quarters, the door closing behind him with final resolve.

Hiding in The Shadows

Andrew stormed into the guest chambers without slowing, the door slamming shut behind him as he crossed the room in long, furious strides. He passed straight through the shadows near the far wall without so much as a glance, missing the still figure standing there entirely. His focus was fixed inward, too consumed by anger to notice anything else.

He kicked off his slippers, sending them skidding across the floor, and tore the mosquito nets aside before dropping hard across the bed.

"Son of a whore," he spat. "What the hell just happened? What in God's name was Nzingha thinkin'? And what the devil was I thinkin'?"

He dragged a hand down his face, shaking his head. "I should've kept my mouth shut. I should've said nothin'."

He stared up at the ceiling, the anger rolling without pause. "And after all that, he didnae even blink at the thought of a granddaughter. Cold bastard. Crown first, blood second. Just like every other king I've ever known."

He pushed himself upright with a sharp breath, the pressure in his body demanding attention. Muttering under his breath, he crossed the small hall toward the privy closet.

He had just begun to relieve himself when a hand settled on his shoulder.

Andrew startled hard, turning on instinct, his heart kicking against his ribs.

"It is only I, your wife."

"Christ, Nzingha, d'ye ken ye've a talent for puttin' a man in his grave?"

For half a heartbeat, his mind refused to catch up. Then relief hit him all at once, fierce and undeniable, a wide grin breaking across his face before he could stop it. The joy barely had time to settle before the anger surged back in its wake.

He turned away, washing his hands roughly, drying them before flinging the rag aside. "Where in hell did ye go?" he demanded. "Ye're sneakin' about like a bloody ghost, ye had me thinkin' ye were..."

She stepped forward and silenced him with a kiss.

The kiss deepened, and everything that had happened that night fell away. All he could remember was the ache of wanting her; it was raw and immediate.

It had been four long months since he had last touched his wife. When he had returned early from his voyage, his only plan had been to make love to her again and again, to lose himself in her until the world made sense once more. Seeing how breathtaking she looked that evening had lit a rage of desire in him, and at this moment, it could not be contained.

Andrew backed her into the corner of the small closet, driving his hips against hers. She felt his hardness and immediately reached for his clothing, tugging at it with urgency. They rushed at each other's hands, fingers clumsy with need as their tongues tangled in a heated rhythm. As he worked at the ties of her gown, frustration flared.

"Christ," he muttered, hot and breathless. "How in hell did yer maid lace this thing? I cannae get it undone."

Impatience won. He tore the fabric free, the sound sharp in the hush of the chamber, baring her breast to the air. His mouth followed instinctively, hunger overtaking thought, while Nzingha's hands worked at the ties at his waist, fingers unsteady with need. By the time his trousers slipped free, he was already guiding her backward, out of the cramped closet and into the open space of the guest chamber.

The room offered no warmth meant for comfort, no hearth, no fur, only an immense bed dressed in silk and veiled by hanging nets, waiting in the half-light.

They came together again, bodies pressing and shifting, the pace building until the heat closed in on him, heavy and relentless. He broke the kiss with a breathless curse, sweat slick along his skin as he dragged a forearm across his brow. "Christ, this heat, tis unbearable, I need air."

He crossed the room and pushed the balcony doors open. Night rushed in at once, a cool breath sweeping through the chamber. Beyond the threshold, the balcony stretched over the sea. A low lounge chair with soft cushions rested near the rail, a hammock swaying gently behind it. Below, waves struck the rocks in a steady rhythm, the sound rising to fill the room.

He leaned against the railing, forearms braced, eyes fixed on the dark water. "Never in a million years did I think I'd be standin' in the same castle as ye and yer father."

Nzingha stepped closer, her smile softened by the starlight. "Never in a million years would I have imagined making love to my husband in my homeland beneath these stars."

She tore away the rest of her bodice, the fabric giving easily beneath her hands. Her breasts spilled free at once, full and heavy, changed by the birth of their daughter. She reached up and loosened her traditional head ties, letting them fall away as her locks slipped down to her waist.

Andrew's smile widened as he took her in, his gaze lingering on the fullness of her breasts, on the woman she had become. He said nothing, only watched, hunger plain in his eyes as she continued to undress before him.

Stepping out of her dress, she stood naked before him, unguarded and sure. She moved toward Andrew and leaned into him, her body fitting easily against his as their mouths met again, the kiss deepening with renewed urgency. Within her, desire coiled low and insistently, aching for his hands, for his touch, for the closeness she had been denied far too long.

She leaned close and whispered, "I want you badly. My womanhood aches for you."

Andrew's smile answered before his words did. He turned her gently but firmly back against the wall, his body closing the distance. "Ah, so that's what ye want, aye? For me to kiss ye there." His smile deepened. "As ye wish."

She nodded, breath hitching as her chest rose and fell, the heat of her need written plainly across her body.

He moved his legs between her knees, opening them wider, causing her to slide down an inch, and without notice, he crept a finger into her moisture; her juices slid freely.

He lowered his voice near her ear, murmuring roughly.

"I never recalled ye this moist before, tis like a warm treat, waitin' tae be tasted."

Hearing him speak drove her insane. He nibbled at her ear while playing with her warmth. Andrew, turned on by her dampness, slid three fingers into her.

She moved her hips with him, each motion drawing her closer. A soft gasp escaped her as release hovered just out of reach, then he withdrew. She went still, breath caught, stunned by the sudden denial. Andrew winked wolfishly and dropped to his knees. He gave her what she craved, rolling his tongue over her knob, not coming up for air. His movements were precise, measured, and rhythmic.

She held on to him, crying out his name. "Andrew, oh Andrew. I am coming."

Nzingha gasped as the rush of euphoria slipped away.

Without hesitation, he hoisted her over his shoulder and carried her to the lounge chair. There was work to be done. He didn't speak as he struggled to pull his pants down. His face gave frustration. "This would have been quicker if I had been wearing my kilt." He then placed her on the soft bedding of the chair. "Come here. I'm not done with my feast."

Nzingha grinned. "You vulgar Scotsman."

He took her by the hand and guided her into position, holding her steady as he settled beneath her. Spreading her hips apart, he resumed tasting her without hesitation. Nzingha moved with him, her hips rising and falling as Andrew continued to work her with practiced intent.

When she reached her peak, her body jerked as the release overtook her. She looked down at him, her gaze dropping to his shaft, the rigid evidence of his desire. Sliding lower, she drew close to his chest, her hand closing around him as she took him into her mouth, her movements eager and unrestrained, breathless with want.

Andrew's toes curled as sensation surged through him. He gripped her firmly, fighting the pull to give in too soon, until at last he stilled her.

She straightened and looked at him. "What is the matter?"

"If ye keep feasting on me in such a manner," he said roughly, "I'll spill in yer mouth."

Nzingha laughed. "Husband, you speak such vulgar words."

"Oh, ye've not heard vulgar yet." He drew her closer. "Come. Let me plant a babe inside ye."

"Another?" she asked.

"Aye, another. I'd keep ye round with child," he said plainly.

She turned her face away for a moment. "Will you stop sailing?"

Andrew sat up and turned her back toward him. "Ye wish for me tae stop sailing?" His brow drew together slightly. "Why?"

"Yes," she said, "I do not like it when you are gone. Destiny is still so young. I would die if something happened to you and she never saw you again. I would be alone in your country, just Destiny and myself. When your uncle came with his men, I was terrified for our babe. Her screams broke my heart, for I could not comfort her while a blade was held to my throat."

She lowered her head against his chest. "My husband," she murmured, "I love you for coming to my aid."

Andrew met her gaze. "Aye, I'll nae sail again. But ye must escape with me tonight. I'll get ye to our babe, even if it costs me my life."

She looked at him with quiet certainty. "I will follow you to the ends of the earth."

He laid Nzingha on her back, and for a long moment they only looked at one another, breath mingling, eyes locked as though nothing else existed. With one swift, certain movement, he joined her gently.

Nzingha closed her eyes, a soft breath leaving her as she felt her husband fill her once more. That joining was all she needed, his body binding to hers, his soul folding into her own.

Andrew moved within her, steady and sure. With each motion, her breasts rose and fell, full and heavy, and he lowered himself to her, taking one nipple into his mouth, drawing it between his lips as he suckled.

He paused suddenly. "Ye're still full," he murmured. "There's milk yet."

A faint flush warmed her cheeks. "Yes," she said softly. "I have ached since the day I was taken. I had to relieve myself from time to time. When we return to Scotland, I may not be able to nurse our babe. My milk flows slowly now. It is likely drying within me."

"I'll see us home to our child," he said firmly. He kissed her and began to move again, slowly at first, then with growing urgency. In and out, deeper each time, wanting to feel every part of her.

Nzingha lifted her hips to meet him, spreading her legs wider as her hands grasped his buttocks, drawing him deeper still.

Andrew could no longer hold back. Sensation surged through him, his body tightening as he gathered her legs over his arms and drove into her with duty.

She bit back her cry, desperate not to be heard, though her body begged for release.

He quickened his pace, the angle driving her breathless, until she cried out despite herself. "Oh, the gods, Andrew! Harder. Please."

Bracing himself on his arms, he thrust deeply, losing himself to the rhythm until the world narrowed to nothing but her. "Oh God… oh God… I love ye," he groaned as release overtook him.

Nzingha rode the crest with him, her hands gripping his hips as she sank into her own pleasure, breathless and trembling.

He collapsed atop her, heart pounding, sweat dripping onto her skin. She drew deep breaths and smiled. "You are my champion."

"I shall always be," he said, pressing a brief kiss to her lips before rolling onto his side. "It's so bloody hot," he muttered, wiping his face. "Summers in Scotland are warm, but this, this feels like the gates of hell."

Seeing his discomfort, Nzingha rose and returned with a cup of water, pressing it into his hand. She followed with a damp cloth and knelt beside him, cooling his skin with careful strokes.

"My thanks," he said, smiling as he kissed her.

She crossed to the hammock and slipped into it, naked, the net swaying gently as she motioned for him to join her.

"What is this contraption?" he asked, eyeing it warily.

"A hammock."

"I ken that," he replied. "But we'll nae both fit."

"Of course we will," she said, holding out her hand. "Trust me."

Andrew climbed in, his weight setting it rocking. "I'm too big. I'll break it."

"No, you will not," she said, smiling up at him.

They settled together, the hammock swaying side to side. He lay back as Nzingha rested her head upon his chest, both gazing up at the sky.

"Oh, look at the moon tonight. A new moon, and so large. We may have conceived this night."

"Aye," he said quietly. "We have shared many nights, but this one... this one I'll remember for as long as I live." He kissed her hair.

"Our bodies joined, and our souls aligned," she whispered. "We called upon lady fertility this night."

"What d'ye mean?" he asked, already drifting.

She spoke softly of the moon, the stars, the cycles her people had followed for generations, of how the light guided desire and life alike. Her words faded into the night as his breathing deepened.

When she looked up, Andrew was asleep, the hammock rocking him as though he were a child once more.

Chapter 23

The Plan

*T*ap. Tap. Tap.

Andrew came awake at once.

Another knock followed, sharp and deliberate, cutting through the quiet of the night. He slid carefully from beneath Nzingha, the hammock swaying as she slept on, unaware. Moving quickly but silently, he stepped inside from the patio, pulling the chamber door closed behind him just as the sound came again.

Tap. Tap. Tap.

The door.

He glanced back once, instinct tightening his chest. Nzingha lay naked in the hammock, her skin pale in the moonlight. He gathered her discarded clothing from the floor and shoved it beneath the pillows, then stripped the top bed cloth from the mattress and wrapped it around his waist. Only then did he cross to the door.

"Who is it?" he asked quietly, his voice low and controlled.

"It is I," came the answer. "Femi."

Andrew opened the door a fraction. Candlelight washed over Femi's face, his expression tight, impatient.

"I have a boat arranged," Femi said at once. "It will take you back to your ship."

Andrew played the fool, drawing his brows together. "Did ye find Nzingha?"

Femi rolled his eyes and shook his head. "Yes... yes, I did. She sleeps in your chamber. Who do you think told her how to get there?"

Andrew leaned out slightly, scanning the corridor for movement. His instincts screamed trap.

Femi caught it and scoffed. "Enough. Get your people ready. Nzingha knows the plan. If you value your life, be quick. My brother is in fury. He spoke of blaming you and carrying out your execution. I convinced him otherwise. We had to drug him to keep him from tearing the castle apart."

Andrew stiffened.

"Stay above the tower stairs," Femi continued. "If his men see you, they will kill you on sight. Listen to Nzingha. She knows the passages. My men are in position and know what to do. The King's soldiers are scouring the beach for her, but they've been sent in the wrong direction. They're searching west, toward your ships. We told them she fled east."

He stepped back, already turning away. "Watch for the King's colors, orange and white. Move before dawn. I will meet Nzingha at the location."

Then he was gone, disappearing down the stairs without saying another word.

Andrew closed the door and lifted his gaze toward the skylight. The stars were thinning, the dark loosening its hold.

First light was coming.

Andrew crossed the hall to Haemish's chamber and rapped sharply against the door. A few moments passed before it opened, Haemish standing there with sleep heavy in his eyes.

"Aye, Laird Barton?" he murmured, voice thick with drowsiness.

"Dress yourself and meet me in the hall," Andrew whispered. "We're leaving."

Haemish nodded once and shut the door without question.

Andrew moved on to Alex's chamber and knocked. No answer. He knocked again, firmer this time. The door finally opened to a woman wrapped only in a bed linen, the cloth clutched hastily to her chest. Andrew halted, brows lifting.

Christ.

He shook his head, unsurprised. Alex's whoring had apparently reached this part of the world.

The woman recognized him at once and bowed quickly. She was one of the bath women from earlier. Andrew gave a curt nod and stepped past her into the chamber.

The stench of sex and smoke hit him full in the face. He covered his nose with his hand.

One. Two. Three women lay sprawled naked around his brother, limbs tangled, skin gleaming in the low light. Every last one of them from the baths.

Andrew stared.

"Even the waxer?" he muttered, spotting Yvonne among them. He shook his head slowly. "God help me, Alex. Ye're a shameless whore."

When his gaze landed on the unmistakable evidence left between the almond-skinned women, Andrew lost what little patience he had left and kicked Alex's foot hard.

Alex jerked awake with a startled groan.

One of the women shrieked and scrambled upright, clutching at her linen. Alex barely opened his eyes, stretching languidly as though waking from the finest sleep of his life.

"Ladies," he drawled, blinking, "thank ye kindly for the… hospitality. But it seems my brother has arrived, so I'll have tae ask ye tae leave while we discuss somethin' important."

The women gathered their clothes in hurried disarray, laughter fading as reality settled back in. One of them smacked Yvonne's backside in passing, a careless, playful gesture meant for someone else entirely.

Yvonne startled at the touch, gasping softly. Her face flushed as she clutched her linen tighter, eyes wide with embarrassment. She did not laugh. She did not linger. She bent quickly, snatching up her garments with trembling hands, fumbling as she dressed, desperate to be gone.

Andrew caught the way she kept her eyes down, the way she edged toward the door as though the room itself might swallow her whole.

She did not look at Alex.

She slipped past the others once she was properly covered, moving quickly, her face pale and tight with embarrassment. The night had left her shaken and unwell, her stomach still churning, her head pounding. She had no memory of how she'd been undressed, only the dull awareness that she had been too far gone to stop it.

As she reached the doorway, a hand caught her wrist.

She froze.

Alex's voice came quieter than before, stripped of its bravado. "I'm sorry," he said, "For all of it."

She turned just enough to look at him, her expression unreadable, then gave a small shake of her head and pulled free.

"Will I see ye later?" he asked, uncertain now.

"Perhaps," she said, the word barely more than breath.

Then she fled the chamber, the door closing behind her with final haste.

Alex watched the door long after she was gone, his grin gone at last.

Andrew turned his head sharply, disgust plain on his face.

Alex dragged a hand down his face once the door shut behind her. "Oh… my… God," he breathed. "I cannae believe last night was real. I barely ken it." He laughed hoarsely. "Clothes came off. They started kissin' each other. I was far too aroused tae refuse. Two of them, Andrew. Yvonne was ill and shy, but the other two! I held out..."

Andrew raised a hand. "Enough. I dinnae want tae hear another word about yer whorish exploits. If ye dinnae curb that appetite, yer cock's liable tae fall clean off. Get dressed. We leave now."

He snatched Alex's shirt from the floor and flung it at his face.

Andrew turned for the door when Alex finally sobered, sitting upright. "Wait... what? Did ye find Nzingha?"

"Aye," Andrew said sharply. "Now hurry, before they decide tae feed me tae crocodiles. Her father kens we're married. He kens about our babe."

Alex's face drained of color. "Holy shite," he whispered. "Then how do we get out?"

I Will Not Falter

Nzingha stood where she was, listening for Andrew before she saw him, aware of every sound below the stairs. At last he entered and drew the door shut behind him with deliberate care. She did not turn at once. She did not need to.

"Your uncle was here," Andrew said quietly. "He's a skiff ready tae take us tae my ship."

She inclined her head once, already moving past the weight of the words as she asked, "Are Alex and Haemish ready?"

"Aye," he answered. "They should be by now."

Andrew glanced into the corridor, where Alex and Haemish waited without speaking, their faces set and watchful. He motioned them inside and closed the door again, sealing the chamber from the sounds below. When he turned back, he found Nzingha already at work.

The bed linens had been torn into long strips, twisted together with practiced efficiency. The gown she had worn earlier lay ruined and abandoned on the floor, stripped of any meaning it once held. What she wore now was the only garment left to her, heavy with fabric and poorly suited for what she intended, yet she bore it as she bore everything else, without hesitation or complaint.

She met Andrew's eyes.

"Give me a hand up."

He stepped closer, his gaze flicking once to the weight of her skirts before returning to her face. "Can ye move in such heavy clothin'?"

"Yes," she said evenly. "I can. Now lift me."

He did not argue. He bent and raised her, steadying her weight as she shifted her grip, her hands already reaching for the beams above.

"Higher," she said calmly. "I need to reach the opening."

When she could reach it, Nzingha slid the glass panel aside and leaned back just enough to look down at them, her expression composed, decisive.

"I will use this as a rope and secure it to a post on the roof."

Then she was gone, her body disappearing through the opening with quiet efficiency. Moments later, her hand reappeared, extended downward, urgent and unmistakable in its command to follow.

The rooftop opened into wind and salt, the low roar of the sea rising from far below. Nzingha dropped into a crouch at once, the movement instinctive, her body already aligned with the danger around them.

"Keep low," she murmured. "Follow me."

They crossed the stone with measured steps, shadows stretching and breaking beneath their feet, the night pressing close on every side, until figures emerged ahead of them.

Soldiers.

Nzingha did not slow. She stepped forward without hesitation and spoke in the Tafari tongue, her voice steady, her posture unyielding.

"Boti iko wapi?"

The soldier pointed west.

"Elekea magharibi, karibu na pwani. Femi anakungoja."

She inclined her head. *"Shukrani zangu."*

They moved on as though nothing had passed between them.

Alex leaned closer as they went. "What did ye ask him?"

"He says the ship waits on the western shore," she answered. "My uncle is there."

At the far edge of the castle, the stone dropped away into darkness, the sea churning far below them. Andrew looked down once, then back at her.

"How in God's name do we get down?"

Nzingha did not answer. She tore strips from her gown instead, the fine fabric ripping cleanly beneath her hands. Alex shot Andrew a look of disbelief, but she continued without pause, binding the cloth swiftly and securely.

"You see the narrow crease between the two walls?" she said as she finished the last knot. "We will brace ourselves with arms and legs and slide down. Follow my lead."

She stepped back and lowered herself into the space between the walls, her descent controlled and deliberate.

Haemish followed, then Alex. Andrew went last.

They gathered in the shadows below, and just before Nzingha stepped into the brush, she lifted her hand. Two of her father's men passed close enough that she could hear the soft scrape of armor. They waited unseen until they were gone.

"We must haste," she whispered.

They reached the shoreline moments later. Nzingha raised her hand toward the dark shape ahead, and her uncle answered with a sharp, urgent motion, signaling her back.

She had no time to understand why.

Mounted soldiers burst from the brush, circling them in tightening arcs. Steel caught the moonlight as horses stamped and snorted, closing the space around them until Nzingha understood there would be no escape.

She lowered her hand.

The night seemed to hold its breath as a white horse stepped forward from the dark, its rider revealed not in haste but with the unhurried authority of inevitability. Moonlight caught the layered cloth at his shoulders, the carved ornaments at his throat, the quiet symbols of rank that needed no metal to command obedience.

Nzingha's breath caught in her chest.

This was not simply a man riding toward them. This was law, blood, and command given form.

Her father.

He reined in before them, the horse settling beneath him as if it recognized the hand that guided it. His presence filled the space, steady and unyielding. For a brief moment, she wondered if this was where love ended, not by blade or betrayal, but by the simple weight of who he was and who she had chosen to be.

No one moved.

No one dared to speak.

The world waited.

Femi swung up onto his horse and drove it forward. "Oshun, help us. It's Afonso."

He rode hard through the circle of riders until he reached them, reining in close, eyes fixed on his brother, rage stirring beneath his control.

"Brother, I..."

King Afonso boomed. "Enough! And to think I placed trust in my own blood. Where did we go wrong, eh?"

Nzingha stepped forward, her voice shaking, her eyes wide with terror. It was a sight Andrew had never witnessed before. He shot a look at Prince Femi; even his chest heaved with fear. The King carried weight.

She dropped to her hands and knees, not in surrender but as one who prayed to the gods themselves. "Father, please hear me. I cannot stay. I cannot. My daughter needs me. Destiny is only eight months old. How do you ask a mother to abandon her child?"

"Silence," Afonso said. "You will come with me. Your pretend husband will return to his land. If you resist, he will die."

"Then I will die with him," she snapped.

A gasp rippled through the garrison.

"Do not force me to resent you more than I already do. When will you understand that you do not own me? I do not want to be a princess. I do not want to be a queen. I want to live. I want my child. I want happiness."

The night swallowed her last word.

Nzingha's father said nothing.

He raised one hand, and at once the King's personal guard unsheathed their swords, steel sliding free in unison as the circle tightened around them.

"Seize the Princess," the King commanded.

Femi rode in hard, positioning himself beside Nzingha and the Scots. He lifted his arm high, and his men mirrored him instantly, swords raised, bodies braced.

"Wait," Femi shouted. "Brother, if she does not leave with her husband this morning, we shall go to war."

The King bellowed with laughter, the sound carrying across the shoreline as though the threat itself amused him.

"You, my younger brother? And what army?"

"The army I built while you sat your lazy ass upon the throne," Femi snapped in anger. "They are loyal to me. You gave me Tafaria to lead after these people were attacked, and you sent no one from Mbemba to fight for them. I built this army from the men, the women, and the boys of Tafaria when you chose comfort over blood."

The King smiled, slow and certain.

"You will continue to govern Tafaria. Nzingha is returning to Mbemba with me. That is final."

One of the King's soldiers surged forward and grabbed Nzingha.

Andrew stepped in without hesitation, his fist striking the man's face hard enough to drop him where he stood.

"Get your bloody hands off my wife."

The King's smile returned, colder this time.

"I see you are stubborn, Scottish man. Do you truly wish to die in this land? We had a deal, and you remember it well. You may still walk away and return to your daughter, or you may choose to challenge my authority. The choice is yours."

Andrew took Nzingha's hand and held it fast.

"Nae, King. You made a deal, and I refused it. I will be takin' my wife home."

The King's eyes narrowed as one brow lifted, his jaw grinding until the veins at his temples stood stark. He spat onto the ground.

"Hmph."

The King raised one arm. His hand closed. The command passed through his ranks without a word.

Ifama, Iney's younger sister, once a close friend and now something harder and more dangerous, broke from the line smiling. Vengeance burned openly in her eyes as she spurred her horse forward, steel already clearing the scabbard while she leaned into the charge.

The animal's weight and speed carried her straight at Andrew. This was the moment she believed would repay her sister's death.

As the horse thundered closer, Ifama lifted her sword high. The blade caught the moonlight before beginning its brutal downward arc, aimed cleanly for Andrew's neck, meant to end him in a single stroke before he could bring his own weapon up.

Time slowed.

Nzingha tried to break free, her body straining against the hands that held her as she screamed his name, the sound tearing from her chest as the distance collapsed too fast to stop. Alex reached for his sword, but his fingers never closed around the hilt. Haemish stood frozen where he was, disbelief locking him in place as the blade continued its descent and Andrew's hand went instinctively to his weapon, already knowing it would not be enough.

The strike never landed.

Femi drove his horse hard into the path of the blow, colliding with Ifama at the last instant and forcing the angle wide. Steel met steel with a violent crack as the horses reared and tangled, and in the chaos of the impact Femi twisted in the saddle and drove his sword through her with all the force of his charge behind it. The momentum tore her from the horse, her body thrown clear before crashing into the sand below, where she lay motionless.

For a heartbeat, no one moved.

Femi dismounted, kicking her free of his sword, his gaze locked on his brother. There was no fury in his eyes now, no hesitation, only a cold, unyielding resolve that made the meaning of what he had done unmistakable. This was not a warning. This was not a threat spoken lightly.

The King's roar ripped through the night, raw and furious, his brother's name breaking from him like a wound.

"FEMIII!"

The prince pointed his blood-stained sword at Andrew, the gesture a wordless declaration of defiance. His voice steady and absolute.

"Unless you wish to die, take your wife and leave this place. Now!"

In three heartbeats, all hell broke loose.

Andrew seized Nzingha's wrist, steel flashing as he tore his sword free and drove forward into the press of bodies. He cut through the first man, then the second, but the numbers were too great, the crush too tight, enemies closing in from every side.

Femi's soldiers surged into position around the Scots and Nzingha, forming a living barricade, blades rising and falling as they cut down any man who tried to break through. The clash of steel rang sharp and merciless, shouts colliding with screams as blood darkened the sand beneath their feet.

The King dismounted.

He stood unmoving as he watched his daughter flee with the foreigner, her hand locked in Andrew's, her skirts gathered as she ran. Rage twisted his features, raw and unrestrained, and his voice tore through the night as he shouted after her.

"NZINGHA! NZINGHA! HOW COULD YOU LEAVE YOUR FATHER?" he roared.

"YOU TURN YOUR BACK ON YOUR FATHER? ON YOUR KING? ON YOUR HOME?"

His voice cracked, fury bleeding into something darker. "YOU ARE A TRAITOR!"

She glanced back mid-stride.

Her father had dropped to his knees.

The sight stole the breath from her chest, but the moment shattered just as quickly as it came. The King turned then, his face contorted with rage, his gaze locking onto his brother. Femi was already fighting, surrounded by four men at once, steel flashing as he battled to keep from being dragged down and taken alive.

Nzingha stopped.

Her heart slammed violently as she saw her father rise, his hand closing around a sword, his steps quickening as he charged straight for his younger brother.

"UNCLE FEMI!" she screamed, terror ripping from her throat. "LOOK OUT! BEHIND YOU!"

Femi did not hear her.

Engaged on all sides, his focus fixed on the men before him, he sensed movement at his back and reacted on instinct alone. He turned sharply, blade already in motion, his sword sweeping out in a brutal arc.

Steel met flesh.

The blade sliced clean across the King's throat.

The battle stopped.

Every sound fell away as the King collapsed into the sand, blood spilling dark and sudden beneath him. Men froze where they stood, swords half-raised, eyes wide as the reality of what had happened settled like ash over the shore.

Femi stared down at the fallen body, horror flooding his features as the truth struck him fully.

"Afonso…" he whispered, his voice breaking as he dropped to his knees beside him. "Brotha. Brotha… No."

Femi dropped to his knees, catching his brother as the blood spilled freely from his neck and mouth, soaking his hands and staining the sand beneath them. He held Afonso close, rocking him as though he could somehow keep him tethered to the world by force alone. His control shattered. Femi wept openly now, his sobs raw and unrestrained.

He spoke in Yoruba, the language of the west, his words breaking apart as grief overtook him.

"*Rárá… jọ̀wọ́… jọ̀wọ́… jọ̀wọ́, arákùnrin,*" he pleaded, his voice cracking. "*Dárí jì mí.*"

No… please… please… please, brother. Forgive me.

Nzingha tore free of Andrew's hand and ran to her father, dropping to her knees beside him as he lay in the sand. She cradled his head against her chest, tears spilling unchecked down her face.

"Daddy," she sobbed. "Daddy… I am sorry. I never wanted this. I did not wish for this to happen."

The King's breathing was shallow now, each breath a labor. With the last of his strength, he lifted his blood-slicked hand and pressed it gently to Nzingha's cheek. His touch trembled, warm and fading, as he exhaled one final breath.

How the Mighty have Fallen

Nzingha let out a wail that rose from somewhere deep within her, raw and unrestrained.

"Why?" she cried. "Daddy, why?"

She rocked her father's lifeless body, clutching him as though her arms alone could anchor him to the world. Nzingha rested her head against his chest, her voice breaking as she spoke again.

"Father… why did you have to be so stubborn?"

Her sobs softened, giving way to quiet devastation. At last, she whispered the words that closed the chapter of her childhood.

"Sleep well, Father."

Tears streamed down her face as she knelt there in silence.

Around her, the soldiers lowered their heads. The King's guard. Femi's men. Warriors who had followed Afonso for decades bowed in reverence to their fallen ruler.

"All hail, Queen Nzingha," they murmured, the chant moving softly through the ranks.

Nzingha shook her head violently, grief spilling into anger as she rose to her feet.

"No," she cried. "No, I do not want it. Stop this!"

She pressed her hands to her chest, breath ragged. "I love Mbemba. I love Tafaria. I love every land my father ever ruled. But he did not agree with my love for Mikel, and he did not agree with my marriage to Laird Barton, all because I never wished to be heir."

She wiped her face with the edge of her dress, refusing to hide her tears.

Love was my choice, and he stripped it from me. First by killing Mikel for daring to love me, and then by demanding that I abandon my family, my own child.

Her voice hardened, no longer pleading.

"No. I cannot."

Months of exile did not break me. Faith carried me to Laird Barton. We fought side by side. We survived what should have killed us. We escaped together. He is my husband now, bound to me by blood, by battle, by choice. We share a child, a daughter still at her mother's breast."

Her jaw tightened.

"My father gave her no place in his heart."

Nzingha turned slowly, her gaze settling on a young soldier standing among the ranks.

"The same way he never cared for his youngest son."

She walked to the soldier and took his hand gently.

"Amadi," she said softly. "This is your father."

The young man's eyes widened in shock.

"I have known you were my brother for a very long time," she continued. "I watched over you from a distance. Today, your life changes."

She turned to Prince Femi.

"Uncle, today I return my inheritance to you, not as surrender, but as trust, you will rule Mbemba as King, on one condition."

The night held still.

Amadi will be recognized before the people as blood of my father's line. He will be raised within the walls of the castle, taught as your own, trained in leadership and protected as royal kin. You have five living children, one son and four daughters. Should you fall, your son Nolo, who stands two years Amadi's senior, will reign. If Nolo is taken before his time, Amadi will stand in his place."

Her voice did not waver.

"If you refuse this, my family and I will remain in Tafaria, and I will rule as Queen. Do you accept?"

Femi studied her, then Amadi, whose face was pale with shock and sorrow. After a long moment, he nodded.

"I accept, before the people and before the ancestors."

Nzingha turned back to Amadi. She knelt and pressed her palm to the sand where her father's blood had fallen, lifting it slowly and placing it against Amadi's chest.

"By blood," she said, "by breath, and by the soil of Mbemba, you are seen."

She removed her father's ring and placed it into Amadi's trembling hand.

"This does not make you ruler; it makes you remembered."

She faced the gathered soldiers and commanders.

"Witness this, Amadi is of our father's blood. He will be raised in the house of Mbemba."

The men bowed their heads, not in chant, but in acknowledgment.

Nzingha then turned to Femi.

"This day, I return the eastern and western lands to Femi Mbemba," she declared. "I release my claim in peace, not in shame."
Her face was wet with tears, she turned and kissed her husband, sealing her destiny in leaving the crown behind. She then lowered herself to the sand and bowed.

"King Femi Mbemba."

Femi remained kneeling beside his brother's body, grief breaking through him in quiet, shaking breaths. Nzingha had never seen him weep. Not for fallen soldiers. Not for lost battles. But now, the hardened prince mourned openly, holding his brother as the night bore witness.

Walking Free in love

Three days later, Femi, Nzingha, and the Barton brothers reached the Kingdom of Mbemba. The journey passed in solemn quiet, the sea carrying them home not in triumph, but in mourning.

On the second day, King Afonso Mbemba was laid to rest.

The rites were long and reverent, filled with song, prayer, and the measured stillness of a people saying farewell to a ruler who had shaped their lives, for better and for worse. The land bore witness as his body was committed to the earth, and the drums spoke where words failed.

When the ceremony ended, Nzingha stood before her people.

They gathered in numbers too great to count, filling the open ground, their faces etched with grief, pride, and an unspoken understanding of what this moment meant. They were relieved to see her alive.

They were proud of her strength. And they were sorrowful, knowing she would soon leave them again.

She lifted her chin and spoke.

"Sons and daughters of the Kingdom of Mbemba," Nzingha said, her voice carrying across the crowd. "Today, I place this great land into the hands of a great king, Femi Mbemba."

A murmur moved through the people.

"I have loved this country with my whole heart," she continued. "I have fought for you, bled for you, and stood for you when the world sought to break us. You are a strong people, born of endurance and bound by spirit."

She paused, emotion tightening her throat.

"This war is not finished," she said plainly. "Do not lay down your strength. Do not forget who you are."

Her gaze swept over them, memorizing faces she had known since childhood.

"I love you," she said, "I will always carry Mbemba with me. And though I leave today, I will return."

The people bowed their heads, not in submission, but in respect.

Back To Scotland

Everyone was safely boarded and sailing back to Scotland. Drake spent most of his days with his wife, rarely leaving her side unless duty called him away. Haemish stood in as captain for the better part of the journey, steady at the helm and unbothered by the weather or the long hours.

But Alex?

Alex was nowhere to be found.

He had taken to his cabin like a man hiding from the law, emerging for nothing and no one. He missed his turns at the helm. He skipped meals. He did not even appear on deck to complain about the weather, which alone made Andrew uneasy.

On the fourth day, with the sea growing rough and the wind turning sharp, Andrew decided he had indulged his brother long enough.

He stopped outside Alex's cabin and knocked.

Nothing.

Andrew frowned and knocked again, harder this time.

The door swung open suddenly, nearly catching him in the shoulder.

Alex stood there blinking, hair mussed, eyes heavy and unfocused, looking every bit like a man who had been dragged out of sleep against his will.

"Aye, brother," he muttered.

Andrew took one look at him and scowled. "Alex, what is the matter with ye? Are ye hale?" He stepped closer, lowering his voice. "Ye've been locked away for days now. Haemish says ye've nae come up once to relieve him of the captain's duties."

Alex shifted his weight, swaying just slightly. "Aye… I'm only tired. I dinnae feel well."

Andrew crossed his arms. "Would ye like me to have Nzingha bring ye some hot cider? Or tea? Or a priest, if this is the end?"

"Nae, I just need sleep."

Andrew leaned into the cabin, his eyes narrowing as he took in the space. The air felt close. Too warm. Alex's skin glistened faintly.

"Brother, ye're sweatin' like ye've run ten miles uphill. Are ye fevered?"

"Nae," Alex replied. "Just… a bit seasick."

Andrew stared at him.

"Seasick," he repeated. "When have ye ever been seasick? I've seen ye drunk, bleeding, and half drowned, and ye still took the helm with a smile."

Alex managed a weak shrug.

Andrew sighed, pinching the bridge of his nose. "Aye. Well. I hope ye feel better soon," he said, already turning away.

The ship chose that moment to lurch violently as a harsh wave struck her side.

Furniture slid. The floor tilted. Andrew grabbed the wall to keep his footing as Alex stumbled backward, swearing under his breath.

And then...

A woman's shriek cut through the cabin.

The closet door flew open, and a body rolled out onto the floor in a tangle of skirts and limbs, landing hard at Andrew's feet.

Andrew froze.

Slowly, he looked down.

"Is that… Yvonne?"

He lifted his gaze to his brother, disbelief sharpening into fury.

"Alex, nae."

Epilogue

It had been eight months since Nzingha and the Scots returned to Scotland.

Andrew laid aside his sea name quietly, without ceremony, choosing to be known only as Laird Andrew Barton when the need arose. To Nzingha, he remained simply Andrew. Titles mattered less now than survival.

The wealth that arrived with them did not announce itself. It came sealed, catalogued, and deliberately understated. Advisors from the Crown moved carefully around the Bartons, urging discretion. Sudden fortune, they warned, drew attention of the wrong kind. For a time, the greater portion of it was placed under watch, distributed slowly, masked through land purchases, improvements, and trusts meant to protect rather than display.

Andrew listened.

Alex did not.

Each man who had sailed with them was compensated well enough to change his future, but never so loudly as to invite questions. Haemish stepped away from the sea altogether, purchasing land and raising stone with a restraint that surprised even himself. His estate grew solidly, sensibly, including a dowager home worthy of Lady Annabella. Yet despite all he had gained, one thing remained unresolved. He never answered the letter she sent, the one that confessed her love and warned that her hand had been offered elsewhere.

Alex used his share differently.

Instead of indulgence, he built.

Tantallon Castle was expanded and reinforced, not merely for defense, but for comfort. Drawing from memory, Alex redesigned the bathhouse after Tafaria Paradise, commissioning flowing water systems and heated stone basins that could withstand Scotland's cold. He improved upon the design further, installing fire channels beneath the pools so warmth could be maintained even in winter. It was innovation born of admiration, and perhaps of regret.

Despite the attention he received from noblewomen, Alex did not return to old habits. Tafaria had changed him.

Responsibility clung to him now, even as recklessness simmered beneath. And though he never spoke her name aloud, Yvonne remained close in his thoughts, her presence already woven into his future in ways he did not yet understand.

Andrew and Nzingha settled near the royal court, though never fully within it. King James VI acknowledged them formally, welcoming Nzingha as Countess Barton of Barton Lands by marriage, without probing her origins. She honored the introduction with a generous offering, one that spoke of respect rather than submission.

They built a castle in Leith and maintained a manor near Tantallon. Nzingha moved easily among Scottish nobles, though their curiosity never faded. Many came seeking a glimpse of Destiny, her green-eyed daughter, now walking and laughing freely. Proposals were whispered early. Nzingha refused them all.

"My daughter's life," she said plainly, "will be her own."

One night, Nzingha lay beside Andrew in their new home, her gaze drifting across the chamber. African artwork from Mbemba lined the walls. Above the hearth hung a portrait of their family, all dressed in ceremonial attire. Andrew wore a white agbada. Nzingha stood beside him, radiant and composed. Destiny sat in her father's arms, solemn as though she understood her place in the world.

Andrew's hand rested over Nzingha's belly, now heavy with child.

"I have something for you," he said softly.

She smiled. "Another secret?"

"Something I nearly forgot," he replied, retrieving a small parcel from his lockbox.

Inside lay a citrine-cut diamond set in warm gold.

"Oh, husband," she breathed. "It's beautiful."

He slid it onto her finger and kissed her hand. "Not wealth," he said, "A reminder. Of us."

She turned onto her side carefully. "Do you remember the night we lay in the hammock?"

"Aye," he said, "You spoke of conceiving. I thought you mad at first. Then I counted the moons."

"You remembered."

Her voice grew quieter. "That night, my mother came to me again. She held a girl. Iney stood beside her, holding a boy. She told me to prepare for a journey with them both. One is night. The other is day."

Andrew sat upright, breath caught.

"Twins?"

Nzingha nodded.

"Yes, husband. Twins."

Authors Note

I have always loved historical and epic storytelling. Yet growing up, I noticed something missing.

So many stories centered European culture, European wealth, European politics, and European beauty, while Africa was often absent, simplified, or stripped of its complexity. Rarely was the continent portrayed in its fullness. Its richness. Its craft. Its power. Its diplomacy. Its internal conflict. Its beauty before invasion and erasure. This story was born from that absence.

Rather than rewriting history or misrepresenting cultures, I created two fictional lands, the Mbembe Kingdom and the Tafaria Kingdom. They are inspired by research into powerful African societies, leadership structures, and spiritual worldviews. While the names and settings are imagined, the intention is not. These lands exist to honor what Africa was and what it could have been, without forcing the narrative into rigid historical constraint.

Andrew and Nzingha do not meet in Europe or Africa. They meet in a place removed from both. A space where identity, lineage, and power are momentarily stripped away. A paradise. In that place, they are simply two people. But the world does not allow that innocence to last. Backgrounds are revealed. Politics arrive. Bloodlines assert themselves. Love is tested not by tenderness alone, but by consequence.

This book is not meant to teach lessons. It is not about tolerance, acceptance, or morality.

It is about grief, betrayal, loyalty, ambition, family, love, and the cost of choosing oneself in a world that demands obedience. It is about darkness as much as devotion. Power as much as intimacy. What happens when personal desire collides with legacy and rule.

If you found beauty here, it exists beside brutality.
If you found love, it survives alongside loss.

This story does not close neatly. It opens outward.

Book Two, *Ravage*, follows Alex and Yvonne, and what unfolds when wealth, secrecy, desire, and consequence can no longer remain hidden.

Thank you for reading.

Kera C. Munnings

This book is a product of SommerSetWay Novels

Copy Right © 2026

* 9 7 9 8 9 9 4 6 1 6 5 0 5 *